STAR TREK®

THE
HAND
OF
KAHLESS

STAR TREK®

THE
HAND
OF
KAHLESS

Star Trek: The Final Reflection
by John M. Ford

Star Trek: The Next Generation® Kahless
by Michael Jan Friedman

Based on
Star Trek and *Star Trek: The Next Generation*
created by Gene Roddenberry

POCKET BOOKS
New York   London   Toronto   Sydney

Dedication for *The Final Reflection*

For J.B.
after fifteen years,
the genuine article

Dedication for *Kahless*

For Valerie Elyse,
who was worth the wait

INTRODUCTION

Klingons—An Evolution

When Kor and his band of Klingons beamed into the *Star Trek* pantheon in the original series episode "Errand of Mercy," they were contentious, arrogant, fearless, and rather smarmy—all miscreant qualities admired in adversaries for Kirk and company. Not surprisingly, these newcomers quickly claimed a prominent position among *Star Trek*'s most memorable villains. Yet even before that seminal episode had ended, the show's creators hinted that the Klingons might not remain strictly adversarial. "It is true," Ayelborne tells Kirk, "that in the future you and the Klingons will become fast friends. You will work together." The Organian's prediction came true, regardless of the Klingon Empire's attempts to maintain a rocky relationship with the Federation. Two years later, in "Day of the Dove," Kirk and Kang were able to laugh their way out of jeopardy together. And a century later, with Captain Picard in command of the *U.S.S. Enterprise* NCC-1701-D, a Klingon warrior named Worf served on the bridge as a Starfleet officer.

Somewhere between *Star Trek* and *Star Trek: The Next Generation*, Klingons had evolved from one-dimensional villains into fully-fleshed characters with a well-defined culture. Along the way, *Star Trek*'s staff had to develop an entire warrior society, including such diverse elements as a unique fighting style, an arsenal, and a language. The process required equal parts evolution and creation. And a touch of serendipity.

In "The Trouble with Tribbles," Korax had bragged that, "Half the quadrant [was] learning to speak Klingonese." While writing *Star Trek III: The Search for Spock*, Producer Harv Bennett discovered that he needed to learn it too. He turned to Marc Okrand, the linguist who had created the Vulcan dialogue for *Star Trek II: The Wrath of Khan*.

"Harv knew that the best way to have a language that sounded like a real language was to actually create a real language," Okrand recalls.

"At the time, the only Klingon words that existed were names, and a few lines of dialogue that had been created by actor Jimmy Doohan (Scotty) for *Star Trek: The Motion Picture*. Harv felt that the Klingons were like Japanese samurai warriors, so I started writing with that in mind, while at the same time trying to match the sounds from the first movie. The cadence, which is kind of choppy, came from those two things."

It was Okrand's job to invent more sounds—and a grammatical structure to hang them on. "Klingons are not humans," he explains, "so their language can't be like a human language. All human languages have certain sound patterns that fall into a system. I violated those rules by picking sounds that cannot exist together in a human language. That's why Klingonese is hard to pronounce—your tongue doesn't want to go in that direction," Okrand says with a laugh.

"I purposely did not model the grammar after any specific language," he continues. "I combined grammatical structures from Burmese and Chinese and Thai, along with a couple of European languages and some American Indian languages, mostly from the West Coast. Plus a bunch of stuff I just made up."

Okrand was satisfied with the results—and a bit surprised as well. "I figured the actors would be able to contort their mouths to say their lines that one time," he says. "I didn't know that people were going to carry on Klingon conversations all over the world years later!"

Star Trek: The Next Generation Visual Effects Producer Dan Curry made up stuff too, including the *bat'leth,* the definitive Klingon weapon, and the flowing martial art style that accommodates its use. Like Okrand, he found much of his inspiration in the Far East. Curry, an expert martial artist, and a lifelong collector of weapons, was intrigued when he read the script to the fourth season *The Next Generation* episode "Reunion."

"It called for a special Klingon bladed weapon," Curry recalls. "I've always been irritated when I've seen weapons in movies that were designed to look cool but in reality couldn't be handled practically. I'd been imagining a curved weapon that was partially influenced by Himalayan weapons like the Gurkha *kukri*. [*The kukri, the wickedly curved knife of the Gurkhas of Nepal, is arguably the most renowned fighting knife in the world.*] I was also thinking about the Chinese double ax, Chinese fighting crescents, and the Tai Chi sword. I combined elements of all those things in order to come up with an ergonomically sound weapon."

Curry made a foam core version of his design, an admittedly flimsy prototype of the *bat'leth,* and showed it to Executive Producer Rick

Berman. "I told Rick that I could create a whole martial arts style too," Curry notes. "And Rick liked it." No one knew at the time that the weapon would become a kind of symbol for the species. "Now you seldom see a picture of a Klingon without a *bat'leth* in his hands," Curry says with a smile.

Curry then began to work with Michael Dorn, the actor who plays Worf, to develop a fighting style to go with the weapon. "We didn't want the Klingons simply to be vicious," he says, "so I thought it would be an interesting dichotomy if they had a very subtle internal quality as well as being incredible fighters—like the samurai during Japan's Tokagawa period, who were dedicated to poetry as well as sword-fighting. We started primarily with Tai Chi, so we could practice in 'slow motion' and have that meditative quality, but I made the style more claw-like and scary-looking by combining it with Hun Gar, a very aggressive Chinese style, and Tai Kwon Do, which is a Korean style." The result: *mok'bara,* the ritual Klingon Martial Art.

About that same time, Curry noticed that the show's writers seemed to be exploring similar inspirational territory as they developed new Klingon storylines. "The writers began to include a kind of Bushido aspect, like a Samurai code for Klingons," he says. "I think they fed off of what they saw Michael Dorn doing onscreen, and one thing naturally evolved into the next."

—Terry J. Erdmann

THE FINAL REFLECTION

Historian's Note

The main events in this story take place over a half century before James Kirk took command of the *U.S.S. Enterprise* NCC-1701 in 2264, "Where No Man Has Gone Before."

Prologue

Enterprise, dormant for nearly a week now, was waking up.

Captain James Kirk had stayed aboard, while the crew took leave on Starbase 12: Dr. McCoy had given him a stern lecture on the perils of overwork, and Engineer Scott a milder talk on the pleasures Kirk would be missing. Even Spock had gone stationside; something to do with new materials for the ship's library computer.

But Kirk was all right. In fact, he felt wonderful. He had given himself a walking inspection tour of his ship, quite alone, at whatever pace he felt like at the moment. It was not work. It had been sheer play.

Now the crew was returning, making *Enterprise* ready for voyage, and that too was satisfactory. Kirk walked the corridors, giving salutes and greetings, feeling almost light-headed, as if he were present at a new creation.

Yeoman Janice Rand came up the corridor toward Kirk, still in a civilian tunic and loose trousers, traveling bag slung over her shoulder. Her hair was in a new, non-regulation style, upswept, quite striking and attractive; Kirk could not remember having seen the style before—

And then he knew he had seen it, once only: on Specialist Mara, the consort of the Klingon Captain Kang.

Kirk gave a clumsy gesture somewhere between a salute and a wave; Rand smiled and waved back.

She's still off duty, Kirk thought, she has the right to wear her hair any way she pleases—but why on earth . . . ? It surely hadn't been that long since the Organian Peace: Kirk wondered if it could *ever* be that long.

He shook his head and walked on. A little farther down the corridor, he heard a crewman use a few words in a foreign language. Kirk did not know the meaning, but knew from the harsh, consonantal sound that the language must be Klingonese. He also knew that only a half-dozen of the ship's complement spoke Klingonese, and this was not one of them.

Kirk went up a level to sickbay. Inside, Dr. McCoy was unpacking a carrier marked MEDICAL SUPPLIES. Kirk's medical training was sufficient to identify Romulan ale, Saurian brandy in the trademark bottle, and a complete set of components for Argelian nine-layer cocktails.

"Expecting an epidemic, Bones?"

McCoy looked up. His expression was odd: slightly distant, slightly sour. "I hope to Lucius Beebe there is—" He stopped short, shook his head.

"Who?" Kirk said.

"Nothing. Something my granddaddy used to say when he got dry." McCoy reverently held up a bottle of Jack Daniel's Black Label. "Bar's still open, if you want, Jim."

Something in the way McCoy made the offer made Kirk hesitate. Bones was always playing the curmudgeon, but when he was really disgruntled he was not pleasant company. "Later, Bones. Too much to do, just now." Kirk smiled. "Promises to keep, and miles to go . . ."

"Uh-huh." McCoy put the bottle down, looking a little forlorn.

"Bones," Kirk said quietly, "what's wrong?"

"Hm? *Oh.* 'Course, you don't know." He reached down into the carrier, clinking bottles and cans, and brought out a book. "Here you go. Read all about it."

Kirk took the book. It was a bookstore edition, in hard covers, not a computer offprint. *The Final Reflection,* the cover said, above a lurid painting showing a Klingon battle cruiser. He turned it over, scanned the blurbs. "This is the one the Starfleet memos were about, isn't it? The novel about the Klingons."

"Novel, yeah," McCoy said. "About the Klingons." His voice was just slightly less tense. "You might like it . . . there's some good space-battle stuff."

"I'll get a print—"

"Take it," McCoy said, and at once his voice cleared, as if there had never been anything wrong at all. "I'd better get my office in order. I'm about to get four hundred cases of station leave."

"All right, Bones. Hold that drink for me."

"Sure, Jim."

Kirk went on down the corridor, looking at the book, half conscious that others were saluting him or dodging out of his way. He tried to remember the texts of the Starfleet memos about the novel: their substance seemed to have been the routine disclaimers about any book not fully approved by the Public Information Office, maybe a little more strongly worded than usual.

Space battles, Bones had said. According to the cover copy, the story was set not long after first contact with the Klingons, just before Kirk himself had been born; back before dilithium, when the best shipwrights in Starfleet thought warp 4.8 was the absolute limit. Before phasers. Before *Enterprise* had gone on the drawing boards. That should be interesting, Kirk thought, even if those days seemed as far away as Captain Hornblower's sails and cannon.

But then, Kirk had always liked Horatio Hornblower.

A name caught his eye: Dr. Emanuel Tagore. A political scientist, Kirk recalled. He had died about a year ago, aged 120 or so; Spock had mentioned it. Spock. . . .

Kirk got into the next turbolift.

Spock was already back in duty uniform, though he had not even unpacked. His small traveling case was on the bed, still sealed; against the wall of the cabin were two large carriers labeled COMPUTER DATA—KEEP FROM ALL RADIATION.

"Captain. I am sorry I have not reported to the bridge. I was . . ."

"Spock. . . . Welcome back."

"Thank you, Captain, though I have not been gone in any real sense." Spock looked down slightly, saw the book in Kirk's hand. "I see you have . . . already obtained a copy of that work."

"Yes. Bones gave it to me."

The eyebrow went up like a flag. "Indeed. I find that . . . well. Perhaps not surprising."

"I wanted to ask you about it."

"It is a work of fiction, Captain. That is, I believe, all that needs to be said."

It's some kind of strange new hangover, Kirk thought, *one leave and my whole crew goes crazy.* "I was going to ask about Emanuel Tagore. Did you know him?"

"He was an acquaintance of my father's. When I was a student at the Makropyrios, we had . . . discussions, though I was never enrolled in his classes."

That said more than perhaps Spock had intended; there were over two million students at the Federation's finest university, too many for anyone to casually "have discussions" outside the classroom.

Kirk said, "So then you did know him."

"I believe that was what I said, Captain."

Kirk almost shook his head. "Analysis, Spock," he said, trying to sound as if he were joking. "Enhancement, please."

"Yes, Captain, I did know Dr. Emanuel Tagore. I admired him, as did my father the ambassador, although in many ways Dr. Tagore was a most illogical man. But I knew him as a human, not a character in a novel."

"I haven't read the book yet."

"Yes, I had just realized there was not time for you to have done so. Is that all you require from me at this time, Captain?" The tone was no cooler than any Vulcan might use. But this was not just any Vulcan.

"Yes, Spock," Kirk said, too puzzled to be really hurt. "See you on the bridge." He looked at Spock, vaguely hoping the science officer would recover as Dr. McCoy had.

But Spock did not. "Of course, Captain." Kirk went out.

The corridor was empty, silent except for the distant chiming of an annunciator. Kirk looked at the book again, at the Klingon ship. *The Final Reflection. Reflection of what?* he thought. He could remember times when he had seen himself reflected in books . . . in Mark Twain, in the Hornblower stories. Sometimes the image was startling. But they were, after all, only stories.

Which was, sort of, what Spock had said.

Kirk went to his own quarters, changed from fatigues into duty uniform, put the book on the bedside table.

First Enterprise, he thought. Then McCoy's drink. Then we'll see what it has to say.

Researcher's Note

"Be a storyteller, an embellisher, a liar; they'll call you that and worse anyway. It hardly matters. The Tao which can be perceived is not the true Tao."

—DR. EMANUEL TAGORE, TO THE AUTHOR

It has been sixty-five years since *U.S.S. Sentry* met *I.K.V. Devisor* in the UFP's first known contact with the Klingon Empire. The final events of the story which follows took place some forty years ago. Some time back we celebrated ten years of *Pax Organia* (of which more in a moment). There are many who are convinced that "the Klingon Phase of Federation history is over." I first heard that phrase used in a lecture at the Makropyrios. No one even smiled.

So perhaps I may be excused a certain puzzlement at the curtains of silence that descended during the research for this work. UFP "Klingon authorities" were unavailable for extended periods, coinciding with my calls and visits. Official records of the "Dissolution Babel" are incomplete, containing little more than the "we kissed and made up" account found in children's books. Important persons have died or dropped from sight—neither rare events, but highly concentrated in this area. While my life was not threatened, my researcher's credentials and my computer's memory cores were. Only one person was willing to speak freely, and that one both warned me that his memory was fallible and gave me the advice quoted above. He was too modest about his memory. But his counsels were always wise.

Thus what follows is a novelist's reconstruction of events, rather than a history, let alone an exposé. (It would be embarrassing to admit the size of the fee I lost from *Insider Illustrated* for not rewriting to their specifications. Sample specification: **More details on Klingon torture please.**) My defenses are fictional license and absence of malice; perhaps if the Van Diemen Papers were not under DOUBLET REGAL classification (two steps higher than the Nova Weapons research files) my tale would be different.

I note in passing that I do not intend to disappear from public view in the immediate future.

An old Italian proverb runs: *Traduttore, traditore:* the translator is a traitor. And it is nowhere more true than when translating between races from different stars; still, I have tried to speak as little treason as possible. For clarity's sake, certain *Klingon* technical terms have been translated as their Federation-Standard equivalents: thus *warp drive, transporter, disruptor,* instead of the more literal *anticurve rider, particle displacer, vibratory destructor* (most literally: the "shake-it-till-it-falls-apart-tool"). After usual practice, directly equivalent ranks and titles such as "Captain" or "Lieutenant" are given as such, while specifically Klingon titles are translated directly (Specialist, Force Leader) or by convention (Thought Admiral, Examiner).

The translation of *kuve* as *servitor* may raise eyebrows, especially among my Vulcan readers, but it is a growing belief among experts on the *Komerex Klingon* (or at least it was) that the usual translation as "slave" is not only inaccurate but inflammatory, much as the phrases "Centaurian lover" and "filthy Ghibelline" of Earth's past.

Anticipating another Vulcan response: I am not a geneticist, and I have documentation that the practice of *tharavul* still exists.

This book would not have been possible without the interest (and frequent forbearance) of two persons. Dr. Emanuel Tagore's notes were indispensable, but no more so than Dr. Tagore himself; the brief time I could spend with him was an education in culture and language, and not only Klingon culture and language. And it was Mimi Panitch, my editor, who first decided that the Federation was ready for this story, and then stayed on Earth while I bummed the warp routes to track it down.

Finally, the work is about more than what (may have) happened four decades ago, in the last Babel Conference to be held on Earth's surface. Inevitably I come back to Dr. Tagore: "The Organian Peace is a peace of the biggest guns: it neither requires nor creates any understanding among the parties. In the absence of that understanding, the most that can be said about the Organian Treaty is that it works.

"For the present."

Those were his last words to me before his death last year.

I still wonder what he had seen, that we have not.

—Stardate 8303.24/JMF

Tempt not the stars, young man; thou canst not play
With the severity of fate. . . . In thy aspect I note
A consequence of danger.

—FROM *THE BROKEN HEART*

PART ONE

The Clouded Levels

If there are gods, they do not help, and justice belongs to the strong: but know that all things done before the naked stars are remembered.

—KLINGON PROVERB

One: Tactics

The children of the Empire were arming for the Game.

Vrenn was a Lancer. He tested the adhesion of his thick-soled boots, adjusted a strap and found them excellent. He flexed his shoulders within their padding—the armor was slightly stiff with newness; he would have to allow for that.

Vrenn's Lance still hung on its charge rack. He leaned into the wall cabinet, read full charge on the indicator, and carefully lifted the weapon out. The Lance was a cylinder of metal and crystal, as thick as his palm was wide. He rested its blank metal, Null end on the floor, and the glass Active tip just reached his shoulder. Then he hefted it, spun it, ran his fingers over the controls in the checkout sequence, watching flashes and listening to answering clicks. The crystal tip glowed blue with neutral charge.

It was a fine Lance, absolutely new like his armor. Vrenn had never before had anything that was new. He wondered what would happen to these things, after they had won the game . . . if there would be prizes to the victors. He took a deep breath of the prep room's air, which was warm and deliriously moist; he lifted his Lance to shoulder-ready and turned around.

Across the room, Dezhe and Rokis were helping each other into Flier rigs, shiny metal harnesses and glossy boots with spurs. Rokis tightened her left hand inside the control gauntlet, and rose very rapidly, almost banging her green helmet on the dim ceiling. Dezhe snorted, grabbed one of Rokis's spurs and pretended to pull her back down.

"*G'daya* new stuff." That was Ragga, who was struggling his immense bulk into the even greater bulk of a Blockader's studded hide armor. "Not a *g'dayt* crease in it, can't *khest'n* move." He did a few squats-and-stretches, looked a little more satisfied, but not much.

"Who said you could move anyway?" Gelly said. Ragga swiped at her; she danced out of the way without the slightest difficulty. "You'd better not move. You might fall down, and I don't think the rest of us together could get you up again."

Ragga showed his teeth and arched his arms, roared like a stormwalker. Gelly skittered away, laughing. Ragga was laughing too, a sound not much different from his roar.

Gelly sealed up the front of her uniform, a coverall of shiny green mesh, with gloves and boots of finely jointed metal on her slender hands and feet. She was the best Swift of their House: the House Proctors said she might be the best Swift of all the Houses.

Others said other things, about her slimness, her smooth forehead, the lightness of her bones and flesh. Vrenn felt a little sorry for her: when they were younger, he had called her "Ugly, ugly!" with the others. But she couldn't help being ugly, and if it was true that some of her genes were Vulcan or Romulan—or even Human!—that was not her fault either. He did not think she was part-Human, though. Vrenn had killed a Human in the Year Games, when he was six, his first intelligent kill, and Humans were slow, not swift.

There had been the one who called Gelly *kuveleta:* servitor's half-child. Zharn had killed that one, and done it well. They had all killed, Zharn and Vrenn and Ragga many different races, but Zharn was the best.

But they were all the best, Vrenn thought. Their positions had not been randomly chosen, nor they themselves: of the three hundred residents of House Twenty-Four, they were the nine best at *klin zha kinta,* the game with live pieces.

Now Zharn was sitting against the wall of the prep room, in full Fencer's armor: smooth green plates and helmet, slender metal staff across his knees. He was humming "Undefeated," a favorite song of House *Gensa.* Segon, a lightly armored Vanguard, was near him, keeping time with his bootheel. A little farther away, Graade and Voloh, the other Vanguards, held hands and kept harmony.

Zharn began to sing aloud, and in a moment they were all singing.

And though the cold brittles the flesh,
The chain of duty cannot be broken,
For the chain is forged in the heart's own fire
Which cold cannot extinguish . . .

The door opened. In the long corridor beyond, lit greenly by small lamps on the walls, was their Senior Proctor, old Khidri tai-Gensa. Khidri was nearly forty years old, very wrinkled; he had been a full Commander in the Navy until vacuum crippled his lungs. Next to him was a Naval officer, in black tunic and gold dress sash and Commander's insignia, with medals for ships taken.

Zharn was instantly on his feet. "Green Team, present!"

The players snapped to attention at once, wrists crossed in salute, weapons at ready-arms.

Khidri gave them a slight smile and one short nod. "This is a high day for the House *Gensa,*" he said. "We are chosen to play at the command of Thought Admiral Kethas epetai-Khemara."

Vrenn felt his chest tighten, but he did not move. None of the Team did. *A planner for the entire Navy!* he thought, and knew then that he was right: they were the very best . . . and others knew it.

Khidri said, "The Thought Admiral is of course a Grand Master of *klin zha* . . . this day we must be worthy of a Grand Master's play." In the last was the smallest hint of a threat, or perhaps a warning. Next to Khidri, the Navy officer stood impassive and rather grim.

"Zharn Gensa, is your Green Team ready?"

"Armed and prepared, Proctor Khidri."

"Then bring them," Khidri said, and as he turned around Vrenn thought he saw the Proctor's smile widen. Then Vrenn looked at Zharn. The Fencer was nine, a year older than the rest of them, and seemed the pure image of leadership.

"House Twenty-Four Green Team," Zharn said, "onward to the victory!"

The *klin zha* players filed out of the room, marching in step down the green corridor, singing.

> *Yet if my line should die,*
> *It dies with its teeth in the enemy's throat,*
> *It dies with its name on the enemy's tongue.*
> *For just as mere life is not victory,*
> *Mere death is not defeat;*
> *And in the next world I shall kill the foe a thousand times,*
> *Laughing,*
> *Undefeated.*

The Arena Gallery was a long, low-ceilinged room, furnished with large soft cushions and small wooden tables with trays of succulents. Servitors, moving silently in clean tan gowns of restrictive cut, replaced the trays when they became empty or messy. Fog hung at the ceiling, humidifier mist mixed with the personal incenses some of the officers present carried. One long wall of the room was entirely of dark glass.

There were slightly more than a dozen of high ranks present, Naval and Marine, and two civilian administrators with a reputation at *klin zha.* Also in the room were a few of the officers' consorts—two for Admiral Kezhke, who was never moderate—and three Vulcans, all *tharavul.*

"The spindles for first move, Thought Admiral?" General Margon sutai-Demma held out a pair of hexagonal rods, of polished white bone with numerals inlaid in gold on their faces. Margon gave them a small, rattling toss and caught them again. They showed double sixes. There was a mildly unpleasant look on Margon's face, but there usually was, and the scar at the side of his mouth only added to it.

Behind Margon, Force Leader Mabli vestai-Galann sat on a cushion, looking quite uncomfortable. One of Margon's *kuve* consorts was stroking Mabli's shoulders, which did not seem to relax him at all, though the female's claws were fully retracted. Mabli kept glancing at the other officers: every one outranked him. Worse, the administrators did as well. Mabli looked straight at his opponent.

Thought Admiral Kethas epetai-Khemara had deep wrinkles in his knobbed forehead, hair very white at his temples. He was fifty-two years old, an age at which Klingons of the Imperial Race should be dead by one means or another, yet his eyes were clear and sharp as naked stars. He smiled at Force Leader Mabli, then faced General Margon. "I grant the option." Kethas reached casually to one side, picked a glass of black brandy from a servitor's tray.

Mabli said, "I take . . ." He broke off, looked around. Only the civilians looked especially disapproving. ". . . I *choose* first position."

Kethas nodded, drank. A side door opened with a whisper of air, and the Game Operator entered the Gallery.

The Operator was a Vulcan, *tharavul* like the others of his race present. He wore a green and gold gown of his homeworld's cut. In his hands was a flat black case; two chains and pendants hung around his neck. The upper pendant was the triangle-circle-gemstone of the IDIC; the lower was a large silver figure of a biped astride a quadruped—a piece of the Human game chess.

The players stood as the Operator entered. "Kethas," the Vulcan said, and gestured with spread fingers.

"Sudok. This is Mabli: he shall have Gold today, and chooses first position."

Sudok inclined his head to Mabli, but did not raise his hand. Then the Operator held the black case level, before the Gallery's glass wall. A metal pedestal rose from the floor to support it. Sudok opened the case. Illuminated controls shone within, flashing color from Sudok's jewelry. He touched a series of buttons; the officers and their consorts began moving toward the glass wall.

Beyond the panel, lights flared, revealing the Arena. It was fifty meters across and high, six-sided, long sides alternating with short; the walls sloped inward slightly, pierced with the windows of other viewing galleries, mostly dark now. This gallery was near the Arena ceiling, which was hung with a mazework of lighting, camera, and projection equipment.

The floor was painted with a triangular emblem of three crooked arms, gold on black. Operator Sudok touched another button, and the floor split into three pieces, panels retracting outward.

"T'tain," General Maida said to the *tharavul* behind him, "what was the price for the last shipment of gladiators to Triskelion?"

"Two point six million in crystals and fissionables," the Vulcan said, in a flat tone.

"That's down, isn't it?" a Naval officer said.

"Twenty percent," T'tain said, and started to say more, but was cut off by a sharp gesture from Maida. The General's mouth twisted, and then he said, "The *gagny* brains that rule the place get bored very quickly. Give 'em new races, they say, or the price will drop to nothing. So when are you going to find us some new *kuve?*"

"We're in a *g'daya* box!" the Admiral snapped back. "Federation one way, Romulans another, Kinshaya one more—where are the *kuve* supposed to breed?"

"You Navy have the Grand Master strategists—"

"Do it elsewhere," General Margon said. His hand was on his dress weapon, apparently casually. There was a long, silent moment; no one moved but Sudok, who continued to work his controls, looking straight out the Gallery window.

"It's done," Maida said finally, without having looked at Margon. Eyes turned back to the Arena.

The game grid was rising from below floor level: a three-sided pyramid of metal struts and transparent panels, a tetrahedral frame nine four-meter pyramids on each edge. Spectra flickered across its facets.

There was a metallic thump, more felt than heard, as the grid locked into place. Then doors opened at Arena floor level, and the Green and Gold pieces filed out: Fencer, Swift, Fliers, Lancer, Vanguards, and Blockader for each side. They executed sharp halts-and-turns and stood, looking upward toward the Gallery.

Kethas waved to the pieces. Mabli saluted his.

Sudok said, "If the players will take their positions." Another key pressed: at either end of the window-wall, small cubicles lit behind glass, one green, one gold. The glass panels slid aside. Within were enveloping, deeply cushioned chairs, like a ship captain's command chair, set before holo displays already showing miniatures of the huge Arena grid.

"A shame this one will be Clouded," Kethas said to Mabli. "I prefer to watch my pieces through my own eyes, don't you?"

Mabli looked puzzled, said nothing.

"Only a thought," Kethas said, and laughed. "A thought." Then he held out his brandy glass to Mabli. The Force Leader accepted it, took a swallow. A servitor appeared to carry the glass away.

Kethas and Mabli spread their arms, snarled and embraced, heads tilted back, throats exposed. The fury between them seemed to radiate; there were grunts of approval from the others.

The players separated, went to their cubicles. The spectators took up comfortable viewing positions, servitors moving cushions and tables to suit. A small, white-fleshed *kuve* folded its body to pillow the head of Margon's consort; she scratched it with a talon and purred. Finally only the four Vulcans and the serving *kuve* remained standing.

Sudok said clearly, "Gold to position first. The clouds descend." At the Arena ceiling, holo projectors came glowing to life.

Vrenn saw the Thought Admiral's wave. He thought, dimly, that it was an odd gesture, not at all like the Marine player's sharp salute, but in a moment it was past, and he was thinking about the game, and the victory. He felt the weight of his Lance, its good balance, the fine fit of his armor.

Prizes, he thought. The House had all the taped episodes of *Battlecruiser Vengeance,* and Vrenn had watched every one of them, and they all ended with the same line. Humans, Romulans, Kinshaya, servitors who had somehow managed to enter space, all of them asked their conqueror who he was, and the answer was always: "I am Captain Koth. Koth of the *Vengeance.* And this ship is my prize."

Not that Vrenn could ever have a ship—not ever a ship, not without a line-name or a line—but perhaps he could have the Lance. A prize of war, his entirely. And like Koth, he would use his prize—

The *klin zha* pyramid was glowing from within, clear panels turning opaque with holo images. Vrenn heard a slight escape of breath from Ragga, that said more than a mouthful of curses. The Clouded Game was hardest on a Blockader. It was not Vrenn's favorite, either. At least Gelly would be pleased, and the Fliers.

And Zharn, perhaps; it was hard to tell. Zharn was always leader-hard and leader-calm. No form of *klin zha* was easy for the Fencer.

On the other side of the Arena floor, the Gold team was moving, filing into the game grid. Green Team had second placement, then, and second move. Vrenn did not know how much advantage there was to second position, when the opponent's set-up was partly hidden; he did not like the Clouded game even when he controlled all the pieces. One could not see the enemy's pieces, or the enemy.

The Naval officer with Proctor Khidri spoke quietly; Khidri gestured, and Green Team entered the grid.

"Green player chooses the left-hand point," Sudok announced. The Gold pieces had been placed as Mabli chose; now the Green pieces occupied another point on the Grid's lowest level, leaving the third point empty.

"I can't *see* them all," Margon's consort said, annoyed. Margon grunted at her, a threatening sound. Sudok said nothing, and moved a control; the Gallery glass darkened, and the grid cleared as the obscuring holos were polarized out. Hazy shimmers remained, indicating which panels were blocked to the players' view.

"Drownfish's teeth, look at that," one of the civilians said to the other. "Old Khemara's got a Lancer Advanced opening. What do you say to doubled stakes?"

The other administrator looked doubtful, turned to his *tharavul.* "Sovin. Percentages of success for the Lancer Advanced?"

The Vulcan said at once, "Nine percent of such openings lead to victory. Adjusted for the three-dimensional game, Obscuration rules, four percent."

"Well . . . let's say redoubled—wait. Sovin, adjust for Grand Master play."

"Data base is small, Manager Akten."

"Coarse data, then."

"Coarse data indicate twenty-two percent success. I cannot correlate for Grand Masters versus Masters of Force Leader Mabli's rating."

"Double and that's all, then," Akten said, giving the *tharavul* a sidelong look. "Sometimes, Atro, you want to cut more out of their skulls than just their mind-snoop. . . ."

Sovin, of course, did not react. Operator Sudok said, "Starting positions are chosen. Goals are being placed." He pushed two slides forward.

General Margon stroked his consort's arm, watched her claws involuntarily extend, and smiled.

Vrenn stood in a triangular cell of metal and light. The floor was a sheet of heavy clear stuff with darkness below, bounded by black metal strips, each with a slot along its length.

He knew he was in the right front space of the starting position. It was a bad place for a Lancer in flat-board *klin zha,* backed against an edge, but perhaps not in this game. *They must follow the Grand Master's lead,* he thought. And be worthy of his play, as Khidri had said.

Voloh, the Vanguard, was to Vrenn's left, and Graade Vanguard was behind Vrenn. A *very* unusual starting position. Just beyond Voloh stood Ragga, still tensing against his Blockader armor. In the center of the position was Zharn; that made sense at least. Vrenn could not see any of the others, nor any of the Gold Team.

There was a flicker of light in Zharn's space. A disk, half a meter across and a handbreadth thick, materialized in midair. Zharn caught it nimbly. The Goal was of polished green metal, heavy by the way Zharn held it. Vrenn hoped he would not have to find out. Zharn put the Goal gently on the floor of his space, put a boot up on it and stood tensed and ready.

The slots in the floor strips lit yellow. At once Vrenn leaned forward, shifting his balance for action; he dropped his Lance from parade to ready position, and moved fingers on the controls. The Lance hummed through his fingers, and the Active tip went from blue to green.

There was a movement before him. A large shape, golden: the enemy Blockader, passing through an unClouded space. Vrenn watched the yellow strip in front of him, waiting for it to change, but it did not.

Ragga's did, yellow to blue, and the Blockader moved, watching to all sides, and even above, though of course no pieces could yet be on the higher levels.

But that was not a bad caution. In non-combat *klin zha,* a Blockader could not be killed at all; but it was different in *klin zha kinta,* and Blocks who forgot that it was different learned again in hard fashion. Another strip turned blue, and Ragga moved on; he disappeared as he crossed the line, which went yellow again after him.

Segon Vanguard walked from a mist into Ragga's empty space. *He did it too hastily,* Vrenn thought, went through the Cloud panel too sure the space beyond would be empty. Segon turned slightly, to wave to Zharn Fencer.

The Gold Vanguard emerged from Cloud and slammed his fist into Segon's chest, all in one motion.

Segon staggered, sank down almost to kneeling—then brought the heels of both hands up hard into the Gold player's chin. The Gold's head went back, and Segon's left gauntlet chopped into her throat. Almost too fast to see, the enemy kicked to the side of Segon's knee; they fell together. The bodies locked, and tensed for a long, long moment, and then there was the liquid-metal sound of a joint failing.

Segon stood up, shoulders pumping as he breathed. He took an unsteady step away from the fallen Vanguard. The Gold's body shimmered, vanished, transported away.

The panel beneath Vrenn's boots trembled, then began to rise, riding on the rails of the game grid. Vrenn returned Zharn's salute, gave one to Segon, who raised a shaking hand to acknowledge.

The panel stopped on the next level above. Vrenn was completely surrounded by Cloud panels. The Elevation move had been toward the grid center, so there was still a board edge to his right—safe to ignore that panel—but he was not in a corner. Two directions to cover—no, four. He looked up.

Spurs flashed by Vrenn's face. Vrenn swung the Null end of his Lance, caught the Flier in the thigh; the swooping Gold rolled in midair and landed on his back, spurred boots pointed at Vrenn. Vrenn reversed the Lance, touched the controls; the Active tip glowed yellow. The Flier twisted his control-gloved hand and was off the floor instantly; his bootheels struck the Lance's deflector shield, and the Gold spun in midair. His shoulder grazed a side panel of the cell, above a yellow floor strip; there was a blue flare and the Flier's jacket smoked, but the player made no sound. *"Kai,"* Vrenn said under his breath, at the same time dropping the shield and checking the Lance's charge counter. It was down by almost a sixth.

The Gold somersaulted forward. Vrenn raised his Lance horizontally, catching the gilded steel spurs against it. The Flier continued his roll. Before the enemy could vault over and land behind him, Vrenn fell forward, twisting to fall on his backside. The Flier whirled, just short of striking the far wall; swooped down again.

Vrenn touched his weapon controls. The crystal tip pulsed green.

The Flier was struck in the left ribs, knocked off course. Vrenn spun the Lance end-for-end, smashing the Null end at the Flier's control gauntlet. He connected. Small bones crunched, and wires. As if swept by an invisible hand, the Gold's harness flung him into the wall of the cell, and pressed him there, outlined in blue fire. The harness spent its charge. The Gold Flier hit the floor, moved just a little, then sparkled and vanished without a sound.

A floor strip turned blue. Vrenn walked through the holo into the space beyond.

Some of the Naval officers, and even one of the Marines, were slapping their thighs in approval. "Good play! Good play!"

Admiral Kezhke said, "Who's the Green Lancer?"

Operator Sudok pressed keys, and the close-up image was printed over with red letters.

"Vrenn," Kezhke read, *"Gensa,* good House . . . *Rustazh?"* Kezhke knocked aside the fruit one of his consorts was feeding him. There was a silence in the gallery.

General Maida had a just-lit incense stick in his fingers; he stopped halfway to the holder on his shoulder. "I thought the Rustazh line was extinct."

"So did I," Kezhke said. "I wonder if Kethas knows."

"Can such things be?" Margon said amiably, and gestured to remind Maida of his smoldering incense.

Kezhke said, "Sudok—"

"The Admiral Grand Master inspected his players' complete records some days ago."

Margon said, "You can hardly assume a Grand Master's play would be affected by his interest in one of the pieces."

"No," Kezhke said levelly, "not Kethas. But it's been . . . seven years since all the Rustazh died—"

"All but one, it would seem."

"It would seem." Kezhke stroked his stomach, turned to the cubicle at the end of the room.

Within it, Thought Admiral Kethas again moved his Lancer.

Vrenn had reached the sixth level of the grid, four cells to an edge. There were only a few Clouds here; about half the level was visible, and several spaces on the level above. Vrenn wondered briefly if the other Gold Flier was still in play, and almost without thinking checked his Lance. The indicator read four-tenths charge. The Fliers could not carry Goals, but surely that did not matter yet; surely they were not so close to endgame.

Behind Vrenn, a player was rising from below. He turned; it was Gelly, bouncing from toe to toe as if she were weightless. There was a film of blood on her metal gloves. She was smiling, like a shining light in her face. Vrenn nodded to her, and she spun round on the ball of one foot.

The other enemy Flier shot upward, through a space two away from Vrenn's, and was lost in the Clouds above.

Huge green-armored shoulders appeared near the far point of Vrenn's level: Ragga was coming up. There were creases now in his heavy leather, and a few rips. Vrenn wondered if he was happier now. He stood as if nothing had ever, could ever, touch him.

The Golden Lancer stepped out of Cloud, faced Ragga directly. Vrenn leaned forward slightly, eager to see.

The enemy's Lance flashed green. Ragga made no attempt to dodge the bolt; he did not even grunt as it struck him. Then he swung.

The Lancer was at least smart enough not to bother with his shields. He reversed his weapon to the Null end. Vrenn smacked a hand on his thigh; it was a bold move. Not that it would save him, not against Ragga.

The Green Blocker's fist smashed at the Lance butt, knocking it down, almost out of the Gold's hands. The enemy staggered.

So did Ragga.

Vrenn stared as the best Blocker of all the Houses sank to his knees. The Lancer stepped back to recover. Ragga barely moved. The Null end struck him, and struck again, and again.

On the third stroke Vrenn heard the pop of a spark, and then he understood: the Lance butt was not Null. There was something hidden in it; a contact stunner, or an agonizer.

It must, he thought, it *must* be a rule he did not know—some handicap against a Grand Master, perhaps—Vrenn checked his controls, touched a finger to the Null of his own Lance; only the grip of training kept him from banging the blunt end against the floor or into one of the wall barriers. Vrenn looked up, toward the window where he had seen the players, but it was blocked now from his view.

An edge of Gelly's space went from yellow to blue. Vrenn turned, saw the path of blue lines leading to the Gold Lancer. Ragga was gone. Vrenn opened his mouth, to warn her. His jaw was tense enough to hurt, and before he could strain out any words Gelly Swift was across the spaces at warp speed.

The Gold brought up his weapon. Gelly danced around it, kicked the Lancer. He stumbled, started to turn. She kicked him again, punched him in the lower back. He seemed about to fall; she tumbled, did a handstand and struck his helmet with her bootheel.

The Lancer fell.

Gelly cartwheeled upright.

The Lancer stood and sent a bolt into her body.

Gelly doubled over. The Lancer hit her with the blunt non-Null steel, hit her twice. There was blood. Gelly's blood was a very dark color.

A snarl came up in Vrenn's throat; he swallowed it back.

Vrenn was Elevated again. When he reached the seventh level, the Goal disk was just being transported into his space; he caught it as it fell. The metal Goal was indeed quite heavy.

The space was opaque on two sides, above, and below; the clear side showed nothing. Where, Vrenn wanted to know, was Zharn? Moving the Fencer away from the Goal was the most dangerous gambit in *klin zha.*

He wanted to know as well if the Gold players were cheating, and if so how they expected to succeed; and if Ragga and Gelly had been transported alive; and he wanted a Gold player, to kill for his own.

"About those odds . . ." Manager Atro said.

Akten, without looking away from the windows, said, "Wagers cancelled, of course. No fault."

Atro waved a hand.

Kezhke had retrieved the fruit from his consort and was chewing furiously. "I don't know about that Lancer," he said, juice running down his chin.

"The Thought Admiral might then be distracted?" General Margon said calmly, reaching for a glass of brandy.

"Not the Green Lancer, the Gold," Kezhke said at once, then turned to face Margon. "I am not a Thought Admiral, and I do not pretend to understand Fleet strategy; but even you, General, know epetai-Khemara's record."

"Oh, yes," Margon said lightly, and made a gesture with fingertips to forehead, indicating mild insanity. The Marine officers laughed. So did some of the Navals. "Does anyone know what sort of fusion that Green Swift was? She was rather interesting, in a skinny sort of way." Margon's consort threw a grape at him.

"The Green Goal's unprotected," General Maida said. "He's sent his Fencer off . . ."

"Operator," Kezhke said slowly, "replay of the last kill by Gold Fencer."

Sudok touched a key, and a small holo was thrown on the glass.

"Lancer Elevated to Seven, covering Goal," one of the Managers said. "Gold Lancer to Seven."

Kezhke said, "Operator, stop replay, and enlarge. . . . General Margon, will you look at this?"

"When I mentioned the Swift, I only had the epetai-Khemara in mind . . . he likes skinny. And green."

"Green Lancer, carrying Goal, up to Eight."

As Vrenn set the Goal disc down, the enemy Lancer rose into view. Now, Vrenn thought, and waited for the yellow space barrier to change. Instead, the floor began rising again. Vrenn put a foot up on the Goal, fingers tight on his Lance; the ache in his jaw was radiating to the side of his head.

From the Eighth level, only two spaces on an edge, he could see downward, see Zharn on the Seventh; now he thought he understood. Zharn would move from Cloud, on the Lancer.

Zharn did. He swung his thin staff in the widest possible arc; the tip struck the Gold Lancer's right arm and wrapped around it. Zharn twisted the polarizing grip and the metal went rigid. Vrenn had seen Zharn execute this kill a hundred times: as the enemy was pulled around, he would be carried directly into Zharn's knifing left hand, and the Gold's own body energy would help to drop him.

Then, impossibly, Zharn stumbled. The Fencer's hand twitched, depolarizing his staff; the Lancer spun in the wrong direction, and shoved the Active Lance-point into Zharn's throat. Green light flashed on green armor.

Zharn's head went back, far back, too far back. His eyes, very wide, looked up into Vrenn's, and his lips moved, spasming—

No, not just a spasm. Vrenn read them, very clearly.

Get this one, Zharn said, and flickered silently out of existence.

"Do you see that flare?" Kezhke said. "Between the Lance and the Swift's body?"

"That's just a lens flare," someone said, without force.

"Assuming that it isn't," Margon said, interested, "what is it?"

Kezhke said, "You know more of personal weapons than I, General. You are an authority on them."

Margon sniffed his brandy. His other hand rested, relaxed, on the grip of his dress weapon. "Are you proposing, oh, anything, Admiral?"

A few of the others stepped quietly aside.

Kezhke waved both his consorts away. He had no weapon visible, but of course no Klingon of rank would be unarmed in public. "Perhaps that you should examine this image, General, and a few others."

"Operator Sudok," Margon said, "did you examine the equipment for this game?"

"I did, General," the Vulcan said.

"And there were no irregularities?"

"None."

Kezhke said nothing. No one would appear so foolish as to doubt a Vulcan's word.

Margon took his hand away from his sidearm, gestured toward Thought Admiral Kethas's cubicle. "If the Naval champion wishes to stop the game, we will naturally accept a draw."

"Kethas," one of the Administrators said, distracted and puzzled, "has *never* been drawn in tournament."

"There is that." Margon went back to the viewing window. "And certainly never by a Marine Force Leader. All that, and the son of the Thought Admiral's good dead friend playing, and the invincible Gold opposing him . . . I do so enjoy *klin zha;* nothing short of living war is so stimulating."

"Gold Lancer Elevated, to Eight."

"There is always," Manager Akten said, "the *komerex zha.*"

"I do not acknowledge the existence of the Perpetual Game," Margon said without turning. "Society is society, war is war. If they are games at all, surely they are not all the same game. I deny it."

"That is a favored tactic," Akten said.

"Green Lancer to Level Nine."

*   *   *

There was no Cloud at the highest level. Vrenn stood in a four-sided pyramid of clear, shimmering panels edged in black steel, and waited for the last move of the Game.

There could only be one move now. Vrenn had carried the Goal to the Ninth Level: the enemy had his next move only to capture the disc. And only the Lancer could reach this space in one. The other Gold Flier might, of course, if she were on an edge space and still alive . . . but Vrenn knew it would not be the Flier. The move would be too easy, not bold enough for a game between Masters.

He was right. A spindle of light, dazzling, soundless, appeared in a point of the space, and the Golden Lancer materialized.

Vrenn smashed his Lance against the Gold's almost before the transport was complete; he felt the displacement field push him back as it did the air. Then the effect died, and Vrenn shoved the enemy back, so that both the Gold's shoulders struck wall panels. Vrenn cursed; he had been expecting shock fields, but here there was only plain matter.

The Gold pushed back, and tried to turn his Lance crosswise to Vrenn's, get freedom to use the Active or false-Null tips. The two Lancers struggled for a dozen heartbeats; then Vrenn was pushed back, by incredible strength. Lances cracked against each other, and against yellow energy shields. Vrenn read his charge counter: one-fourth. He dropped the shield and used the Lance as if it were a plain metal fighting stick, striking sparks, connecting with blows to the enemy's limbs that seemed to have no effect at all. He would have howled, but there was no breath to spare.

He looked into the enemy's face. Their eyes met. The Gold was clearly full Klingon, as much Imperial Race as was Vrenn; the broad dark face was scarred heavily, and there was a strange high tension in the look, like electricity in the yellow eyes.

Vrenn knew that it was desperation that he saw, and thought the Gold must see the same. They were images in a mirror, only the colors of their clothing different.

No, not only. The Gold had his dishonest Lance. And with his desperation, Vrenn *Gensa* Green had his rage.

Vrenn struck downward to disengage, then spun full circle on the ball of his foot, extending his Lance as Zharn had swung his slender staff. The startled enemy had blocked high, and the crystal tip of Vrenn's Lance caught him just below the right armpit.

Vrenn fingered his controls, and the whole remaining charge in his weapon went into a single green bolt.

The Gold player dropped his Lance. Vrenn kicked it aside, then threw away his own. And then he stopped still, and stared.

He had been wrong. There had been no hidden weapon in the Gold player's Lance. Not in his *Lance,* at all.

The Gold's right arm lay on the floor, twitching, its fingers spasming one-two-three-four. Above it stood its former owner, wobbling on his feet. From his right shoulder, wires dangled and sparked, and coolant and fluidic oil dripped from broken tubes.

Vrenn drove a fist into the enemy's body, then another. He felt tissue give beneath: only part-robot, then. Good. Very good. The enemy fell back, against a wall panel.

"Kai!" Vrenn shouted, only half meaning it as mockery, leaped and drove both feet into the Gold-thing's midsection.

Plastic splintered outward, and the cyborg Lancer went out and down, down fifty meters, and hit with a sound neither fleshly or mechanical. Blood and oil ran together.

"Gensa, the victory!" Vrenn shouted from the apex of the grid, out the open panel. He looked at the officers watching from their gallery, across space and a little below him now. *"Gensa,* a thousand times, undefeated!"

He wondered if any of them were listening.

"What an extraordinary endgame," Manager Akten said. General Maida coughed and snuffed out his incense. One of Admiral Kezhke's consorts turned and was sick; a servitor caught it in the hem of its robe. Kezhke said, "I should call it more than—"

"Yes," Margon said, and his pistol was out. Consorts and officers went for cover.

"Tokhe straav'!" Margon shouted: *Willing slave,* the vilest name Klingon could call Klingon, an insult only death could redeem. Then Margon fired, a bolt of actinic blue light that starred the glass door of Force Leader Mabli's cubicle. Mabli had just turned when the second shot blasted the panel apart, showering the player with fragments of crystal. The third shot tore apart his chest. Margon's pistol was holstered before the last shard of glass had struck the floor. The mist overhead swirled, and there was the sharp smell of ozone. Kezhke's left hand was tense on his leveled right forearm; slowly, he relaxed.

Margon raised the brandy glass he still held. *"Kai,* Thought Admiral. Another victory with your many."

Kethas stood in the open door of his cubicle. "Yes." He looked past Margon. Servitors were already sweeping up the fragments. "And for every victory, a loss, Margon?"

"There was nothing else for him," Margon said plainly. "Certainly not life. What could be accepted as truth from one who would commit fraud at *klin zha?* I would suspect that, when the plodders of Security finish with this *straav*'s record, it will be found full of lies as well."

"I would not doubt that," Kezhke said, without sarcasm.

"But the corruption ends here," said General Maida.

Kethas was looking out the window, at the figure on the top of the pyramid. The Green Lancer had arms upraised, and was shouting something the glass filtered out. It was barely possible that Mabli had heard Margon's challenge, before his glass was broken; but it hardly mattered.

Kethas said, "There is a last thing, sutai-Demma. . . ."

Margon said, "Epetai-Khemara?"

"A pleasing game. My compliments to a worthy opponent."

Margon nodded. Kethas turned away. "Manager Akten," he said, "I should like to discuss a matter with you. An adoption from one of the Houses of Lineless Youth."

Akten gestured to his *tharavul.* "I took that to be the context of your message, and Sovin has a set of—" Akten stopped short. "You said an *adoption?* Not just a transfer of residence?"

Kethas gave the faintest of smiles. "You are a good player, Akten . . . but even I did not know in advance how the game would end."

Two: Strategies

Vrenn was in his sleeping room of the House Twenty-Four, alone. The six beds were all neat; the other occupants were at a morning instruction. Vrenn had a sudden, deep flash of wishing he were with them. But he was no longer Gensa, but Khemara. Shortly a transport would be here, to take him away to his destiny.

Vrenn crouched on the edge of the bed that he had slept in all his life, leaned forward, slipped his fingers beneath it, feeling out of sight of the room monitors for the slot between metal frames.

He found nothing.

His jaw tensed, and his lips curled back from his teeth. So the one thing he would have kept was gone as well. He thought that it was not right for the Proctors to take it; it did not really belong to the House. If he found Khidri, Vrenn wondered, could he convince him to give Vrenn that one thing? Or if he could not take it away, at least give it to a Housemate. . . .

That would be a poor strategy, Vrenn knew at once. It had been old Khi' who had cautioned Vrenn not to demand privileges too soon in the name of Khemara, not to call a victory what was not.

Let the House have the envelope, then. Let them burn it. And he would see it again, in the next life, when he captained a ship of the Black Fleet.

Vrenn left the room. The halls were very quiet; the walls were of smooth castrock, hung with a few machine-copy tapestries, good traps for sound.

"Khemara."

It was the sound that made Vrenn turn, not the name. Proctor Muros was standing not far away, hands folded. His control wand swung at his side: Vrenn could not think when the wand had seemed both less of a threat, and more.

"Are you lost, Khemara? Guests of this House are normally provided with guides. I will guide you if you wish, honored and exalted guest." *Epetai-zana:* an honorific so high it became absurd, an insult.

"I am not lost, Proctor," Vrenn said firmly, then hardened his neck muscles and said, "You may go about your duties."

Muros smiled faintly, showing points of teeth. "Of course, *epetai-zana.*" He nodded politely, turned and walked silently away. Vrenn felt his liver relax.

Newcomers to the House often thought Muros was demanding their deference, and gave it. It was the wrong answer. "Are you *straave?*" he would snarl, and use the wand.

When Muros snaps, snap back: it was one of many secret rules of the House. When one arrived, one's five roommates, and only they, could tell the rules. Or not tell, as they chose. Usually they would tell a part, leave a part to be found out at the end of a wand. Zharn had warned Vrenn of Muros, and it was said he had ordered Gelly's mates to warn her, which for her strangeness they might not have done.

Zharn and Gelly had not returned, after the *klin zha kinta.* The others game-killed had, including Ragga, but Ragga was sullen and distant now, hardly speaking even to curse.

Vrenn came into the front common room. The light was lower here, the air moister; there were plants and a shallow dark pool for meditations. Panels of colored glass in the ceiling formed a large Imperial trefoil, the *komerex stela,* glowing with angular morning sun. A *klin zha* table was idle near the wall; Vrenn went toward it.

"You are Vrenn Khemara." Again, it was the sound of someone speaking, not the name he was called, that made Vrenn turn: and this voice was not Klingon, though the language was *klingonaase.*

A tall, very thin figure was approaching: he wore a black and gold Navy uniform, without insignia. Vrenn did not know the race. A little behind him was Proctor Khidri, carrying a folded pile of dark cloth.

"My name is Tirian," the tall male said. He had an extremely

angular face, very broad shoulders, a narrow waist. "I am Transporteer to Thought Admiral Kethas. I am now honored to serve you
as well."

Khidri held out the bundle. "Epetai-Khemara has sent clothing for
you."

Vrenn took the clothes. There was a long, loose tunic and trousers
of deep blue fabric, very soft. Vrenn tugged open the seams of his gray
House uniform and began changing on the spot; Khidri was after all a
House Proctor, and Tirian, whatever his exact race, was obviously
kuve. He had spoken of serving—and more telling, Khidri had said
epetai-Khemara sent the clothes, not that Tirian brought them.

A thought occurred as Vrenn was dressing. "These are like Cadet's
clothes, aren't they? Navy Cadet's?"

Tirian said, "Somewhat. A Cadet's tunic is less long or full, so that
it does not balloon in no-weight."

Vrenn moved his shoulders. He had never touched cloth so soft. He
picked up his discarded uniform, folding it automatically, and gave it
to Khidri. "When do we depart, Transporteer?" he said, feeling his
voice tremble just a bit as he tried for the sound of command.

"At your convenience, *zan* Vrenn. Do you have baggage?"

"No . . . nothing, Transporteer."

"If you wish, call me Tirian. *Kuvesa tokhesa.*" *I serve willingly,* the
alien said, and yet Vrenn knew it for an instruction. "Then you shall
call me Vrenn," he answered, a request.

They went into the House forecourt. There was a small flier parked
there, short-winged and graceful, green-backed and white-bellied. The
viewports had armored shutters ready to drop, and under the wings
were mounted disruptors and missile pods. Vrenn knew it from the
recognition books as a Teska-2: not just an armed transport but a real
combat craft, able to meet a spaceship in orbit.

Around the flier, admiring it from a careful distance, were the residents of the House Gensa; at Kidri's appearance all turned, and fell
neatly into ranks.

They sang "The *Vengeance* Flies at Morning," the theme from
Vrenn's favorite tape series: "Undefeated" was the House favorite, but
it was about facing enemies and death. This was a better song for today.

The guns are hot, the hull is ringing,
The engines sing the sound of triumph;
And every one aboard awaits
A prize upon the high horizon.
Hand and weapon! Heart and power!
Cry it with the voice of Empire!

Victory and prize and plunder!
Vengeance flies at morning!

It was the perfect song for today, and Vrenn's neck hurt with holding his jaw steady and his lips tight shut . . . but Zharn was not here to sing it, nor Gelly.

Rokis stepped forward, limping a bit; she had hurt her leg in the *klin zha kinta,* making a grand swooping kill. She held out her hands to Vrenn: in them was a brown paper envelope. "A gift from us," she said. "Some things to remember."

Vrenn almost smiled. So that was why he had not found it beneath his bed.

A hand intruded, and Vrenn stopped as he reached for the envelope; a Proctor passed a device over the package and withdrew again without touching it.

Vrenn took the package, held it as tightly as he could without wrinkling it. "This is . . . an honorable House," he said, and looked up, but of course sunlight and clouds clothed the stars.

Then the crowd parted, and Vrenn and Tirian went to the flier; the Transporteer touched controls on a wrist device, and the door opened and stairs swung down. Tirian gestured, and Vrenn went aboard.

Vrenn had seen pictures and tapes of ships' interiors, but he was not at all ready for this. He was in a tunnel, barely wider than his shoulders and not much higher than his head, lined with equipment of metal and plastic and rubber, alive with small lights and noises.

"Go on forward," Tirian said, turning his wide shoulders to follow. Vrenn emerged into a slightly larger space, fronted with thick tinted glass. There were two large padded chairs, each caged by equipment. Small displays flickered, and ducted air rushed by.

Tirian said, "You're left seat. That's—"

"Gunner's seat," Vrenn said.

Tirian clicked his teeth together. "Sure, you'd know that. Can you get belted in?"

Vrenn climbed into the seat, pulled the parts of the harness together and locked them over his chest.

"Fine job. Can you get out now?"

Vrenn slapped at the knob on the harness buckle. Nothing happened. He slapped again, hard enough to hurt. Nothing.

Tirian reached across. "Turn, then push." He demonstrated, then relocked the harness. "Anything could bump open those old locks they show on the tapes. This is safer, and just as fast." He leaned against his chair, tapped his thin, pale fingers on his knee. "Now. I'm your Transporteer. Do you know what that means?"

Vrenn struggled with himself. Could this really be a servitor? Or was Vrenn's new status not what he had believed? He looked at Tirian, who waited, no expression on his bony face. Vrenn knew he must answer, and he would not lie. "No. Will you tell me?"

Tirian nodded gravely. "Of course, *zan* Vrenn. My duty is to keep you safe, while you are aboard any vehicle. If you travel by particle transporter, I will set the controls, that you may be properly reassembled. It may also become my duty to inform you of desirable or undesirable actions while in transit; as my master you must decide how to act on this information. Is this explanation sufficient?"

"Yes, Trans—Tirian." It was more than sufficient. A Captain lent his life to the one he trusted as transporter operator, each time he used the machine: the one chosen must be of special quality. It was reasonable that an Admiral should have a special officer for the purpose—and a *kuve* one, who could have no ambitions.

Now Vrenn realized he had insulted one he must trust. He was not sure how to correct the error; surely he should not express error, not to a servitor. He simply had no experience of *kuve;* on tapes they were so easily dealt with . . .

Finally Vrenn said, "I seem to have misunderstood you at first."

Tirian said, "I regret that this is common. I am a Withiki—" more a whistle than a word—"and I do not speak well." He got into his seat, fastened his harness, began bringing the flier to life.

Vrenn looked at him, wondering at what he had just heard. He had seen Withiki, real ones, at the Year Games, and Tirian could not possibly be of that race.

The flier began to lift. Through the windshield Vrenn could see his once-Housemates waving, and he waved back, though realizing they could not see him through the dark glass.

He waited until Tirian had brought them to cruising altitude, then said, "Could you provide me with some information on this equipment?"

Again Tirian's teeth clicked; Vrenn supposed it was his race's form of polite laughter, but he was not offended. "The weapons are indeed loaded, Vrenn, but are all on safety. However, you might enjoy the view through the gunsights. A moment to get us on guide-beam, and I'll show you how it works."

The Khemara linehold was almost a quarter of the world away; it took half a day airborne, beam-guided around reserved airspaces, military and private. Had they intruded, they would have vanished from the sky in an instant.

The Teska had a tiny, unenclosed waste facility, and a food locker stuffed with cold meat and fish and fruit nectars. Vrenn took a swallow and was astonished at the taste: the juice was real.

They swung near mist-cloaked hills and low over green lakes, crossing the Northwest Sea as the sun was setting. The clouds broke for a moment and showed the star, a white pinpoint; Vrenn shielded his eyes at once. Then the light was gone, and they were over the Kartade Forest. Tirian was dozing in his chair, breath whistling. Vrenn had no notion of sleep. He switched the gunsight to night vision and scanned the forest; the intertwined trees showed up in startling clarity, and now and then an animal streaked by, burning bright on the infrared screen.

A beep from the communications board woke Tirian instantly. He touched a switch, and a web of light was projected on the windshield: the image of a landing grid that lay, invisible, on the ground ahead. Tirian hung an audio pickup behind his ear. "Center Space, this is Flier 04 . . . Aboard, affirm . . . My password is Tailfeather. What is your password? Affirm, off beam and landing now."

They touched down very gently. Outside the flier, a pathway lit up; then lights came on behind large windows. Tirian said, "You're to go on inside. My duty's here."

Vrenn nodded. "It was a good trip," he said, sure it was not too much praise.

Tirian did not click his teeth. He said, "Thank you, master Vrenn," with clear satisfaction. And he had said *master,* not the neutral *zan.* He indicated the brown envelope: "May I bring your package?"

"No . . . I'll take that."

Vrenn went down the steps, holding the envelope. The path wound out before him through a garden, with shrubs and pools, and knotted-trunked trees as grew in the Kartade. There was a heavy scent of flower perfumes.

The house was quite high, at least three stories, with a V-shaped roof: the huge front windows seemed a little like angled eyes looking down on Vrenn. Behind the windows was what appeared to be one large room, with red light flickering within.

Without any pause at all, Vrenn went inside.

There was indeed one vast, high-ceilinged room, with wooden beams cutting across the space overhead, and iron-railed stairs to balconies on either side. In the center was a broad, black pillar, open at the base: a fire, fed by wood, burned within. Around the fireplace were cushions, and tables topped with wood inlay and black glass.

A figure stood, silhouetted by the fire. "Welcome, Vrenn. Be welcome in your house."

"Thought Admiral . . ." Vrenn said, and saw the tilt of Kethas's head.

". . . Father."

Kethas nodded, took Vrenn's free hand in both of his and drew him into the firelight. "Sit, if you like, though I suppose you've been sitting too long already. Are you hungry? Thirsty? We need a glass of something to talk over . . . you're nine, aren't you?"

"Nearly nine."

"Yes. Do they have strong drinks, in the Houses? I really don't know that much about them."

"I drink ale."

"Dark ale, then, that's the best when you're tired. Not the scorch of a distillate and less risky than brandy." Almost before Kethas finished speaking, a servitor had appeared with a tray.

Vrenn had never much cared for ale, but it was all he had experience of: this drink, however, was wonderful, as much as the fruit nectar had been. Vrenn began to wonder if he would simply have to relearn eating and drinking.

Another being, a female, came into view. She wore a long gown of some pale stuff that shimmered. Her skin was quite dark, and Vrenn thought for a moment she was Klingon, but then a white ceiling light showed the green cast to her complexion. Light gleamed on fingernails like polished green opals.

And then Vrenn felt something very strange, like an invisible hand squeezing inside his chest. It was not painful . . . not quite. He spilled a little of his drink.

"Pheromonal shock," Kethas said. "At your age, the rush of hormones could be deadly." Vrenn had no idea what Kethas was talking about. He knew from the female's color what she must be: half the ships Koth of the *Vengeance* captured had an Orion female aboard, all green, all beautiful past imagining . . . but Vrenn realized now that they were all just Klingon females in makeup. And compared to this one, they were all dead things.

"This is Rogaine," Kethas said. Vrenn forced himself to listen. "She is my sole consort. Rogaine, this is Vrenn, whom we have taken into the line."

Vrenn bowed. Rogaine returned it, and sank with an impossibly smooth motion onto a cushion by the fire. "Please don't stare," she said, in a fluid voice, one not at all suited to *klingonaase.* "It makes me feel that I have committed an error."

Kethas sat next to Rogaine, covered her hand with his. "In this House you are infallible," he said, and then said something in a language as ill-suited to his tongue as *klingonaase* was to hers. Rogaine laughed, a sound that melted in the air.

Kethas said, "Sit down, Vrenn. This isn't an examination."

Vrenn sat, very carefully. "Thought Admiral, a question."

"Of course; the first of many, I'm sure."

"Why am I here?"

"A fair enough opening," Kethas said. "You do not know your parents, do you? Your actual parents, not us."

"No . . . I do not remember anything but the House. We were told that was better."

"I cannot disagree. But listen now. Your line was Rustazh, your father Squadron Leader Kovar sutai-Rustazh."

"I have a line?" Vrenn burst out. "I—that is—"

"An understandable response. But the Rustazh line is extinct. Your once-father was leading a convoy of colonization; the line had received an Imperial grant of space. But the ships were ambushed, by Romulans. Kovar fought well, but there were problems . . . colony ships are a handicap in combat. There were no survivors, as one expects of Romulans."

"How do I . . . then live?"

"I don't know. Kovar's youngest son was named Vrenn, and he would be your age . . . and I see some resemblance, for whatever that's worth. But how you came to be in the House Twenty-four . . . that is a mystery. Records have been lost, or altered, enough to buy at least one death, could we find the actors."

Kethas drank his ale, and Vrenn did likewise. Kethas spoke again, in a very serious tone. "But you asked why you were here, and I have not answered yet. Under me, Kovar served Empire well, and because of certain things he did in that time I am disposed to do a thing for him."

Vrenn said, "I am—" Kethas cut him off with a raised finger.

The Thought Admiral said, "I have had eight children, which ought to be enough to preserve a line. But seven of them are dead in seven parts of space; and the eighth has changed his name to begin a line of his own, and when his last brother died it was too late to reverse this course. And I have spent many years in space, on the old thin-hulled ships, when the power came from isotopes, and I have taken too much radiation; my children now are monsters, that bubble and die."

Rogaine turned sharply away. Kethas touched her hand, but did not turn toward her. He said, "For Kovar's sake I took you out of the Lineless' House; one life was my debt to him. But for my sake I will make you heritor of the line Khemara, and to this linehold and all its property; and the price is that you will be Khemara and forget that you ever were Rustazh."

Vrenn felt slightly dizzy, but he had heard every word clearly, and there was no Cloud in his mind. He said, "I was never Rustazh until now . . . but now I am already Khemara. And so I will stay."

Kethas stood, put both hands on Vrenn's shoulders. "In you the *klin* lives, this is certain! Odise." A servitor appeared. "Take Vrenn Khemara to his rooms." He gave Vrenn's shoulder a squeeze, then let go.

Vrenn stood, retrieving his envelope. Kethas said, "What's that? Discharge papers?" He held out his hand.

"*No* . . . these are . . . just some things of mine."

Kethas nodded. "We'll talk again tomorrow, then. And . . . I saw you on the board; do you play *klin zha,* when you are not a piece?"

"Yes, Grand Master." Vrenn supposed the title was appropriate now.

Kethas smiled slightly. "Then we will do that." He went back to Rogaine, who sat very still by the fire; he spoke to her in her own language.

The servitor Odise bowed crookedly to Vrenn. It was a small being, a little over half Vrenn's height, with spindly legs and arms and a turret head, covered all over with smooth black fur. It turned, and Vrenn followed it, up stairs to a corridor above.

The *kuve* opened a door, handed the key to Vrenn, then gestured for him to enter the dark doorway. As Vrenn did, lights came on.

The chambers inside were fully the equal of a Captain's quarters. There was a study the size of Vrenn's shared room at the house, with a library screen and books on shelves; an equally large bedroom beyond that; a private wash-and-waste. Odise demonstrated some of the controls—silently; it apparently did not speak—bowed and went out, closing the door.

Vrenn wandered around the rooms for several minutes. The similarity to a Captain's cabin was not just superficial, he realized. He had seen pictures of ships showing the same furnishings: the cylindrical closets, the angular desks and chairs, the tracked spotlamps. The bed even had a concave surface, though there was no restraint web. There was a meal slot in the wall, with programming buttons. And the walls were covered with clearprints of stars and planets, lit from behind, exactly like viewports to Space beyond.

Vrenn sat down on the lumpless bed, weighted down with too many enormities for one day.

On a small table next to the bed was a *klin zha* set. The pieces were of heavy green and amber stone—jade and quartz, Vrenn guessed, having heard of those materials. The board was black enamel, with inlaid brass strips marking off the spaces. Vrenn looked at it for a long while, not touching it, then opened his brown envelope and slid its contents out onto the table: a triangular piece of heavy card, and some discs of soft wood.

Vrenn had found the board on the ground next to a recycling bin, and inked the triangular grid with another piece of scrap for a straight-edge. The discs were hole-punchings from some packing material, scrounged in the same way. Vrenn had engraved the symbols for the pieces into the soft grain with a writing stylus. They were Green and Black, since he had no yellow ink.

Vrenn set up his pieces to match the stone set. He made a few moves, then looked up at the corners of his room. There was nothing overtly a monitor visible. He felt the key in his pocket, thought about getting up to lock the door, but did not.

Finally he scooped the paper board and pieces into their envelope, reached beneath his bed, and found a slot where the package would fit.

Morning light filtered through skylights, vines, and fog into the house's indoor garden. Vrenn felt the warm, wet air like a solid substance around him. Fog parted as he moved.

Kethas was armpit-deep in a sponge-tiled pool, watching text flicker by on a small viewer at the water's edge. "Come in, Vrenn," he said, and touched the display off.

Vrenn approached. His tunic and trousers were damp, impeding him. He stood on the edge of the water, on which bright plants were floating, giving off a sweet scent.

"Well, come *in,*" Kethas said, smiling.

After a moment, Vrenn undressed and slipped into the water. It was an oddly neutral sensation, not cool, not hot, just . . . enveloping, and very comfortable.

"Now we're civilized," Kethas said. "Have you eaten?"

"I . . . just a little." The meal slot in his room served nine flavors of fruit nectar, and he had gone through a large glass of each. But they had not stayed with him. And he had soon been more interested by the library screen, which also served as a starship action simulator.

"Two meals," Kethas said, to the apparently inert monitor. "You were up early."

Vrenn wondered then if his room was watched. "We always woke before sunrise, at the House."

"There's no such rule here. It would never work. I live midmorning to midnight, and Rogaine needs many little sleeptimes, and Tirian sleeps when it's convenient, like a Vulcan. If you like mornings, fine, but find the time you're best at and live there. That's the payoff strategy. The most efficient, that is to say."

That was exactly the opposite of what the House Proctors called efficiency, but Vrenn was already thinking of something else. "Are there Vulcans here?"

"No, I do not have a *tharavul.* Can you use a library unit?"

Watched or not? Vrenn thought, and said, "Yes."

"Then you have no need for *tharavul*. Here's food."

There were light fried anemones and crisp salt fish, sweet gel pastries (Vrenn was careful to take only two) and a hot dark drink he thought at first was heated ale, but which was something harsh and incredibly bitter. Vrenn nearly choked.

"Human *kafei*," Kethas said, laughing. "They bring it to me in course; I should have warned you. Awful, yes, but you learn to drink it. Some years back, I was on a deep mission, taking supply by forage, and for half the voyage we had nothing to drink but a case of that stuff taken as prize . . . that and the white fire the Engineer brewed up. They're not bad together, too." Kethas drained his cup. "*And* it has a mind-clearing effect, which you're going to need."

The Thought Admiral reached to the display unit again. As he rose slightly from the water, Vrenn could see rippled scars on Kethas's flank. He had watched enough tapes of battles to know that only delta rays left marks like that: Kethas had been burned by either an unshielded warpdrive, or Romulan lasers.

"Bring down my green tunic," Kethas said to the unit, "and for Vrenn, the gold."

Vrenn and Kethas walked around the fireplace in the large front room. Along the walls were boards and pieces for every game Vrenn had ever heard of, and even more that he had not. For *klin zha* there were many sets, for all the variations.

"I've seen you in the Clouded Game," Kethas said. "Do you know the Ablative form?" He gestured to a board that was elevated on posts, pressed a finger on one of the spaces; the triangular tile fell out, into a tray below.

"Yes. And Blind, too." Vrenn wore a long coat of gold brocade, with the multicolored crest of a forest lizard sewn across the shoulders. Kethas's coat was of thick green cloth, with an Admiral's haloed stars on the sleeve.

Vrenn thought about his clothes; both the wardrobes in his rooms had been filled. This gown was too new to have been the Admiral's; it must have belonged to one of Kethas's children. Vrenn put the question away to ask later, if at all.

Kethas pointed at boards marked in squares instead of triangles. One was square overall, spaces alternately black and white; the other was rectangular, a tan color with gold lines.

"The *human zha, chess.* And the *rom zha,* which the Romulans call *latrunculo.* They are both fine games, though not so interesting or varied as *klin zha.*

"Do all races have a game?"

Kethas smiled, evidently pleased with the question. "Kinshaya have no stylized game, though they are excellent at small-war with model soldiers. Vulcans find games 'illogical,' though they create computer simulations that amount to the same thing, and labor at other races' games for some reason of the Vulcan sort. Do you know the saying 'Less pleasant than torturing Vulcans'?"

Vrenn laughed, which was enough answer. Kethas said, "Among Masters of the Game it goes '. . . than *klin zha* against a Vulcan.' "

"And the *kuve?*"

"The *kuve* do not. They have games, yes, and some of them are worth a little study—I will show you, another time—but no *kuve zha* can be truly great."

"That is only sensible," Vrenn said, embarrassed. "I should have understood it."

"An obvious question is better than obvious ignorance," Kethas said. "In this house questions may always be asked. Only in the larger universe must one be cautious not to show one's blindness."

Vrenn nodded, silently resolving to be more cautious at once. He said, "What variant is this?" realizing he was showing more ignorance.

The board and pieces before them were of *klin zha* pattern, but there was only one set of pieces, colored green and gold combined.

"That is for the Reflective Game. It is the highest form of *klin zha,* and the most difficult. Barring of course the *komerex zha*—or do you deny the Perpetual Game?" Kethas shook his head, smiling; evidently a joke was intended. "Come here; I'll show you."

Kethas picked up the Reflective set, carried it to one of the tables by the fireplace. He punched up a cushion and sat against it, then swept the single set of two-colored pieces to the side of the board.

Vrenn sat, folding his tunic beneath himself, and waited.

"In the Reflective Game," Kethas said, "there is a single group of pieces which either player may move in turn. All pieces move in the fashion of the normal Open Game."

"How does one win?"

"In the same fashion as the Open Game: by making it impossible for the opponent to move legally. . . . We begin by setting up. Choose a piece and place it: any piece, anywhere. Then I shall do so, and so on, alternating."

Without hesitation, Vrenn reached for the Fencer, placing it in the corner of the board nearest himself. He watched Kethas: but suddenly nothing at all, not even a smile, was readable from the Grand Master's face. Kethas selected a Vanguard, placed it some distance from Vrenn's Fencer.

When all the pieces were placed, in what seemed to Vrenn a totally random fashion, Kethas said, "I move first. This is a disadvantage." He shifted a Vanguard. "Now, your move."

"*Any* piece? And I may kill as well?"

"Of course. *Remember only,*" he said, still without expression, "that you may not voluntarily put your Goal in danger of attack. Even though it is *also* my Goal."

Suddenly Vrenn began to understand. He examined the board, realizing that most of the moves he had thought were possible actually endangered the Goal disc. If he even moved the Fencer off the Goal, it would then become the enemy's Fencer, and give the enemy an instant victory.

The game lasted only three moves after that.

Kethas sat back. "A pleasing game," he said. "My compliments to a worthy opponent."

Vrenn felt frustrated, angry. He felt he had been used, to win a cheap and honorless victory. Controlling his voice, he said, "I am a good player, at the forms of *klin zha* which I know, but I do not know this one, and I could not play well against you."

Kethas answered in a voice that seemed to reach out and physically take hold of Vrenn. "I am an undrawn Grand Master of the Game, and you cannot *lose* well against me, no matter the form. But as with all my children, I will play this game or another against you every day that you are here, and in time you will learn to lose well, and you may even learn to lose brilliantly."

Vrenn held his hands below the table, keeping them from clawing into fists, kept his lips from curling back. He wanted to understand, but was not sure at all that he did, or ever would. "And if in time I learn to win . . . however badly?"

"*Kai Kassai, Klingon!*" Kethas said, laughing, and slapped Vrenn's shoulder. "Then I will make you a Thought Admiral in my place, and retire to my consort and my garden pool forever!"

That night, after a long and useless assault on sleep, Vrenn touched on the bedside lamp and stared at the stonecut *klin zha* set in the pool of light. Then he reached beneath the bed, took out the envelope, shook its contents onto the table and set up a game.

It was an afternoon deep in the cold season, and the perpetual fireplace was stoked high; there had been a trace of real white frost on the garden outside, just at dawn, and Vrenn had watched until the day reclaimed it. He had never been so far north, and found the change of seasons amazing. He had been Khemara now for two-thirds of a year.

Kethas had been away from the house for ten days, at a meeting of the Imperial Council, in the Throne City on the other side of the world. Today, the morning's message said, he would be returning.

Tirian had at once gone to check the working of the house's transporter station; he seemed satisfied, and now sat in the front room reading a printed book, while Vrenn experimented with *klin zha* positions on a computer grid. Music drifted down from a balcony: Rogaine was playing the harp in her chambers. The sound was pleasing, but it was not like Klingon music; there could be no words to it, and it did not inspire.

The harp fell silent. A moment later, Tirian's belt annunciator chimed. He tucked his book away inside his clothing. Vrenn blanked the game display and followed Tirian out of the house.

Beyond the formal garden and the flier landing, all to itself, was a small hexagonal pavilion, much newer than the main house. The particle transporter had been safe for Klingon use for less than thirty years; only very recently had anyone, even an Admiral, the luxury of a home station.

Inside the small building, Tirian unlocked two banks of controls. On the first, he dilated an opening in the deflector shield covering the estate, set to scramble any unauthorized attempt to beam in. Then he went to the second console and began setting to receive.

There were three discs on the floor before the control consoles, matching three on the ceiling. Between one pair a column of sparkling golden light appeared, entirely without sound.

Kethas epetai-Khemara, in black silk tunic and full-formal gold vest heavy with medals, stepped off the disc, and sighed. The grooves in his face and forehead stood out very darkly. Vrenn could not remember seeing him look so tired, or old.

"Well done, Tirian," Kethas said. "The war continues, on every space of the board." He nodded to Vrenn, and went out of the transporter pavilion, toward the house.

Tirian began locking up the console. Vrenn thought of what he had wanted to ask the servitor, for a long time now: suddenly, perhaps because of the quiet of the mood, or their distance from the life of the house, it seemed the right time to ask. "Tirian, do you believe in the Black Fleet?"

"My people mostly believe in a next life," Tirian said, without looking from his work, "though there are not starships in it. But we evolved separately, and if one world's idea is true, I suppose all must be."

It was much more answer than Vrenn had expected, but he took it as affirmation. "When my father has gone to command there . . . will you then be his Transporteer?"

"What," Tirian said quietly, "does the Empire's hold extend so far as that?"

"Any race may reach—"

"I know. Kethas has told me. I will have a place on his Black Ship. Even if I do not want it."

"You are Withiki," Vrenn said. "You would have wings again."

Tirian turned. His skull face was drawn, pure white. "So my younger master is a strategist as well," he said flatly. "The Thought Admiral will be pleased.

"But I wonder if you are right, Master Vrenn. I had fine wings once, blue-feathered, if you know what that means, and of spread twice my height. But such broad wings are awkward in the corridors of a starship. So a Force Leader of Imperial Race told me, when he had his Marines pull my wings from their sockets. Do you think that officer is also in the Black Fleet, waiting to maim me a thousand times? Laughing?

"*Kuvesa tokhesa.* Your father. While I live." Tirian walked out of the room, toward the flier hangars, not the house.

After a little while, Vrenn went back to the house, thinking that he had in fact won a victory, gotten the information he wanted. But it did not have the taste of victory.

The female Rogaine was seated among the web ferns of the indoor garden, playing her harp. There was no light from above, and she was no more than a dark shape outlined in light, almost one with the reflections on the pool beyond. Thick mist floated, glowing, diffuse.

Rogaine turned, playing a complex chord, and Vrenn could see that the mist was all that covered her. He felt a stitch in his side, as if his air was short. It was not quite pain, and then it was something worse than any pain Vrenn had ever known. Rogaine's long nails stroked the strings, and Vrenn heard himself groan.

Then a cold hand touched him, and all his nerves cried out at once.

Vrenn lay on his back, in his bed. Above him, touching Vrenn's shoulder, was Kethas, wearing his dress uniform. Only the bedside lamp was on; it seemed to be still the middle of the night, when Kethas slept.

"Get up, and dress," the Thought Admiral said. "It is a night for decisions. Meet me in the garden outside." He went away.

Vrenn lay still a moment longer, not entirely certain he had not simply slipped from one dream into another. But his senses told him otherwise; surely, he thought, the relics he felt of his last dream would not carry over to this one. So he rose, and put on his adoption-day clothes that were like a Cadet's, and went outside.

The night air was very cold, and Vrenn's breath misted. The sky was very dark. . . .

The sky, Vrenn saw, was cloudless. Overhead were stars, hard and white, all the thousand stars of the world's sky standing naked, as they did on less than one night in a hundred.

So whatever Vrenn and Kethas said here, whatever they did, would be remembered for all time to come.

"Shortly you will be ten years old," Kethas said, a figure of gold and darkness—but no dream, Vrenn knew. "It will be time for you to choose what you will be. Have you thought on this?"

"The Navy," Vrenn said instantly.

Kethas did not smile. "You know that I do not require this of you? That you may, as you wish, be a scientist, or an administrator—or even a Marine?"

"I know, Father. And I would not be anything else."

Then the Thought Admiral smiled. "And so you should not. You captain the machine like you were made for it. I am pleased to find you wise as well as skillful."

Vrenn said, "Was my father sutai-Rustazh a great captain?"

Kethas tilted his head. "You have no father but myself." After a moment he added, "Though it is true I once knew one called sutai-Rustazh, who was great."

Vrenn bowed his head, ashamed at the stupidity of the question. And still Kethas—indeed his only father, his whole line—had answered it; Vrenn wondered what this strategy was.

Kethas said, "There are assistances I can provide. You will be assigned directly to the Academy, of course, and the Path of Command. A cruise can be arranged at the earliest—"

"I would make my own path, Father."

Kethas's hand slashed crosswise. "Don't talk like a Romulan! What, do you think you are the only son of an Admiral who will attend the Academy? Half your mates will be Admirals' sons; and some of them will be *kuvekhestat* unfit to *serve* aboard a ship, and those especially will use every advantage their lines can win them. You are still not a good enough player to give your enemies odds." He paused, said more gently, "And surely you do not deny the Perpetual Game?"

Vrenn stood entirely still, feeling his jaw clench, his lips pulling apart. He knew then that he must have a ship, a command, and he would have them, and he would never know shame again. He looked at the stars, stark burning naked, and knew the oath was sealed.

"Let's go inside," Kethas said, his manner easy again. "We'll play *klin zha.*"

They went into the house. The fire was uncommonly welcome after the cold of the night. Vrenn sat at the game table, reached to turn it on.

"Not that set," Kethas said. "The one in your room. The one beneath your bed."

Vrenn felt his eyes twitch with staring. Kethas's look was bland. Vrenn went to his room, brought back the envelope with the set of wood and card.

"There is never time to teach everything, so the important things must take precedence," Kethas said, as they played through a standard opening. "And example works quickest . . . you do know the proverb: If you do not wish a thing heard—"

"Do not say it."

"Yes. This will always be true; it will be so if you are a Captain, or an Admiral, or the Emperor. You will be watched, so live as if you are watched. Beds are a terrible place for secrets . . . you are about to lose your Vanguard." And Kethas moved, killing it. He picked up the dead piece, turned the disc over in his fingers. "You know that there is a form of *klin zha* we have not yet played."

"What is that, Father?"

"It is the form least often taught, less even than the Reflective, but in a way it is the most important of all to a Captain. I think we should play it now." Kethas flicked his fingers, and the wooden Vanguard sailed through the air, into the fireplace, where the flames absorbed it with the smallest of whispers.

It had happened faster than Vrenn could think, and now he did not know what to think. He wondered if Kethas had flipped the piece through the fire, and out the other side, but he did not believe that.

Finally the Thought Admiral said, "Your move."

Vrenn looked around the room, and the gameboards along the walls. He started to rise. "And which set will the Thought Admiral risk?"

Kethas waved a finger at Vrenn's seat cushion. It looked like a casual gesture. It was not. Vrenn sat.

Kethas said, "You are not ready to count your enemy's losses until you have learned to count your own. And remember that some enemies will never have learned to count."

Vrenn looked at the board and pieces that he had made so carefully, kept so long; he tried to see them as nothing but scraps of fiber, bits of waste saved from the bin, and he could not. "What happens, then, when I kill a piece of your side?"

"Keep it," Kethas said. "Eventually there will be only one set left. And then we will play the Reflective Game."

Vrenn moved his Fencer and Goal, feeling the wood very warm and fragile against his fingers, like a living thing.

Three: Gambits

Romulan plasma hit Klingon shields: power leaked through in second and third harmonics, and the target cruiser shook.

"Damage?" said the officer in the command chair.

Vrenn Khemara ran his finger down a screen, bright in the red-lit Bridge; a schematic of the cruiser *Blue Fire* flashed into view, yellow blocks marking areas hit. Vrenn read off the reports in a few short phrases of Battle Language.

Below Vrenn, the Commander spat an acknowledgment and turned back to the main display. Vrenn looked up: across the Bridge, another Cadet flashed a hand at him, fingers spread. The gesture symbolized a Captain's starburst of rank: in words it would come out approximately as "You'll have a command by morning!"

Blue Fire rolled to starboard. She was pulling Warp 3, and the floor-plates whined and the bulkheads groaned; a Cadet grabbed a strut to steady himself under the shifting gravity. The Commander caught sight of it. "Environmental?" he said, tone deadly even, eyes like disruptors.

The unbalanced Cadet strained toward his board. "Point eight six two, nominal," he said.

The Commander acknowledged, turned back to the main view. All the Cadets understood very well: fall down, fall asleep, do as you like, as long as you've got the Captain's answers when he wants them.

It was not the Captain of *Blue Fire* in the Chair. Squadron Leader Kodon was five decks above, in the Primary Bridge. Commander Kev, the Executive Officer, sat with the Cadets in the Auxiliary Bridge, call-ing for situation reports and helm responses exactly as if he were Kodon, and the Cadets worked their locked-off consoles just as if they controlled the ship.

Only the data were real.

There was a flash in the corner of the display as the cruiser rolled; Vrenn's instruments picked up the wave of energy as a plasma bolt passed less than forty meters below their ship's port wing. It had not been fired when Kodon started the maneuver: he had somehow fore-seen the enemy action. Vrenn watched, and tried to learn.

The Klingons were outnumbered, five to three; but the Klingon D-4 cruisers were individually much more powerful than the Romulan War-birds. "So we win, on numbers," Kodon had told them, before the raid began, "but there's a few things the numbers don't count."

Two Fingers, the portside ship of Kodon's Squadron, had picked up three of the Warbirds, which swarmed around it, firing plasma in con-tinuous cycle, two ships' tubes cooling while one blazed, trying to bat-ter their victim's shields down from all directions at once.

"One thing," Kodon said, "is that ships *move*. Tactics are real, and if you don't move right, you die."

Blue Fire was now turned perpendicular to *Two Fingers*. Commander Kev gave a firing order, and the Cadets on Weapons followed just as the officers above them. Six disruptors fired, making two pyramids of blue light whose points were Romulan ships. Romulan hulls buckled, as the forces holding their molecules together were suppressed and restored ninety times a second. That was disruption: or, as the big ships' batteries were nicknamed, the Sound of Destruction.

Two Warbirds lurched out of their loops, and *Two Fingers* went to work on the third. *Blue Fire* came about again, to find a prey of its own.

There was a sudden swelling spot of white light in the forward display: the screen darkened, and it was still too bright to look at. Then the flash faded, and was gone. Stars came back on in the display. Ahead, the other ship of the squadron, *Death Hand,* had turned into the blast, to take it against her strong forward shields.

"The other thing," the Squadron Leader had told them all, "Is that Roms have some pretty odd ideas about dying."

Kev said, "Communications, signal Code KATEN to Squadron. Helm, when KATEN is acknowledged executed, I want Warp 4 at once."

The Cadets tensed, almost as a unit. There would be no boarding this time, no prizes, not even a creditable kill they could stripe on their sashes. But this was only the first skirmish of the raid, as Kodon had outlined it to them all. Their goal was farther into the Romulan sphere. Vrenn certainly understood; it was not an elaborate strategy, even for the frontier squadrons.

Still, he wanted a kill as much as the rest of them.

Perhaps more.

Both enemy squadrons were trying to regroup, to disentangle from each other's ships. The Klingon cruisers had more power, which counted most in large-ship maneuvers; *Death Hand* was able to bounce a Rom off its shields like a small animal off a groundcar's fender.

Formation lights flared on displays, drifting toward marked target positions: the three D-4s moved, silently as all things in space, into a triskele formation, port engines inward. A Rom fired, the bolt glancing from *Blue Fire*'s shields.

"You may give him one for vengeance, *zan* Tatell," Kev said, and as helm counted toward formation lock-on Weapons trued his crosshairs and his firing keys. Blue light reached out to the Rom, to the bronze raptor painted on its belly.

The bird was cut open from wing to drumstick.

Lights met their targets. "Warp 4," the Helmsman remembered to say, and the Romulans—what was left of them—streaked by and were gone, as Kodon's squadron pierced yet deeper into the space the Roms claimed as theirs, three times faster than their ships could follow.

Commander Kev stood, inspected the Cadets. He touched the phone in his ear that had sent him all of the actual Captain's orders. "A good engagement," he said, "damage done, no ships lost, only minor injuries to crewmen and none to officers . . ." Kev looked at Zhoka, the Cadet who had almost lost more than just his balance.

Kev paused, eyes narrowed, apparently getting some message through his earphone. "I am instructed to tell you that, by consensus of the Squadron Captains, *Blue Fire* is to be credited with one Romulan kill. May this be a favorable sign."

Kev stood silent then, watching. The Cadets did not move. Vrenn thought the collar of his blue tunic must surely be contracting, but kept his hands firmly on his console.

Finally the Commander decided they had had enough. "Alert over. Stand down to cruise stations." And he saluted. "*Blue Fire,* the victory!"

"The victory!"

Vrenn and his roommate, an engineering cadet named Ruzhe Avell, were playing Open *klin zha* in quarters. Vrenn had not played *klin zha* against a live opponent since halfway through his Academy year; until Ruzhe, everyone had too much minded losing.

Maybe Ruzhe didn't mind because he didn't pay attention anyway. "I still say it's better in Engineering. We get to work on the real ship, not dead controls."

"If something happened to the main Bridge, it'd be real enough."

"And you know how long we'd last after that? You know, you can still get off that Command Path, and do something with honest metal and current."

Vrenn felt a little annoyance at the word "honest," but only a little. It was only another game between them, and he could hardly fault Ruzhe for being better at it than at *klin zha.* "I think I'll stay up front in the pod. Away from the radiation."

"There's no radiation back there! We just keep the Drell design because it works!"

"All right, up front away from the Marines."

Ruzhe growled, stared at the board. "You're going to win again."

It was true enough. Vrenn said, "Maybe you'll get lucky, and the Roms will attack." He moved a Flier. "After all, we got lucky enough to get assigned to a raid, on our first full cruise."

Ruzhe said, "I heard one of the Lieutenants say everyone gets assigned to a raid, unless they're just so hopeless they have to put 'em on garbage scows or runs to Vulcan."

"Why?" Vrenn said. He had heard rumors like that, but only from superior-sounding Cadets. Never officers.

"Same reason all the frontier captains go privateer: if you *khest* it, it's your fault, not the Academy's."

Vrenn knew that was true. "So I guess we better not *khest* it?"

Ruzhe laughed. "Sure you don't want to work aft?" He bumped the board. Pieces tipped over. "*Gday't,* I lose."

"Well, you *khest't* it." Vrenn picked up a fallen piece. "Want to *khest* it again?"

"I'd like to *khest* just once on this trip," Ruzhe said. "Got an Orion female in your closet?"

The piece slipped out of Vrenn's fingers, bounced on the floor.

Kodon's Squadron had been inside Romulan claims for seventy-eight days. There had been two more skirmishes, early on, and a kill for *Death Hand* and another for *Blue Fire,* but nothing, not even a contact, for over fifty days now. They were eating salvage from the third battle, Romulan rations, solid enough food but dull on the tongue. Vrenn at last understood his father's story about Human *kafei,* and found it actually made the alien stuff more edible; but the trick didn't work for the other Cadets. Some of those from old Navy lines had been given sealed parcels of food, with vague warnings about not opening them too soon; now anyone who had obeyed the warning had power, of a sort. Vrenn rather quickly saw the limitations of a fruitcake-based economy, and knew why Kethas had not so supplied him.

Still, it could be hard to be a strategist.

Vrenn was in the Junior Officers' Mess, chewing determinedly at a piece of vacuum-dried sausage, when the sounds of a discussion floated in his direction. There were three Ensigns at a table across the room, and they had gotten on the subject of Orions, and (inevitably) Orion females. One of them, the Helmsman Kotkhe, was insisting he had actually been with one, prize of a Cadet cruise. "I admit I was lucky—"

"*Nobody* gets that lucky on a Cadet cruise," said an Ensign with Medical insignia.

"I suppose you two think I care if you believe me."

"Suppose we do." That was Merzhan, the youngest Security officer on the ship. He kept to himself less than the other Security crew, and he showed a nasty sense ot humor on all occasions. "You wouldn't have some evidence? A lock of her hair, tied up with a green ribbon?"

"Well, I—" Kotkhe's hand stopped on the way to his pocket.

Merzhan's smile was thin as the edge of a knife, and the other Ensign looked nervous. Vrenn dumped his tray down the disposal slot, started for the door. He had seen the souvenirs you could buy in a leave port, knew how easily the green dye rubbed off. And he had heard, easily thirty times in his first Academy term, the tale of exotic delights that Kotkhe was now clumsily telling again. He'd have done better, Vrenn thought, to just quote some text from a volume of *Tales of the Privateers;* every other book in the series had the same scene in it.

"But there's a thing they never tell you in the books," Kotkhe said. "And that's the place, the only one place, where an Orion female's *not* green."

Vrenn paused. He wondered where it would be, this time.

Merzhan's eyes flickered over. "Well," he said, "you've got *something* convinced."

"I was just leaving," Vrenn said, and knew at once it was the wrong response: he should have just gone out the door. *Ensigns love Cadets,* he had been warned at the Academy, *like you love jelly pastry. They won't talk to the crew and there's nobody else they can damage.*

"Don't go yet," the Security officer said. "You'll miss the best part."

Vrenn took a step toward the door.

"I said, *don't go,* Cadet."

Vrenn stopped. It was a legitimate order.

Merzhan said, "Well, 'Khe, we've got something here to educate. Finish the story."

Kotkhe seemed pleased; baiting Cadets was much safer than whatever game Merzhan had been playing. He went on to detail exactly where Orion females were not green. It was the usual version. "Now, Pathfinder, have you learned something to help you walk?" The title and the phrase referred to the Path of Command: the statement was thoroughly insulting without containing any explicit insult.

Vrenn said suddenly, "No, Ensign."

Kotkhe's jaw opened, snapped shut. "Say that again, Pathfinder. For the record this time."

"If I hadn't wanted it heard I wouldn't have said it." Vrenn had not realized just how angry he was. They had, without realizing it, pushed him into an area of his mind he had very carefully walled off. Now Vrenn wondered how much his strategic blindness would cost him.

There was a coldness in the room, the Ensigns still not quite believing what they had heard. *Sometimes to show teeth is enough,* Vrenn thought, *but if you bite, bite deep.* "What was there to learn? The lesson's wrong. There's no place they don't have a little green. No place at all."

"Kahlesste kaase," the surgeon's aide said, "he's right."

It was no improvement, though Vrenn wondered if anything short of a Romulan attack could be. Now not only was Ensign Kotkhe made out a liar, his boast of conquest had been upstaged—by a Cadet.

"I guess it is true," Kotkhe said, sounding almost desperate; "they *will* open to anything—"

Vrenn leaped, knocking Kotkhe from his chair, taking both of them to the deck. Kotkhe was unready, and Vrenn gave him no chance: Vrenn punched four times rapidly to nerve junctions. Kotkhe went rigid. Vrenn struck once crosswise, neatly dislocating the Ensign's jaw. Then he stopped—and realized the medical Ensign was holding his arm in a wrestler's pinch above the elbow, shaking his head *no, no*. There were more Klingons in the room now, Security enforcers in duty armor, shock clubs out and ready. Merzhan was tucking away his communicator with his left hand; his right held a pistol casually level.

The look on the Security officer's face was that of one starving, suddenly offered a banquet.

Squadron Leader Kodon vestai-Karum sat behind his desk. Commander Kev sat a little distance to Kodon's right. Vrenn Khemara stood, in the crossfire between them.

"And that was when you assaulted the Ensign?" Kodon said, in a completely disinterested tone.

"Just then, Squadron Leader."

Kodon reached to the tape player in his desk, took out the cassette with the Ensigns' and Vrenn's testimony. "I know the epetai-Khemara somewhat," he said, not quite offhand. "Is the one well?"

"At my last hearing, Squadron Leader."

"And his consort?"

Vrenn hesitated, only an instant. "And the one, Squadron Leader."

Kodon nodded. "The line Khemara is not to be insulted, even ignorantly by ignorant youth. Do you wish to enter a claim of line honor?"

"No, Squadron Leader." Vrenn was suddenly thinking of Ensign Merzhan's look, and his words, and wondering if complete ignorance had really been there.

"That seems best. As much as we need diversion, the duel circle does not seem right, just now. And I do not know Ensign Kotkhe's father; there are so many Admirals. . . ." Kodon sat back, turning the tape over in his hands. "The Ensign didn't even scratch you, Cadet. How do you account for that?"

"I had the advantage of surprise, Squadron Leader."

Kodon laughed. "Ah. Well, I can hardly assume that the other Ensigns held him down for you." He leaned over his desk again, held up the cassette as if weighing it. "Brawling aboard a ship under cruise is a violation of regulations, as is striking a superior office . . . but injuries sustained during a lesson in personal combat are of course not actionable."

"Combat lessons are usually given in the Officers' Gym," Kev said.

"It was occupied," Kodon said. "*I* was using it."

Kev said, "Of course, Captain."

Kodon dropped the cassette. It struck a pair of doors on the desktop, which opened to swallow it, and closed on the flash of destroying light. "It simplifies matters enormously when honor claims are absent."

Vrenn waited.

"Still, a disturbance was created, and Security was dispatched without cause. Commander Kev, I think you know what punishment is appropriate." Kodon stood, and Kev. Salutes were exchanged, and the Squadron Leader disappeared into his inner cabin.

Kev, a portable terminal under his arm, walked to the desk. He brought the black panel up to working position, pressed keys. Green light flashed in his yellow eyes. "The Surgeon reports that Ensign Kotkhe will be unfit for duty for several days. Given your responsibility for this, your punishment detail will be to assume his duties aboard."

"The Helm, Commander?"

"That is *zan* Kotkhe's current duty."

At times like this, Vrenn came close to denying the *komerex zha:* for the universe to be a game implied that it had knowable rules.

Kev looked at Vrenn. The look was very cool, very sharp. Vrenn had realized some time ago that Kev used his eyes as needles; he liked to watch others writhe, impaled on their points.

Finally the Executive said, "You seem to realize that you haven't won anything. That's good. It was necessary that the *g'dayt*-livered Kotkhe be replaced. You forced the Captain's hand; don't think he likes that. Just remember: he's made you a Helmsman. He can make you raw protein if he wants." Kev pushed more keys on his console. In a quieter but no less threatening voice, he said, "You'll be breveted Ensign for the rest of the cruise . . . or as long as you last. Don't go changing your name yet. . . ."

"I understand, Commander."

Kev looked up sharply. In a wholly changed tone he said, "Yes . . . it's just possible that you do. But if you did plan this, Khemara, do not ever let anyone know it. *Dismissed.*"

Kodon's Squadron hid, literally, behind a rock. The three cruisers, in Spearhead formation, hung behind a two-kilometer planetoid, shadowed from enemy sensing. A drone, too small to register at this range, orbited the rock, relaying image and data to the D-4s.

"Keep the guns cold until I call for them," Kodon said, not for the first time but without audible annoyance. "*Zan* Vrenn, watch the shadow."

Vrenn's console display showed a yellow-gridded sphere, the planetoid, and a larger blue arc, the electronic penumbra. "Margin seventy meters, firm," Vrenn said.

"That's good," said the Captain. It was only acknowledgment, not approval. But it was good work, Vrenn knew: he was successfully holding the cruiser to a mark less than a third of its length away. Ensign Kotkhe had been out of Sickbay for ten days now, but this was the climax of the raid, and Ensign Vrenn had the helm.

The Communications Officer gestured. The drone operator touched a control, adjusting the satellite's orbit: on the main display, a planet came into sharp focus, blue and brown and cloud-streaked. Keys were pressed, and data lines overlaid the visual, with a bright three-armed crosshair over the site of the Romulan groundport.

Tiny flecks appeared near the planet's edge, and were annotated at once: "Cargo tugs," the sensor operator announced. Then: "Shuttle launches confirmed."

Kodon watched the main board, scanned the repeater displays near the foot of his chair. "Helm signal 0.2 Warp," he said, in the short syllables of Battle Language.

"0.2 Warp read," Vrenn said.

"Show mag 8," said the Captain.

The picture on the screen swelled, sparkling as the sensors reached their limit of resolution. The image still clearly showed the Romulan shuttles rolling over, to dock with warpdrive tugs already in orbit above the port.

The schematic display drew in four yellow crescents: Warbirds moving into convoy positions.

Kodon said, "Helm, action. Affirm, action."

"Acting," Vrenn said, and pushed for thrust. The planetoid fell away, the target world dawning above it.

"Weapons preheat," Kodon ordered. "Shields attack standard." Each command was no longer than a single word, the acknowledgments just snaps of the tongue.

"Warp 0.2," Vrenn said.

"Squadron—" Kodon said, on relay to all the ships, and his next word was the same in plain or Battle Language: *"Kill!"*

They fell on the Warbirds from ahead and above, out of the danger cone from their plasma guns. Rom lasers, warp-accelerated into the delta frequencies, stabbed up, to detune against shields. Triplet disruptors knifed down, blue light sweeping across the enemy ships' wings. *Two Fingers* severed a Romulan warp engine neatly; its other fire missed by meters. *Death Hand* cut almost entirely through a Warbird's wing, and tore its spine open, splashing fire and debris.

"Precision fire," Kodon said. "Helm, coordinate."

"Affirm," the Weapons officer said. "Affirm," Vrenn said, eyes on three different data displays at once. There was no vision to spare for the controls: now his hands had to know the task.

They did. *Blue Fire* scraped by a Warbird barely twice its length away, and cut both warp nacelles away in a stroke. The flat Rom hull, unable to maneuver or even self-destruct, wavered and began to tumble.

"Stern tractors," said the Squadron Leader.

"Locked." The beams pulled the crippled Rom away from the planet, slinging it on a slow curve toward deep space; the prize would still be there when they were ready to claim it.

"Five more coming, Squadron Leader," the sensor operator said, then, in a tighter voice, "Correction, ten more." He dropped out of Battle Language. "They must have been hiding in—"

"Show it," Kodon said.

Finger-fives of Warbirds were swinging into high strike-fractionals above the planet's east and west horizons. The Klingons were caught between.

Vrenn thought suddenly of white and black pieces on a square-gridded board: but this was no time for the image, and he shoved it away.

"Helm, Warp 0.3. Keep us well sublight, this close to the planet. Vector." Kodon stroked a finger on his armrest controls, drawing the path he wanted on Vrenn's display. It was not an escape vector. "Weapons, free fire," the Squadron Leader said, then, "*Zan* Kandel, reopen the Captains' Link."

Blue Fire caught plasma to starboard, and shook as the harmonics leaked through; Vrenn drifted off Kodon's line, by a hair, for a moment, then brought the ship back again. It was not responding normally: Vrenn scanned his readouts, found the power graphs dropping.

"Engineer—"

"You'll have to share with the deflectors," the Engineer said, as another bolt hit the cruiser. Power fell again. The Engineer turned. "Squadron Leader, commit?"

"Power to shields and weapons," Kodon said, clipped and very calm. "We still fight."

When Koth of the *Vengeance* said something like that, his Bridge crew usually raised a cheer. No one started one now.

Three Warbirds were in a precise, right-angled formation just below *Blue Fire*. Disruptors tore one open: trailing hot junk, it slid narrowly past another and dipped into air. There was a cometary flash. The remaining Romulans kept their formation.

"This Admiral is an idiot," Kodon said. "He's got the ships, and he must have had a warning, but he is still an idiot."

On the screen ahead, Romulan ships were bracketing *Death Hand*, ahead, on the wings, behind. *Death Hand* fired back and did not miss—it was hardly possible at such ranges—but the number of Roms tipped the balance. A plasma bolt struck the Klingon cruiser's hangar deck from the rear, and detonated inside: there was a jet of incandescent gas from the dorsal vent.

Kandel on Communications said, "Squadron Leader, the Force Leader wants to know if you intend to land his Marines."

"Can't he see we're *expected?*" Kodon stared at *Death Hand* ahead, dying. "What shield shall I drop to transport him down?" Kodon's teeth showed. "Just tell him we are engaged, and that he is to stand by."

Death Hand killed one of her harriers. "Weapons, *that* one," Kodon said, stabbing a finger, and *Blue Fire* poured its namesake into another Rom. "Flat-thinker!" Kodon snarled, and as the Rom blew up there was finally a cheer on the Bridge.

The word closed the circuit in Vrenn's mind. It explained the lockstep formations, the flat-plane attacks, the way *Death Hand* had been surrounded. Now, if there was time to make any use of the knowledge—"Squadron Leader, a thought," Vrenn said.

"Squadron Leader," Ensign Kandel cut in, "*Death Hand* sends intent to abandon and destruct."

There was a pause. A Captain did not abandon until the gravest extreme.

But not yet, Vrenn thought, not just yet—

"Affirmed," Kodon said. "Only a fool fights in a burning house." Then, with what seemed to Vrenn an infinite slowness, Kodon turned to him. "Proceed, *zan* Vrenn."

"Squadron Leader, I know the *rom zha, latrunculo*—"

"He wants to play games," the drone operator said.

Vrenn did not stop. "—which is played on squares, on a flat board. Pieces kill by pinning enemies between themselves—" Vrenn knew there was no time to explain the game, the thoughts behind it; Kodon must *see*. Vrenn pointed at the main display: the alignments of Warbirds and D-4s were as clear to him as the naked stars around them all. If there were some way to show square references upon the triangular grid of the display . . . perhaps Kandel could. . . .

Kodon turned away. Vrenn felt eyes on him from all directions, felt the shame he had sworn under naked stars he would never know again, felt death in his liver.

"I know of the game," Kodon said. "It is a fair observation. . . . So, if this is the sort of idiot the Rom Admiral is, Thought Ensign Vrenn, what shall we do to him?"

"There is a single piece in *latrunculo*," Vrenn said, speaking almost faster than thought, "with the ability to leap over others, like a Flier of *klin zha*. Other pieces must be concentrated against the Centurion. . . ."

Kodon laughed loudly. "Signal to *Death Hand,* priority! Drop shields and transport, and separate, I say once more separate; *hold destruct.*"

"Helmsman—" A line appeared on Vrenn's display. Vrenn took *Blue Fire* to Warp 0.5 and skimmed the cruiser over Warbird, almost close enough to touch.

The Rom moved.

"Number 3 shield down."

"Troop transporters energized to receive," the Engineer said, and the power graphs dove as a wave of *Death Hand*'s Marines were beamed aboard *Blue Fire.*

Blue Fire jumped two more Warbirds, taking only token shots at them. Then, as Warbirds turned in place, a shudder went through *Death Hand* at the center of the enemy cluster: there was a brilliant ring of light at the junction of the cruiser's narrow forward boom with her broad main wing. The two structures parted, and the boom began to crawl forward on impulse drive.

The Roms hesitated, turned again inward.

"Number 4 shield down, 5 up."

"Transients in the signal," the Engineer said, his hands running over controls. Power curves spiked, and warnings flashed yellow. He said, "We've got some scramble cases."

"Affirm," Kodon said.

Marine no-ranks did not have personal transporter operators watching for them.

Blue Fire glided on toward *Death Hand,* directly toward it. Vrenn watched as his boards showed tighter and tighter tolerances, less maneuver power as the mass transports stole it from engines.

"Transport arc's changing again," the Weapons officer said. "5 shield down, 6 up."

"Transients clearing from the signal," the Engineer said, as the two ships closed.

"Signal to *Death Hand,*" Kodon said. "Invitation to Naval officers aboard."

Moments later the main display lit with a picture of *Death Hand*'s Bridge. Smoke obscured the scene. The Captain's left arm was tucked inside his sash. Behind him, someone was lying dead across a sparking console.

"Your invitation received," the Captain said. "My Ensigns are transporting now. I hope they find much glory with you."

"I am certain," Kodon said.

For the first time since the battle began, Vrenn thought about the damage to *Blue Fire:* who might be dead on the lower decks. But he had less time for such thoughts by the second. The two cruisers were less than a thousand meters apart, on collision course. An alarm screamed; Vrenn snapped it off.

He shifted power between port and starboard engines: *Blue Fire* began to roll.

Kodon said to the other Captain, "And your Executive?"

"Dead," *Death Hand*'s Captain said. "And I, of course . . ."

"This need not be said," said Kodon. "Kill Roms, with your Black Ship, Kadi."

The other Captain grinned. "Not these Roms. They're too stupid. After this death, no more for them. . . ." His lips pulled back from his teeth, and his arm spasmed; blood soaked through the sash. The picture broke up.

Blue Fire slipped sidewise through the gap between the parts of *Death Hand.* Roms still surrounded them, some still firing into the dead ship's hulk.

"Naval officers aboard," the Engineer said. "Ready to receive second Marine unit."

"Squadron Leader," Communications said, "they're breaking formation."

Vrenn heard, registered, ignored: He *was* the ship now, seeking out the one gap in the formation of Roms they never would have thought to cover: how can two ships be in the same place at once?

Kodon looked up from his foot repeaters. "So, not all their Captains are such fools as their Admiral. . . . Cancel transport. Signal Code TAZHAT. Action!"

"Acting," said all voices on the Bridge.

The planet whirled over on the display as Vrenn, clear at last of *Death Hand,* brought the ship about. Yellow lines cut across his displays, then green ones, then a blue. Vrenn pushed for thrust, the first set of levers, then the second.

Blue Fire engaged warp drive, and the stars blazed violet, and black, and were past.

"Flash wave aft," said the Communications officer.

"Shield 6—" said Weapons, and a rumble through the decks finished the statement for her.

"Power," Vrenn said, and the Engineer gave it to him. *Blue Fire* reached Warp 2, and the rumble died way: the ship had just outrun the sphere of photons and debris that was everything left of *Death Hand*. And of the Roms around it.

"Kai!" Kodon cried out. Vrenn felt proud, then embarrassed: it surely must be Captain Kadi that the Squadron Leader hailed.

Then Kodon said, "Navigator, course for the nearest outpost. Dronesman, trail one to flash. Communications, have *Two Fingers* home on the drone signal."

Kandel said, "Sir, the cargo ships—"

"Dust, like all good Roms," Kodon said, quiet but intense. "I am not now interested in prizes. I want an answer, and I do not think it is to be found back there."

"Squadron Leader, shall I signal to the Fleet—"

"Signal them *anything* and I'll have your throat out!"

So that, Vrenn thought, *is what a* real *threat from Kodon sounds like.*

After a moment, Kodon spoke again, in his normal tone. "Engineer, raise the heat and moisture on quarters decks; we're going to be hungry but we might as well be comfortable. And I want Warp 4 power as soon as possible." He got out of his chair. "Kurrozh, you have the conn. Vrenn, you will come with me."

Vrenn stood, not knowing what to think and so trying to think nothing. It was an old trick to threaten the one and punish the other: this had an intensified effect on both subjects. He could not think of what he had done wrong, but knew far better than to be reassured by that.

And then he knew too well what he had done: he had suggested a strategy to a Squadron Leader during battle, and worse, the strategy had worked.

But then, as Vrenn followed Kodon to the lift, he saw one of the Bridge crew flash him the spread fingers of the Captain's Star, and then another, and another. And he knew, then, that he would have his ship, even if it flew in the Black Fleet.

The Ensign's tunic was torn, and smelled of smoke. He slung his bag on to the empty bed, sat down hard, and saluted with a bandaged hand. "Kelag, *Death Hand*," he said.

"Kai Death Hand," Vrenn said. "Vrenn—" He paused. "Brevet Lieutenant."

"Vrenn . . . ?" Kelag looked at Vrenn's rank badges. "But you're an Ensign?"

"Brevet Ensign."

Kelag shook his head. His eyelids were drooping. "I don't understand. What'd you . . ."

"I was *Blue Fire*'s Helmsman. I am, I mean."

"Oh," said Ensign Kelag, awake at once. *"Kai* Vrenn. *Kai Blue Fire."*

Vrenn nodded. "That was Ruzhe's bed," he said. "He was aft, in Engineering."

"Bad battle."

"He got through the battle all right . . . but when they were working on getting the power back up, some tubes blew. It was intercooler gas. Almost plasma, they said. Anyway, there hasn't been time to clear out his things."

Kelag was contemplating the floor. After a moment, Vrenn realized he was asleep sitting up. Vrenn stood, took a step, meaning to stretch the Ensign out flat on the bed, but then he stopped. He did not look up. Security did not like any signs that one knew they were watching. They were much more likely to find something wrong with what they saw.

Vrenn turned out the lights—let them watch by infrared—and went to bed himself. He was instantly asleep.

Security had a Rom in the cube. It was running live on ship's entertainment channel, and in the Inspirational Theatres. Most of the newer officers had traded duty to watch, but Vrenn had stayed on the helm. Kodon laughed; "You've gotten to like the conn quick enough. I know what that's like."

The Weapons Officer had the Examination picture on her repeater screen, sound too low for Vrenn to hear. If he looked that way, he could see it clearly enough. The right side of the screen showed the information display: a green outline of the Rom's body, with blue traces of major nerves and yellow crosses where the agonizers were focused. On the left, the Romulan sat in the chair—very firmly so; *Blue Fire*'s Specialist Examiner had set the booth foci so the Rom's muscles shoved her down and back into the seat cushions, leaving all the restraint straps slack. It was the work of a real expert, showing off just a little.

Vrenn supposed his view was really no worse than that in the Examining Room itself: the agonizer cubes were supposed to be entirely soundproof, with phones for the interested observer to listen at any chosen volume.

There had been three Romulans at the Imperial outpost where Kodon's Squadron stopped. They claimed diplomatic protection; Kodon was hardly interested, and the outpost Commander was only too happy to stay out of the Squadron Leader's way—especially after the Executive made clear that *he* was next in line for cube time.

The Ambassador cut her own throat, by Romulan ritual and admirably well. The Romulan Naval Attaché tried to be a great hero by overloading his pistol, but mis-set the controls. Kodon gave him to the surviving Marines from *Death Hand.* That left the Mission Clerk, who was in the cube, while the Security analysts did similar electronic things to the coded recordings she had carried. Security was pleased with their catch: clerks often knew more useful things than the bureaucrats they served.

The Rom slumped over. The Weapons Officer yawned and turned away; on the screen behind her, the agonizer foci shifted to new nerves, and the clerk's head snapped up again. "So hey, Krenn," the Gunner said, "how long before we get someplace with thick air? I hate these little outposts, flatulent rocks."

Vrenn was getting used to the officers ennobling his name, though it couldn't be final until the Navy made his promotions official. Which might, he knew, never happen. Not everything a privateer captain did, lasted. But for now, it made the conversations easier. "Three days to Aviskie, Lieutenant, if the Squadron Leader wants Warp 4."

"He will. Got any plans?"

The Romulan was bleeding a thin green trickle from the corner of her mouth.

"I hadn't," Vrenn said.

"I think you do now."

Vrenn tried not to laugh, but did anyway. The two other Lieutenants on the Bridge were carefully watching their boards.

"So what am I supposed to make of that?" the Gunner said. "There may be too much Cadet fuzz on your ears to know it, but you're on the warp route, Thought Ensign." Kodon's half-mocking title for him had spread. "Ever hear of the Warp 4 Club?"

"I *have* got duty."

"You can't conn the ship for three *khest'n* days."

Vrenn grinned. The Gunner had no serious faults he could see—except, perhaps, the rank badges on her vest: Vrenn wondered if he ought to wait, just until his Lieutenancy came through in cold metal.

But then he wouldn't be a full member of the Club.

The Romulan began to convulse, then went rigid: her lips moved, forming words. The Gunner turned up the sound: it was barely understandable as a string of Romulan numbers.

"Here come the code keys," the officer said, slapping his thigh.

"You see?" the Gunner said to Vrenn, laughing. "I hope your timing's *always* this good."

*   *   *

The rental room in Aviskie Column Five was dark, and finally quiet, and damp with room fog and perspiration. The incense in the bedside holder had burned out a little while ago.

Light lanced in, and cold outside air. Vrenn rolled off the bed, fingers arched to claw: on the other side, the Gunner had been just a little faster, and was already saluting.

"Come with us, *Lieutenant,*" Ensign Merzhan said. Behind him were a Navy Commander with a silver Detached Service sash, and two armed enforcers, from the port complement, not *Blue Fire's.*

Vrenn saluted: it did not occur to him to disagree. "I'll dress—"

"Why?" said Merzhan. The Commander made a tiny gesture, and Merzhan's face froze. The officer said, "Go ahead."

Vrenn pulled on trousers and boots and tunic, and finally his vest and sash, waiting for someone to stop him donning the rank marks. No one did. The Gunner stood at parade rest.

"Let's go," the Detached Commander said, in a voice with less character than a ship's computer's. He looked at the Gunner, eyes not so much appraising as measuring her. "We weren't here."

"Nobody was," she said, and as Vrenn was led out he thought that she did not sound frightened at all: just rueful.

Vrenn sat in a bare conference room, windowless, with three Naval officers: Koll, the Commander who had come to his rental room, Commander Kev of *Blue Fire,* and Captain Kessum of *Two Fingers.* Vrenn had not seen Kodon. All the Security men had gone, so they were certainly watching by other means.

"This is not a tribunal," Koll said, "nor any other sort of official meeting. In fact, this meeting is not taking place, and never will have taken place. Is this understood?"

"Perfectly," Vrenn said.

Kev nodded. Koll put a rectangular object on the table; an antenna rose from it, and several small lights began to flicker. Vrenn realized that the Detached officer, whatever he was, was quite serious about the nature of the meeting: now, not even Security would be listening.

Commander Koll said, "As a result of certain Romulan decrypts, we have learned of a series of secret negotiations between the *Komerex Romulan* and a faction within the *Komerex Klingon.* Had these discussions resulted in a treaty, a neutral zone would have been established between the *Komerexi,* supposedly inviolable by either side. While such a treaty has often been proposed in the Imperial Council, and discarded, this group might have been able to enforce the support of an agreement presented as an accomplished fact. . . ."

Vrenn felt his liver shift in his chest. He knew one proponent of Rom Neutral Space, only one. The idea was related to the principle of center control in the game called *chess*.

". . . an excuse for destruction of Klingon frontier vessels on charting or colonization missions, having no effect at all on Romulan incursionary forces—"

"Commander," Kev said, "that's background." Kev looked at Vrenn, with his impaling eyes; Vrenn tried to puzzle out what the look said.

"Yes, correct," Koll said. "The point is that now the treaty conspirators have been identified. Among them is Thought Admiral Kethas epetai-Khemara." Koll gave Vrenn his mechanical, measuring look. Kessum tapped a hand on the table, the two-fingered right hand that gave his ship its name.

Kev said abruptly, "The point is this. Squadron Leader Kodon thinks that you are not involved in this conspiracy, and are too good an officer to be disposed of for the sake of mere caution. I agree with both points. Now, we have worked very fast, faster than Security can follow, *we think,* so listen carefully. There's an independent command waiting for you, if you want it. A small frontier scout, but it's Navy, and it doesn't have to be a *khesterex thath* if you stay as clever as you've been."

Vrenn sat very still. He wondered if the stars above this world were clothed or naked now. Here was his ship, then; here too was its price.

"If the one hesitates," Captain Kessum said formally, "for the breaking of the chain of duty, let certain terms of the negotiation be stated."

Kev said, "The Roms wanted some proofs of the negotiators' intent. They wanted information on the next frontier raid. They got it."

Vrenn said, "Did the one—"

"The one knew," said Commander Koll. "The one verified it."

So there was only the *komerex zha,* Vrenn thought, and the pieces of the game were only bits of wood in the fire. "The Navy honors me," he said, "and where I am commanded, there I shall go."

"Kai kassai," Kev said softly, but his look was still steel needles.

Vrenn said, "If I might take formal leave of Squadron Leader Kodon—"

Captain Kessum said stiffly, "This one is here for Kodon."

Yes, of course, Vrenn thought. *Blue Fire* lived, but *Death Hand* was dust. And there was the question of strategy, that least Klingon of Sciences, whose practitioners made strange things happen; as Kev had said once before, *If you did plan this, do not let it be known.*

". . . it is of course understood that you will not operate in this part of the frontier."

"This need not be said," Vrenn said.

"Then it's done," Koll said, and reached for his sensor jammer.

Commander Kev said, "You'll have to change your name now."

Scout Captain Krenn was eighty days out on an exploratory cruise when the recordings arrived, scrambled with Krenn's personal cipher; there was no originating label.

He watched the taped deaths of Kethas and Rogaine twice through. They were competent kills, as the law of assassination specified: that indeed was the reason for taping at all.

Krenn was pleased to see that Rogaine fought very well, stabbing one assassin, blinding another with her nails after her body had hypnotized him. It served the fool right for such carelessness.

Kethas fell near his gameboards, firing back as he collapsed, upsetting the Reflective Game set that had been his favorite. Kethas's hand closed on the green-gold Lancer, and then did not move. The camera swung away. On the second play, Krenn stopped the image, enlarged it; he realized that the epetai-Khemara had not been reaching for the game piece, but toward his consort's body.

Krenn stopped the tape again, thinking to rewind and watch for Kethas's look, exactly as Rogaine died; but he did not do so.

The record covered only two of the house *kuve*. Little black-furred Odise was shot from a balcony, fell, landing in a wet and messy heap. Tirian they stunned, and agonized for a time, then carried aloft in a flier. His tunic was slit down the back, and the scars of his wings shown to the camera. Then they flung him out, perhaps twelve hundred meters above the dark twisted mass of the Kartade Forest. Krenn did not rerun that scene.

He burned the cassette, thinking, *It simplifies things enormously when honor claims are absent.*

Krenn stepped out onto the Bridge. The Helmsman saluted, not too sharply, and the Science officer turned. They were enough Bridge crew; it was a small ship. But a Navy ship, and perhaps not a dead command.

"Anything of interest?" Krenn asked Sciences.

"Dust and smaller dust," Specialist Akhil said. "Your message?"

"Some bureaucratic housecleaning."

Akhil laughed. Then he said, "Is this a good time to ask a question, Captain?"

"As good as any."

"My oldest uncle was on a ship under a Captain of the Rustazh line. Are you any—"

"They're all gone," said Krenn tai-Rustazh. "The name was free for use."

"So you *are* starting a line," the Helmsman said.

"Why else would anyone be out here?" Krenn said. "To play the Perpetual Game?"

Then he laughed, and the Scientist and the Helmsman joined in.

PART TWO

The Naked Stars

Negotiation may cost far less than war, or infinitely more: for war cannot cost more than one's life.

—KLINGON PROVERB

Four: Spaces

"We've got the ship on tractors, Captain."

"Pull it in. *Zan* Kafter, keep the guns hot: one through the command pod if her energy readings change."

"Affirm, Captain." The crew of *Imperial Klingon Cruiser Fencer* went to work, towing in the depowered but intact Willall starship: it was their twelfth such prize, and they knew the drill.

Captain Krenn vestai-Rustazh sat back in the Command Chair, folded his hands and rested his chin on them. The Willall vessel showed up magnified in the forward display: a boxy thing, without a hint of Warp physics in the design. Willall ships all looked like outdoor toilets with warpdrive nacelles wired on. But those ridiculous-looking ships had made a very serious dent in Imperial space.

They didn't have any strategy, beyond just raiding the next planet they stumbled across. They didn't know any tactics, either, other than shooting and swooping. *Willall* was shorthand *klingonaase* for their name for themselves, which fully translated said in much more grandiose fashion that they were the race which would command all the possible realities.

But they fought like—"like drunken Romulans" was a popular expression, here on the other side of Empire from Romulan claims. And their junk ships could absorb a lot of fire, and put out a respectable volume.

Still, even determined shooting and swooping only did so much. "Tactics are *real*," Krenn told his crew. *Fencer* had proven it, destroying Willall until Krenn was bored with that.

He and his Engineer had put on environment suits and gone probing through one of the Willall wrecks. They found a couple of weak structural points, where low-intensity disruptor shots would break the main superconducting lines to the warp engines, sever the Agaan Tubes. So now they didn't destroy Willall; they wrapped them up and sent them to the Emperor.

"Got her readings, Captain," Akhil said from the Sciences board. "Life, armed, all small weapons. No ship's systems above emergency levels."

"Transporter clear?"

"No spikes, no transients. Safe enough for the Emperor."

Krenn nodded. "Communications, open to the prize's Bridge."

The image was fuzzy, made up of scan lines: Willall vision technology was no superior to the rest of it. Half-a-dozen aliens were looking up at the monitor. They always reminded Krenn of unbaked dough, or putty sculptures; soft and colorless. *Kuve.*

"I am Krenn of the *Fencer,*" he said, slowly enough for the translation program to keep up. "I have destroyed your ability to resist the Empire. If you attempt any further hostility, I will destroy you. Is this understood?"

The Willall spoke, a sound like bubbles in stew. Several of them were talking at once; they had some kind of group command structure, and the Security analysts had not decided which of them did what. The cube was worthless: agonizers made Willall nerves fall literally to pieces.

"It is understood," the translator finally said. "The group is in isolation. It ceases." The aliens put their hand weapons in a pile on the deck.

Kuve, Krenn thought again. Yet they were correct, of course; had they not disarmed . . . well. There were several things he had done, in the course of a dozen captures.

This game was beginning to bore him as well, he knew.

"I will put Klingons aboard your ship. Some of these will repair the damage to your engines. When this is done, your ship will proceed to a world of the Empire, and there surrender.

"You may, as you choose, pilot the ship yourselves. However, there will be Klingons aboard to prevent errors in navigation, and others to protect the navigators and engineers. You will interfere with none of these, and aid them as you can."

The Willall crew flooped agreement. Krenn broke the link.

He went aft to the transporter room, for a last word with the prize crew. They were in a high enough mood: it would be easy duty, with a good welcome waiting for them when they turned the ship in.

"Ensign Kian," Krenn said.

"Captain?" Kian looked like he had just won a banner in the Year Games. He would, however briefly, have full charge of a starship: never mind that it was not a Navy ship, or even a Klingon ship.

Krenn indicated the portable computer Kian carried. "Don't use that unless you have to. You'll be in command; *command.*"

"Of course, Captain."

The small computer contained a special set of navigational routines, in the event that the Willall refused to cooperate. They had never yet done so, at least, not as far as anyone knew. Two of Krenn's prizes had never arrived, but many things could have happened, and in tin-plate ships like the Willall, who could tell?

Klingons would have found a way to attack their captors. Romulans or Andorians would have, even if they were all certain to die. Humans and Kinshaya were almost too devious to leave alive as prisoners. Even Vulcans, Krenn supposed, would use all their logic to find a flaw in the terms of surrender.

But these Willall just obeyed. Like any servitors. Perhaps the geneticists were right, and something in the *kuve* blood and flesh made *kuve.*

Krenn thought that was a stupid idea, but it was a private thought.

Akhil stepped out of the lift, went to the transporter controls; the petty officer there stepped aside at once. The prize crew straightened up to full attention: the Captain's own transporter operator made this an authentic heroes' sendoff.

"Ready to transport," Akhil said.

"*Zan* Kian," Krenn said.

"Captain?"

"Take care of our ship." He had chosen the possessive very carefully.

"This need not be said, Captain."

Krenn nodded. "Energize," he said, and Akhil pushed the control levers. The crewmen and Marines dissolved into spindles of light and were gone.

Krenn stroked his forehead ridge, his jaw. "I'll be in quarters, 'Khil."

"I've still got some of that Saurian brandy," Akhil said.

"Not this time." Krenn got into the lift car. "If I'm still there when Kian calls, ring me. Won't do to give formal leave from the bath."

Akhil said, not at all lightly, "You're thinking too much again, Thought Ensign."

Krenn grimaced as the lift door closed. He'd never found out where Akhil had heard of that title. But the Executive was careful never to use it except when they were alone. Just Krenn and Akhil and Security's monitors.

It was just possible, Krenn thought, as he undressed and slid into hot salt water, that he did think too much. Could a Scientist believe that? Even a Klingon Scientist?

Of course, he thought, as his senses began to dim. He had only known one Klingon who trusted all in thought. And the epetai-Khemara was dust six years.

Chiming woke Krenn. "I'm awake, 'Khil, I'm awake," he lied, stumbling out of the bath; he remembered to suppress vision before turning the intercom on.

It was not Akhil, but Kalitta, the Communications officer. "Captain, I have a yellow-2 priority from Navy command. It's an immediate recall of *Fencer.* To Klinzhai, Captain."

"Yellow priority," Krenn said. It was not a question: he could see the lights on Kalitta's board. Yellow-2 didn't mean the galaxy was exploding, but it was close enough. And to the *homeworld?* "Open link to Ensign Kian, aboard the prize."

"Acting." The picture stuttered and blanked: Kian appeared, through Willall scan lines. "Acknowledging *Fencer,*" he said, looking slightly puzzled.

"Stand by, *zan* Kian." Krenn grabbed a gown and tossed it on, then switched on his vision pickup.

"Captain?"

"We've been called home, Ensign. Warp 4 plus. No more time to spend on that thing, and we can't drag it along; prepare to transport and we'll cut it loose."

Kian looked startled, and angry. Krenn thought that was reasonable; he felt the same way. The Ensign said, "We've got less than a third of a shift's work left, Captain. Zero problems so far."

"This is a priority recall, Ensign. We don't have a third of a shift to wait."

Kian stared up at the screen. Krenn saw him chew his tongue. Then he said, "A moment, Captain. We've got some transmission problems." He reached for his portable computer. "You're breaking up very badly, Captain. I don't know if it's safe to transport—"

Krenn almost laughed. "That's a good try, Kian, but you're perfectly clear to me."

Kian stopped with his hand on the black case. "Yes, Captain," he said calmly, "I suppose I am."

Krenn did laugh then.

Kian said, "Leave us behind, Captain."

"You're still depowered. Suppose you can't start the engines? This is the frontier; you might eat each other, but you can't breathe vacuum."

"We'll get power. I'll take responsibility."

Krenn's smile froze. Even bold young Ensigns did not say that very often. Not and mean it, and Krenn could see Kian meant it. "And the rest of your crew? What about them?"

"It's my command, Captain Krenn."

Krenn looked into the hot yellow eyes on the sketchy screen, wondering if he had really looked like that, when Kodon first gave him *Blue Fire*'s conn. When he became a full member of the club.

"Yes, Ensign," Krenn said finally. "Your command. Bring home glory. The *klin* is already in you."

"Captain." Kian saluted, and then broke the link on his superior officer: Krenn had to grin. He wouldn't have given the old starburst time to rethink, either.

Krenn killed vision again, hit the Call key. "Captain to Bridge. Prepare to cut tractors and get under way. Tell engineering Warp 4 is expected, 4.5 would be better."

Akhil's voice said, "Transport signal's clear."

"No one's transporting. The prize goes as she is."

"Affirm," Akhil said, sounding cheerful, or satisfied, or both. Krenn wondered if Kalitta had left the link open, on the Bridge . . . well, if he hadn't wanted it heard, he wouldn't have said it.

Kalitta said, "Statement to the crew, Captain?"

"Just tell them we're ordered to travel. Krenn out." He snapped the link, said to the air, "Unless you know something I don't?"

Just this once, he hoped Security was listening.

It took *Fencer* 112 days to reach the Klingon homeworld: she had been far enough on the fringe of the spiral arm that Warp 4.85 was possible for the first twenty-plus days, and the Engineer was muttering about a record. The officers and crew were talking too: not many had visited Klinzhai itself, and fewer still had lived there: to them it was the ultimate of leave worlds, paradise with hotel service.

So the three-cruiser escort waiting for them in high orbit was a surprise to most of *Fencer*'s complement. So was the strict warning about leaving the escort's "protection"—that is, their cones of fire—or launching shuttles, or transporting down. Only one aboard was authorized to leave the ship—and Krenn was not surprised, not really. He was in fact rather pleased to be beaming down alone; it meant his crew was safe, for now.

He was met at the discs by a Security team in dress armor, wearing light weapons; they were polite, which did not at all mean that Krenn was not under arrest. He did not waste effort asking the team leader questions.

Krenn was taken through empty corridors to a room that might have been in one of the Throne City's better hotels. But its door would not open after the Security team departed. The communicator and the computer screen were both *khex*. There were no windows.

The meal slot did function: Krenn punched for pastry and fruit juice, and sat contemplating a clearprint on the wall of a D-4 cutting up a Kinshaya supercarrier.

The thing he liked least about particle transporters, Krenn thought, was that the signal could be relayed; one could not really know where one was going. He *might* be in the Throne City, or someplace very different. Even aboard a ship: but he felt the gravity and doubted that.

The door opened, and three Klingons came in, and Krenn got his first real surprise.

One of them was Koll, the Commander who had come for him six years ago. He still wore the silver sash of Detached Service, but now had a Captain's stars. There was a heavyset Admiral with a parcel under his arm, and a tall, powerfully built Security officer without badges of specific rank—which meant, very high rank.

"Captain Krenn, I am Captain Koll."

Of course, Krenn thought; *we've never met.* Krenn was a little glad, in a backhand way, to have the Security supergrade there: whatever this meeting was, at least it would exist.

"Captain Koll. Honored."

"This is Admiral Kezhke zantai-Adion . . . and Operations Master Meth of Imperial Intelligence."

Intelligence? Krenn thought, feeling muscles tense. He knew Navy officers who feared Imperial Intelligence as they did not fear to die cowards; he had heard that Security feared them. And high rank indeed. Meth would be answerable to no one but the Emperor . . . and if II functioned as Krenn supposed it must, perhaps not the Emperor.

Admiral Kezhke had his package on a table and was unwrapping it; he set out four spherical glasses and a bottle of Saurian brandy. "Pleased to finally meet you, Captain Krenn," Kezhke said as he worked at the brandy stopper. "You've got a stormwalker's dinner of a record, you know." The plug came out. "Drinks?"

Only Koll declined. Krenn took a very small sip, on the small chance that it was genuine Saurian. It was. Krenn felt as if he had been kicked in the liver. But (as Akhil said, over glasses of the reasonable fake he kept in his desk) it was a *wonderful* kick in the liver.

Kezhke stoppered the bottle again. "Only one of those to a meeting," he said. He smiled at Krenn, a bland look that might cover anything.

"Good rule," Meth of Intelligence said, and put down his half-emptied glass. He was not smiling, but his voice was pleasant enough.

Krenn felt his own voice coming back. "May the one ask the reason for urgent recall?" he said, perhaps a little too quickly.

"That much formality isn't necessary," Meth said. His expression was very still—not empty like Kezhke's or frozen like Koll's, but literally immobile. As Meth spoke, Krenn realized that most of his facial flesh was cosmetic plastic—whether a prosthetic, or a disguise, Krenn could not tell.

"The Admiral mentioned your record," Meth said. "It is rather extraordinary. No one, within my knowledge, has a similar rate of captures of intact ships."

"There are several with more captures," Koll said, not a correction but a machine annotation. "But none in so short a time. And none with a single ship."

"It's a talent," Meth said, "which shouldn't be wasted."

Krenn looked at Koll, but if the phrase registered in the Detached officer's mind, there was no sign. Not for the first time, Krenn wondered if the Aviskie meeting really had been nonexistent: if only he remembered it at all.

"We have a mission for you, Captain," Meth said, still echoing. "It's rather particular in its requirements, and no one seems better qualified than you."

Krenn squeezed another sip of the brandy down his throat. He knew perfectly well—and these officers must know that he knew—how often *best qualified* for a special mission meant *most expendable.*

If that were the case now, then if he refused, they would simply expend him and call the next name on the list. *So, bite deep.* "I am honored," Krenn said. "What is the mission?"

Meth touched his glass, but did not lift it. His hands were also surfaced with plastic. "We need one brought to this world. It will be a rather long cruise."

"On the frontier all cruises are long," Krenn said.

"This one will exceed a year, at Warp 4 speed."

"In each direction?"

"In each direction."

That meant it was to somewhere outside Klingon holdings. Krenn had a sudden thought of just how they might have chosen to expend him. "To Romulan space?"

"Not the Roms," Admiral Kezhke said. "The Federation." He gave the brandy bottle a hard look. "They want to send us an . . . *Ambassador.* A ship must travel, under peace signals, to bring the one."

"Peace signals," Krenn said.

Captain Koll said, "The Imperial Council has, for the situation, agreed to the Federation idea that a ship bearing an Ambassador must not have combat."

"But this calls for a Squadron," Krenn said, trying to think moves ahead in the game. Why would the Council consent to disarming a ship, and how could they expect to find a Captain for it? "With escorts, who may use their weapons—"

"One battlecruiser," Kezhke said. There was an authentic-sounding distress in his voice.

"And if we are attacked by . . . perhaps, Romulans?" Meth looked at

him, and Krenn was suddenly afraid to even think what he never would
have said: *Or, perhaps, Klingons.* Imperial Intelligence was said to
know things they could not know by any natural means; they were said
to know thoughts. Krenn did not believe this, and still he was afraid.

"A Romulan attack would be a diplomatic incident between the
three Empires," Koll was saying. "By the *komerex federazhon* law, an
act of war."

Krenn wondered if that were the strategy. He imagined it would
please certain of the Imperial Council very greatly if the son of Kethas,
who had died trying to make peace with the Romulans, were to die
igniting a war with them.

Meth said, "Are you declining the mission, Captain Krenn?"

"I am questioning it," Krenn said. "Only a servitor goes blindly to
the death: I serve the Empire, but I am not the Empire's servitor."

"Kai, klingon," Kezhke said, with something like relief.

"We do not think it is the death," Operations Master Meth said. His
tone was almost conciliatory. "The Federation has strong ideas about
its own laws." He picked up the brandy glass. "But the mission is not
commanded. Only offered."

"I would take *Fencer* and my crew?"

"Fencer and any crew you like," Kezhke said.

"But time is short," Meth said. "Some of your crew will doubtless
need leave and rest; they may need replacement from the pools."

Of course Intelligence would put its people aboard; if Krenn tried to
fight that, II would still get them aboard, and Krenn would have even
less idea who they were. "I'll need my Science officer; he's also my
Executive."

"You'll get him," Kezhke said, before Meth could speak.

Meth said, "You accept the duty, then."

"I accept."

Meth nodded. Koll reached into his tunic, brought out several computer cassettes. "Your navigational tapes. A message of introduction
from the Council. And a dream-learning tape of the Federation language."

Meth said, "If you would rather take the language by RNA transfer,
it can be arranged. We have a native *fedegonaase* speaker, freshly spun
down."

"This will be adequate," Krenn said, taking the cassettes.

Kezhke said, "There's a dock space waiting for your ship, and priority orders. She's in good order?"

"Yes."

The Admiral smiled. "I knew she would be. Tune and trim, then.
Image will matter, this cruise."

Meth said, "Tell your crew that leave has been arranged for them, at the Throne City port. At Imperial expense, naturally."

"They will be pleased."

Meth gave his unreal, dead-faced smile. It was impossible to tell if irony was meant. "Then hail the mission and its success." He drank the rest of his brandy. "We'll let you return to your ship, then. There's a lot to do, in a little time."

The door opened for the officers. The Security team leader was standing in the hall, without his team; Krenn had not seen anyone summon him.

Krenn was taken back to the transporter room. Just before the underofficer energized the disc, Admiral Kezhke came into the room. "Leave us for a moment," the Admiral said.

The Security man looked unhappy, but obeyed.

Kezhke motioned for Krenn to step off the transport stage. After he had, the Admiral pushed the transport levers halfway up. The discs flickered.

"Loose energy *khests* the monitors," Kezhke said. He looked straight at Krenn. "I knew the great of your line, vestai-Rustazh." He held out the bottle of brandy.

"This is a misapprehension I often find," Krenn said. "The name was—"

Kezhke was shaking his head. "No error, Captain. I knew *both* your fathers."

Krenn accepted the bottle, took a swallow.

"Listen to me, vestai-Rustazh, Khemara. You must bring the Federation Ambassador here, and you must bring him alive, and without any incident. No matter what you are told, or *think* you are ordered, you must do this."

Krenn felt he was listening from light-years away. If this one was close to the sutai-Rustazh and the epetai-Khemara, then what was he doing alive, speaking to the one with the secret of both lines?

Krenn began to wonder if a Rom war would be such a bad thing to die for. Kahless, the greatest of all Emperors, had died so, and Kahless was known as The One Who Is Remembered.

What Krenn said was, "I understand the mission, Admiral. I do not mean to fail in it."

"I hope so," Kezhke said. "I hope you understand."

Krenn held out the bottle. "Keep it," Kezhke said, and went to the door; he let the Security transport operator in, then stood in the doorway. "Much glory, Captain Krenn," he said, which was the last thing Krenn had expected him to say.

The homeworld faded out.

Fencer faded in.

"Did you meet the Emperor?" Akhil said, smiling.

"Not unless he goes around in clever plastic disguises."

"What?" The Specialist's look fell on the object in Krenn's hands. "That *isn't* really—"

"Have some," Krenn said. "Let's both have some, right now, 'Khil. And then I'll *really* make your head spin."

The air turned to fire above the diamond grid of the cargo transporter, and a crate materialized, displacing a small breeze. *Fencer's* Cargomaster ran a coding wand over its invoice plate and registered the load on his portable computer.

"What's that one, Keppa?" Krenn asked.

"More whitefang steaks," the Cargomaster said, with something close to awe. "Well, if we're captured, we can just eat ourselves to death."

"It's a two-year cruise, with no stops to forage."

"That wasn't a complaint, Captain," Keppa said quickly. "Any time they want to load meat instead of Marines, I'll clear the space."

Krenn laughed. "I know how you'd do it, too. But decompression's hard on the hull." Akhil was approaching, making notes on a small scribe panel. "Keep the steaks coming, Keppa."

"Affirm, Captain." The cargo module was lifted on antigravs; Krenn turned away.

"Keppa says another quarter-day to load stores," Krenn said to Akhil. "How are the other preparations?"

"The weapon interlocks are installed," Akhil said.

Krenn pointed a finger, and he and Akhil passed, quite casually, between two cargo modules. Krenn said quietly, "My way or theirs?"

"Yours. Any time outbound, your personal cipher will get us disruptors."

"Good."

"And I got these last night." Akhil handed Krenn a pair of cassettes.

"Where did you get them?"

"A friend in the Institutes of Research for Language. That's their latest revision of Federation Standard, set up for dream-learning. And that's *all* that's on them."

Krenn took the black plastic boxes. "They offered me an RNA drip, too."

Akhil tapped his scribe on the board. "Human?"

"That's what Meth said."

"Do you really think they were planning to program you?"

"I *know* they meant to program me," Krenn said. "I don't know if there was anything clever on the dream-tapes."

Akhil nodded. They came out from between the crates, turned a corner; Akhil pressed for a lift car. The two Klingons got in. "Bridge," Krenn said, and they started the long ride from the cruiser's lowest tail deck, up the shaft of the boom to the command pod forward.

"And the crew?" Krenn said.

"They enjoyed themselves, but nobody's dead," Akhil said dryly. "Koplo and Aghi put in for long-term leave; they were entitled, and you said—"

"It's all right. This trip, everyone's a volunteer. They were replaced?"

"I've got the pool files on all the new crew. Krenn . . . there are a couple of things you're not going to like."

"Only a couple? What a relief."

"Kalitta was beaten up, outside a bar. The port patrols say they ran off some Marines—"

"But no one was caught, and it was very, very dark."

"As the void, Captain."

"I suppose we were fortunate, and an experienced Communications officer was available?"

"Blue lights, Captain."

"How's Kalitta doing?"

"That's the other thing you won't like."

Krenn growled deep in his throat. "They never take chances, do they." He said suddenly, "What about Maktai?"

"He checked aboard this morning, all lights blue."

Krenn thought about that. Imperial Intelligence could have just ordered the Security Commander replaced, and no one, least of all Mak, could have said anything. That they had not meant . . .

Nothing. Either Maktai belonged to II, or he did not, but they had someone else aboard. Someone unsuspected.

Someone in a good position to communicate his reports.

Krenn found himself staring at Akhil.

The Exec did not seem to notice. "I've got a hospital address for Kalitta, if you want to send her a tape."

"Tape?" Krenn said absently.

"They said she'd be conscious in a few days."

"G'dayt," Krenn spat. "Yes, let's do that. Let's do it from the Bridge, and get everyone's face on it. And let's do it now, before the gossip link figures out what happened to her." The lift car slowed. "Besides, we can see our new Communications expert in action."

The car doors opened on *Fencer*'s Bridge. All stations were occupied, as the crew checked the ship down for cruise. Akhil and Krenn went to the Communications board.

"Captain, presenting—"

Krenn looked up, and disbelieved.

"Lieutenant Kelly, Electronics, Communications," Akhil said, and saw Krenn's face, and took a step backward.

"Captain Krenn," Gelly *Gensa* Swift said—though of course she was no longer any of those things—and rose from her chair, a smooth motion, and saluted. The movement of her arm was somehow wrong, and Krenn could see in his mind the steel Lance coming down, and the dark-colored blood.

"Welcome aboard *Fencer,* Lieutenant," Krenn said. "It has been quite some time."

Kelly nodded slightly. Krenn thought she relaxed, but he was not certain; he had never seen her when she was not dancing with energy—except for the one time, with the blood.

"You know each other?" Akhil said, more curious than surprised. All around the Bridge, work stopped, heads turned.

"Yes," Krenn said, wondering if it was the truth.

"But Zharn was alive after they transported you off the grid?" Krenn said. He and Kelly were alone in the Officers' Mess, talking, over warm black ale and plain pastry with pale butter.

"Alive, yes," she said. "His neck was broken, and of course he couldn't move . . . they put him into a frame and took him away. I was wrapped all up in something . . ." She touched her arm. "I remember not liking being wrapped. But the care was really very good. It took two years." She straightened her elbow, lifted her arm; her shoulder swiveled, stopped, swiveled.

"Metal implant?" Krenn said.

Kelly nodded. "There weren't any grafts to match my fusion, so it had to be metal. You know, before that, I used to think I was half-Romulan. But they have lots of material for Klingon-Rom fusions, since they use so many on the border now."

Krenn had heard of that development, though of course he had been nowhere near that space.

Kelly said, "And they took samples, but . . . I still don't know what I am, really. I suppose I never will."

She drank some ale. There was still an astonishing grace to all her movements—even of her rebuilt arm— and Krenn found himself wondering if the medical geneticists had matched her against an Orion template.

He pulled back from the thought. She had been sent here, he knew, and those who sent her might have planned on exactly that reaction from him.

She said, "And you? How did you come to have a line, and a ship?"

She said she had not returned to the House, after the hospital released her, but had gone straight to Naval Technical School. She knew nothing of what had happened to him. She said.

"I was adopted out," Krenn said. "But I took another linename, to start new."

"Oh. You have consorts, then."

"No."

"Oh."

She stood up. *No,* Krenn thought, *she was not Swift any longer:* there was a deliberation that she had never shown before. It was not the calculated, mind-blinding stimulation of an Orion female, either.

Though Krenn could not deny that she affected him.

"Permission to retire, Captain?"

"Muros's *nose,* Kelly. . . ."

She nodded, trying either to force or restrain a smile. "Pleasant rest, Krenn."

"Pleasant rest, Kelly."

Early in the following dayshift, Akhil said to Krenn, "Do you think Imperial Intelligence sent her?"

"If they did," Krenn said, a rumble in his voice, "would we know it so soon?"

Krenn staggered out of his bed, almost falling over the loose restraint web. He felt his way to the washroom, turned on the sink, then ignored it, tumbled into the bath and hit the fill lever. Water flowed over him; his arms twitched at the stimulus, throwing water across the room.

"Is," he said, "are, was, were, be, been, am. Excuse me, citizen, but where may currency be exchanged? *Pozhalasta prishl'yiti bagazh.*"

He started to sink, into the dreams that were mutually exclusive with dream-learning, into the hot water. Both felt good.

I am drowning, he thought, in Federation Standard. *Please inform the UFP Consulate.*

Eventually he noticed that the communicator was chiming, and managed to answer in *klingonaase* with only a slight Federation accent.

"Disputed Zone coming up, Captain."

"Strategic," Krenn said, using Battle Language automatically. The main display showed the area of space ahead in large scale, the Disputed Zone—what the Federation wanted to call a "border"—marked in white.

A set of yellow symbols appeared on the far side of the Zone: five ships in echelon.

"Kagga's crown, *Roms*," the Weapons officer said, and reached for his board; his hands hovered, shaking, above the sealed-off controls.

They were only off, not sealed, but the Gunner didn't know that. "Not Roms," Krenn said. "All but the *kuve* have five fingers. Akhil?"

Sensor schematics flashed on the display: four ships with flattened-sphere hulls, mounting Warp tubes directly aft; and one that was a saucer connected to an oblong block, the Warp engines in stand-off nacelles.

"Federation cruisers," the Science officer said, watching his sensor telltales, calling recognition data to the displays. "Two types . . . four *Mann*-class, one unknown."

"*Human*-class?" Krenn said.

"Different spelling, a Human proper name, probably. Imperial code-name HOKOT." But Akhil was smiling; Krenn had not been the only one to give up many nights' dreaming.

Nor just the two of them. "Signal from the lead ship, Captain, the unknown one," Kelly said. "They're asking our name and intentions."

"Open the link."

The display showed a Bridge of the circular Federation design. In the Command Chair at its center sat a broadly built Human, with red-brown skin and very black hair. His face seemed to be cut from rock.

Krenn said, "I am Krenn, Captain of *I.K.V. Fencer*. My intention is to enter your space, on a prearranged diplomatic mission."

The Human's eyes narrowed slightly; he looked for just a moment at an Andorian Krenn supposed was the Communications officer. Then the Human said, "This is Admiral Luther Whitetree, command-ing Task Force K, aboard *U.S.S. Glasgow*. Do you have proof of your identity?"

"I have authorizations from the Klingon Imperial Council. Shall I transport them?"

"Launch anything and we'll *burn* it," said Admiral Luther—no, Krenn thought, Admiral Whitetree. Krenn wondered what in Keth's hundred years the Human meant. Then the Admiral said, "Play your tapes."

Krenn gestured to Kelly; she plugged the cassette into her board.

"Five *khest'n* cruisers," Security Commander Maktai said. "Are they cowards of such *great* degree?"

On the display, Whitetree's head snapped up; Kelly at once broke the Bridge-to-Bridge link. "Captain, I—"

"No fault, Lieutenant," Krenn said. "I'm pleased they heard it." He turned to Maktai, who stood rigid with embarrassment. Krenn did wonder at a Security officer who was so careless of who might be listening, but that was Mak's way. "I don't think they're cowards, Mak. Cautious, yes, but . . ." He turned back to the display, where the Human Admiral was again watching the Council's message. Krenn said, "I think that one would make a good Klingon, don't you?"

Kelly warned them of the end of tape in time for the laughter to fade away.

"If you are ready, Captain Krenn," Admiral Whitetree said, less challenging than before but no less hard, "we will escort you to Starbase 6."

The disc-and-block starship, *Glasgow,* came about, flashing formation lights; the four spheroid ships moved apart, to surround *Fencer.*

Whitetree said, "Can you cruise at Warp Factor Four, Captain?"

"Quite comfortably, Admiral," Krenn said, thinking, *Of course you knew that, just as my computers are filled with data on your ships. But we will play the game as if it were Blind, instead of only Clouded.*

Thermal sinks on the *Mann*-class cruisers glowed dull red, and the convoy moved toward the space the Federation claimed as its own.

Five: Players

Fencer held station ten thousand meters off Federation Starbase 6. The Klingons had an excellent view of the Starbase, a dished circular hull some five hundred meters across, mounting an antenna-and-sensor cluster at its center. The web forms of work docks floated beyond the hull, marker lights flashing. The docks all seemed to be empty. Kelly had reported no subspace traffic in or out, even encrypted.

There was a squadron of small, hunter-type ships, all built for speed and firepower; Krenn supposed they could be frontier patrol on normal station leave. But there were those empty docks: ships could not need so little maintenance, else why build so many docks? And there were the five cruisers still englobing *Fencer.*

"You say, Captain Krenn, that your total ship's complement is less than three hundred?" Admiral Whitetree said. The disbelief in his voice was not open, but it was there.

"Your recognition data are correct, Admiral. Our normal complement is larger. But this ship is carrying only a few Marines as honor guards for the officers. It did not seem necessary to bring more. . . . I believe your sensor systems can verify the number of living organisms aboard?"

The Admiral said, "In that case, permission granted to deboard your crew. We'll give you approach routes for your shuttlecraft."

"From which we will not deviate. Until we meet face to face, Admiral. Krenn out."

Kelly broke the link.

Maktai said, "Shuttlecraft?"

"The Admiral's suggestion," Krenn said, thinking hard.

"It'll take eight trips with all shuttles running, if we don't have a *kherx* on the staging floor. Are they afraid we'll use the troop transporters and overrun them?" He pointed at the Starbase. "There must be thousands of troops on that thing. If the whole hold was full of *frozen* Marines, we—"

Akhil said, "They may just not want to drop shields, even a crack. Or there's another possibility." He looked at Krenn. "Are you thinking what I am, Captain?"

Maktai caught on in a moment. "They don't *have* particle transporters."

Akhil said, "We haven't had them for so very long."

Maktai said, "If that's true—"

Krenn said, "If it's true, they still have shields. And there's another possibility: they have transporters, but they don't know that *we* do. . . . I think we ought to avoid mentioning transporter systems while we're on this leave. Mak, you'll let the crew know—and tell them that they might, without attracting any notice, be looking for anything that might be a Federation transporter?"

The Security Commander grunted agreement.

Krenn's shuttle entered a landing deck that could have held thirty such craft; tractors pulled it to a lighted square on the dark surface, and an elevator carried it down to a pressurized staging room larger than *Fencer*'s entire shuttle deck.

The ship's doors opened. Two honor guards preceded Krenn out.

A small, slim Human and a Vulcan were waiting. Behind them were six beings of assorted races, all carrying sidearms. All wore dress uniforms of glossy fabric, with bright gold trim; the Human and Vulcan showed a large number of award pins on their tunics.

"Welcome aboard Starbase 6, Captain," the slender Human said, in rather good *klingonaase,* not machine-translation. "I am Takashi Onoda, senior Diplomatic representative to this station. May I introduce Captain Sinon, the Starfleet attaché." The Vulcan bowed slightly.

Onoda said, "The rest of your officers are coming? We're of course pleased to accommodate your crew; if Admiral Whitetree expressed himself badly—"

"My officers are coming. My Executive, the Security Commander, and I do not ride in the same shuttlecraft."

"Of course. A sensible precaution. And this is your . . ." Onoda paused. ". . . Consort?"

"This is Lieutenant Kelly, my Communications Officer," Krenn said. He stepped aside, so that Kelly's uniform and sash were clearly visible, and thought, *This is one of their* diplomats?

Onoda paled slightly. "A moment, please, Captain." He turned to the attaché, said something in the Vulcan language. Krenn wondered if Sinon were *tharavul*.

Onoda said, "If you and your company will follow me, please? We have a reception planned. I hope it's to your liking."

"Diplomat Onoda," Krenn said, "are you the Ambassador we are to take to Klinzhai?"

"Oh, no," Onoda said, "oh, no." He gestured, and the group started out of the room. As they funneled toward the door, Onoda turned to Sinon and said, in Federation, "Whitetree's going to *explode.*"

Then they have not contacted him, Krenn thought. *Which means he is coming by shuttle as well.*

Perhaps we should not have used their language so soon.

One of the Federation guards was speaking to one of his companions. He was discussing Kelly, and clearly he did not know she could understand him.

Krenn said to her, in Battle Language, "Subspace silence. Hold fire."

"It doesn't bother me to tell you," Admiral Whitetree said to Captain Krenn, "I wanted you quarantined here. Give you the Ambassador and send you home again. But the Diplomatic Corps overruled Starfleet."

Krenn said, "I have no disagreement with your caution."

They were sitting in a private lounge on the rim of the Starbase; the lights within were dim, and a panoramic window showed a solid wall of naked stars.

The Admiral got up from his chair. "Another?" he said, pointing at Krenn's glass.

"Please," Krenn said. He had had a hard time getting used to the word. But after a day on the Starbase, Krenn had realized that the Humans used it continually, across all levels of authority, for requests of any or no importance: the word simply had no meaning.

"Apple or orange?" Whitetree said. "We've got pineapple and grape, too . . . and prune, but the Medical Corps would have my ass for antimatter if I gave you that."

"Apple juice is fine."

Whitetree came back from the wall unit with two glasses. "I understand the climate here's a little out of range for you."

"It is acceptable."

"Onoda wanted to reset temp and humidity for the whole damned base. We just couldn't do it; you know the size of this place, you can imagine the inertia in the enviro system. It'd take a week and a half to even try, with a good chance of making it uncomfortable for everyone."

"This is understood." And, Krenn thought, Starfleet was not always overruled by the Diplomatic Corps.

"I'm glad. I've stayed in enough alien cabins to know what it's like. . . . I suppose your homeworld's star is a spectral class . . . F-something? Or is the orbit very tight?"

"I am not an astronomer. My Science officer would know. But I am not certain that he could tell you."

After a pause, the Admiral said, "Yup. I can think of a dozen different things I'd usually talk about, with a Captain just off a cruise like yours, but most of them would violate military security. And I'm not sure I want to go near the others."

"I have killed a few who insulted me," Krenn said, "but I do not think you mean any insults. Please speak."

Whitetree said, "Well, there's your Communications person . . . I never knew your Empire used female officers."

"Your Empire does. Why would we waste an intelligent one with talent?"

"You have women . . . females in command, then?"

"Lieutenant Kelly's orders are obeyed."

"I mean, in command of ships. Independent command." There was a set to Whitetree's creased, dark face, a light in his eyes.

Krenn said, "No."

Whitetree said, "My daughter commands a survey ship. The *Avebury*."

Krenn said nothing.

Whitetree said, as if pressing the same point, "How does a Klingon Captain get chosen for duty like this? Was it a reward? Or punishment? Or did you just draw the short straw?"

Krenn's taped learning did not include the last idiom, but he supposed it meant bad luck. "The Empire ordered me here; I came. The mission is not dishonorable."

"So you were just following orders?"

"Do officers of the Federation not follow orders?"

Whitetree leaned forward, about to say something; then he sat back slowly. His expression had changed wholly, though the shifts of flesh were small. "I'm . . . sorry, Captain."

Krenn had heard that word too: it seemed to have more of its meaning left than *please* did. And, watching the Human, Krenn thought he intended that it should have meaning now.

"I am not insulted, Admiral."

"Maybe you should be. I was—" Whitetree shook his head. "My son was killed by Klingons."

"Did the one fight well?" Krenn said.

"He was on a ship called the *Flying Fortress,*" the Admiral said. "You may have heard of the incident. The ship was one of our *Rickenbacker*-class, what we used to call Maximum Security Transports. Only one of them was ever hijacked . . . pirates broadcast a fake distress message from a fake Federation scout. When *Flying Fort* answered, the pirates put a shot straight into her crew compartment.

"There was an automatic subspace alarm aboard, though, that the pirates didn't know about. A patrol was scrambled, and when it showed up, the pirates dropped the loot and ran."

"I have indeed heard of this incident," Krenn said. "Those who fled were executed, for cowardice."

Whitetree said, "I didn't know that. I suppose . . . it ought to please me, or at least satisfy me, but . . ."

In a low voice, the Admiral said, "You see, Captain, Starfleet sent me out here because they thought I'd really show you the hot end of the lasers. And I really thought I would.

"So what happens? I show up with a task force that could level half a planet, to meet one cruiser with a light crew and sealed guns. You don't drip spittle from your bloodied fangs, you don't keep your women in chains—Spirit, you speak the language better than some of my crew, and you're a damn sight politer."

He stood up, went to look out the window. No ships were visible. Krenn wondered if Humans believed in the power of the naked stars. Whitetree said, "So everyone involved with the hijack is dead?"

"The one who planned it was named Kethas. He also is dead."

Whitetree turned. "Kethas? We've heard of him. The Klingon Yamamoto. Dead too . . . damnation."

"My family," Krenn said, "was killed by Romulans. It was also an ambush of a ship not at war."

"Don't misunderstand me, Captain," Whitetree said, his voice hardened again. "I still hate you, and all Klingons. I don't think I'd stop hating you if I found out Jesus Christ was a Klingon. But you've . . . made me think. It's as if . . . dead things were alive again."

The only truth about death, Krenn thought but did not consider to say, *is that it is death, and the end.*

The wall communicator chimed, and the Admiral went to it.

"Whitetree . . . Yes, I see. The Captain's with me; we'll be there shortly."

Whitetree turned to Krenn. "Some of your crew are in a brawl with some of mine. We'd better go and untangle them."

Krenn said, "Was the combat started by Klingons?"

"They didn't say." Whitetree swallowed the last of his juice. "And I really don't think it's going to matter a damn. Do you?"

Krenn, Akhil, and Maktai had Lieutenant Kalim in a three-way fire: Krenn was aware it was probably harder on the young officer than time in the cube, but they could not afford even the usual leave tolerances just now. The Klingons had left the Starbase under the tubes of guns and eyes hardly less threatening, and *Fencer*'s authorization to proceed to Earth had come none too soon.

"We were just talking," Kalim said, "with some of those fringe-patrol Feds. Some of them had fought Roms, you see, Captain, and they knew good Rom stories, like 'How many Roms does it take to change a translator?' "

"Don't digress," Maktai said. His usual easy manner made his growl all the more effective.

"Yes, Lieutenant," Krenn said calmly, "you were talking with the Starfleet beings. Did the fight start over old Rom stories?"

"No, Captain, it wasn't that. One of the Feds mentioned Lieutenant Kelly—"

Not *that* again, Krenn thought, surprised at the strength of his feeling.

"—he didn't know her name, not then, but he talked about her, and that translator-pipe of theirs isn't very subtle, *if* you know what I mean, Captain, and it was clear who he was talking about. And I said, 'That's our Lieutenant Kelly, and you be careful how you talk.' "

"You said that?" Akhil said.

"Well, Commander, it may have been Konli, but I was about to say it."

According to the taped testimonies, every one of the twenty-six Klingons involved in the brawl had been first to defend the Communications officer. Krenn said "Proceed."

Kalim said, "So one of the Feds said, 'Personal deity, they have an Eirizhman in the crew.' That's what the translator-pipe said."

Krenn said, " 'Irish' is a place of origin on Earth."

"I thought it was an insult, Captain."

"A reasonable assumption. Proceed."

"So then a Human said, 'That makes nothing. I heard there is a Skots'man also, a . . . Maktai.' And then the Feds started arguing with each other."

"That was when the fight started?"

"No, Captain. We didn't even know what the argument was about, not then. But then Ensign Kintata said—"

If the speaker was a Lieutenant, it was an Ensign who had said the key phrase; if an Ensign, a Lieutenant had. It was that, or admit one had been drinking with non-officers. Krenn supposed they were fortunate to have no Cadets aboard.

Akhil read from the computer screen in his lap, "Asked a Starfleet Human his name. Was told it was 'Marks.' Announced that he knew many Klingons named Marks, and all were Marines."

"Yes, Commander," Kalim said, nodding vigorously.

"And *that* was when the fight started."

"Affirm."

Krenn said, "A small surprise."

The Lieutenant started to nod, but instead came to laser-locked attention.

"This is not a raid," Krenn said. "We are not to provoke combat, though we have the right to defend ourselves." He paused. "*Did* we defend ourselves?"

"Oh, yes, Captain," Kalim said. "Humans can take a lot of hitting, but they're slow. And those stunners of theirs, the beam ones, they don't work well at all. I was hit, oh, eight or nine times and I still took down—"

"That's sufficient, Lieutenant." Krenn stood up. "The Exec has a punishment detail in mind for you."

To his credit, Lieutenant Kalim did not react at all as Krenn went into his inner office, followed by Maktai. The door closed; Krenn touched on a monitor with a view of the outer office.

". . . confined to quarters during non-duty or meal hours until the ship reaches Earth," Akhil was saying. "Confined to the ship during the duration of the Earth stay . . ."

"It'll be a Security directive when it comes," Krenn said, "but no one's going downside on Earth but the landing party . . . me, 'Khil, you if you want, but I'd rather have you in command here." And away from the Feds, Krenn thought.

"How about Communications?"

"I'll have a communicator. I'll want Kelly listening for me." And away from the Humans, doubled.

Beside which, Krenn thought, if she is from II, the two of you are best kept in the same place . . . in fact, if either of you are, or both.

Maktai said, "How many guards?"

"None. Akhil and I will carry dress weapons. If they want to kill us, they have a whole planet to do it with."

"It isn't the bite, it's the showing of teeth."

"They expect us to show teeth—*khest,* they expect us to bite. It doesn't scare them. But they feel wrong when they send out a great force, and are met by a small one. They feel . . ." Krenn found the Human word. ". . . *silly.* This has enormous power over them. I want them to feel as *silly* as possible while we're there."

Maktai said, "Oh, that Vulcan attaché—the one you thought might be *tharavul* to the diplomat?"

"He wasn't, was he."

"No. One of my people saw him mind-touch one of the Starfleeters, after the fight. A Human. She seemed to consent to it."

"Humans seem to consent to a lot of things," Krenn said. "But then, the Vulcans consent to having a piece of their brains cut out, just so they can live among us, watch how we live."

"What do Vulcans care?" Maktai said. "And, no one reported seeing or hearing anything about particle transporters. Not that they gave us much freedom to look."

"I wonder what they'll let us see on Earth," Krenn said.

Akhil came in. "That's the last of the disciplines. At least there weren't any deaths . . . I think we're lucky the crews didn't know much of each other's anatomy. The Surgeon had to set six dislocated jaws, did you know? Humans like to punch at the jaw. . . ." He shook his head. "In Keth's years, I've never heard such a story."

"Speaking of stories, 'Khil," Krenn said.

"Yes?"

"How many Roms *does* it take to change a translator?"

Akhil stared. So did Maktai. Almost together, they said, "You don't *know?*"

"I never much liked Romulan jokes."

Maktai said, "One to change the 'stator . . ."

Akhil said, ". . . and 150 to blow up the ship out of shame."

And Krenn, who had not laughed at a Rom joke in many years, found himself full to bursting.

Seen from parking orbit, most of Earth had been ocean, and clouds covered it in vast white ruffs and whorls.

So how, Krenn wondered, *could such a planet have a place so incredibly dry, with so much bald white sky arching over?*

"Don't breathe deeply," Akhil warned, as they stepped from the shuttle onto the hard soil. "There's no moisture at *all;* it'll burn your lungs out."

And it was hot, like a fusion torch is hot. Krenn's head was aching in a moment. He looked around, feeling his eyeballs beginning to cook: there was a ring of Humans and vehicles all around the shuttlecraft, all waiting for something. Krenn saw that all the Humans had weapons; so did all the vehicles, except for one, a blocky thing the size of the shuttle, all white metal below and black glass above. NORTH AMERICAN PRIME STARPORT, said letters on the metal side, WHITE SANDS, CIBOLA, USA.

"Bloody Ishtar," a Human voice said, "if they have heatstroke it's our tails," and four of the soldiers ran to help Krenn and Akhil toward the half-glass vehicle. "I thought they *liked* it hot," one muttered.

Within the vehicle it was dark, and moist, and cold: but as Krenn recovered, he realized it was only the effect of sudden change. The interior of the vehicle was actually very close to a Klingon ship's environment.

"Sit down," another Human voice said. "It isn't that they were afraid of you; they just didn't know what they might have to be afraid *of.*"

Krenn sat. Then he realized that the Human voice had spoken in quite casual *klingonaase.*

Krenn looked up. There were leather swivel seats along both sides of the vehicle, which was moving now: an operator was visible through thick glass in the front. There was no door to his compartment. With him was one of the Human soldiers, rifle at ready arms, head encased in some kind of breathing helmet.

Krenn turned again. In a seat opposite him sat the smallest, frailest Human Krenn had yet seen, including some who had spent days in the agonizer cube.

This Human was dark-skinned, almost as dark as a Klingon— Kelly's color, Krenn thought. His hair was thin, gray-silver, almost white. His face was bony and lined, but his eyes were brilliant behind discs of glass in a wire frame. He wore a long belted tunic of smooth white fabric; there were single traceries of gold wire on collar and cuffs, and a supernova of award triangles on the breast. If they were the medals they represented, Krenn thought, they would outweigh the wearer.

"There is no more absolute zero of land," the Human said, looking through the heavily tinted windows, "not since we have begun to live on the icecap. Only white sun, white air, and a pan of industrial abrasive the size of Chesapeake Bay, with no good line dividing them."

The Human looked at Krenn again, and his face made Krenn uneasy: the bright eyes in the old face made him think too much, far too much, of Kethas.

"Things are done here," the Human said, "*you* are here, because this place is nothing, and nothing can ever happen here. When we were inventing reaction-drive spacecraft, the fueled rockets were allowed to crash here. Nuclear weapons were set off here, just to satisfy curiosity as to what would happen, because *it would not matter,* you see. There is no mind in this land, and no memory. And that is why you were caused to land here.

"I am Dr. Emanuel Tagore," said the Human, "Ph.D. several times, University of New Bombay, Universities of Chicago, Edinburgh, Akademgorodok and the Ocean of Storms, late of the Makropyrios College of Political Science, and probable candidate for the Museum of Antiquities on Memory Alpha. I will have the honor of accompanying you on your return home, Captain . . . if we reach the lands of memory."

Krenn watched a monitor, showing Humans fighting one another in the streets of a city. The city's location was not given, and its name was meaningless to him. He, and Akhil, and *Fencer,* were the subjects of the riot; Krenn wondered how far away the Humans were rioting.

He also wondered what their purpose was in letting him see this.

The Klingons and the Ambassador Dr. Tagore had been transferred, at a place called Juarez–El Paso Station, to a gravity-suspended train of cars riding elevated tracks. Akhil had asked one of the train crew their speed: the Human seemed startled to hear the Klingon speaking his language, but then rather proudly gave the speed as three hundred kilometers an Earth hour. Akhil gave a suitably impressed thanks.

The sun had set; Dr. Tagore assured Krenn it was safe to watch, and the colors were indeed dramatic. Now Krenn was alone in the last car of the train. Akhil was one car forward, dozing in a small bedroom. Dr. Tagore was further ahead, in conference with the other Federation officials aboard. There was a soldier visible through the door to that car, not threatening, merely armed and ready.

The door to Krenn's car opened, and two Humans came in. The first was a Starfleet Admiral, Marcus van Diemen; the second was a Colonel of the Earth Surface Forces named Rabinowich.

Van Diemen was a large, impressive male with yellow hair and light skin; he wore a Starfleet dress uniform with plenty of gold braid, more by far than Admiral Whitetree had worn. Jael Rabinowich wore a uniform like those her soldiers wore, with rank badges of dark fabric that would not show to an enemy's scouts or snipers, and a sidearm of dull black metal that was clearly not for show. She was darker than van Diemen, much smaller, though not slight. Krenn thought about Whitetree's comments on female Commanders. He looked at Rabinowich's face, and wondered what tools she would use to lead.

Admiral van Diemen said, "We have a change of plans." His voice was large as well. "A gentleman of some importance has asked to speak with you, and the diversion and meeting have just been approved. It will delay us perhaps half a day . . . will your crew become alarmed, if you are stopped for a few hours before reaching Federa-Terra?"

Van Diemen looked at Krenn's communicator. Krenn had supposed the Federation would be screening them from search; but then, no one could ever quite know what the enemy's sensors could sense past. And if they did not in fact have the transporter . . . "I will inform them. To where is the diversion?"

"The city of Atlanta, State of Georgia, United States of America."

Wherever that was, Krenn thought. "And whom are we to meet?"

"His name is Maxwell Grandisson, the Third. He is a private citizen, but, as I say, influential. In fact, it was partly through Mr. Grandisson's efforts that the embassy to Klingon is being established."

"Klinzhai," Krenn said.

"Excuse me?"

"The Homeworld's name is Klinzhai."

"Ahh. I see." Van Diemen acted as if he had just discovered a major military secret. Krenn wondered if the Admiral understood any *klingonaase.*

Krenn said, trying not to sound too curious, "Will the stop in this city complicate your security arrangements?"

Van Diemen looked past Krenn, at the monitor screen, and took on a vaguely distracted expression. Colonel Rabinowich said, "Complicate them, yes. This citizen insists on meeting you at the place of his choosing. And the Atlanta Metroplex is very large. But we can control our people." Her voice was surprisingly soft, though not smooth. She nodded toward the rioters on the screen. "To protest, to demonstrate, these we may not interfere with. But we will not let them cause lasting damage."

Admiral van Diemen said, "You must understand, Captain . . . many of our people have lost relatives and friends to Klingon action. I myself had a brother killed on the frontier. This is why we must have peace."

Both the Humans had used the phrase "our people"; the same possessive, yet Krenn felt they did not mean the same thing by it.

"I assure you, Admiral, I shall do my best," said a voice from the car ahead. Colonel Rabinowich instantly moved to let Dr. Tagore pass. She would be a good Swift, perhaps, Krenn thought. But her bearing seemed more that of a Fencer.

"Yes," van Diemen said, uncertain for only an instant. "Well. We'll be returning to our car now; there's still a lot to do and not much time to do it in. Good night, Captain . . . Mr. Ambassador."

"Good night," Dr. Tagore said. Krenn bowed slightly. The Admiral went out. "Peace," the Colonel said, and followed.

When the door had closed, Krenn said in *klingonaase,* "Peace? Was that sarcasm? At you?"

"Not at all. It's a common greeting, or exit line. I see your companion has retired; do you need to rest?"

"Not for some time."

"Your day is longer than ours?"

"Somewhat."

Dr. Tagore smiled. "I ask only as one who expects to live there soon. Shall we sit and talk, then? You said you drank coffee, so I brought some."

Krenn turned the monitor off as Dr. Tagore filled cups. When they were settled, Dr. Tagore said, "You are vestai-Rustazh. Is the line a large one?"

"No. . . . Only I am this line."

"Then you are a founder."

"You have authentic knowledge," Krenn said, surprised that the Human had so quickly drawn the conclusion.

"There are reports, mostly from Vulcan. And there are books and tapes . . . they filter from your space into ours, in Orion loot and Rigellian trading hulls. I suppose I shouldn't say this, but a spy was captured on Argelius III, and the one had dozens of books and tapes, a closetful of them. Starfleet Intelligence was convinced the one was using them in an elaborate code scheme, and as the nearest available reader of *klingonaase* I was called in to read the lot."

Krenn sipped the *kafei*—he found he was actually coming to like the stuff—and wondered that the Ambassador should so casually reveal his connection with the Intelligence service. "Were they a code?"

"Not at all. They were solely for his pleasure. As he said, as soon as the matter was found: but Intelligence did not believe this. I told them, once he was discovered, and no longer a spy, the one would say nothing, or tell the truth. But I was not believed, either."

Perhaps that was the point of the story: indirectly, the Human was discounting his tie to Intelligence.

Dr. Tagore said, "I'm pleased to find my knowledge is valid. There are some famous fictions about our history that I should not like an alien ambassador to take learning from. . . . Though I confess I have become quite fond of *Battlecruiser Vengeance.* Is it still in production?"

"Yes," Krenn said, trying not to choke.

"I was correct that you are founder of a line, Captain; do you have a sole consort, or many?"

At least this one asked in private, as one with a concern. "I have no consort at this time."

Dr. Tagore paused, said, "I see. My own wife—" he used the Human word—"is dead."

Krenn waited: every Human seemed to have a close relative killed by marauding Klingons.

"A disease of the nerve sheaths," Dr. Tagore said, looking away from Krenn. "Gualter's neuromyelitis. There is a chemical therapy, but one patient in twenty cannot tolerate it; that one dies in a few years." The Human looked at Krenn, said in a very mild, almost apologetic tone, "I am told the symptoms are similar to the effects of your agonizer device. . . ." In Human he added, "I'm sorry; I meant nothing by that."

That made still another inflection of the word *sorry*.

Dr. Tagore said, still in Federation Standard, "I know your race has no tradition of ghosts or revenants, no rites for the dead. Ours has too many of them. I say this to explain certain of our actions, that might otherwise seem strange. I have a theory . . . but this isn't the time for it. Please, let's find another subject."

Krenn waited a moment. The Human's eyes seemed even brighter than before, yet the face was older, more crumpled. At once Krenn also wished to change the subject. He pointed at the darkened monitor. "Those people . . . who hate us . . . how many of them are there?"

"Enough," Dr. Tagore said. "Always enough. The Klingon Empire has been a very convenient devil, these twenty-odd years. Whenever a ship vanishes in that general direction of space, someone claims, with or without evidence, that it's 'fallen prey to the savage Klingon.' All too often the claim is made on the floor of the Solar Senate, or even the whole Federation." He sighed. "From the Galactic Bermuda Triangle to the Klingon Twilight Zone."

Krenn said, "Twenty odd years?"

"An idiom, pardon. In *klingonaase,* twenty-plus—which is also an idiom of ours; I must be sure to use that one from now on. First contact with the *komerex klingon* was, if I can unwind it from the Stardate system, twenty-two Standard years ago. That would be twenty years Klingon standard, if I have the ratios right."

"Yes, that is the difference as I understand it." Krenn was not really thinking about year lengths, but the fact that the first Federation ships had been taken by the Empire fully thirty years ago: thirty Klingon years. Obviously no prize had reported its fate for a long time.

"There was a novel, written long before we had starflight and even longer before warp drive," Dr. Tagore was saying, "in which the accidental loss of some starships coincided with first contact with nonhumans—who had also lost ships. Both sides resorted to the communication that needs no translation. The war, in the story, lasted a thousand years."

"A war of a thousand years . . . ?" Krenn said. It was an astonishing idea, still more so from a Human. Yet Krenn could, thinking on it, see how it might be conducted: dynastic lines ruling over lines of battle, fifty generations born and dying in the pursuit of a single glory. A war like that would mark worlds deeply so that if, a million years after, when all the warriors were dust, a new race should come upon the space, they would know what had happened there.

Dr. Tagore said, "Perhaps we will not take so long to communicate. I do not have a thousand years left in this life, and I fear I have about used my karma up."

"I do not know the word."

"Neither do I." The Human was smiling whitely; his teeth, Krenn saw, were square-cornered, without points. "At least, not so I could explain it properly, and that's the same thing. My enlightenment is all of the immanent sort."

Krenn wondered at this little Human, who seemed to think he could dismiss an idea as potent as a war of a thousand years in a single moment . . . who would stand between two Empires, like waves of the sea, or colliding stars, and hold them apart. It was absurd; it was *silly;* perhaps it was insane.

Krenn thought then of the Willall, and the Tellarites, all hollow great words . . . but no, he did not think this Dr. Tagore was *kuve.* He drank more *kafei;* it had gone cold. It was not good cold. Dr. Tagore saw Krenn's grimace, tasted his own drink, said, "I see what you mean. I'll get another pot."

When the Human had gone, Krenn turned on the monitor again, set it to the channel that gave continuous news reports. There was a report of an industrial accident, a display of new clothing by "famous designers" that was little short of bewildering, and then more tape of the rioters. They were breaking windows of buildings, which seemed strange, since Krenn and Akhil were the only Klingons on Earth—at least, the only Klingons known to be on Earth. A group burned a wooden model of a D-4 cruiser. Krenn laughed; no one had told him Humans believed in primitive magic.

Then the picture changed again, to two streaks of light in darkness, and Krenn leaped to the train window; slowly, he opened a curtain.

The train's guideway was elevated on castrock piers, twenty to twenty-five meters above the ground: below, as the train flashed by, were long dashes of light. With difficulty Krenn resolved them into Humans with torches, electric and flaming and cold chemical. He tried to calculate their number: Akhil said the train covered five thousand meters every local minute. Krenn looked at his communicator's time display.

Krenn turned as the door opened. It was Akhil. He did not look rested at all. He pointed at the glass. "I saw them from the window. They've been with us for at least an hour."

"How many, do you figure?"

"A hundred thousand, probably more. I suppose they could be relaying a smaller group, behind us to ahead; a flier could just outrun this train. But what I'm really thinking is what a couple of good shots into one of those support towers would do."

"That is also Colonel Rabinowich's thought," Dr. Tagore said from the doorway. "She does tell me that the construction is very strong, and hand weapons would not serve, and they have sensor vehicles searching for any larger weapons." In a smaller voice he said, "She also says that a certain number of the demonstrators are actually her troops, disguised."

"*Kai* Rabinowich," Krenn said, impressed.

"Yes," Dr. Tagore said, speaking *klingonaase* again. "Her family have been soldiers for more than ten generations, and I think your praise would please her, if it were properly explained." He looked down at the torches streaming by. "It is the explanations which are hard . . . especially in a culture which knows no difference between a machine translation and an understanding of language."

He paused, filled two cups with *kafei,* then a third for Akhil, who seemed genuinely glad to have it. Dr. Tagore said, "You have noticed, perhaps, that in Fed-Standard *klingonaase* is pronounced a little strangely?"

" 'Klingoneeze,' " Akhil said.

Dr. Tagore nodded. "That suffix is common in several of Standard's root languages, including, dear me, Rigellian Trade Dialect, to turn a nation-name into the nation-language—which itself is a less than wholly useful notion. And so we have Japanese, Terchionese, F'tallgatri'itese, and, when the circuits got the word in their clutches, 'Klingonese.' The whole significance of the *aase* suffix, that the language is the tool for manipulating the embodiment of the *klin* principle . . . all that is lost, in the leap of an electron across an Abramson junction."

Krenn said, "What do the lights out there mean? The flames? Can you translate those? Or is it your language that needs no translation?"

"They need to say something," Dr. Tagore said calmly, "but they do not know just what. Not yet." He went to the monitor, which was showing close views of the chains of Humans, showing their faces, lit by torchlight and searchlight and the flash of the train's passing. Krenn could see the strong emotions there, and knew that he must be seeing fear, and hate, and pain, because those were the only things he knew that could bend the face so, but he was not at all sure which was which, or what else might be there as well.

"You understand, now," Dr. Tagore said in *klingonaase*. "You do not know yet, either, what to say. There must be a little time."

Krenn said, "And if, in time, they still hate us?" He was aware, even as he spoke, that he said it only to get a little time to think.

Dr. Tagore put his thin-fingered hand across his eyes, as if to hide them from the faces on the screen; but at once he took it away, and looked at Krenn and Akhil. "I said that Colonel Rabinowich's was a line of warriors. That line is rooted in a hate that ran deeper than blood runs in the liver, that many people of the best intention though could only end in the separations of walls and wire, or in the mass grave. And there were those things. But the walls are down, and the graveyards . . . they are remembered, and kept, which is a thing our race does.

"And Admiral van Diemen's people had their war, too, for hate instead of territory. And the walls, and the graves. But finally the peace. The city of Atlanta, to which we are making a side excursion, was burned to nothing a hundred years before nuclear explosives made it so much less laborious a task. . . . And my own ancestors were the second nation of Earth to use a nuclear explosive against an enemy, though not the last, not the last.

"We know what hate is, Captain, and we practice it with great finesse. But sometimes we achieve things in spite of it."

Akhil said, without force, "But if they want the war?"

"If they do, Commander, I will oppose them. I am a public servant; I am not a servitor."

Krenn saw Akhil's eyes flick. He realized that he had failed to take this Human's measure. And the advantage he had found was—at least with this one—gone: this one could have no concern with being made absurd. He might die—they all might, Krenn thought, as another hundred Human fires flashed by—but silly he would not be.

Wondering if he had now been twice maneuvered into changing the subject, Krenn said, "This diversion . . . do you know this person we're to see? This *important* person?"

"Maxwell Grandisson the Third," Dr. Tagore said, stretching out the syllables. "I know *of* him, who doesn't—sorry, Captain—but we've never met. I have only once been to Atlanta, and he never leaves the city. Which indirectly answers your indirect question: he is powerful enough that he does not have to leave. If he wishes to see a mountain, the mountain comes to him." The Human smiled. "Figuratively speaking, of course. Though I do not doubt he has the resources to move mountains. Small ones, at any rate."

Akhil said, "How much wealth is concentrated with this Human?"

"Enough . . . always enough, somehow. But faith is the power that moves mountains, and of that he has access to a great deal more than enough."

Krenn said, "What does he want from us, then? Trade? Or just the satisfaction of his curiosity?"

"Certainly not the first, and not just the second." Dr. Tagore hesitated. "Mr. Grandisson is a leader of a large—still growing, I regret to say—movement, spread throughout Human space. This . . . movement is not known so much for what it wants, as what it does not want."

"War?" Krenn said, and then remembered that Dr. Tagore had *regretted*.

"The stars," Dr. Tagore said.

The sun was rising behind the city called Atlanta. The entire city seemed to be built of glass and crystal and bright metal, cylindrical columns and truncated pyramids endlessly reflecting one another, all tied together with flying bridges at every level. Morning light colored all the glass a pale red: Krenn thought of Dr. Tagore's comment, of the city burning. A century before nuclears, the Human said, however long ago that was. It was a Vulcan calculation that a culture's lifespan was either some fifty years after basic fission was discovered, or else indefinite.

There were still Humans at the base of the guideway as the train hurtled into the city, now holding colored flags instead of torches. Colonel Rabinowich said, "We'll be going underground a few klicks before the terminal. And an identical train will come out of the southbound pipe. We'd have done it at the Baton Rouge shunt, but there wasn't time."

"And the change of course?" Dr. Tagore said.

"Let 'em think we tried to fool 'em, and failed."

"An excellent strategy," Krenn said, careful to draw no comparisons with Klingon methods, though any Imperial officer would have hailed the trick. "You honor your craft and your line." He understood well now which of the leader's paths she had mastered: the way of greater cunning.

Rabinowich cast a side look at Dr. Tagore, who sat across the dining car, placidly drinking coffee. He had had no sleep, Krenn knew. Admiral van Diemen was in the sleeping car now.

The Colonel said, "Thank you, Captain," in her customary soft-coarse voice. "That's more than Starfleet usually gives us dirtballers."

The terrain rose past the train. Interior lights came on, and then the windows went black, except for flashes of light that were gone before the eye could catch what was illuminated.

"Sit down, please, Captain, Commander," the Colonel said, going to a seat herself; Dr. Tagore gulped the last of his coffee, held tight to the ceramic cup. "Gravitic braking," Rabinowich said.

It was not a bad deceleration—certainly nothing like a combat maneuver when the deckplates were already straining—but Krenn was glad of the chair as invisible drag pulled him toward the front of the train.

In less than two local minutes they were at a full stop. Cool blue lights showed a platform beyond the windows, and more soldiers.

"All out," Dr. Tagore said lightly, "change here for the *Southern Crescent.*"

Colonel Rabinowich looked at the Ambassador for a moment, then said, "Your escort to the hotel's on the platform. We'll be meeting you at a different platform: right now we've got to get the numbers scraped off this train and a different set on. Enjoy your breakfast."

"You aren't coming with us?" Krenn said. "Or the Admiral?"

"Or the Ambassador," Dr. Tagore said.

Rabinowich paused. "You must—no, of course you don't know. The invitation wasn't to us. Grandisson doesn't like Starfleet people."

"You are not with Starfleet."

"Never been off Earth, in fact. Max Grandisson doesn't like me for a reason I thought was extinct until I was twenty-eight years old." She gave a flat smile. "It goes a long way back. Unto the tenth generation, and then some. *Shalom aleichem,* Captain Krenn, Commander Akhil."

"Aleichem shalom," Krenn said, and as the Colonel's mouth opened in surprise, and then a grin, Krenn caught Dr. Tagore's nod in the corner of his eye.

The building was ancient, dull stone among all the bright glass, with new entry steps that led down where it had settled into the earth. The Klingons' escorts—Humans in plain clothing, driving a vehicle that was like a dozen others on the street—surrounded Krenn and Akhil as all walked briskly inside.

Within, the hotel was a hollow box, balconies lining its interior; the roof, many floors above, was of an age-darkened glass that let only a few shafts of light through. Spindle-shaped lift cars rode up a central black pylon. The lobby was quite empty, and quiet. Bright green plants stood next to dying ones.

All this Krenn saw on the move. Within seconds they were at the glass-walled lifts, which more Humans in plain suits were holding ready; Akhil and half the guards went into one glass capsule, Krenn and the rest into another.

A young Human male in a red and white uniform walked past

Krenn's lift just then, carrying a tray. He looked up. Krenn looked back. The tray fell with a crash Krenn could not hear, as the car moved upward.

They emerged into a curved room: windows ran around the outer wall, giving what must have been a panorama of the city when the building was new, but which now showed only a curtain of glass.

A tall, slender Human came around the curve. The cut of his clothing was almost as restrained as the Security guards' suits, but the tailoring was much sharper, the fabrics more exotic by far. His shirt had a high collar and a lace front. His face was rectangular, with a large jaw, a high forehead from which brown hair fell back straight to the collar. His nose was a blade, his eyes sharp enough to draw blood. There was a wireless phone in his ear, and a black device, the size of a communicator, clipped to his breast pocket.

"Good morning, gentlemen," he said, and the device in his pocket repeated it in *klingonaase.* Not only was the black device much smaller than the usual Federation translator, its sound quality was better. "I'm Max Grandisson. Glad you could join us."

Krenn thought a moment about his answer, not only what to say but which language to say it in. Finally he decided that, while speaking Federation might cost them some interesting side comments, a deception might backfire. "Thank you for the invitation, Mr. Grandisson. We're here to make peaceful contacts. I am Krenn, Captain of the *Fencer;* this is Commander Akhil, my Science officer, and also my Executive."

Grandisson held quite still, his sharp eyes narrowing slightly; he touched his earphone, then extracted it, smiled. "Pardon my surprise, gentlemen. No one told me you spoke our language." From his tone, Krenn was certain that someone would regret the lapse.

Grandisson said to the guards, "Why don't you fellows go on down. Have breakfast if you like; I don't suppose you're allowed to drink on the job, but anything you like, just charge it to me." He waved a hand before an objection could properly be raised. "I don't think you need worry about our guests; I'll vouch for the gentlemen with me, and no one comes up here without my approval. Go on down, now, and relax."

It was one of the most gently delivered absolute commands Krenn had ever heard. And, though they looked doubtful, the Security people got into the lifts and descended.

"Now, Captain, Commander, if you'll come with me, we can get started. Pardon me a moment." Grandisson took another black device from inside his coat, pressed buttons on it. "Sally? This is Max. There's some boys coming down right now, you won't be able to miss 'em, they've got Government written all over 'em in big red letters. You see they get what they want, but give 'em a seat with a good view of the kitchen."

There was a sound from the speaker. Grandisson said, "That's right. Don't annoy them. But keep them out of mischief.

"And, Sally, if anyone from the *Constitution* comes by, there's nothing happening here, and there certainly aren't any Government hound dogs around. . . . I know you will, Sal. That's what I pay you for." He put away the communicator.

Akhil said, "*Constitution* is what class of starship?"

"*What?* Ah. Not at all, Commander. The *Atlanta Constitution* is a news service. Honest men, but not always prudent ones. Now, if you'll all come this way." As they went around the curve, past partitions, desks, and bookshelves, Grandisson said, "This was originally a restaurant, built to revolve, you see. But after two hundred years the mechanism became rather delicate . . . not that there was anything left to see by that time. I wish I could show you gentlemen the old city."

"Before the fire?" Krenn said.

Grandisson stroked his smooth brown hair. "I daresay, Captain, you have me at a loss." Krenn thoroughly doubted that. "No, Captain, I wasn't thinking that far back. That's a sight I'd like to see myself. Do you know of—ah, here we are."

Three Human males were seated at a table set for six. Two of them rose as Grandisson and the Klingons approached; the third, Krenn saw, sat in an antigrav chair, because he had no legs. One of the standing men was young, with eyeglasses and a thin mustache; the other had a neat gray beard, and a gold chain across the front of his coat. All were well-dressed, though not so expensively as Grandisson.

Grandisson said, "May I present Commodore Amos Blakeslee of the Starfleet Exploration Command, now retired." The legless Human nodded. Krenn wondered about Colonel Rabinowich's comment: how *did* Grandisson feel about Starfleet personnel?

"Doctor Samuel Landers, of the Inner Space Corporation." That was the young Human. "And T. J. McCoy, M.D., Chief of Medicine at the Emory University Medical Center."

Introductions completed, all sat down. The chairs were carved wood with leather padding; not really comfortable for Klingon anatomy, but tolerable. The table was of highly polished wood, the service of heavy ceramics, apparently solid silver, and cut crystal that broke the indirect light into rainbows.

"I understand that you gentlemen can eat our cooking," Grandisson said, as platters were unloaded onto the table. Krenn wondered, if Grandisson should be told the words, if he would consider the Human servers *kuve* or *straave*.

"We've done so without harm," Akhil said.

"That's fine. Of course, just in case, I called T.J. up here to join us. Best doctor in the state."

Dr. McCoy turned, slowly. His accent was much stronger than Grandisson's. "Actually, Captain, I'm just a G.P. from Union County, not a xenophysician at all. And I doubt there's anyone inside of twenty parsecs with any experience of Klingon medicine. I would, however, give you the medical advice not to eat those."

"What is that?" Akhil said.

"Those, sir, are called grits."

Krenn had already tried a forkful. They were, he decided, no worse than Romulan emergency rations. But it was a near thing.

The soft-cooked eggs in silver cups required mechanical mastery, but tasted good, if bland. The peach nectar was blood-thick and incredible. The coffee was void-black and incredibly strong.

The places were cleared; the Humans, except for Commodore Blakeslee, sat back in their chairs.

"I've asked you here, Captain," Grandisson said crisply, "because you're about to be hustled down to that Florida land swindle they call a Federation City, and double-shuffled past some diplomats and Starfleet officers, and sent home again heavily weighted with one point of view. I'd like to expose you to another, one that a great many Human beings subscribe to."

He turned, settling into a comfortable three-quarter pose. "For a long time, our leaders have been telling us that we had to progress in certain directions: greater speed, greater height, greater sheer mass and volume. There was a time when this city was filled with architectural masterworks, like the building we're in now; but progress tore them down, *blasted* them down, and gave us *that* in their place." Grandisson pointed out the window, at the sheer glass cliffs. "We have seen the future, gentlemen, and it is vastly more expensive.

"The other direction we were told we must go was out. A *long way* out. First to the Moon, then Mars, and some gravitational holes just as far away as the Moon but no more hospitable: and now, the stars. On every one, we were told, we'd find the answers to all our problems. But when we got there, somehow the answers had moved on."

Dr. McCoy burped lightly, excused himself, and said, "It seems to me, Max, that it started with Columbus, or maybe Lucky Leif, before the Moon got into it. Or maybe it was when some little thing that lived in a pond decided that it had better try the dry land, before the pond took it to dry up."

"If it was Space he'd had to cross," Commodore Blakeslee said in a rasping voice, "cold, hard Space, Columbus would have been a shoe-maker and glad to have the work."

Grandisson was watching both the other Humans, with a faintly calculating smile. Krenn wondered if he were delivering them cues. Finally Grandisson said, "When I spoke of expense, I also meant the personal kind. Amos was . . . hurt, looking for one of those worlds full of answers that always seem just out of reach. As it was, he was caught out of reach . . . with an injury that, if he'd only been nearer home, would have been fixed—"

"People die on the front steps of hospitals," Dr. McCoy said. Krenn saw the physician's hands were folded very tightly in his lap.

Grandisson said pleasantly, "Tom's always being modest when he doesn't have to. That's why I keep him around; I need a conscience." McCoy tapped a finger on his gold vest chain. Grandisson went on: "I'm not a mathematician, but I know the ratio between a sphere's diameter and its volume. And I know how much of my money the Federation taxes away every year, trying to fill that bottomless bucket."

Krenn wondered, if this Human were so powerful, how the Federation managed to take his wealth.

Grandisson was looking directly at Krenn. His eyes were very blue, and very cold. "Captain," he said, "in Federa-Terra they're going to tell you that we've got to grow in your direction, that if we *don't* grow we'll die, and so on; and I'm telling you it's a bill of goods. We don't need your space. We don't need the space we've got now. All we need is the Earth. And I speak for almost one billion Human beings when I say that the Earth is all we want."

"Well, you don't speak for me, Max," Dr. McCoy said, and stood up. "You want your goddamn neutral witness, invite those *Constitution* reporters up here." He turned to Krenn and Akhil. "You officers will kindly excuse my bad manners, but I've had my intelligence insulted enough for one day. Good day to you; I hope the rest of your stay here is pleasanter and more productive than this morning has been for me . . . and if your ship's doctor should feel like visiting, I'd admire to buy him a bottle of whatever he's drinking."

"And good day to you, too, Max. I'm gonna go change my grandson Leonard's diapers now, but I'll be thinkin' of you the whole time." He turned, and walked toward the lifts.

"Oh, come on back, T.J.," Grandisson said, smiling. McCoy did not break stride. Grandisson's smile wavered. "*Tom,* come back here."

McCoy did stop then, and turn. "I'll see you at the Clinic on Thursday, won't I, Max?" he said, rather quietly. And then he walked away again.

"*McCoy!*" Grandisson shouted, but the Doctor was already out of sight. Grandisson pulled out his communicator. Commodore Blakeslee looked violent and Dr. Landers looked baffled.

"Sal? *Well, get her.* . . . Sal, Tom McCoy's coming down, and he's in another of his moods. You just—no, *listen*. You just make sure he doesn't talk to any reporters. No, *don't* have Billy follow him, if he doesn't do it right off, it'll blow over. Yes, honey, your job and then some."

Grandisson looked up; Krenn was looking at him. To have looked at anything else would have been an absurd gesture.

"I have," Grandisson said, recovering with amazing speed, "a somewhat dramatic conscience.

"But I assure you, Captain, that I, and the Homeworld Movement on whose behalf I speak, are entirely serious and committed. Dr. Landers heads a multi-megacredit corporation that is, right now, developing the technology to make the Earth not only habitable for the many millions who will return, but a self-sufficient paradise for them."

Akhil said, *"Komerex tel khesterex?"*

Grandisson turned, reached to his ear. He took the phone from his pocket and inserted it. "I'm afraid I didn't—"

Krenn said, "What of the Humans who do not wish to return?"

"Naturally we can't explain everyone's motives. But we also cannot take responsibility for those who choose irresponsible paths. A Human not on Earth will be . . . homeless. As, in a way, they always have been.

"Now, all I ask is that you take this message back to your leaders, along with the 'official' one. Will you do that?"

Krenn said, "Which message do you mean, Mr. Grandisson?"

The Human stared, then laughed shortly. "I suppose I have gone on a bit. Tell your people that not all Humans want their territory, and endless rounds of gunboat diplomacy and saber-rattling."

Krenn had no trouble understanding the idioms. He rather liked them. But he was tired of this meeting.

Grandisson's *dramatic* was an interesting choice of words, Krenn thought. The stage was effective, the lead performance good, the three Human props adequate . . . though Krenn wondered about the character of the physician McCoy.

It did not matter. What mattered was whether Krenn and Akhil were supposed to take the presentation at its face value, or find some secret meaning.

It was simpler in the Empire, Krenn thought. One had the *komerex zha:* one was always safe in assuming the other player was enemy, the next move a trap.

Well. He would show the Human a Klingon face. But perhaps not the face he was expecting.

Krenn said, "If you wish, I will take that message. But there is something I ought to tell you. We have a word, *komerex:* your translator has probably told you it means 'Empire,' but what it means truly is 'the structure that grows.' It has an opposite, *khesterex:* 'the structure that dies.' We are taught—by those you wish to receive your story— that there are no other cultures than these. And in my years as a Captain, I have seen nothing to indicate that my teaching was wrong. There are only Empires . . . and *kuve.*" Krenn saw Grandisson's long jaw go slack; he knew how the Human's machine had translated the last word. "And this is the change you say you wish to make in yourselves. . . .

"So, yes, Mr. Grandisson, if you wish I will take your message. But I tell you now: there are none Klingon who will believe it."

Six: Games

Krenn had some vague ideas about what a diplomatic conference might be. None of them prepared him for the reality. He shortly began to doubt that he could have been prepared: there were ideas so new and strange, as the epetai-Khemara had taught him, that they must be shown by example.

There were two days of "opening ceremonies," during which the delegates showed short dull tapes of their planets and held long dull parties at which everyone pretended to be drunker than they actually were, presumably hoping to catch carelessly dropped information. Krenn did discover that Earth made some excellent black ales, and whenever an "important secret" was tossed in his direction he dutifully caught it, as he was meant to.

After the opening came meetings with political representatives and military ones—Krenn was startled to discover how different the two sorts were, even when they represented the same population. Akhil reported that the scientists were just as isolated from their "colleagues" in the other branches.

Each meeting took half an Earthly hour to begin, with recitations of each present delegate's credentials for being present, invocations to three Federation religions chosen randomly, and a song. Krenn was certain that he was misunderstanding the anthem's lyrics. At least, he hoped he was.

The shape of the meeting table was different for every session: now round, now polyhedral, now scalloped, now long and narrow . . . "Part of the system," Dr. Tagore said. "Used to be, you could hold up a conference for weeks over the shape of the table."

No one shot anyone else, at least while Krenn was present.

For all the protocols, the meetings did not seem to be *about* much of anything. Trade was mentioned, but not what might be traded. Peace was a constant topic (". . . but there is no peace," Emanuel Tagore said once, and silenced the room, and departed it with a small strange smile). It was suggested that a true Neutral Zone in space be established. *They could not,* Krenn thought with distasteful irony, *have known just how empty a thought that was.*

There seemed to be a huge game going on, with dozens of pieces on an indeterminable number of sides, and most of the board obscured. Krenn did not deny the *komerex zha,* that was not his strategy, but the *komerex zha* was *for* something. Each night, after the long ritual of ending the day's discussion and an aimless social function, Krenn returned to his hotel room and sank into a warm bath . . . the Humans *did* know how to build a bath . . . and wondered what any of it was for.

And if perhaps Maxwell Grandisson III was not such a fool after all.

During the sixth day, or perhaps it was the seventh—Krenn was losing track—a diplomat offered an elaborate plan of exchanging prisoners across the boundary—he kept saying Neutral Zone, of course; Krenn had forgotten whether that plan was a precondition of *this* plan—anyhow, at the recitation of the twenty-sixth Point Governing the Treatment of Federation Prisoners, Krenn stood up from the table, excused himself in Fed-Standard, said in *klingonaase* that he must have time to think, and used all he knew of the Kinshaya language to curse the Humans and their riding animals.

Krenn sat down in a small lounge, expelling the Human servitors and xenophysician sent after him.

Dr. Tagore came in. "The one is well?" he said, then tucked his hands inside his gown and sat a polite distance away. He said, "The one asks the wrong question."

"Does the one know what will happen," Krenn said, feeling rage tearing at him, "if this proposal is set before the Imperial Council? *Orion pirates* take hostages for ransom. *Kuve* in desperation take hostages for their lives. And now the Federation shows us more rules than a Vulcan would make, about selling hostages! I will tell you what the Klingon law of hostages is: A dead thing is without value."

Dr. Tagore said, "Klingons do take prizes. For the Year Games, and the Thought Masters of medicine."

"Of course," Krenn said. "How else to supply them?"

"And prizes have a value."

"This need not be said." Krenn was puzzled.

"Then might not the sale of prizes be arranged? I do not speak of a universal rule, but only a case for discussion. Either side might refuse the trade, but that is the nature of trade. And the one taken as prize might refuse to be part of a sale . . . or might refuse to be taken."

Krenn had an unsettling thought. "Are . . . many Klingons taken?" He thought about the Human fondness for stunning weapons. And he knew that the Federation kept its criminals in cages, for years, or their lives. The idea made him slightly sick.

"There are not many," Dr. Tagore said. "But it is a common belief that the Klingons take no living prizes at all."

"But you know this is not true—you just said—"

"*I* know," Dr. Tagore said. "A very few know. If more than a very few were to know, then it would not be this one going to Klinzhai, but a thousand warships. And if you were to see the pain of those we take, and keep in the places without memory . . ."

Dr. Tagore paused, hands to his eyes. Krenn could not react: the little Human seemed huge before him. The Ambassador uncovered his face, and began to speak again, and while his voice was like no Commander's Krenn had ever heard, still it held him tight.

"It is not the one with his thousand rules who must speak to the Imperial Council, but I, and I must have the right thing to tell them, for while too many are dying for fear's sake right now, it is nothing compared to those who will die if those fears take their true shape, and if the naked stars see what we have done to one another."

A clear fluid was running from Dr. Tagore's eyes. *Tears,* Krenn thought; he vaguely recalled that pain brought them. The Human wiped the fluid away with his sleeve; his gaze did not leave Krenn.

Krenn said, "It is that you do not want the war. You do not want it, even if your people should be certain of the victory. You do not want the war *as a thing.*"

"Yes," the Human said, and his voice was thick with the fluid but still very strong. "I do not want it, as a thing. And if it comes, I will have no part of it, except to save what peace I may."

Krenn stared. The other diplomats, and they had been many, made clear that the war stood behind their plans, as a cruiser squadron escorts a convoy of freighters. But this one denied that, and this was the one who went to Klinzhai.

Why would the Federation send one who cared not enough to fight for it?

Unless, Krenn thought, this was the trapped move in the game. Krenn remembered Admiral Kezhke's strange advice: *You must bring him alive . . . no matter what you are told.*

This was such a little Human, to start a war of a thousand years: but only a little antimatter started a great reaction.

"I don't . . . understand," Krenn said finally.

Dr. Tagore sat down, his eyes no longer running, but red-colored. "That's all right," he said. "There's still a little time."

The only good thing about the Embassy reception, Krenn thought, was that it was not also a dinner. Those present were free to wander around a large building, starting or avoiding conversations as desired.

It was now common knowledge that the two Klingons understood the Federation language without translators, and discussions tended to sputter and shift as Krenn approached. This made little sense to him. Not only did half the beings present carry translating machines (or have servitors to carry them) but Krenn could not even hear very well. Akhil said it was the thinness of the air.

The air seemed thick enough to Krenn, but not pleasantly so. The Federation beings preferred talking around him than to him, but when he was asked questions, they were the same. Yes, he had been a privateer. No, he had never taken Federation prizes. Yes, he had killed with his hands. *And* his teeth. Krenn thought he should have a tape recorded.

In one of the larger rooms, the Vulcan Ambassador to Earth stood near a fireplace, speaking to a moderately large circle of guests of a dozen miscellaneous races. A Human female, even-featured and light-haired, stood near the Ambassador: Krenn recalled from the first day's shock wave of introductions that she was the Vulcan's sole consort. Interested, Krenn went that way, not quite joining the group; no one turned to notice him as the tall Vulcan talked on.

Krenn could not understand any complete sentence of the lecture. The Ambassador's Federation Standard was Vulcan-flawless, of course, but there was no machine program that could make a Vulcan's technical conversation intelligible. Krenn supposed the other listeners must all be Thought Masters, or one of the equivalent Federation degrees. Or perhaps they had other reasons for standing in the barrage of words.

Krenn watched the Human female. There seemed to be a tightness in her expression; if it was humor, it was not any sort he had seen. It looked more like distress, but at what? Krenn? No, she was not looking at him. She was not, Krenn saw, looking at anything.

A few of the Vulcan's words registered on Krenn: something about *chromosomes* and *interspacing.*

Krenn withdrew, and wandered from room to room until he found Akhil, who was amusing himself with an electronic pattern-matching toy.

"Where did you get that?" Krenn said.

"There's a games room upstairs. Want to try this? It helps if you drink something strong."

"How does that help?"

"You don't mind losing. Here."

"Not now. Come with me. I need a Specialist to listen to something."

They went back to watch the Vulcan Ambassador, and listened until the two Klingons together began to attract the attention Krenn alone had avoided.

"What was he talking about?" Krenn asked Akhil.

"I'm an astronomer, not a geneticist." There was a hesitation in his voice.

"That still tells me more than I knew. What was he talking about, even generally?"

"Oh, I know more than generally. He's discussing genetic fusion. Don't you remember, when we were meeting half the Federation, that son of theirs—seven or eight years old? He's a fusion, and the Ambassador was describing the process."

"With his consort present?" Krenn said, astonished and disgusted.

"What? Was she there?" Akhil said, distracted. "He said something really interesting, in with all the technical detail."

Krenn said, carefully, "Interesting?" He had heard Akhil call off incoming fire as if it concerned him not at all; he had heard the Exec tear a slacking junior officer into raw protein with his voice. But only very rarely had he heard Akhil angry. It was not a loud effect. The sharpest knives are the quietest. And 'Khil was angry now.

"He was saying that the fusion techniques were 'only recently perfected by Vulcan scientists.' *Recently perfected?* If that gets back to the Imperial Institutes of Research, there are going to be some *tharavul* headed back to Vulcan, Warp 4. Without a ship around them."

"How can he say that? If he lies—" Krenn thought that, if it should be found that a Vulcan could lie, the *tharavul* would soon be more than just deaf telepathically.

"Lies?" Akhil said, and stopped short; the anger slipped out of his voice. "No. He doesn't lie. He reports scientific results." Akhil laughed. "Scientists know some tricks Imperial Intelligence will never master."

Krenn asked Akhil the way to the Embassy game room, and they separated again. Krenn climbed a curving white staircase, carpeted in black velvet with tiny crystal stars, and turned down the corridor Akhil had indicated. He passed a door, and despite that it was closed and his hearing diminished, he could clearly hear a Human voice within, saying, ". . . not whether Tagore's a competent negotiator, we're not even that far along in the argument. First I want to know if the bastard's *sane.*"

There was an unintelligible reply.

"I'll *grant* you that . . . volunteering for this should be grounds for confinement. But you know his record . . . all right, sure, but would you send Gandhi to argue Hitler out of . . . How do we *know* he won't?"

The rest was lost in a sound of plumbing. Krenn moved on to the room he wanted.

It was dim within, pleasantly so after the Earth-level lighting of the main rooms. Spotlights shone on tables set for several different games; Krenn examined the unfamiliar ones, and sat down at a chessboard with pieces lathe-turned from bright and dark metal.

"Would you wish an opponent, sir?" said a voice behind Krenn. He turned, hand dropping to his weapon. There was a small being a few meters from him, in a spotlit alcove of the room; it had been reading a book. It came forward.

It was only a child, Krenn saw at once. The hair was cut in the Vulcan style, and the ears were unmistakable.

"My parents are downstairs," the young Vulcan said. "I did not wish to be an annoyance. I will leave."

This must be the Ambassador's son, Krenn thought, the fusion. "You do not annoy me," he said, as the boy moved toward the door. "And I would welcome a chance to play this game."

Krenn won the chess game, but he did not win it easily. "A pleasant game," he said. "My compliments to a worthy opponent."

The child nodded.

Krenn said, "That is a phrase we use at the conclusion of our game, *klin zha*. In my language it is *'Zha riest'n, teskas tal'tai-kleon.'* "

"*Zha riest'n,*" the boy said, carefully copying Krenn's pronunciation, "*teskas tal . . . la . . .*"

"*Tal'tai-kleon.*"

"*Tal'tai-kleon.*"

"*Kai,*" Krenn said, and laughed.

"Are you the Klingon Captain, sir, or the Science officer?"

"I am the Captain . . . of the cruiser *Fencer,*" Krenn said. He had been about to give his full name and honorific, but it had suddenly seemed unnecessary. *Rather silly.* And he was tired of introductions. "Have you ever thought of being a starship Captain?"

The boy's lips compressed. Then he said, "I plan to be a scientist. But perhaps I will join the Starfleet."

"The sciences are a good path. I'm sorry my Specialist isn't here to talk to you."

"No insult was meant, sir—"

"None was assumed."

"There will be a logical choice."

"Sometimes there is," Krenn said. "Another game?"

They talked as they played. It did not affect the boy's play, but Krenn let a bishop get away from him, and lost. The boy gave him the whole *klingonaase* phrase, perfectly accented.

"Sa tel'ren?" Krenn said.

"What does that mean, Captain sir?"

"Two out of three."

Krenn wondered what Vulcan children said to a fusion in their midst. The two races were similar to start with, and this one's physical characteristics leaned to the Vulcan. The ears especially. Krenn tried to think what would have happened, in his House Gensa, to one with Vulcan ears. He seemed to feel the blood on his fingers. *Would it be green,* he wondered.

The boy moved a knight, taking one of Krenn's rooks. He waited.

Krenn slid a pawn forward.

"Given the established balance of our skills, Captain, and other factors being equal, you cannot defeat me with the odds of a rook. It would be logical for you to resign."

"Klingons do not resign," Krenn said. Seven or eight years old, Akhil had said. Krenn had killed his first intelligent being when he was this one's age. A Human starship crewman, a prize, in the Year Games.

"The sequence of moves is predictable, and barring suboptimal strategies, inevitable. The time consumed—"

"If I go to the Black Fleet, what matter that I go a little slowly?" Krenn thought of the Human, who had shouted challenge into Krenn's face even as he died. It was an honorable death, and a glorious kill.

"What is the Black Fleet?" the Vulcan asked.

Krenn was pulled back from his memory. "One who serves his ship well, in the life we see, will serve on a ship of the Fleet when this life ends." Krenn's Federation vocabulary was not right for this; the words would not fit together as Dr. Tagore could make them to fit. "In the Fleet there is the death that is not death, because not the end; there is the enemy to be killed a thousand times, and each time return; and there is the laughter."

"Laughter?" the boy said. "And enemies?" His eyes were calm, and yet almost painfully intense to Krenn, who struggled to make the languages meet, and wondered why he so badly needed to.

"Fed, Rom . . . others," Krenn said. "Without *kleoni,* what would be the purpose?"

"My mother says that the spirit is eternal," the boy said. "My father says this is true in a purely figurative sense, as the wisdom of Surak is not forgotten, though Surak is become unstructured."

"We have one who is not forgotten," Krenn said. "His name was Kahless. When his ship was dying, he had his hand bound to his Chair, that no one could say he left it, or that another had been in the Chair at the ship's death. Then all his crew could escape without suspicion, because Kahless had taken on all the ship's destiny.

"*Kahlesste kaase,* we say. Kahless's hand."

"This would seem a supremely logical act."

"*Logical?*" Krenn said, and then he understood. The boy was raised in his father's culture. It was the highest praise he knew. "I think you are right," Krenn said. "I had not perceived the logic of the situation."

"My father says that this is his task: to communicate logic by example."

Is that why you were caused to exist? Krenn was thinking. *As an example?* He could see that the boy was proud of what he had just done—communicated to a Klingon! Was that not the victory? And yet he could not shout it. Vulcans did not shout.

"My mother is a teacher," the boy said. "She also communicates. My parents are—" He looked away.

"My mother," Krenn said, "was not of my father's race."

The boy turned his eyes on Krenn once more. It could not be called a stare, it was absolutely polite, but it did pierce, and the arched eyebrows cut.

"It is a custom on Earth," the Vulcan said, "on concluding a chess game, to shake hands."

Krenn's liver pinched. That was not a Vulcan custom, he knew well enough. Touching a Vulcan's hand opened the path for the touch of their minds. And *that* touch could pull out thoughts that the agonizer or the Examiner's tools could never reach. It was said by some that it could burn the brain; Krenn did not believe this, but . . .

The touch, Krenn thought, *the touch.* And he raised his right hand, slowly held it out over the chessboard, palm up.

The boy extended his own hand, above Krenn's, palm down. A drop of water fell into Krenn's palm.

A Vulcan sweating. And I am drenched already.

There was a choked cry from the doorway, a scream stopped at the last instant. Krenn and the boy turned together, and saw the Ambassador's consort standing there, her whole body rigid, her knuckles bone-white against the sides of her face.

"*What is this?*" the Human said.

The boy said, "We were playing a game—"

"Game!" It was half a gasp. The female looked at Krenn, and the hatred in her look was like a blow against his body.

Then she said, very calmly, without looking away from Krenn, "Your father's looking for you. Go to him now."

"Yes, Mother." At the door, the boy stopped, turned, held up his hand with fingers at an angle. "Live long and prosper, Captain."

Krenn nodded. He could still feel the hate and fear radiating from the Human. He raised his hand and saluted the boy, who bowed and went out.

"I don't . . ." said the Ambassador's consort, still angry and frightened, but now with the tension of confusion as well.

"You would fight for your line," Krenn said. "That is a good thing. I think that is the best honor I know. That one is . . ." He tried to think of a praise the Human could not misinterpret. ". . . worthy of the stars." He was, now, a little relieved that events had ended when they had.

The woman's face had softened, though her stance was still rigid. "Perhaps I misunderstood," she said. "I am sorry. It can be hard to . . . protect a child, on Vulcan."

"You fear the Klingon," Krenn said. "In this is no need for apology."

The meetings dragged on for three more days. Krenn had a sort of waking nightmare that the Federation had lost or forgotten the procedures necessary to end their conferences, and the sessions would continue until all those present crumbled into dust around rotting tables.

Then, rather suddenly, a hammer came down on a wooden block and it was all over, and even more suddenly diplomats and attachés were headed for their homeworlds, each packing a shuttle-load of luggage . . . each but one.

"These are all the goods you require?" Krenn asked Dr. Tagore. "We do not have such a mass constraint."

"There's more there than I can carry, and that's already too much. But I've become used to having certain things around . . . softer than I used to be." Krenn looked at the Human, who seemed made of dry brown sticks, and wondered at that.

The Ambassador bent over one of his cases, examined the label. "They're going to seal my apartment, I hear, and fill it with nitrogen. If I don't return, I suppose they can just bolt a plaque on the door." He pointed at one of the smaller cases. "This is a data encryptor. I'll have to warn your Security people that it'll destroy itself if the case is opened. Starfleet wanted me to take a complete subspace radio rig, three hundred kilos plus spares, not that I'd know what to do if it needed spares. The ComInt man said a Klingon set would be bugged." He looked up, smiled. "Monitored, that is. Of course it will, I said. What would I be saying that I would not want heard?"

He sat down on a suitcase. "I've brought quite a few clothes. *Zan* Akhil tells me your ship's laundry doesn't synthesize from basic fiber, as ours do. And I'm not built much like the Imperial Race." He looked at the time display on his wrist. "That 'demonstration' of Marcus van Diemen's, whatever it is, is in twenty minutes. Shall we go, Captain?"

"It would please me, Thought Master, to be called Krenn."

"Honored, Krenn. And you must call me Emanuel." He laughed. "Hoping that isn't blasphemy."

They went to a small auditorium, half full of Starfleet Naval and Technical personnel. Akhil was already there, in a front-row seat; Krenn sat next to him. As Dr. Tagore prepared to sit, a junior officer whispered in his ear. "A moment, Krenn. I seem to be wanted." The officer led him away. Krenn looked after them until they were lost in the crowd; he was remembering that the people along the train route, the ones with torches, had been called *demonstrators*.

The Humans all found seats. Admiral van Diemen stepped onto the dais, looking the very image of heroism in his full-dress uniform and weapon with gilded hilt. "Good afternoon, fellow officers . . . and our honored guests. It is a Human custom to provide something special at a guest's departure, so they may carry with them an enduring memory.

"Now, through the latest breakthrough in Federation scientific research, we wish to present to you something very special indeed. *Lights.*"

The room darkened. "Another *gagny* hologram show?" Akhil muttered.

There was an electronic squeal, a rising, oscillating hum. On the dais, three columns of light appeared, took shapes.

Three armed soldiers were transporting onto the stage.

Krenn went for his pistol. It was, he thought, a crude trap, but deadly enough; but there were many targets behind him, and he would die spitting challenge at them, and not all of them would live to hear his last words.

His arm would not move. He turned his head. Akhil had three fingers tight on Krenn's arm, pinching the nerves, blocking the muscle. "No," he said, not loud but urgently. "Not yet."

"What are you doing?"

"If I'm wrong," Akhil said coolly, "kill me first."

The armed Humans solidified; the mechanical noise died away. The soldiers did not move, nor did their weapons come to bear on the Klingons; Krenn saw they were frozen in a sort of heroic tableau.

The lights came up. Krenn winced. No one was moving yet.

"The most important development in translator applications in fifty years," Admiral van Diemen was saying. "Thirty years in development, and now certified safe for intelligent life."

The Humans were applauding. Krenn looked at Akhil. Akhil released Krenn's arm, said very quietly, "Now we know."

As the clapping subsided, Admiral van Diemen said, in a completely friendly tone, "I hope, Captain, that you and your Science officer will take word of this breakthrough to your own physicists."

"Of course I will, Admiral," Krenn said. He took out his communicator, glanced at Akhil; the Specialist nodded.

"Captain to *Fencer*."

Kelly responded. Krenn snapped a line of Battle Language.

"Captain, are you—"

"The situation is stable, Kelly. Action."

"Acting."

Akhil stood, muttering, "Don't want to land on my butt," and flickered golden, and evaporated without a sound.

Around Krenn, there was a silence like the silence of vacuum. Then there was a single sound of applause: Krenn turned to see Dr. Tagore clapping furiously, the fluid called tears rolling down his cheeks as he laughed.

"Our physicists will indeed be interested," Krenn said to Admiral van Diemen, who stood gripping the podium with both hands. "They will want very much to know why your system makes that terrible noise."

"All right, *why?*" Krenn said.

"Specialist Antaan worked it out," Akhil said. He seemed extremely pleased, and Krenn could hardly argue: they were bringing back a major piece of scientific intelligence, and they could hardly be accused of having pirated it.

"Antaan got a sensor lock on the corona leakage from the Feds' 'demonstration.'" Akhil pushed a key, and a multicolored trace appeared on the display of Akhil's Bridge station. "Do you see this line?"

"You're pointing to it, I see it," Krenn said patiently. He was thinking that since they had this data, *Fencer* had indeed had sensors trained on them the whole time. Just like home.

"Antaan calls it a super-carrier wave, polarized in three dimensions plus warp-time. They're overlaying it on the ordinary transporter signal. At reassembly, it superheterodynes with the main signal; the heterodyning produces a set of parasitic sound frequencies. Like the fact that a disruptor beam is blue, even though the disrupting wave itself is invisible."

"So it's noisy," Krenn said, wondering if 'Khil might secretly be a Vulcan fusion. "Is it better?"

"I can't see how," Akhil said flatly. "The super-carrier repeats the main signal information, but the reduction in assembly error is trivial, maybe one percent. And the power cost is twenty percent higher, not to mention the cost of extra equipment. *Plus* being able to hear a boarding party a boom's-length away."

Krenn leaned against one of the main ceiling struts. He looked at the main display, just past his empty Chair, at the stars passing at Warp 4 and the Federation ships surrounding *Fencer.* They had only three escorts for the voyage from Earth, all of them the new-model cruisers with the saucer hulls and outriggered warp engines. There was *Glasgow,* that had led them in, and *Savannah,* and *Hokkaido.* Admiral van Diemen had said with quickly recovered pride that they were of the *Baton Rouge*–class, and they also were on Starfleet's leading edge of technology. And all of them did have transporters, Krenn was told.

"One percent, you say?"

"One percent of the error rate, Captain, not the number of transports."

"Yes . . . I'd thought that was what you meant." Krenn looked at Kelly. She had been watching him; quickly she turned away. "Still," Krenn said, "they seem to have a powerful desire for personal safety."

"Humans?" Akhil said, disbelieving. "Most of them weren't even armed."

"Maybe their idea of danger isn't the same as ours."

Amused, Akhil said, "How many things are there to fear?"

"I don't know," Krenn said. "That's what scares me."

Akhil took it as a joke, as Krenn had intended.

"The room is comfortable?" Maktai said.

"Very much so," Dr. Tagore said, looking around, at the clearprints on the walls, the newly installed furniture, and his still-sealed baggage. "Much larger than I had expected. This isn't normally a stateroom?"

"It's my office," Krenn said. "I'll be using the Exec's office down the corridor."

"I hadn't meant such an inconvenience."

Krenn said, "An advantage of this cruise is that there isn't much office work. Anyway, we had to put you somewhere; this has its own washroom, and an individual lock code. There aren't any regular passenger facilities, and you can't have expected us to give you Marine quarters." Krenn noticed Maktai watching him; as casual as Mak was, he had not expected the informality between his superior officers and the alien.

Dr. Tagore said, "Starfleet has done just that, on occasion." He turned to Maktai. "And I have had my bags examined by a number of Federation member worlds, including Earth. I'll gladly assist your crew in a search, Commander Maktai."

The Security chief scratched his forehead. Krenn was amused, and interested: if Mak's style aboard were really only a mask, this cruise might put some wrinkles in it.

Maktai said, "We do not search others' property without cause."

"I hadn't meant to suggest you would. Many cultures consider my profession itself not only sufficient cause, but necessary."

"We . . . do not," Maktai said. "You're aware that you will be the only resident of this deck . . . besides this office, and the Executive's, there are only the forward transporter rooms at the corridor ends. And the ship's computers . . . but I must advise you not to enter those compartments."

"The doors to the computer room are secured, I assume?"

"This . . . need not be said."

"Then it need not be said that I shall not enter. The same for the transporter rooms; I find it a fascinating invention, much pleasanter than shuttlecraft rides, but I should not like to accidentally disassemble myself."

"It is good that you understand."

"Commander, that is the reason I am here."

Krenn said, "Mak and Akhil and I are three decks below. You're not alone in the pod." He gestured at the wall. "We've disabled the priority call on your communicator, but it'll call any open location. And we'll have a computer screen in here in a day."

Dr. Tagore said gently, "What you may have heard is true: my kind die if we are isolated. But you need not worry." He pressed the seal on one of his cases, and it folded itself open. Within were books, more than a hundred of them, and a case of crystal slides with a reader. In the bottom of the case was a flat black plane, like a computer terminal, but with very different controls that Krenn recognized at once: he had played a thousand games of *klin zha* on just such an electronic game grid.

"You see," Dr. Tagore said, selecting a book, "I am not isolated."

Maktai said, "There is one Security matter . . ."

"Of course, Commander."

"Your weapon."

"Weapon?" Dr. Tagore said, sounding slightly distressed.

"Of course you may keep your personal arms. But I must know their type, for the record. So that if an incident occurs, yours may be . . . eliminated from consideration."

"Commander . . . Captain . . . I have not carried a weapon in forty-four years. Since I would not use one, I would not tell the lie of wearing one."

"On Earth," Krenn said, startled, "I saw your people with dress arms—" He had assumed the Ambassador carried his weapon well concealed.

"It is permitted," the Human said, "though many of us hope it ceases to be the fashion."

"I may," Maktai said slowly, "be forced to search your bags, to confirm this . . ."

"My offer to assist you still stands."

"I think that's all for now," Krenn said. "I would be pleased if you would join me for dinner, Dr. Tagore."

"Honored of course, Captain."

In the lift, Krenn said to Maktai, "As strange as it sounds, Mak . . . I don't think he has a weapon."

Maktai shook his head, plucked at his hair. "I *know* he doesn't. We scanned his equipment for weapons, routine, you know the drill. *Nothing. G'dayt,* I'd been thinking he had something that our scanners couldn't pick up."

Krenn could see how Mak felt: he felt *silly.*

"So tell me, Captain, *why* doesn't he have a weapon?" Maktai spread his hands. "He's not *kuve* . . . Kagga's crown, he's not *kuve.* So what *is* he, Captain?"

It was the late watch, and *Fencer* was quiet; quieter now than in a long time. The ship was ten days across the Zone, in Klingon space again.

Krenn moved a pawn upward one space. "Do all Humans play chess?"

"No," Dr. Tagore said. "Actually very few play, though everyone knows the pieces, and most have an idea of the moves. There is a common belief that truly exceptional chessplayers, grandmasters, must also be . . ." He touched a rook, moved it downward. ". . . insane."

Krenn took a bite from a gel pastry, washed it back with *kafei.* "Is this belief true?"

"I don't know. At least partially, I suppose. Certainly some grandmasters were mad, or went mad. But so have any number of people who never touched a pawn. . . . The other factor is that computers play chess. In solitaire mode, this unit—" he tapped the game grid—"plays so well I cannot beat it. And one of the new duotronic computers cannot be beaten at all, not even by a Vulcan."

"What difference does that make?" Krenn said. "What honor is there in playing a machine whose only function is to win?" Krenn shifted a sub-board, the projected pieces descending through his fingers.

Dr. Tagore looked up, pleased. Krenn stared at the position again.

"Oh, don't worry, I'm mated in two or so," the Human said. "I'm just delighted to hear you say that. Not even Vulcans seem to be able to see that it is not the game, but the player."

The checkmate actually took five moves. *At least the Ambassador never tried to resign,* Krenn thought.

Dr. Tagore blanked the board. "Another? Or would you like to give me another lesson in *klin zha?*"

"I would like to have another lesson in *pokher.*"

"Gladly." Dr. Tagore went to his library, returned with two decks of cards and a rack of tokens. "You realize that I've still got nothing of value to play for, and I doubt that Strip would be of more than academic interest."

"It is important that the stakes be real," Krenn said. He had been waiting for this, trying to perfect his strategy for the moment when it came.

"As I've said, Chess and Poker between them sum up the Human psyche. And Chess is the supreme game for itself, just as Poker is the supreme game for stakes."

Krenn stood up, went to the library shelves, pulled out one of the thin, plastic-covered books. "There are these," he said.

Dr. Tagore laughed. "Krenn, if I've ever grudged the loan of a book, may the spirit of Ben Franklin choke me with a kitestring. You're welcome to any of those."

"No," Krenn said, and walked to the services wall. He tapped the book against the spring doors of the disposal slot.

Dr. Tagore said, "One of the hardest parts of xenoculture is understanding humor. . . . Are you joking, Krenn?"

Krenn started to put the book through the slot. It would have taken only a snap of the wrist, but he looked down, and read the title on the cover, and his hand did not move. After a moment he said, "No, Emanuel. I am not joking."

Dr. Tagore nodded. He said, "And what will be your stake, Krenn?"

"The books are my stake," Krenn said. "I already hold them; you may win them back."

"Despite that they have no value to you?" The Human's calm was like an unexpected cold wind.

"It was you, was it not, who told me one might trade for hostages, that also have no value."

"Very well. Cut for first deal, Krenn."

Krenn said, "If you were armed, you could fight me for this."

Dr. Tagore paused in his shuffling; then he resumed. "But I am not." He split the deck. "Jack of spades. Your cut."

"Perhaps I have selected one that means nothing to you. I shall destroy it and select another." The book seemed to twist in Krenn's hand, and would not enter the slot. Krenn resisted looking at the title again.

"That one is as precious as the rest, as I imagine you know. Take your cut, so we may begin."

Krenn went to the table. He put the book facedown, picked up a block of cards, turned them.

"Nine of diamonds," Dr. Tagore said. "Dealer chooses five-card draw, nothing wild."

"Is *that* what you will say to the Imperial Council?" Krenn said. "When they ask you why you go unarmed like a *kuve,* when they ask you what the Federation can be worth to you, since you will not fight for it—" He had not meant to shout, but he was shouting. "When they ask why they should deal with you, will you tell them it is because you have drawn a higher card?"

"If that is the game we are playing."

Perhaps this one was insane, Krenn thought. Perhaps he went into the Empire like a Romulan, to find his death close to the enemy's heart. "The game they play is the *komerex zha,*" Krenn said, "and if you lose, it will not be your books that burn, but yourself."

Dr. Tagore reached for the book.

(Kethas reached for the dead green hand.)

The Human said, "There is no difference." He picked up the book, held it out to Krenn. "Here. It's yours. Read it or destroy it; but if you destroy it, you will never know what it had to say to you."

Krenn took it. He did not even look at the disposal slot. He knew he had been beaten, by one unarmed. He read the book's title: *Space Cadet,* it said. The book could say nothing to him; how could it? He was no longer a Cadet.

And still he knew he would have to read it.

Dr. Tagore was casing the decks of cards. "Pleasant rest, Krenn," he said.

Now Krenn was being ordered out of his office. "It was . . . a good game, Emanuel."

"An excellent game, Krenn. *Teskas tal'tai-kleon.*"

Krenn took the lift down to his cabin. He put the book on the bedside table, unfastened his vest and was about to slip out of his tunic when there was a tap at the door. Krenn looked at the communicator panel; the idle lights were on. He went to the door.

Akhil was in the corridor, his portable terminal under his arm. Krenn was about to ask if whatever it was could wait, but the expression on the Exec's face said it would not. Then Krenn saw that Akhil was wearing, not his usual duty arms, but a heavy disruptor pistol.

"What is it, 'Khil?"

"Not here. Get something to shoot with and come with me."

"Where's Mak?" Krenn said, but the suspicion was already rising.

"Mak's asleep. At least, I hope he is. Now *come*."

They took the lift aft, down the boom to the cargo hold. The deck was lit only by small directional lights; indicators flickered in the darkness.

Akhil said, "Wait." He paused by a communicator panel, put a key into the access lock. Krenn held the terminal as Akhil swung the wall panel open, exposing a maze of components. Akhil took a rectangle of green circuit board from his sash, slipped it between two junction blocks. He said, "Now if one of Maktai's crew takes a look down here, they'll get noise. It'll look like normal circuit transients for a little while, but not long. Over here."

They stopped again at one of the cargo modules, an insulated food box. Akhil took his terminal, opened the black case, and uncoiled the cord of a coding wand. He ran it over the cargo module's invoice plate. "This is the one." He stood, gave the terminal to Krenn. "Better read it for yourself."

Krenn wiped the wand over the code lines, and read the terminal screen.

"Cold-sleep capsules?" he said, and looked automatically toward the invisible ceiling, the invisible monitors.

"Should be fifty Marines, if this is the only one," Akhil said. "Instant mutiny. Just thaw and serve."

"How did you find this?"

"Checking the cargo manifest." Akhil gave a toneless laugh. "The Feds consider zentaars an intelligent species. I thought it might bother our passenger if a zentaar haunch showed up on his dinner tray . . . I suppose it's an honorable debt we owe him, for this."

"If it's on the label and manifest, then the Cargo-master has to know," Krenn said. "Who else?" He counted through his officers.

"Someone's got to command this instant army."

"Maktai . . ."

"Would they trust a lower rank?"

"I haven't decided who 'they' are yet." He thought of Meth of Imperial Intelligence, with his plastic face.

He thought of Kelly. "But I don't suppose it matters. Let's go."

"Who . . . ?" said the voice from the other side of the door.

"It's Krenn, Mak." He pushed the heavy disruptor inside his sash, out of sight.

Maktai opened the door. *"Parkhest . . ."*

"Just the way I feel, Mak. We've got trouble aboard."

"The passenger?" Maktai looked at his wall monitor. "There's no alert."

"Not yet. Get some clothes on, and come with me. Rapid action."

"Acting, Captain."

"And, Mak—light weapons."

"*Khest* diplomacy."

Krenn stepped into the cabin, letting the door close, and watched Maktai dress, noting carefully where the Security chief put the small projectile pistol he favored for light work. *If Mak were not Klingon, this would be easier,* Krenn thought. But he could not show Maktai the gun. And he could not order Mak to come unarmed; the one would have known he went to arrest, if not execution, and that must not happen until Krenn knew who else was part of the mutiny.

And it was possible still that they would not have to execute more than a few crewmen, as strong example. It was not necessarily a crime to *consider* mutiny.

Krenn and Maktai met Akhil and Kelly in the lift. Kelly looked confused and sleepy, at Krenn; then she looked at Maktai. Mak gave a faint shake of his head.

Krenn felt his lips pull back, his liver turn to lead.

They arrived in the hold. Akhil went to the cargo module, plugged in a keypad and pressed buttons. Seals cracked, and the thick insulated door swung open; a cloud of white vapor flooded out.

"What in the name of the Nameless Emperor *is* this?" Maktai said, shivering in the wave of cold air.

"See for yourself," Krenn said, and motioned Maktai and Kelly forward. Akhil brought the deck lights up as they reached the door, and the glowing white fog was blinding. Krenn thought briefly about what Admiral Whitetree would have said, if he were told fifty Klingons had entered his space without even rippling his sensors.

Krenn's vision cleared, and he looked into the module.

Whitefang and zentaar carcasses stood ranked along the inner walls, impaled on frost-covered rods.

Akhil's fingers thrust into the base of Krenn's skull; a shock ran down Krenn's spine, and he fell forward, carrying Mak and Kelly with him into the freezer. He felt ice burn his face, saw the arc of light from outside sweep down to nothing as the door swung shut.

Maktai crawled from beneath Krenn, reached for the opening, got two fingers on the frame. The door closed regardless. There was a hiss as the gaskets resealed, and then total darkness.

Krenn rolled over. His legs were still paralyzed: they struck a carcass. Maktai said, *"G'dayt, v'kaase,"* in an almost disinterested tone. *Shock,* Krenn thought.

"Freeze it, Mak," Krenn said. "Freeze the stumps before you bleed out."

"Right . . ."

"Kelly, can you reach Mak?"

"He's got it," she said.

Krenn felt muscle control returning to his lower body. He realized the floor was sucking heat from him; knew he would freeze to it in a moment. He levered himself up, burning his hands.

"Kelly to Bridge," she was saying. "Kelly to Security. Kelly to any station, priority call." A flash of light came from nearby; Kelly had done something to her communicator so the blue-white call light shone bright and steady. "That won't last long," she said, "but it might as well be good for something. I can't call out through this thing."

Even in the darkness, it was still not much light, and it was cold and pale. Kelly reached inside her tunic, produced a palm-sized object. "I've got a light sonic. Will that do any good on the door?"

"We'll try it," Krenn said. "Mak, you've . . ." But of course he knew.

"Slug-thrower. You said small weapons."

"I did." Krenn drew out the heavy disruptor. Its grip froze to his fingers; he pulled it free, wrapped it in the end of his sash.

"Small?" Maktai said, as Krenn's pistol caught the light.

Krenn held the gun close to the doorframe, thumbed fire. The blue flash was dazzling, and fragments of plastic erupted; Krenn felt them shower his arms. He examined the target spot. It was disappointing: the insulation had absorbed much of the blast energy. But Krenn had heard metal tear. The sonic would be worthless, but the disruptor would work, if there was enough charge.

And enough heat, and enough air.

"Could you explain," Maktai said, his voice very tight, "what we're doing here?"

Krenn tried to do so, shouting to be heard as he cut the door.

Maktai said, "All right," and there was no condemnation in it; no Klingon would require excuses of a Captain threatened with mutiny. "What does Akhil want, then? It can't be the ship, not this way."

"It has to be the ship, or else the passenger," Krenn said. "And I don't think it's the ship, either."

"Captain, permission to speak?"

"For the duration of the crisis, Kelly."

"Did the Captain suspect this one from the first?"

"Yes," Krenn said, and bore down on the disruptor. The cold was in his lungs like death's own hand now, and only the flash of the disruptor gave any warmth at all.

Maktai's head rolled to the side. Kelly moved toward him, shook him. Maktai grunted, stirred, then slumped again.

"In his sash, near his pistol," Krenn said. "He's got . . ."

Kelly knew. She had the metal cylinder out, and was tugging Maktai's tunic open at the collar. She held the agonizer to the communicator's light, checking the setting, and applied it. Maktai's limbs twitched.

Krenn said, "I'll tell you when I need a touch of that."

As Kelly had warned, the communicator's battery died shortly. A knife-thin light came in around the doorframe, where Krenn had made his cuts. Kelly began firing her sonic into the frozen meat; the noise was worse than the disruptor on the door, but it seemed to generate a little bit of heat.

After years of darkness Krenn reached the last corner. He struggled to stand; his skin hurt as he moved. He wondered if the blood was frozen in his small surface vessels. He had seen that happen. The flesh went greenish-black, and sloughed away like bark from a dead tree.

Krenn slammed his shoulder against the door. Pain exploded inside him. Frost crashed. The panel did not move.

Maktai got up, wavering, Kelly helping him. The three of them leaned together.

"Action," Krenn said.

With a tearing crash the door fell out. The Klingons staggered onto the cargo deck. Krenn felt his lungs open up to receive the hot air, tried to control his breathing so his heart would not burst.

The wall communicator had been shot apart. At the lift doors, Maktai hit the call button. The indicator did not light. "He's locked them off," he said, hammered the panel with his maimed hand, then looked at the stumps of his fingers and said, "I didn't even feel that." He took a step, then leaned against the wall. Ice crystals fell from his shoulders. "The stairway's around the corner . . . we'll have to take the boom corridor forward."

Krenn said, "That's two decks up, then the length of the ship, *then* up three more decks to Emanuel's room." Ignoring Maktai's look, Krenn looked back the way they had come. "But there's a stage right back there."

"I'll set the controls," Kelly said.

"Krenn," Mak said, "there are only cargo transporters on this level. . . . Oh, *khest* it, I'm coming." He took one step, two, then slumped against the wall again. Krenn knew it wasn't muscle keeping him up, but pure *klin*.

"You're no use to me as you are," Krenn said, "and less use dead."

Mak slid down to the deck. He wrapped the fingers of his good hand around the other wrist; it might have been to slow the bleeding once his blood thawed, but Krenn saw Maktai's look. *Kahlesste kaase,* it said. Kahless's Hand.

Krenn and Kelly made for the transporter stage. He had not seen her run since she had come aboard Fencer: it pleased him to know that she still could run.

"Your arm," he said then, because it hung like a dead thing nailed to her body.

"My shoulder froze," she said, and Krenn knew it was literal truth; she was metal there, within. He remembered the feel of the pistol butt in his hand, for only an instant.

There was not enough pain in Akhil's body to pay for all of this.

They reached the transporter, a flat plane of rhomboidal segments. Krenn could not remember the scramble rate for living things sent by the less finely tuned cargo units, and was glad of the lapse. "Starboard stage, Pod Deck 4," he said.

"Acting." She worked the controls one-handed with an ease that was more than manual dexterity: Krenn suddenly realized that he had not known she even knew the transport routines. He supposed those in the Unassigned pool must master as many skills as possible, to more often get out of the pool and on a ship.

She would not be going back to the pool after this cruise, Krenn thought.

"Energizing," she said, and pushed the levers. Krenn held dead still; it couldn't hurt.

He turned golden and vanished.

Krenn flickered in on the disc of the passenger transporter: Deck 4 Starboard, the room sign said. He still hurt in all the same places, and now he had a headache, but a scramble error never left the victim able to notice his problem.

The corridor was empty, its far end, with the portside transporter, just out of sight around the curve. One door along the forward wall was open, and Earth-bright light spilled out. Krenn moved to the open door. No sound came from within.

He might, he knew, be a long time too late. But *Fencer* was still his. He went through the door.

The outer room was empty. Dr. Tagore's game grid was in pieces on the table, shattered by a disruptor bolt. A book lay on the floor, by an overturned chair; *The Innocents Abroad,* its cover said. The door to the inner room had been burned open.

Krenn heard the sound of a fresh charge slide going into a weapon. He moved, quickly, to the inner door.

Akhil stood by the bathroom door, which was closed; he spun as Krenn entered, disruptor level. He fired. The doorframe exploded next to Krenn; metal struck him, and the shock wave knocked him down, took the gun from his hand.

Akhil said, "I knew you'd get out of the freezer," he said, "but how . . . oh. The cargo stage. *Kai* the Captain."

Krenn groped for his disruptor. Akhil fired again, high. Molecules of wall tore themselves apart. "Don't, Krenn. Don't force me to kill you. It isn't *necessary.* Is Maktai dead?"

"Not . . . quite."

"It can be an execution, then. Too bad for Mak, but someone has to die for killing the Human, and it's not going to be me, and why should it be you? The Navy won't mind—it's the Security chief, after all. But it has to be one of us; anyone any lower, and they'd fry us for incompetence."

"Why?" Krenn said.

"You *can't* see, can you?" Akhil said, sounding very tired and sad. He gestured at the bathroom door. "How that thing in there has you . . . *enslaved?"*

"What did you call me?" Krenn said, and almost succeeded in sitting up; but he fell back again.

"Not willingly," Akhil said, shaking his head violently. "Maybe it's psionic, I don't know. The rest of the race we saw on Earth—we'll have no trouble with them. But we're taking *this* one to the Imperial Council. That just mustn't happen, Thought Ensign." Akhil turned back to the door, pressed the cone of his disruptor against the panel, thumbed fire.

There was an explosion that blew the door out of its frame, throwing Akhil backward in a cloud of steam; he clutched at his face with scalded hands, fell nearly on top of Krenn as a wave of water drenched them both. Krenn grabbed for the Specialist and missed; Akhil crawled away, staggered to his feet, went for the corridor door.

Krenn found his pistol, pulsed the trigger. The shot shattered a clearprint on the wall. Krenn pulled himself up; his midsection felt like a bowl of lumpy pudding.

Akhil disappeared through the door. Krenn stumbled after. When he reached the corridor, Akhil was working at one of the Computer Room's security doors. They dared not use weapons in the machine room, Krenn knew; if Akhil got inside he would have to be pried out with bare hands. And long before that could happen, he could kill *Fencer* and all of them, by killing *Fencer's* brain.

Krenn braced against the office door, fired. The pistol buzzed dry of charge. Akhil did not even look up from the lock.

The heavy shielded door moved inward, then slid aside. Krenn tensed to leap; it hurt enough to make him dizzy.

Kelly stepped around the curve from the portside transporter, pointed Maktai's pistol and fired. Akhil was slammed against the edge of the door, but stayed on his feet. Kelly shot him again. He took a step, and she ran to where he stood and kicked, Swift-like, to the back of his knee.

Akhil fell down and did not move.

Kelly turned to face Krenn; her arm still dangled. Krenn felt hands touching him: Dr. Tagore, his clothing wrinkled and wet but otherwise undamaged, was guiding Krenn to a chair.

"You weren't . . . in the bathroom."

"I closed the drains and opened all the taps, then went out again, closing the door. I'd merely hoped the water would distract him, but Commander Akhil did not even check that the door was not locked."

"Klingons always lock doors," Krenn said. "Where were you?"

"A custom of my race, in the presence of danger. . . . I was underneath the bed."

"You almost convinced me," Krenn said. "I thought you would not fight. It was . . . a good trick."

"I did not fight," Dr. Tagore said calmly. "I simply did not allow myself to be too easily killed."

And Krenn laughed, not because it was absurd but because he saw the reason of it. "Emanuel . . . are you psionic?"

"No, Krenn. I have been tested, on Vulcan. I am not."

"Then Akhil was right," Krenn said, feeling his senses fading, as in a warm bath. "The Imperial Council must beware. Now that their Imperial Intelligence has failed to protect them . . ."

"Akhil did not act for II," Krenn heard, and though he could no longer see, the voice could not be anyone's but Kelly's.

"I do."

Krenn and Dr. Tagore were playing *klin zha,* with Krenn's set, when the call came to announce that Akhil's body had been transported into space at maximum beam divergence. Krenn acknowledged and made his next move.

Dr. Tagore said, "I believe I once told you I had a theory, about the Klingon observance of death."

"You did not say what it was."

"Well, it isn't popular among my colleagues. . . . At any rate, when one of our race dies, we hold a ceremony, sometimes simple, sometimes very elaborate."

"You *celebrate* a death?"

"Commemorate, rather."

"And the one dead appreciates this."

Dr. Tagore smiled thinly, said, "That depends on the culture. But the practical function is to allow the survivors a vent for their grief, a time when emotion may be released, shared."

"Sharing diminishes the . . . grief?"

"Such is our experience."

Krenn said, "We do not do this."

"I know. And I wonder what happens to the energy, the stress. . . . I think it helps to drive your culture. To expand . . . to conquer, if you like."

"Nal komerex, khesterex," Krenn said, distracted from the game, annoyed to have even such a small reminder of Maxwell Grandisson III.

"I know that, too. And your environment is hostile, and your life-cycle is short and rapid. As I say, my hypothesis is not popular."

Krenn massaged his jaw.

"Klingons do not weep, as many races do," Dr. Tagore said idly. "A different set of facial nerves is stimulated by stress. The Klingon in deep emotion bares his teeth, as if to say 'stay away, until this feeling is past.'"

"The isolation that results is . . . not unknown among Humans."

Krenn won the game, congratulated Dr. Tagore on his growing skill at *klin zha,* and went out.

He found Kelly in the Officer's Mess; she was alone, her plate empty, watching the naked stars flow past.

She did not turn as he approached, and he knew she was being politely deaf; twenty days after the incident there was still a plastic splint on his hip, and he made a good deal of noise in motion.

He understood, now, why her movements had become deliberate, un-Swift-like: she had been imprisoned in her body for far longer than he would be.

Now there was a sheathing of surgical plastic on her shoulder, where *Fencer*'s Surgeon had again replaced the joint with a new metal one. This time it was minor, though. Only the changing-out of a part.

Krenn sat down. She greeted him.

Neither of them spoke for a while.

"I wonder," Krenn said finally, "what Meth of Imperial Intelligence will say about this whole affair?"

"Operations Master Meth is never concerned with methods," Kelly said. "Only results."

Krenn nodded, watching her: the curve of her throat, the slant of her white eyes. He reached over and touched her arm, carefully avoiding the nerves.

She stood, looked at him. Her face was quite empty, though never so dead as Meth's. "You are the founder of a line," she said. "I can be no part of that; I am a fusion, and I do not even know what manner of fusion, so that children might be created."

Krenn said, "Does Meth have that information?"

She said, "You know that Meth only uses those he controls. I have been part of injury and death to your crew. And . . . you are injured; I would cause you . . . pain."

"I know that," Krenn said.

She began to walk away. He caught her hand, held it; she shook at the movement of her shoulder. She said, "I cannot be trusted, and I am not Klingon."

"Akhil was Klingon."

"What do you want?"

"I want you to tell me," Krenn said, "something that I do not already know."

He released her hand. She looked at the stars racing by, and nodded, and went out, walking again slowly, each movement carefully chosen.

But if one knew how to look, Krenn thought, she was dancing.

He followed in her steps.

PART THREE

The Falling Tower

Only a fool fights in a burning house.

—KLINGON PROVERB

Seven: Mirrors

Twenty-six select members of the Imperial Council sat and reclined facing Krenn. There was a large Navy faction, some Marine officers, several political Specialists, and two Imperial Planetary Governors.

The Audience Chamber was an enormous, multisided room. Random panels of colored and reflective glass dissected the space near the ceiling, bouncing and diffusing soft light. The air was pleasant, though not so warm and damp as to induce sleep. Woven into the carpeting was an Imperial trefoil some ten meters long: Krenn stood behind a narrow glass podium at the figure's center.

"Supply of arms to the worlds Tcholin III and Wilda's Planet has caused the dominant factions to favor the Empire as a partner in development," Krenn said. He had no notes to read from: he was allowed none. He watched the audience. Admiral Kezhke was there, aging and still overindulgent. And there was Admiral Kodon, the hero of the Romulan Frontier. Krenn did not look directly into Kodon's face.

"These arms are of course all inexpensive sonics. No translator technology has been supplied. The sale is aided by the fact that Federation machines translate all *vird'dakaasei* as *disruptor*, regardless of their actual operating mode. . . ."

There were half a dozen *tharavul* standing like sculpture behind the Klingons they served-observed. A few servitors carried trays with food, drink, and incenses: they were *tharkuve*, deaf in a more literal sense than the Vulcans.

"Four more worlds along the Alshanai Rift have made advances of peace. They will not commit to abandoning the Federation, but they have been made to understand that the Federation cannot protect them from Orion pirates.

"If this technique is to be expanded, it will be necessary to simulate Orion attacks, as the cost of purchasing actual pirate raids will become unacceptable."

There was a throne in the Chamber, but it was empty. A crown rested on it, in token of the Emperor's presence. Kadrya had chosen iron as the substance for his crown. It was generally a free choice by each Emperor, though none since Keth the Centenarian had presumed to wear imperishable gold. And none had imitated General Kagga, who despite that he was under sentence of death for rebellion had been granted the accession, allowed to reign for the twentieth part of one day, and executed upon the throne: a grand end move of the *komerex zha*. Kagga's crown had been branded, on the flesh around his skull.

"The Federation authorities propose to convene one of the meetings of all members they call *Babels,* to discuss their terms of union. Such meetings require roughly one year to assemble all delegates, because of travel time.

"That concludes this report of the Imperial Contacts Branch, Captain Krenn sutai-Rustazh reporting."

There were polite nods. Krenn saluted and went out of the Chamber. There was a transporter link to his hotel; he nodded to the operator and stepped onto a disc.

Krenn found himself standing on the smallest transporter stage he had ever seen: there was only a single disc, which was enormously wasteful of control equipment; even home stations had three. The only other things in the room were an unattended control console for the transporter, and a blank metal door.

The door receded a few centimeters, then slid aside. It was a good fifth of a meter thick. Supposing his presence was either invited or commanded, Krenn went through.

He entered a small, dim room. The only furnishing was a desk, with a computer and a flask of pale liquid on its top. The far wall was all glass, tilted slightly outward. A tall, broad-shouldered Klingon, dressed entirely in black, stood looking out the window, his back to Krenn.

Without turning around, Operations Master Meth said, "Do join me, Captain Krenn."

Krenn took a step; the door closed behind him, and he heard it seal. He went to the window.

He was looking down on the Audience Chamber he had just left. The Council members had changed slightly; more Administrators were present, fewer Navy. Approaching the podium was Dr. Emanuel Tagore, dressed in a straight-lined white gown with a dark red sash.

They were hidden among the glass panels of the ceiling, Krenn understood; *how* they could be here, he did not know.

Dr. Tagore bowed, began to speak. His words were inaudible.

Meth held out a wireless earphone to Krenn. He took and inserted it, noticing that Meth did not wear one. Krenn wondered if he had a direct implant. Klingons rarely had such things, wary of taps, of mind control, of feedback signals to set the mechanism burning. But Meth . . .

"The exchange of athletes between the Year Games and the Pan-

Federation Olympics," Dr. Tagore was saying, "would reduce the need for prizes to fight in the Games, and allow trials other than deadly combat. There are already many such events in the Year Games, and they are honorable.

"As for the passage of damaging medical data, the required screenings could be conducted entirely by medical tricorder, the machines' recording function being disabled: even if a contestant were to be disqualified, none would know the exact reason. Dr. T'Riri, *tharavul* to Thought Master Ankhisek, tells me this is easily possible for Vulcan technicians . . ."

Meth said, "It is remarkable to watch him. Given only a little more time, the Council would approve this proposal. . . . After four years, most of them believe he has taken their part. When in fact they have taken his." Meth's lips curled in his plastic smile.

Krenn said, "Does he know he's been called back to Earth?"

"Oh, yes. Since you were so readily available, there was no need to delay the message. . . ." Meth looked down again. "He knows, and still he delivers the speech, as if there were still a Federation united behind him. One could almost believe the one believes in his proposals for their own sake."

"Perhaps the one does."

"Ah, I had forgotten you were close," Meth said. Krenn knew he had done no such thing. "No, I don't think so. That technique is useful, on the lower levels. The assassin's gun may believe it is a surgeon's laser. But the assassin must know the task." Meth gestured toward Dr. Tagore with a disguised hand. "I have become very respectful of this Human, Captain, and I think he is a craftsman, not a tool. . . . His reaction, when he received his message of recall, was interesting to watch. If you would care to see it, a tape may be arranged."

"No," Krenn said. "Is the ship ready?"

"Quite ready. Kezhke was most helpful, again. . . . He has strong beliefs about you, sutai-Rustazh." There had been no change in Meth's tone. Krenn realized, for the first time, that he had never heard the Intelligence chief's linename.

Before he could say something dangerous to himself, Krenn said, "And the ones requested?"

"Commander Maktai and Lieutenant Commander Kelly are of course yours, and excellent choices."

"Commander Kelly?"

"As of tonight, yes. Ranks are not difficult to obtain. Authority is rather more so . . . but that, of course, is your problem. As for the other, it has been arranged. You understand the limitations?"

"Thought Master Ankhisek himself explained them."

"And you understood him? *Kai* the thought, Captain." It was almost a joke: Thought Captain. Krenn wondered if it were meant as one.

Meth said, "I'm certain that you understand the mission, so I suppose you are ready for cruise. The Red File will be transferred aboard just before you depart."

"I will be ready whenever the Ambassador is."

"He is already. He is leaving all his effects, except for some clothing and his library. He explained that he is only traveling to a conference; the Embassy remains in existence." Meth looked down at Dr. Tagore, as did Krenn. Krenn found that even from the high angle, the Human did not seem diminished. Krenn turned, a very slight movement, to watch Meth, but Meth's face gave away nothing, his eyes might as well have been glass behind holes in the plastic, even his powerful body— or was that another concealment?—was neutrally posed.

Meth was a black hole of information: he drew it in from everywhere, with a reach as infinite as gravity, but nothing ever escaped the event horizon around him.

There was, in theory at least, one way to get information out of a black hole. It involved high energies just at the event horizon, and for every particle that escaped one of equal value must be lost.

Akhil had told Krenn that.

Meth said, "I shall regret the departure of the epetai-Tagore." There did not seem to be any irony in the honorific. "Like myself, he is absolutely loyal to his Empire, and will do anything at all to protect it."

"Perhaps not anything," Krenn said.

"A natural error, sutai-Rustazh. You do not understand, because you are not absolutely loyal."

"*I am—*"

"It is not an accusation, Captain. Only the truth. You *serve* the Empire, and very well. But some of your loyalty is always reserved for yourself. . . . This is true of all Klingons but I. It is true of the Emperor." He pointed downward. "I suspect that it is also true of all Humans. Except this one."

Krenn recalled what Meth had said about the Council, wondered if the Intelligence Master had also come to see himself reflected in the Ambassador. He said, "Still, I have come to believe that the one would use no weapon."

Meth smiled, and Krenn thought there was somehow amusement in it. "Have you ever seen my weapon, Captain?"

Krenn was too startled to answer.

"You think there is a *komerex zha,*" Meth said calmly, "but there is only the *komerex.*" He indicated the throne, the iron crown upon it.

"Kadrya is nearly sixty now, and Kadrya is no Keth. Though it may be criminal now to speak of rust on iron, in time he will die, and the Council will fight for the crown, and I will fight for the Empire.

"And if the Federation should choose to war with itself, then it must occur while there is an Emperor, and we may take advantages."

Meth filled two glasses from the bottle of pale liquid. There was a strong scent of herbs. "Speaking of loyalty . . . I noticed that the Contacts Branch did not tell the Council their next speaker had been recalled? . . .

"And you know your mission, and it is not my habit to repeat myself. Pleasant voyage, Captain."

Kelly moved the levers, and Dr. Tagore silently flickered in. Krenn thought perhaps the Human's hair had become whiter, but there was no great outward change.

The Ambassador stepped off the disc, nodded to them all. "Honored again, Captain Krenn. I was pleased to hear it would be you taking me home. And Kelly . . . full Commander, now? *Kai*. And Maktai. Good to see you all. I'm in need of good signs, this cruise."

Then Krenn saw the tiredness—but it was a small thing, where Krenn had expected a greater.

"This is a new ship, isn't it?" Dr. Tagore said, and while he spoke the small tiredness was not visible. "*Mirror*, they said. Is *Fencer*, then . . ."

"*Fencer* still exists, still mine," Krenn said. "She is in the docks. *Mirror* is new, a Class D-5, though the changes are mostly not visible. The interior is the same, with only small exceptions . . . one being that we have a stateroom for a passenger, on the officers' deck."

"With a private bath," Maktai said. There was a moment's cool silence, and then Dr. Tagore began to laugh, and then they were all laughing.

"You see," the Human said, "I have learned to know when you are joking."

"The reason I was recalled?" Dr. Tagore said. "To . . . now what was the exact phrase . . . 'reevaluate the mission, and expose the Ambassador to the mood, as well as the decisions, of the Babel Conference.' How many cards?"

Krenn took three cards. He adjusted his hand: a four, a King, and three nines. Maktai tapped his three-fingered hand on the table and took one card. Mak caught his tongue between his teeth and let his cards fall, facedown. Krenn looked at him; it had taken a long time to teach Mak that folding was not the same as resignation: that the courage of the game was not in throwing resources into a pot already lost. Still, they were losing to the Human.

Dr. Tagore said, "The gentleman drops. And dealer takes two. Bet?"

"Check," Krenn said.

"You've stayed in practice."

Maktai said, "I paid for it."

Dr. Tagore said, "All right. Dealer bets three." He separated three fruit drops from a pile near his elbow, pushed them into the pile at the center of the table. "Of course, the actual reason for the recall is that many UFP members do not want a single negotiator to represent them to the Empire. They want to make their own deals."

"Call, raise two," Krenn said. "As I understand it, you have won the Federation a number of points."

"Thank you, Krenn. I'll see that, raise you five. But of course the Federation is a coalition, not a super-government, though sometimes it forgets that . . . if the members do not wish the Federation to act for them, then it must not do so."

Krenn looked at his three of a kind, at Dr. Tagore's face. He was wondering what the Operations Master of Imperial Intelligence would have said to that.

He let his cards fall. Maktai looked sidewise.

Dr. Tagore put his hand facedown. Maktai reached out; Dr. Tagore's finger came down on top of the cards. "You didn't pay to see those," he said.

Maktai withdrew. "I forgot the rule," he said quietly.

Dr. Tagore nodded. "No insult was assumed. But not every game is as friendly as this one."

One ship was waiting for them, at the far side of the Zone: a single saucer-fronted cruiser, the *Savannah II.* The first of that name, Krenn recalled, had taken them outbound from Earth, years ago. He wondered who had destroyed it.

The Human in command was younger-looking than the other Human Admirals Krenn had seen. He had reddish hair, moderately pale skin by Human standards, and a remarkable, bushy growth of hair down the sides of his face and over his upper lip.

"Captain Krenn," he said, in reasonably good *klingonaase* without translating machine, "a pleasure to meet you. I'm Douglas Tancred Shepherd, commanding this Task Force, such as it is. Starfleet is spread somewhat thin just now, ferrying delegates."

Krenn wondered about that: would the Human so casually admit to a Klingon that the frontier patrols were stretched thin? Yet there were still the hunter-killer squadrons. So perhaps it was a challenge, however slight.

Shepherd said, "Chief of Staff van Diemen sends his respects, Captain, and regrets that he could not meet you. And please give my regards to Dr. Tagore; I was once a student of his."

Krenn said, "And my respects to Admiral Luther Whitetree."

Admiral Shepherd said slowly, "Lou Whitetree . . . died two years ago, Captain."

Krenn wanted to ask if he had died well, but Shepherd already showed discomfort, and Humans had too many ideas about death to be all comprehended. Someday, he thought, I will meet you, Whitetree, in the Black Fleet, and kill you a thousand times laughing. And perhaps you will even kill me, for the glory of your son.

What Krenn said was, "I regret to hear that. My Executive also is dead . . . I would have liked for the Admiral to meet his replacement." He looked at the Communications station, but Ensign Kreg was in the seat.

"My . . . sympathies," Shepherd said, sounding very puzzled. "Your authorizations are fully in order, so if you're ready, Captain Krenn . . . Warp 4?"

"Warp 4, Admiral."

When the ships were under way, the Bridge-to-Bridge link broken, Krenn said, "Lieutenant Klimor, you have the conn," and nodded to Maktai. They took the lift down eight decks within the pod, to the Intelligence Operations level.

All doors here were heavily shielded. To Krenn's left was the Interrogation Room, empty now. Krenn and Mak went right; Maktai inserted a key in the lock. Only Maktai's personal key could open this door; those within could not even leave at will. The door opened. Within were three rows of consoles, each with an elaborate cluster of displays.

In every other cruiser of the Navy, this was the Internal Surveillance Room, from which Security could monitor any part of the ship at will. Here the room was called Special Communications. *Mirror* did not in fact have continuous Internal Surveillance. Most of the crew did not know this, and would not have believed it if told. It was the least of the ship's secrets.

Kelly came around the consoles. "They're sensing us, Captain. I'm maintaining the level of screens they expect; they've found the guns off and the hold empty . . . power level's taking care of itself, and mechanical shielding covers the rest."

"Perfect, Kelly. What are you reading from them?"

"Normal subspace traffic. Admiral Shepherd is pleased to report you courteous as described to him."

Krenn laughed. "Soon they'll lose their fear of the Empire, and then what shall happen? . . . Nothing further to the Red File?"

"Not since the Section Two confirming message several days ago."

Krenn nodded. "You should put in an appearance on the Bridge. I'll be in quarters. Emanuel expects me for *klin zha.*"

Dr. Tagore moved the Lancer on the Reflective board.

Krenn examined the position, sat back, letting out a long breath. "You have also stayed in practice, Emanuel."

"Zha riest'n," Dr. Tagore said. "And compliments indeed; in four years I do not think I found a finer opponent. Certainly not for the Reflective Game."

"I was well instructed."

"The name of Kethas was mentioned. A Thought Admiral, the epetai-Khemara."

Krenn said, "In what connection?"

"Reflective *klin zha,*" Dr. Tagore said, as if the question were unexpected. "I would mention the game to a potential opponent, and more than half the time the one would say 'that was Kethas's game.' Did you know the one?"

"I of course know of him. He died when I was young."

Dr. Tagore sighed. "I still have not lived among Klingons long enough. I still think of you as aging as we do . . . you must be, what, twenty-five?"

"Nearly so."

"And I will be seventy-nine on my next birthday. And still we aren't so far apart . . . we both have twenty or thirty years left, if we avoid violence." Krenn was not insulted by that. "Maybe even longer. Coffee?"

"Yes."

"We work slowly on improving our genes, except for what we've borrowed from the Vulcans. Ever since the Eugenics Wars . . ." He shook his head. "Anyway, to return to the original point, Kethas had a reputation with Starfleet, I recall. They called him the Klingon Yamamoto, after a strategist of our history . . . the one was an extraordinary poker player. And he had three fingers on one hand."

"I'll tell Mak." Krenn was wondering if this discussion was about games.

"He seems in an ill mood lately," Dr. Tagore said. "Is the one well?"

"He's lost dreams. We both thought he should learn Federation."

"Ah. My sympathies."

Krenn said, "The Commander of our escort is an Admiral Douglas Tancred Shepherd. He mentioned your name."

"Doug Shepherd's an Admiral now? Now that does make me feel old. Reminds me of when . . ." He paused. "Did you read the book about Arthur and Camelot? The long one?"

"With the changing into animals."

"Yes. Well, when I was teaching boys like Doug Shepherd, I tended to think of myself as Lancelot . . . the terrible sinner, looking for a miracle, just one miracle of his own." He touched one of the Reflective pieces. "I have spent a large part of the last four years with the Imperial Council. It became apparent long ago that I was not the only Ambassador to the Council from Federation worlds, though I was the only one with portfolio."

Quietly Dr. Tagore said, "Although I hope I will be returning to Klinzhai when the conference ends, still you could have saved a long voyage by transferring me to Admiral Shepherd's ship at the Zone. Are you proceeding to Earth . . ." He paused. "Are you being allowed to proceed to Babel because I am aboard, or because you were yourselves invited?"

"The Empire was asked by several to send an observer."

"Yes . . . I'd supposed that was it. You see, I gave up believing in miracles.

"Shall we play again? I don't know anyone on Earth who plays *klin zha.*"

This arrival at Earth, there was no game with shuttlecraft. Krenn, Maktai, and Dr. Tagore beamed down directly to Federa-Terra. They were met at the stage by a heavily armed Security force, and an official wearing Babel Conference insignia who seemed in an extreme hurry.

"Admiral van Diemen sends his regrets," the functionary said. "He's been delayed in San Francisco, but he'll be sending a visual message tonight. We have rooms ready for you, Captain, and you, Commander . . . and, Doctor, you'll be in the delegates' quarters."

They were almost instantly separated. Krenn and Maktai were loaded, with several armed and uniformed Starfleet Military guards, into a small vehicle with curtained windows, and moved off at speed.

The car stopped a few minutes later, and the guards practically leaped out; Admiral Shepherd entered, the door closed, and the car started moving again, at a somewhat lesser speed.

Krenn understood now, as he had not six years ago, the term *double-shuffle.*

"Welcome to Earth, truly this time, Captain Krenn," Shepherd said. "I find I've been appointed as Marcus van Diemen's deputy until he arrives, so I won't be able to spend as much time with you as I'd hoped. I suppose you're aware that you're the most in demand of all the non-Federation observers?"

He produced several sheets of computer printing. "These are the delegates who have asked for interviews."

Krenn flipped through the listing. "How many names are here?"

"One hundred thirty-one."

Maktai said, "And how many members has the Federation?"

"Five hundred forty," Shepherd said, with just the right *klingonaase* inflection for irony.

Krenn said, "This is an impossible number."

Shepherd said, "In several senses I agree. It's entirely your decision whom you wish actually to see, if anyone. The delegates' worlds are listed there; if you need more data, there'll be a computer terminal in your hotel suite."

"Where may we meet . . . such of these persons as we decide on?"

"Your suite is electronically scrambled. If that's not sufficient, we can arrange a secured conference room at Starfleet Headquarters." He paused, said delicately, "The hotel will be shielded against transport, of course. . . ."

"This need not be said." Krenn read through the names of planets. Contacts Branch knew most of them. Some they knew very well indeed. Krenn mentally crossed those off at once. He said, "You are being very cooperative with us, Admiral."

Shepherd put his hands together on his lap. "I'm against dissolution, Captain Krenn. And I know perfectly well that the beings on that list are for it, a little or a long way. But I can't think of a better way to guarantee their votes than to put pressure on them, or even give the appearance of pressure." He reached out, tapped the paper. "If Starfleet tried to tamper with the vote . . . the Federation wouldn't deserve to exist."

Acutely reminded that Dr. Tagore had taught this Human, Krenn looked up; Shepherd's look was quite intent, but there was nothing of a threat in it.

Krenn and Maktai walked into the hotel suite. A uniformed Human shifted their traveling bags from an antigrav carrier to the deep carpeting, went silently around the room indicating closets, lights, and environmental controls, opening the heavy drape across the windows: the fiftieth-floor view of the city and the sea was dramatic. The porter stood by the door for a moment, as if expecting something, then gave a small quick bow and went out.

"Humanai kuvest'?" Maktai said.

"A paid worker," Krenn said, though he had been thinking of Odise, in his father's house so long ago. *"Tokhest*—I don't know."

Maktai grunted. "They have anything that passes for a bath here?" He disappeared into the next room.

"I saw some good ones, last time . . . they call them 'Roman,' after an Empire from their history."

Mak stuck his head back around the corner. "A what?"

"Komerex Romaan."

Mak made a hands-up gesture and turned around again. Krenn followed him, into a room with two enormous beds.

"I've been on ships smaller than these quarters," Maktai was saying. "This must be the—Maskan's *liver,* Captain. . . ."

The Security officer stood in a doorway that opened on a circular room, the size of a small ship's Bridge; it was decorated with columns of veined white stone, mirrors around the walls and on the ceiling. Green vines trailed down from a wooden lattice that diffused the overhead light. In the center of the floor was a sunken bath wider than the span of Maktai's arms, with golden taps and sprays in bizarre shapes.

"We've got to meet those delegates, Mak. . . ." Krenn heard his mouth saying, and wondered why his mouth was saying such a stupid thing.

Maktai had a wildly dreamy grin. "But you really ought to relax before then, Captain. And I've got to check this thing out first. Security rules."

"Captains put up with a lot," Krenn said. "All right, make sure it isn't a Romulan trap. I'll find the computer . . . we'll see who wants us badly enough to wait a little while for the privilege."

"When the Federation was incorporated, ninety standard years ago," the Rigellian delegate said, "we requested the sum of eight billion credits to cover the administrative and other costs of in-federation. This sum was, however, never paid; instead, crude threats of Andorian reprisal were used to coerce our signature to the Articles of Federation."

The Rigellian brushed the fur on its nose, and curled its silver-ornamented tail across its shoulders. "The original amount, invested at four percent annual interest compounded annually—a modest rate of appreciation, you must agree—would now equal . . ." The delegate consulted a wrist computer. ". . . two hundred and seventy-three billion credits. Unfortunately, the membership as a whole still shows no understanding of our position, and in fact has reverted to its original approach—except that now we are threatened with Klingon devils instead of Andorian ones."

"Klingons do not believe in devils," Krenn said.

"A very pragmatic approach."

"Klingons also do not believe in bribery."

"That's a *terrible* word to use for—administrative expenses."

"In our experience it is the most accurate one."

"Perhaps . . . the interest could be discounted for risk."

Krenn showed the points of his side teeth.

"Or even waived," the Rigellian said. It tugged at its tail, which had somehow become wrapped around its throat. "Or perhaps a certain positive consideration—"

"I have only a single diplomatic cruiser," Krenn said. "I doubt there is room in its holds for two hundred seventy-three billion credits." He stood up, bowed slightly. "This concludes the interview."

"Of course," the Rigellian whispered, and left with its tail around its neck.

Krenn went into the suite's bedroom, Maktai was watching a monitor; the pictures were of delegates arriving at Babel, with extra tape allotted to those of particularly non-humanoid forms. Mak said, "I'm glad now I learned the language. They showed a tape of the *g'dayt* ugliest Klingon I'd ever seen, all fangs and scars, and were talking about him as if he was just run of the Imperial Race. Then I saw it was me."

"Have you tried the entertainment channels?"

"What's this?"

"News."

"I thought it *was* the entertainment channel. The others all look like children's indoctrination tapes."

The picture changed again. A crowd of Humans was seated on a hillside. There were long banners stretched above them, reading ONLY ONE SPACESHIP: EARTH and LOOK HOMEWARD HUMAN. Balloons, painted to resemble the Earth, floated on strings.

"In major cities on all points of the globe," a disembodied voice said, "members of the Back-to-Earth Movement met peacefully to protest . . ."

"Points?" Maktai said.

"They don't like to go into space."

Maktai had his tongue between his teeth, watching the crowd of Humans. "There must be thousands of them, all there together."

"They turned out a quarter million for just two Klingons."

"I remember 'Khil . . . you saying that . . . but . . ." he shook his head. "I don't think I've ever seen ten thousand of anything in one place before. Not even *kuve*." He pointed at the blue sky above the crowd. "A few fliers with weapon pods, and a cordon force around them . . . not fifty would get away. But they don't . . . and that mob doesn't even look like they've thought of it." Maktai looked up at Krenn. "Is that what you meant, when you said we weren't afraid of the same things?"

"Partly."

The picture changed again, to an old building against a sky of glass, with a blue-domed disc on its roof. "In Atlanta," the announcer said,

"Maxwell Grandisson III, leader of the well-supported Homeworld faction of Back-to-Earth, was unavailable for comment. But a tapetext release to the press, signed by Grandisson, included the phrases 'a major development is near' and 'years of faith are about to be vindicated in action.' " The words appeared on the screen. "Speculation on—"

Krenn struck the monitor's off switch. Maktai was silent for a few moments, then said, "How did it play, with the Rigellian?"

"Well enough. We wouldn't buy and we wouldn't sell, so they don't know what to do about us; they're off balance, and it won't take much to push them over." He looked at the curtained window; it was fully dark outside. The clock beside the bed read 22:36. "I think it's time."

Maktai nodded, began unfastening his tunic.

Krenn said, "There are two more interviews set for tonight, and three tomorrow morning. Think you're ready?"

"I think I'll enjoy it." Mak gestured toward the monitor. "If any of them saw those tapes, the real me ought to scare them to death."

Krenn laughed. "Don't do that, or they won't be able to vote."

Mak reached inside his loosened clothing, drew out a flat black display panel, then a small keyboard, and finally a metal box that unfolded itself in four stages to become a meter-wide antenna array. Cables linked all the devices together: indicators came to life, and the display screen showed first noise, then a data line.

Maktai worked at the keyboard, then said, "Shepherd gave me the key to shut off the spy screens."

"How convenient," Krenn said. "I'm sure someone's waiting for us to use it. Besides, Kelly'd be insulted."

"She's the proudest female I . . . um."

Krenn laughed.

"They're answering," Maktai said. "Decrypting the shields now. . . . *Mirror* has lock-on. At least, as locked as we can expect."

"Have them energize," Krenn said.

"Captain . . ." Mak said, "I think one gets only so much luck with transporters, this side of the Black Fleet. You understand?"

"I understand, Mak. Action."

"Acting."

The golden flicker was very slow, and pulsed much brighter than normal, as the warp-accelerated transport signal found the dead oscillations of the standing shield wave, and cycled through them.

Science Officer Antaan had devised the technique, though Kelly's hands were on the console. Antaan claimed the Federation could not have guessed at the technique, because their transporter's super-carrier (or, as Antaan called it, the Noise Wave) could not get through the null spots. That was his thought, anyway.

Krenn felt his head throb with the transport pulse, wondered if they should not just have announced some unnamed emergency, and beamed up openly: the Federation surely would not have dared to forbid it. That was Mak and Kelly's thought.

But it was necessary that no attention at all be called to *Mirror,* not while it was within reach of Earth, and Earth's Specialists, and whatever equipment they might have. There were secrets aboard that must be kept.

Including, Krenn thought as he finally faded, *from Kelly and Mak.*

Eight: Images

Krenn stepped off the disc, felt himself sway, put his head against the wall. A hand tried to touch an agonizer to his ear, and he snarled and swept it away: then he realized it was the Surgeon, and the tool was a neural scanner. It wasn't so much of an error after all, Krenn thought; they were the same device, only wired differently.

Kelly said, "You were almost nine minutes in transit."

"It would have been . . . a long swim."

"Artifact errors build up geometrically while you're in the system."

Krenn nodded, almost caring. "Have I missed van Diemen's message?"

"No. It's being open-channel broadcast; I routed it to the forward Theatre. Unless you'd rather lie down and watch it in your cabin."

"I'm all right. Auloh."

"Captain?" the Surgeon said.

"I think you'd better go down to the hold and get started. There's a data tape in the container."

"I've thawed out more Marines than a squadron can carry," Auloh said diffidently.

"Not like this, you haven't. Run the tape. We'll record van Diemen for you."

Marcus van Diemen, Chief of Staff for Starfleet and Chairman of the Babel Conference, stood before a panoramic view of the city called San Francisco: lighted buildings stretched away for kilometers, and the moon shone on water beneath a long bridge that was strung with lights in a double arc. Van Diemen wore a uniform that stated his rank in unrestrained terms: Krenn supposed there were enough Federation members who needed to see the metal.

"Though unforeseen events will keep me from the Conference until tomorrow, I am with you in spirit, through this message."

The Chief of Staff himself was no less dramatic a figure than he had been at Krenn's first visit: a wind seemed to lift his yellow hair as he spoke, and his hands gestured like fists striking blows.

"Perhaps, all unintended, this may be a symbolic opening for this Babel; for what we are to discuss is keeping contact between peoples who are sometimes held apart. This Babel is, more than any before it, about sending messages to ourselves.

"There are those who say that Starfleet cannot protect the Federation members. I cannot deny that we have been spread thin, that there have been losses on the frontiers; and we must find a better answer to this problem. But is that answer to disband the Fleet, each world defending itself in isolation? I think the frontier would find itself imperiled indeed without the ships of the line provided by the inner worlds, and the trained crews produced by Starfleet Academy.

"Conversely, the claim that the frontier defense bleeds the inner worlds simply misses the fact: the frontier defense *is* the defense of the inner worlds. Has Earth ever been raided by Romulan or Klingon? Has Centauri, or Rigel, or Vulcan?"

Above the skyline behind van Diemen, a small ship was rising on gravs, marker lights strobing. Krenn reached for his communicator. "Special Communications, Commander Kelly," he said.

"And finally there are those," van Diemen said, "who claim the Federation is unresponsive to the needs of its members. I could give several answers to this; casually say 'The Federation is its members,' callously say 'The members get the Federation they deserve.'

"Instead, I will mention some events of Federation history. The halting of Rigellian Fever. The evacuation of entire planets doomed by supernovae. Peace with the Romulans—peace forged with blood and iron, certainly, but a real peace nonetheless. Concessions won from the Klingon Empire, which not ten years ago was thought to be beyond the reach of reason—"

In the Inspirational Theatre aboard *Mirror,* there were several comments from the officers listening on translator. Krenn only smiled.

Van Diemen said, "The truth is that we do not, from one day to the next, know what our needs will be. Medical aid, disaster relief, united defense against an unimagined new enemy or a resurgent old one— these have been our needs, and who can say what will follow them?

"As a great Human said centuries ago, at the joining of another great Union, 'We must all hang together, or we shall assuredly all hang separately.' "

Krenn heard more comments from the Theatre audience, and wondered how the translator had converted the hanging line.

"Delegates to Babel . . . until we meet . . . good night."

Krenn kept his seat as the others filed out of the Theatre. Shortly Kelly came in, holding two clear prints. Krenn took one; the film was still warm from the printer. The image showed the spacecraft he had seen behind Admiral van Diemen, enlarged so that its markings were clearly visible. "Cargo tug?" Krenn said. "About a kilometer altitude."

Kelly nodded, handed Krenn the second print. It showed San Francisco from Mirror's orbit; the city was easily identifiable by the bay and bridge. Krenn held the print to the light of the Theatre screen, flexed it for maximum depth effect. A ship a thousand meters up should have stood out clearly, floating above the landscape. But there was nothing but a few wisps of cloud.

Krenn checked the reference strips along the prints' edges; they were simultaneous exposures.

"So it was a recorded message," Krenn said. "Was the window real, or a display?"

"It seems to have been real. The resolution matches that of van Diemen's image. But the analysts are still working. We may be able to find out when the tape was made, from light cues in the city and the angle of the moon."

"*Kai* Special Communications."

Krenn's communicator chimed. "Captain. . . . Yes, Auloh. I'll be there." He switched off, said to Kelly, "He's almost ready. Shall we go?"

"I'd . . . rather not, Captain." She held very still: Krenn realized it was to keep herself from trembling. Involuntarily, Krenn looked at the ceiling, though he knew very well there were no watchers on this voyage. Sometimes death is better, he thought, death is the end. But the thought did not improve his feeling.

Krenn said, "No reason why you have to. Finish assembling the Red File, and put these into it." He handed back the clearprints.

"Section One or Two?"

"Section One. Then do a full sort, and download a copy of One."

"Affirm." Kelly went out, walking cautiously, holding her arm to herself. After allowing her time to get a lift car, Krenn left the Theatre and rode up three decks to Sickbay.

A male Klingon lay naked on the surgical bed, strapped down securely, still half-surrounded by thermowave projectors and scanning gear. An empty cold-sleep capsule stood against the wall.

Surgeon Specialist Auloh pulled a contact away from the body, cleaned off the conductive paste. "You were right about the tape," he said to Krenn. "If I'd gotten these neural readings on anyone else, I'd have figured he was a candidate to go back in the freezer, not on duty. And some of these 'recommended procedures' aren't recommended by any authority I know of." He picked up a pressure injector. "This is one."

Krenn said, "What is it?"

"Masiform-D, Tri-Ox, *and* four times the therapeutic dose of Cordrazine."

"Lethal?" Krenn said, looking at the body on the bed. The sleeping Klingon appeared to be about Krenn's age; in a way, that was right, but it was also very, very wrong.

Auloh said, "This wouldn't just kill you; you'd *explode*." He gave the injection. "I'll be in my office. I need a jolt of something strong, too. Call if he goes over the lines."

After a few minutes, the body began to stir. The bed displays ticked higher, many of them into the yellow critical ranges; Krenn saw that Auloh had marked new lines onto the display with a wax stylus, and the indicator bars hovered near the marks.

The Klingon on the bed twitched. A wrist tore through the heavy plastic of the restraint as if it were wet paper. Then the arm stopped moving, lowered again. The eyes opened; Krenn imagined he heard a click.

"Welcome aboard, Zharn," Krenn said. "I am Krenn, Captain of the *Mirror*. Are you well?"

"I am indeed so," Zharn said. "You have a mission for me, Captain?"

"I do," Krenn said, and began unfastening the bed restraints.

"You are Captain . . ."

"Krenn."

"Captain Krenn. Have I acted for you before?"

"Not I. But I know your record."

"Is it a good record?" The question was almost absurdly eager.

"It is full of glory." Krenn released the last strap. Zharn began to sit up; Krenn started to assist him.

"Do not touch me, Captain. I have a reflex to attack anyone in physical contact, and I might become distracted and fail to suppress the reflex. You would die."

"I . . . understand. This was in the background tape."

"It is a thing I always remember," Zharn said. "Do you have my target briefing?"

"Yes. But we have a little time. Would you like anything—food? Something else?"

"I will need to eat. . . ." Zharn stood up. He moved like oiled machinery; naked, he seemed not at all vulnerable. "And of course I appreciate your hospitality." He smiled vaguely. "But after the mission, I will be more . . . able. And I will . . . remember it longer. The sleep damages memory."

"As you wish, *zan* Zharn."

"You are gracious, Captain . . . Krenn. Are you . . . certain I have never acted for you?"

"It is not impossible that we have met. Perhaps long ago. In the Year Games?"

"I was in the Year Games. Perhaps then. Was it long ago, that you were in the Games? For me it was not."

Krenn looked casually at his chronometer. In Federa-Terra, on the Earth below, it was 03:14. "I have your equipment ready," Krenn said. "And your target briefing."

"How did you get such precise coordinates?" Krenn asked Kelly, as they rode the lift to the transporter room.

"We tapped into their public communications grid at an open microwave link. It's a very easy system to use, there are any number of directories. I called the University of Emory, and they connected me directly to his office: we locked on the call impulse."

"You *spoke* to him?"

"He wasn't there. But a secretary told me when he would be."

They stepped out of the lift. They were wearing long hooded cloaks over their dress uniforms: Krenn's was black velvet, Kelly's a metallic gold.

In the transporter room, she handed Krenn a computer cassette. "These are the settings for Antaan's transmission technique. We've held lock on Maktai's focal referent since you beamed up . . . don't let Antaan try to set the transporter manually."

"Why?"

"Because the Captain's transport is my responsibility," she said, and began working at the console. "Energizing," she said, and stepped onto a disc next to Krenn's.

They flickered into an office with wood-paneled walls, and wooden furniture with the dark tone of age. Along the walls were glass cases, holding peculiar devices of glass and wood and metal; Krenn saw a few that were similar to Auloh's instruments, and supposed they were a collection of medical tools. A pendulum clock's hands pointed to 10:25.

On the wall above the office desk was a large framed document, with script so ornate Krenn could not read most of it: he made out DOC-TOR OF MEDICINE and THOMAS JACKSON MCCOY.

Beneath his credentials, Dr. McCoy was seated, staring, hand frozen in midair on its way to a stylus plate. After a moment he said, "That's quite a trick, gentlemen . . . excuse me, sir, madam."

"Doctor McCoy, I am Captain Krenn . . . we met some years ago, at Maxwell Grandisson III's table. This is Commander Kelly, my Communications and Executive Officer."

"Well, I'll be damned," McCoy said.

"Do you remember, Doctor . . ."

"I'm not likely to forget that breakfast," the Human said, and stood up. "Won't you all please sit down?"

The door to the office opened, and a woman came in, carrying a stack of note plates. She was wearing eyeglasses on a cord around her neck; she stopped short, and the glasses fell off.

"Not just now, Lucy," Dr. McCoy said. "I think I'm in consultation."

The woman put back her glasses, took a very long look at the two Klingons, and another at Dr. McCoy. Then she smiled. "Of course, Doctor. Hold your calls?"

"Sounds like a good idea."

The woman nodded to Krenn and Kelly, still smiling. "Since I've already barged in on you folks, can I get you something? Coffee?"

"Coffee would be most pleasant, thank you," Krenn said.

Dr. McCoy said, "Bring the pot, Lucy. And I hope to Lucius Beebe there's something strong for it."

Krenn thought of Auloh, and smiled to himself.

When they were supplied and seated, Dr. McCoy said, "Now what can I do for you?"

Krenn explained briefly.

Dr. McCoy was sitting back in his chair, stroking his square gray beard. He said, "I assume this isn't a professional referral?"

"I don't understand," Krenn said.

"The legally constituted authorities don't know you're here. And if they find out you *are,* it's gonna make the Last Trump sound like a tin whistle."

The phrase was bewildering, but its tone was clear enough. "The Federation will not be pleased," Krenn said.

Dr. McCoy said, "And if even some of what I hear about your culture is true, *they* won't be any too happy either."

Kelly said, "This is true." She began to stand up.

"Good!" McCoy said. Kelly dropped back into her chair. McCoy said, "I won't play anybody's politics. But for the lady, that's just fine." He picked up the communicator handset on his desk. "Lucy? Get me Dr. Nesheim in the path lab."

Krenn had never seen any being but Dr. Tagore smile so warmly.

Krenn took out his own communicator. "I have to meet other

appointments," he said. "The Commander will call for transport when you are finished."

"You understand, this'll take a few days," Dr. McCoy said. "We'll have to use some of our research gear, and do a little midnight requisitioning."

Cargomaster Keppa had used exactly that phrase in *klingonaase.* "I understand, Doctor."

"Then don't worry, Captain. We'll take the best care of her."

Kelly said, in *klingonaase,* "Use the control cassette."

"All *right,* Kelly."

"And use caution."

"Affirm." Krenn pushed the call key. "*Zan* Kreg, this is the Captain . . . ready to beam up."

Krenn materialized in the hotel room, took a few steps, and sat down hard on the bed. He put down the pouch containing the Red File, Section One.

"You look terrible," Maktai said.

"It is a good thing to be so cared for," Krenn said. "The interviews?" Maktai's laugh was enough answer. "Good," Krenn said, and looked at the bedside clock. 11:18. He had been nonexistent for eight minutes since leaving *Mirror.* "Turn on the monitor . . . news channel."

The screen showed the dedication of a housing unit in a place called Antarctica: Krenn remembered Dr. Tagore saying that was the planet's south polar cap. He felt cold just looking at the pictures. Maktai was rubbing his three-fingered hand, and had a rigid expression.

The screen changed abruptly to a sign reading URGENT BULLETIN. The next image was of a crowd of Humans, some of them armed soldiers in the Earth Forces and Starfleet Military uniforms. The picture shook, evidently taken by a hand-held camera; the camera seemed trying to go forward, and the troops were holding it back. In the background, a concrete pillar was just visible. Then the soldiers pressed in again, and the picture retreated.

A Human wearing a headset dodged into view. "This is Judith Rozmital, in . . . where? . . . Byron, Georgia, USA. We have word that Admiral Marcus van Diemen's train has been attacked. . . ." An insert appeared in the corner of the screen, with a still picture of van Diemen. The cordon of soldiers continued pushing outward.

"We're trying to get some pictures . . . there's no official statement yet.

"Admiral van Diemen was on his way to Federa-Terra, where he is to be Chairman of the Babel Conference. He left San Francisco this morning . . ." The reporter turned her head sharply, said in a low voice,

"Jack? This line doesn't go to Frisco . . ." Rozmital turned back to the camera. "I'm told we're about to get an official statement."

The URGENT BULLETIN sign appeared for a moment. Then the unsteady camera showed a group of civilians, all wired in some way, around an Earth Forces officer in field uniform. Lines of superimposed type read COL. WALLACE DUQUESNE and EGF SECURITY. Krenn was glad it was not Colonel Rabinowich.

"I regret to announce," the Colonel said, "that Admiral Marcus van Diemen . . . is dead."

The reporters crowded in. Someone screamed in the distance.

"The cause of death . . . is unknown at this time.

"*Attack? No* . . . no, the train was *not* attacked . . . *heart attack,* someone may possibly have said, and if so it was totally without authorization, or responsibility.

"No, other than that I don't . . . We're looking into the route. . . .

"No, there is *no* evidence of an attack. Not by aliens, not by Humans, not by killer bees. There is . . . Oh, that *concludes* the goddamn statement." Colonel Duquesne turned, drew a finger across his throat.

The screen went white.

"*Him* I understand," Maktai said.

Marcus van Diemen appeared on the screen, frozen-framed, standing in front of San Francisco by night. A voice said, "For the benefit of our viewers who did not see the original broadcast, we present again Admiral van Diemen's last message . . . once again, Starfleet Chief of Staff Marcus van Diemen is dead at 67. More details as they become available."

Krenn turned off the sound, but not the monitor. He picked up the hotel communicator, watching the screen. On the bed, Maktai was dismantling the transporter referent.

"Good afternoon," Krenn said. "I would like to arrange a meeting with the Deputy Conference Chairman, Admiral Douglas Shepherd. . . . Yes, I am certain he is very busy. Tell him this is Captain Krenn sutai-Rustazh of the Klingon Empire.

"Thank you. Tell him also that one other Human must be present at this meeting. His name is . . ." Krenn reached into his tunic, produced a small plastic card. ". . . Carter Winston, delegate to Babel from the planet Deneva.

"Yes, I shall be pleased to have the Ambassador there, but it is not required. Mr. Winston's presence is *required*.

"It is indeed related to that. I suggest a place more secure than my suite. I suggest the most secure place Admiral Shepherd can arrange.

"Thank you."

Krenn broke the link. He flexed the card with Winston's name between his fingers, cracked it across, and dropped the pieces into a metal wastebasket. They glowed orange as they fell, and were burning whitely before they touched the bottom.

On one wall of the conference chamber, a display panel showed colored wave patterns, continuous proof that the room's electronic defenses were functional. Overhead, a circular ventilator moved cold, damp air with a continuous rush.

Krenn supposed all Security meeting rooms looked alike: all blank and bare, as if any hint of warmth or comfort were an entrance for the enemy. This room even had access by transporter only, like Meth's window on the Council: but there were three discs on the stage, and of course it was the screeching Federation device. Krenn listened to the irritating sound of the ventilator and wondered if, should the power fail, they would all suffocate, sealed inside the Starfleet Tower. He had no disruptor to burn an exit.

Krenn sat at one long side of the long black table. The Red File rested near his left elbow. At the narrow end to Krenn's right was Douglas Tancred Shepherd, for the last forty minutes the Acting Chief of Staff for Starfleet. At the other end Dr. Tagore sat, a little back from the table, fingers interlaced in his lap.

The door hissed open, and another Human came in: he wore a narrow-waisted suit of purple velvet, with a white silk scarf at his throat. There was a silver ring on his left hand, of simple and elegant design, mounting a red-gold stone. His hair was a medium brown, long, caught at the back of his neck with a plain silver band. His face would have been smooth, except for the lines of worry in it.

"I understand that the situation is difficult, Admiral Shepherd," he said, firmly, not angrily. "But I don't appreciate being rousted from a business lunch in a public place by rude men in cheap suits. We don't do that on Deneva, and I certainly didn't expect it on Earth. I'm going to—" He turned, saw Krenn. "—Oh, my stars."

"We apologize for any embarrassment that may have been caused, Mr. Winston," Admiral Shepherd said, "but I doubt that troops in uniform would have been any less so, and the matter is very important.

"This is Captain Krenn, of the Klingon cruiser *Mirror*. And Dr. Emanuel Tagore, our Ambassador to the Klingon Empire."

"Carter Winston," the young Human said. "Resources Corporation of Deneva . . ." He looked at Shepherd, then Dr. Tagore. "I don't, ah, have a translator with me . . ."

Krenn said, "I understand you, Mr. Winston."

Shepherd said, "Please sit down, sir."

Winston sat.

Krenn said, "Admiral, what is the latest word on the death of Admiral van Diemen?"

Shepherd said, "We're still investigating—"

Dr. Tagore said gently, "I think, Doug, that if Starfleet knows anything, it had best be said."

Shepherd tensed. Measuring the words, he said "At 1552 hours Universal Time today . . . 1052 locally . . . an electrical fault in the guideway control system stopped Admiral van Diemen's train, just south of Macon, Georgia. Colonel Duquesne, the Security officer in charge, sealed the cars at once.

"Six minutes twenty seconds after the stop, Colonel Duquesne checked on Admiral van Diemen, who was in a sleeping compartment. When the Admiral did not respond, the Colonel had the compartment door forced.

"The Admiral was on the bed inside, wearing his dress uniform, with a holstered, fully charged pistol. He appeared to be asleep, and the first assumption was of a stroke or heart attack.

"However . . . the military physician who examined the body a few minutes later discovered that cause of death was a clean cervical fracture."

"What?" Winston said.

Dr. Tagore said, "The Admiral died in bed of a broken neck."

Shepherd said, "In the physician's opinion, death had occurred within the last twenty minutes, which is to say, no more than ten minutes before the train was stopped, or immediately afterward."

Winston said, "Couldn't they have frozen him—or something?"

"The spinal cord was entirely severed. As by a knife, the doctor's report says, though the skin was unbroken. Even if the Admiral had not suffered irreversible brain damage from loss of oxygen, there would be little hope of restoring function to his body below the neck." Shepherd paused. "Marc van Diemen wouldn't want that."

"So he was murdered," Winston said.

Admiral Shepherd said, "I've seen men die of broken necks, and they . . . twitch when they die. Not for long, but . . . Marc's body was as composed as if he was sleeping. Which means someone composed it."

"And your suspects?" Dr. Tagore said.

"There were eight soldiers, including Colonel Duquesne, three train crew, and two members of the Chief's personal staff. The blow was very precise, but superhuman strength wasn't necessary, only knowing how, and anyone could know how. All of Duquesne's troops admit they do know. The compartment was latched, but a screwdriver could open it, and all the train crew knew how to do *that*. As for alibis, a train is a very small place, distances are short. It would have taken perhaps a minute, perhaps thirty seconds or less. And in the confusion of the sudden stop . . . well.

"We have thirteen suspects, and unless one of them confesses, we are not likely to have a prosecution. And a confession is unlikely." Shepherd looked at Krenn. "As the means we may use to extract confessions are strictly limited."

"Our facilities are at your disposal, of course," Krenn said, in *klingonaase*.

Winston looked at Krenn, said to Shepherd, "You haven't mentioned a motive. But I don't suppose I need to ask that, do I? He was on his way to Babel."

"Via the eye of the needle, it would seem," Dr. Tagore said very quietly.

Winston said, his voice rising, "Why are you *sitting* on this? Don't you realize what'll happen when the truth comes out? The Dissolution forces will be discredited completely—anyone who voted to dissolve would be linked to the murderers."

Dr. Tagore said, "I think you underestimate the flexibility of the members. The greater the excess of an act, the more easily it is disassociated from oneself."

Winston looked rueful. "Yes . . . I suppose you're right." He gave a short, unhappy laugh. "What am I saying? I've dealt with the Pentalians, not to mention Rent-a-Rigellian. I *know* you're right."

"Please do not congratulate me," Dr. Tagore said.

Krenn said, "Are you then in favor of Federation unity, Mr. Winston?"

Winston looked up. He seemed to have forgotten Krenn's presence until now. "Of course I am. I wouldn't be in business if it weren't for my Federation contracts. If it weren't for Starfleet, I wouldn't *be* here; my parents were nearly killed by . . . well, pirates."

"And peace concerns you."

"No businessman in his right mind wants a war. Trade patterns go to perdition, goods get seized, currencies devalue . . ." Winston laughed again, somewhat less bitterly. "Even my friends in the arms trade prefer a wide-open market."

"Yet Dissolution seems quite popular."

"I didn't say we were all in our right minds."

Krenn reached into the Red File pouch, brought out a tape cassette. "Is there a means to play this?"

Shepherd took the tape, went to the light panel on the wall. He touched a button, and a panel slid open to expose a playback unit. He put in the cartridge.

A section of the gray wall brightened, showed visual noise. The swirling dots resolved into small squares, then into a picture: here and there, squares still dropped out black, but the Human on the screen was clearly Marcus van Diemen.

"What's wrong with the picture?" Winston said.

Shepherd said, "It's a descramble . . . an unauthorized descramble." He looked at Krenn, who looked back with a slight smile.

"Standard procedure, as before," van Diemen was saying to the unseen recipient of the message, "no names, numbers, coordinates. Burn any recordings or notes." He touched keys on the desk before him, and a transparent starmap appeared in front of him. Stretching from one corner to the other was a wide amber band.

Krenn said, "That is the zone of space which the Federation calls the Klingon Neutral Zone."

Shepherd said, "That could be tested."

"A hunter squadron and two scouts to these points," van Diemen said, indicating them with a fingertip. "Engage, exchange fire, and break off. If you're pursued, signal code TRIPWIRE for support in strength."

Krenn said, "Is there such a code, Admiral?"

"That would be . . . classified," Shepherd said, staring at the screen.

Van Diemen said, "Your desirable losses are one-third of the hunters and moderate damage to one scout. Loss of one scout is acceptable. However, if a TRIPWIRE directive appears certain to result, any loss may be—"

Shepherd snatched the cartridge from the machine. "This is a fake," he said. A burr had come into his voice. "Sweet Mary O'Meara, it's got to be a phony."

Krenn took a document from the file pouch. "This is a voiceprint and image-source analysis. I do not understand all the technical aspects, but my Communications officer tells me that your signal-intelligence staff will be able to reach the same conclusions." He touched the File. "There are more intercepts, all of the same general meaning."

"If these are real," Shepherd said, *"if . . ."*

Krenn said, "Speaking as a Naval officer, I would think the best way to test their validity would be to examine the pattern of skirmishes across the . . . Neutral Zone."

Shepherd's voice was thick with confusion and anger. "You're sayin' he was tryin' to draw you . . . *the Klingons* . . . into a war. Sendin' crews out deliberately t'be killed. You tell me why the Chief would do that, Captain. An' it better be a damned good reason."

Winston said quietly, "Every delegate to Babel knows *why*, Admiral. We'd never dare dissolve the Federation if we thought some alien menace was waiting to gobble us up piecemeal. I admit, and I'm not proud of it, one of the reasons I was for unity was that I was . . . afraid of the Klingons."

"In this," Krenn said, "there is no need for apology."

Shepherd said, tightly controlling himself, "Are you telling us, Captain, that the Klingon Empire has no desire for war? That every shootout on the frontier has been provoked by Starfleet? For that matter, are you telling us that the Klingons even *minded* having an excuse to attack across the Zone?"

Krenn smiled, showing teeth. Winston paled slightly; Shepherd stood impassive; Dr. Tagore's face was calm. Krenn wished that Emanuel were not here; the Ambassador was the only one here who might see through Krenn's performance.

Krenn said, "I am telling you one thing only. I intend to release this file to the Babel conference. Being no diplomat, I cannot calculate its effects. But I would expect them to be strong. And the killing of the Conference Chairman may seem then to be no more terrible a crime than . . ." Krenn paused, as if searching for the phrase. ". . . the shooting of a mad dog."

Shepherd flushed red, and he was shaking. The plastic cassette creaked in his grip. "I don't care what you've found out wi' your dirty window-peeping, *Captain*. You say another such thing about Admiral van Diemen an' we'll have it out, right here between us."

Krenn said nothing. But he saw the tilt of Dr. Tagore's head, and thought, Emanuel knows, of course. He understands that the Klingon who comes as a friend will always be thought a liar.

Carter Winston pulled gently at his hair, said, "All right, Captain Krenn . . . what's the asking price for these documents?"

Shepherd said, "You've no authorization—"

"Of course, trade with the Klingon Empire is illegal," Winston said coolly, "even though it happens on a regular basis. But under the Uniform Law of Space Salvage, any item recovered by a ship Captain from a wreck abandoned by its owner becomes ship's property. This is certainly a wreck we're looking at: does Starfleet want to claim it?

"And Federation law is quite clear that the right of individuals to hold, transfer, sell, use, destroy, or otherwise manipulate nonliving personal property may not be infringed. I told you, Admiral, I've been to Rigel and come back with most of my shirt." He looked at Krenn. "Besides which, there must be a reason I was . . . invited here. Tell me, Captain, do you know our word, 'blackmail'?"

"I know it."

"Good. That saves all the threats and counterthreats. What do you want for the original file, and destruction of all copies?"

Krenn said, "Dilithium."

There was a silence. Winston pulled off his ring, set it on the table in front of Krenn, with the red-gold stone showing. "There's a piece," he said. "Five carats, worth about eighty thousand credits. Or how much did you have in mind? I warn you, it's a horror to cut; tougher than diamond. You need high-output lasers."

"Or antimatter," Krenn said.

Winston said, "That sounds *very* dangerous."

Krenn said, "Over two years ago, a geophysicist at the Lalande 8 mining complex discovered that dilithium crystals could focus and channel the energy from antimatter annihilation reactions. The difference in output, his preliminary report said, was similar to the difference between white light and a laser."

"I think I read about that," Winston said. "In some mining journal or another. Pretty dull stuff."

"Yet the Federation immediately began an engineering development project, which was highly classified. A few months ago, this project issued a report, also very secret.

"Mr. Winston, Resources Corporation of Deneva owns Lalande 8. You were the contractor for the dilithium development project, and you have access to the report. I want a copy."

Winston put his ring on again, examined the stone. "Yes, I guess that explains my invitation well enough. My compliments on your research, Captain."

Dr. Tagore said, "Not being an engineer, would someone explain this invention in political terms?"

Admiral Shepherd said, "It means a new generation of warp drives. Warp 6, at least . . . maybe Warp 8 or 9." He looked very black. "And the same sort of advance in weapons systems. Is that political enough, Professor?"

"Yes, Admiral. Those terms I understand."

Shepherd said, "Then you understand why we can't possibly do it."

Winston said, "It'll take the rest of today to get hold of one, Captain. Is that acceptable?"

The Admiral said, *"What in God's name are you saying?"*

"I'm closing a deal, Admiral. That's what I'm here for."

"The Dilithium Report is still under Starfleet classification—and if you think you can space-lawyer your way around *that,* you're wrong. As a Federation citizen—"

"Admiral," Winston said calmly, "there are over five hundred Babel delegates out there, and every one of them is scared of the Klingons, even the ones that weren't scared a couple of days ago. I don't suppose the Vulcans are, but they've only got one vote.

"I assure you, if those tapes are released, in forty-eight hours there won't *be* any Federation citizens, or any Federation, or any Starfleet: just five hundred tiny little Empires. And the Klingons, and the Romulans. And if you think *this* deal is rotten, just wait and see what happens *then.*"

Shepherd sat down. "I know now," he said, exhausted. "I know why Marc wanted the war."

Dr. Tagore said, "But you don't want it, Doug."

Shepherd looked down the length of the table. "Not you too, Emanuel . . . you of all people haven't started believing in the balance of terror."

"You know what I believe in, Douglas."

Shepherd nodded. "You're right. I don't want a war." He stood again. "Gentlemen . . . let's all go back to our hotels and betray our trusts."

Krenn almost laughed. But the Humans would not understand. Not even Dr. Tagore, this time.

Admiral Shepherd's hand paused on the way to the door control. "I suppose I understand, now, where the Chief's train detoured to . . . who he was meeting. Who else would demand a meeting at the last minute and get it?"

"The File contains evidence," Krenn said, "not all of it recent."

"If you were watching . . . are you selling us that too? Will that file tell us who killed him?"

Krenn smiled. "Sorry. You didn't pay to see those cards."

Nine: Reflections

It was morning over Federa-Terra and Atlanta when Kelly beamed up. Krenn pointed at a cloth bag she was carrying: it had a pattern of flowers embroidered on the side. "What's that?"

"They called it my 'discharge kit,' " she said. "One of the nurses gave it to me, to carry all the records. . . ."

"They found it?"

She nodded slowly. "They gave me some . . . 'pattern slides,' they called them. Auloh can . . . match a shoulder joint to me now." She looked at him. "Or anything." She took a step toward the door, a little crookedly. "Too much time in bed . . . it's been three days; I'd better check the station. Both of them."

"Kreg's done all right on the Bridge, and we haven't needed Special Communications," Krenn said. "But it will be good to have you back."

"Pleased, Captain." There seemed to be a light in her, as if the glow of transport had not entirely faded.

On her way to the door she stopped, said, "Is Zharn still . . ."

"For the rest of the day."

She nodded. "I'll find him."

"Kelly—he doesn't know us. He's only still called Zharn because he had to have some name."

"I understand," she said. "But I'd like to see him anyway." She reached into her bag. "Dr. McCoy sent this to you . . . and a message with it." Kelly pulled out a roll of densely printed paper.

"What's the message?"

" 'I guess I oughta be happy,' " she said, in a fair imitation of McCoy's accent. " 'But I'm not.' "

Krenn felt a coldness as he took the paper; he nodded as Kelly went out, then unfolded the sheets. But there was nothing there about the Communications Officer.

THE ATLANTA CONSTITUTION, read heavy type at the top of the front page. There were several columns of text, each with its own heading shouting for attention. KLINGONS LEAVE BABEL, one said, DELEGATES EXPRESS RELIEF. But Krenn had no difficulty deciding which story he was meant to read.

ATLANTA INDUSTRIALIST DIES

Maxwell Grandisson III, billionaire local businessman and key figure in the "Back-to-Earth Movement," died early yesterday afternoon in a freak accident at the Atlanta Regency, where he had resided for several years.

Grandisson plunged through the glass wall of one of the hotel's scenic elevators, falling more than twenty stories to his death. It was suggested that fatigue stresses in the glass and frame, parts of which are more than two hundred years old, caused a sudden fracture when Grandisson leaned against the elevator wall. Ms. Sally Parker, a spokesperson for the hotel, said that as a historic building the Regency is exempt from certain types of safety certification.

The Fulton County Coroner officially declared cause of death as "death by misadventure." No inquest is expected. It was established that Grandisson was alone in the elevator at the time of the incident, nor were any other persons in the deceased's penthouse apartments.

Acquaintances could offer no likely motive for suicide, discounting the recent sharp decline in support for Back-to-Earth following the yet-unsolved murder of Starfleet Chief of Staff Marcus van Diemen. Ms. Parker noted that Admiral Douglas T. Shepherd, van Diemen's successor as Chief of Staff, had breakfasted with Grandisson on the morning of the incident. Admiral Shepherd was unavailable for comment.

Grandisson's personal physician, Dr. T. J. McCoy of Emory Medical Center, said, "Mr. Grandisson was a very healthy man, considering that he was nearly one hundred years of age. He'd had some reconstructive surgery that kept him from space travel, but otherwise he was a very well man, a very satisfied man. I can't imagine anything so damaging that satisfaction as to make him take his own life."

Memorial arrangements have not been made public. The Atlanta office of Back-to-Earth Inc. announced that it is seeking contributions for a Grandisson Memorial Fund. . . .

It was almost painful to watch Zharn in action; he moved faster than the eye could comfortably track him. He seemed to flicker between the machines in the officers' Gym as if transporting, rather than moving; only the rush of air gave away his passage.

Kelly stood up from her seat near the door and walked toward him; Krenn stayed behind. Zharn stopped as she approached, an effect as if a running tape had frozen on a single frame.

"Do not touch me," he said, in a friendly tone. "I have a reflex—"

"The Captain told me."

"Do you have a second mission for me?"

"No. My name is Kelly. I am the Executive Officer aboard this ship."

"Honored, Executive Kelly. I am Zharn . . . I have not seen you, and I have been awake . . . for some days. Though there was the time I spent on my mission."

"I was receiving medical care. My shoulder was badly damaged."

Krenn leaned forward, wondering.

"I was badly hurt once," Zharn said. "I'm told it was many years ago, but I don't know." He moved again, around the Gym and back to Kelly in seconds. Then he bent his head, pulled down his loose training jacket to show the back of his neck. Scars like ropes ran down it. "My nerves were all broken," he said. "But the Thought Master Ankhisek mended them."

"Ankhisek is known for his brilliance."

Zharn smiled broadly. "Yes, brilliant! When he fixed them, they were better than new. The Thought Master says my nerves are four times as fast as they were before. And five times as fast as a Human's. Have you ever seen a Human, Executive . . ."

Kelly replied, "Yes, I have."

"They're slow. Really slow. I did well, this mission . . . but soon they'll freeze me, and I'll forget." He stopped still again. "I don't like to forget, but it's important that I not be wasted. So between missions they freeze me, and I don't get any older."

"You look almost my age," Kelly said.

"Well, I've had a lot of missions. Even if I don't remember them all, others do. And they say my record is glorious." Zharn flew into the boxing ring, triggering a holographic sparring dummy: he knocked down the projection in a moment, punched it three times as it fell, kicked it before it could vanish. Another projected fighter appeared, and Zharn demolished it as well. He did not look back at Kelly. He had forgotten her.

Kelly went back to Krenn, and they left the Gym.

She said, "How fast does he age, when he's warm?"

"Sixty-four times. Like the warp relation, to his nerve impulses."

"Then he must be only . . . a few months older than when we knew him. In his mind, I mean."

"He doesn't know. Or care. Are you sorry you saw him?"

She shook her head. "But I'm glad it was now, after the hospital. Before, I . . . it wouldn't have been good, to meet someone who was happy with not knowing who he was."

Krenn's communicator chimed. "Captain."

"Captain Krenn, the Ambassador is ready to beam up."

"Tell him there'll be a brief delay." He turned to Kelly. "Call Auloh. It's time to put Zharn back in his box."

*   *   *

Krenn pressed the door annunciator.

"Come in," Dr. Tagore said.

Krenn went in. Dr. Tagore was seated in a corner of the front cabin, reading. He put the book down without marking his place. "Hello, Krenn."

"Emanuel. I wondered if you would care for a game."

"My regrets, Krenn . . . I don't feel like playing just now."

"Is the one well? Or . . . does the one ask the wrong question?"

The Human smiled. "The one is well. And is honored by the question. Sit down, if you will, Krenn."

Krenn sat.

Dr. Tagore said, "I've told you about Admiral Yamamoto, have I not?"

"The three-fingered one, who played *pokher* well."

"Yes. Did I tell you how he died?"

"No."

"The Admiral was traveling by flier, alone but for attendants and a few escort fliers. There was a war, and it was a secret flight, but the enemy had broken the codes, and knew of it. And they sent out a squadron of hunters, to destroy the Admiral; which they did."

Krenn nodded.

Dr. Tagore said, "It must be understood that the Humans who ordered this did not . . . hate the Admiral. There were some who did . . . and there had been lies told, that he had no respect for his enemy, that he thought them *kuve;* but in the end, it was not hate that did it, it was the necessity of the war, that had already killed hundred thousands. Next to hundred thousands, what is the one, when none are *kuve?*"

Krenn said, "Did the one die well?"

"In his ship. With his hand on his weapon."

Krenn said, "Then perhaps we will meet. I will tell him of Maktai's three fingers. And another I know, who had only two." He understood the story, what it was supposed to say to him; he wondered if Dr. Tagore had told it to Admiral Shepherd.

Dr. Tagore said, "Diplomacy is the art of the possible. Have I said that?"

"Yes."

"But not the art of the necessary. So why . . . *why* are the deaths necessary, when I know something better is possible?" Dr. Tagore was staring, not at Krenn but past him, tears standing in his eyes.

Krenn said, as gently as he could, "There is death, Emanuel. If you had carried a weapon, if you had ever killed, you would know—"

"What makes you think I haven't?"

Krenn laughed, and said, "You told me, when you told Mak, that for all forty-four of your years . . . oh, I . . . misunderstood, Emanuel. Your ages are not like ours . . . you were older than forty-four."

"I was seventy-three then. I'm seventy-nine now. In three months, two days, six hours . . . you see, this I keep apart from Stardates . . . it will be fifty standard years since I held a weapon."

"You were a warrior, then," Krenn said, satisfied. *Now* he understood—

"Oh, no. Though the state did arm me. They gave me the key, you see."

"Key?"

"I put it in a slot . . ." He mimed the action. ". . . and turned it . . . and my wife was not in pain any longer."

The disease, Krenn thought, that was like the agonizer. He looked at Dr. Tagore: the Human was weeping freely now, bent forward in his chair with his hand still extended, turning the key in the life-support machine. For the first time Krenn saw him as small, helpless; but Krenn did not feel strong by comparison. He felt sick.

"You must," Krenn said, in Federation because *klingonaase* would never do, "you must have loved her very much, to do that."

"Did I? But it wasn't her I killed, you see. She had been dead a long time, her mind was gone . . . all I turned the key on was pain.

"I waited so long, while she suffered," Dr. Tagore said, his voice thin but steady, "because I thought, there must be a resolution, both moral and compassionate . . . it was selfish, literally damnably selfish, if I believed in Hell. Which I don't, any more than a Klingon. What extra purpose would it serve, in a universe already so backwards that death can be an act of love?"

His tears had stopped. He sniffled, a ridiculous sound. He said, "I don't ask you to understand, Krenn."

Krenn said, "I do not know if I do . . . but will you listen to a story of mine, that perhaps you will not understand?"

"Of course."

"Then I will tell you about Kethas epetai-Khemara," Krenn said, "and about Rogaine."

"Serkash II," Navigator Kepool said. "One light-day out from the Disputed Zone."

"*Zan* Klimor, parking orbit," Krenn said.

"Acting," said the Helmsman.

"*Zan* Kreg, signal to the surface: prepare to receive a Federation Ambassador."

Dr. Tagore stepped out of the lift. "We're out of Warp early, aren't we—*Pardon me?*"

Krenn said, "Grand strategic display."

A large-scale map, on which the Zone was no more than a streak, appeared on the display. Mirror was a white three-armed cross, Serkash II a circle.

Just crossing the Zone were three blue crosses. Annotations read BEST ESTIMATED POSITION.

Dr. Tagore said, "But . . . we've recrossed the Zone. We're in Federation space."

Krenn pointed at the blue marks of ships. "That is a planetary assault squadron," Krenn said. "It will arrive at our present location in approximately two hours. Its assignment is to destroy the colony on this planet's surface: twelve million Federation citizens."

"How do you know that?"

"It was in the Red File," Krenn said. "Section Two. Which was deleted before the File was turned over."

"Van Diemen's war," Dr. Tagore said softly. "How did he arrange *this?*"

"Our Admirals are not different from yours."

"No. I suppose not. And it doesn't matter if Starfleet arrives, does it . . . the result's just the same."

"Starfleet will not arrive, now that our escort has been evaded," Krenn said. He touched the communicator key on his Chair. "Special Communications, is subspace jammed?"

"On all frequencies, Captain," Kelly's voice said.

"You intend," Dr. Tagore said, "to fight them?"

"I intend to defeat their purpose," Krenn said, "by whatever means are necessary."

The Bridge crew turned, almost as one, to face Maktai. Mak stood up slowly from the Security console, pointed his hand past Krenn, at the Strategic display. "The Admirals have conspired to throw away Klingon lives as if they were *kuve,*" he said, in the coldest voice Krenn had ever heard him use. "This is no more than mutiny, and less honorable. Security stands with the Captain."

The sound that followed was not so much a cheer as collective relief.

Krenn said, "Since there is the possibility that the squadron will attack this ship, I must put you ashore, Emanuel."

Dr. Tagore said, "I . . ."

"You are the Ambassador. With you aboard, I may not unlock my weapons."

"Yes . . . I know. Will you, however, do a thing for me first? Will you open a subspace channel to Earth, for one hour—time for a message and reply?"

Krenn opened link to Kelly, gave the order. "Ready," she said. "Your message?"

"What is the Conference's decision," he said, "on Referendum 72?"

"Transmitted."

Krenn said, "What is Referendum 72?"

"To close the Embassy to Klinzhai, and recall the Ambassador."

"But—" Krenn said. "If they meant to hold such a vote, why wasn't it done while you were still on Earth?"

"Because there was a Klingon ship in orbit above the Earth," Dr. Tagore said, "and its guns were under diplomatic seal. They could not pass 72 until you were a long way off."

"*Kai* the Babel Conference, tower of courage," Maktai said.

"Strange you should call it that," Dr. Tagore said.

Krenn said, "Would we have been any better? And we would not have trusted the diplomatic seal."

"Perhaps you're both right," Dr. Tagore said. "There: that may be my last official diplomatic statement." He went toward the lift. "I'll be in my cabin . . . call me when the reply comes."

Krenn went to him instead, along with Kelly, and Maktai.

Dr. Tagore opened the door, saw the three of them, said, "Oh, my, is it as bad as all that? Please come in, don't mind the mess." The Human had been folding clothes, stacking them on the furniture: his library was already folded into its case and sealed, sitting in the middle of the floor.

Kelly said, "The referendum to recall has passed. The final vote was—"

"Don't tell me that . . . not yet. I'll find it out soon enough. Just tell me—was it close?"

"Neither close nor overwhelming."

Dr. Tagore sighed. "Not even with a bang. Well. Under the circumstances, I don't suppose I will be allowed to travel to Klinzhai; someone else will have to close the Embassy office." He said to Maktai, "Tell them to be careful, disposing of the encryption machine; it's obsolete anyway, and it really does contain a destruction charge."

Krenn said, "The squadron will arrive in seventy minutes. We have made arrangements to put you ashore . . . they'll probably meet you with weapons drawn, but I don't think they'll harm you."

"I'm sure they won't. I'm the most harmless of men."

Krenn said, in the Federation language, "Trouble rather the tiger in his lair than the sage amongst his books. For to you Kingdoms and their armies are things mighty and enduring, but to him they are but toys of the moment, to be overturned by the flicking of a finger."

Dr. Tagore had stopped still, a half-folded shirt draped over his arm. "So now you understand," he said, very quietly, "what it is the books have to say."

"It is a Klingon faith as well."

Dr. Tagore put down the shirt. "Yes . . . you told me. . . ."

Krenn tensed. He had not intended that speech for Kelly or Mak. Yet he had said it, as if he wanted it heard.

". . . that there were no more Thought Admirals."

Krenn relaxed, nodded. "How soon will you be ready to beam down?"

"Oh, everything important is packed," the Human said, indicating the library case. "But I'd like to ask the Captain's permission to remain aboard. Until . . . whatever happens, is over."

"And if there is a combat? I will not be able to lower shields, to transport you to safety." It was only the truth: Antaan's penetration technique would not work through *Mirror*'s shields. Nor anyone else's, soon enough.

"Well, I am no longer an ambassador, which eliminates that objection. If there is a combat, I will do my best not to interfere. And not to be killed too early . . .

"Our destinies are already interlocked, Krenn. It is too late to separate them."

Krenn nodded slowly. He turned to Kelly. "Have engineering rig a Flag Commander's Chair on the Bridge."

She said, "Dr. Tagore may use my station; I can control communications from the Special Room."

"Which you cannot leave, if it burns?" Krenn said. Then, more calmly, he said, "No. We will all be on the Bridge. Emanuel is right; there are destinies that cannot be separated."

Mirror hung still, shadowed by a planetoid, wrapped in electronic silence.

"Hostile squadron two thousand kilometers and closing," the Helmsman said.

Krenn said, "Subspace is jammed, Communications?"

"On all frequencies, Captain."

"One thousand kilometers and closing."

"Tactical."

The display showed three D-4 cruisers in echelon; they filled the screen.

"Five hundred kilometers and closing."

"Weapons?" Krenn said.

"Preheats completed, Captain. All circuits show blue lights."

"Take pre-locks, then. But wait for it. Communications, on my command drop our sensor jamming, and open RF link to the squadron."

"Affirm."

"Range to squadron approaching zero."

The three ships passed over the one, barely twice a cruiser's length away. The tactical display seemed to show every weld and bolt and panel. In a moment they were past, impulse drives glowing. Triangles bracketed them on the display. "Prelocks," the Gunner said.

"Communications . . . action."

The main display showed a cruiser's Bridge, the face of a Klingon Captain. The view sparked slightly, radio-frequency communication rather than subspace.

"What ship is that?" the Captain said. He was young, and familiar to Krenn. "This is Kian, of *Fury,* commanding a special attack squadron. If you are a privateer, you may join us—"

"This is Krenn, Captain of *Mirror.* Pleased to know of your advancement, Captain Kian."

Dr. Tagore looked puzzled. Maktai went over to the Human, spoke softly into his ear. Dr. Tagore nodded, sadly.

"Captain Krenn? I . . . was not told you were in this sector. Are you not commanding the . . . diplomatic mission?"

"I was. But no longer."

"Then you may join us," Kian said, excited. "There will be high glory—"

"No," Krenn said, "you are mistaken." He turned to *Mirror's* Weapons officer, spoke a phrase of Battle Language.

Disruptors flared from *Mirror,* punching through thin rear shields on all three of the cruisers at once.

"This is mutiny!" Kian shouted, his teeth showing to their roots.

"Kelly, countermeasures," Krenn said, and the display picture broke up. "Helm." Krenn sketched course plans, and *Mirror* responded, rolling sidewise, keeping forward shields to the squadron.

"Incoming fire," Antaan said from the Science console, "three-eight, three-five, three-three—" He was almost as cool as Akhil, Krenn thought. The tactical display reappeared in time to flare blue, and *Mirror* shook with damage.

"One impact, two misses," said the Engineer.

"Damage report."

"Acting."

Mirror fired again, slashing across the starboard wing of the center cruiser. The scar glowed yellow, then white as the fuel plant began to burn: but the warp nacelle did not separate. Klingon cruisers were larger, stronger, than Rom Warbirds.

More shots came past. *Mirror* was hit again. "Engineer, that report?"

"Crew's quarters hit. Engineering, some damage."

"Special assemblies?"

"No damage there."

"Keep me informed. Weapons, repeat that last shot, target portside." Blue light cut into the cruiser's other wing. "Maktai."

"Captain?"

"I call for Security Option Two. Set for automatic destruct if we lose the Bridge."

Maktai pushed buttons, took out his key and inserted it in the board, touched another set of controls. "Option set. Security password entered."

"Kelly?"

"Executive's password entered."

Krenn worked his armrest console. "Captain's password entered. Option in force." There was a sound of weapon-shield harmonics, and curves bent on the Engineer's displays.

The Engineer stood. "I'd better get aft. If we lose any more inter-cooler capacity, I'll have to switch out a main, or we'll melt."

"Do it," Krenn said, and turned to the Helmsman. *"Zan* Klimor, I want *this."* His finger traced across the board. "Gunner, precision fire."

Mirror rolled again, sideslipped vertically past the lead D-4. *"Action."*

Light lanced from each ship to the other. *Mirror* trembled. On the other ship's forward pod, the Bridge deck exploded in a crown of fire. "Hit to our flight deck," Specialist Antaan said. "We were decompressed already: no explosion."

Dr. Tagore said clearly, "And if that ship had been set to destruct as we are?"

"Then we would all go to the Black Fleet together," Krenn said, not annoyed. Humans met Death too late in their lives. In many senses. "Is this not an acceptable outcome? *Zan* Kepool, pressors on the *khex,* before their second Bridge can assume control."

"Acting, Captain," the Navigator said.

The damaged ship began to drift, slowly on pressor thrust toward the other two. They continued to fire past it, then through it.

"Kai kassai, klingoni," Krenn said. "Gunner, two projections on the far cruiser. Your discretion."

The other Captain broke high, to avoid drifting hulk. *Mirror*'s disruptors found its ventral surface: there was light, and violent out-gassing, and the wound released cargo modules into space, some of them glowing with incident heat. Then the modules began exploding.

"That's bombardment ordnance, Captain," the Gunner said. There was an eruption inside the holed ship, and she shook from wingtip to wingtip.

Maktai said, "You were right. They didn't intend to capture the colony."

"What great glory that would have been, raining bombs," Krenn said, finally angry. "What a prize. I told Kian he was wrong."

"Captain," Antaan said, "*Fury*'s shields are dropping."

"Is he surrendering?" Dr. Tagore said.

Krenn turned. "This one would not. *Boost—*"

The center ship, Kian's torn-winged cruiser, fired all its disruptors at once, six blue lightnings at *Mirror*. The display darkened with light-overload.

Fire arced around *Mirror*'s bridge, and every light went out. Some-one cursed, in *klingonaase;* Krenn could not tell who. But it was a male voice.

The consoles lit again, then the dim red emergency lighting. Krenn felt lancing pain in his left leg, looked down: one of the repeater screens in the Chair near his boot had shattered, fragments ripping his trouser leg and the skin beneath. He looked around: there were small cuts and burns, no one seemed seriously hurt. Kelly was injured slightly as well, but that was all right; now they could mend her.

Krenn looked at *Fury*, growing huge on the screen. "What are their shields?"

"Still low," Antaan said, clutching a cut hand. "They're recharging to—"

"Hit the pod!"

The Gunner acted, firing without sensor locks: beams tore crooked paths across the curve of *Fury*'s pod, skipping off metal into space, leaving traces burning red.

Fury did not fire.

In the pause that followed, Dr. Tagore said, "Weren't we supposed to have exploded, a few minutes ago?"

Kelly said, "The verification cycle takes forty seconds. We recov-ered in thirty-one."

Dr. Tagore said to Maktai, "*Kai* Security checks."

Mak laughed.

Kelly said, "*Fury*'s trying to open link, RF channel."

"Accept," Krenn said.

The enemy Bridge was burning. Captain Kian was slumped in his Chair; it was not apparent what had injured or killed him. The Security Commander came into view, pushed Kian out of the Chair. He sat down.

"Krenn," the Commander said, "Krenn sutai-Mutineer, do you remember who I am?"

"Yes, Commander Merzhan. I remember you."

"Before you claim the victory," Merzhan said, "I have a message for you. It was given to me by General Margon zantai-Demma. Are you listening?"

"Captain," the Navigator said, "*Fury*'s boom is separating."

Without looking away from the screen, Krenn stroked his fingers on the command board. "I am listening, Merzhan."

"General Margon said there would be a time to tell you this, Cadet. I think this time is good. Listen well: there were no survivors of the line Rustazh. *None.* There was only a lineless one of certain attributes, which zantai-Demma had a use for.

"Do you understand, *tokhe Human-straav'?* Does your crew understand? Does your *kuveleta* consort?" He was screaming.

"Communications," Krenn said, "jam all frequencies. Weapons, action."

The display showed *Fury*'s boom moving forward from the main hull, on its internal impulse engines. Then *Mirror* fired on the vector Krenn had ordered, and cut the boom in two; the impulse unit, running light of load, tumbled and shot past the command pod, and was gone.

Dr. Tagore said, "Can he still execute a destruct? By remote control?"

"You understand well, Emanuel," Krenn said. "But he must do it by laser link; everything else is jammed. And it will take him a little time to think of it. *Zan* Klimor: this course."

The Helmsman looked at his order repeater. "Affirm," he said, not too steadily.

"When I was younger than you," Krenn said, "I did not hesitate."

"Affirm, Captain."

Mirror began to roll, her dorsal side to *Fury*'s hull, ventral toward the slowly tumbling pod, sliding into the gap between them.

"*Kai* the helm," Krenn said.

"Laser pulse," Kelly said.

"What's the phrase, Emanuel . . . about doors."

Dr. Tagore said, "We make a better door than a window." His voice seemed to come from far away.

Krenn nodded. "Gunner, free fire."

Mirror cut *Fury*'s command pod into scrap.

There was a cheer on the Bridge. Krenn heard Kelly softly singing "Undefeated." He turned around.

Dr. Tagore's chair was empty.

Krenn stood up, too late remembering his leg; but he caught the Chair arm, and did not fall.

Dr. Tagore was sealing the last of his bags. "You're hurt," the Human said, as Krenn limped into the room.

"I am well," Krenn said. Auloh had removed the splinters and sealed the skin. "And you?"

"Well enough."

"Did you find the fight dishonorable? I knew Captain Kian, as Mak must have told you: there could be no talking his prize away from him. He was filled with *klin* . . . I take no pleasure in his death."

"I understand this," Dr. Tagore said. "I am pleased that the colony lives. And I am pleased that you are alive, and the others of the crew. And yes, *yes,* I was thrilled, in the thick of the battle. But the universe is still backwards. Don't ask me to be more pleased than this." He sat down on one of his cases. There was a long, quiet pause.

Krenn said, "You are correct, Emanuel. I destroyed Merzhan in anger, and not for any war that might or might not have been."

Dr. Tagore said, "I did not understand all the one said. But I think the epetai-Khemara would be proud of a student who could defeat three ships with one."

Krenn said nothing.

"I am a man of the Federation," Dr. Tagore said "not its center, but its fringe, yet still within it. But not all people born in Federation space belong. Some go off to the Pioneer Corps, or alone to mine planetoids. Some find that dark country which is madness, and we cannot bring them back, because they are happier there than ever they were sane.

"When a Klingon is born, Krenn, and the one cannot be a Klingon . . . where can the one go?"

Krenn touched the wall communicator. "Dr. Tagore's baggage is to be taken to the Transporter Room." He released the call key, smiled. *"Pozhalasta prishl'yiti bagazh.* One of the first things I ever learned to say in your language. I have never had the chance to use it."

Dr. Tagore smiled, said in *klingonaase,* " 'Where are the secret military installations?' I never got to use that one, either."

Krenn laughed aloud. He took Dr. Tagore's arm, and led him from the room; he was laughing too hard to speak.

They took the lift down the boom to Engineering; crew were busy making repairs, cleaning up debris and burn marks, moving wounded and dead. Few of the workers even noticed Krenn to salute. Krenn keyed a shielded door, and went through, motioning for Dr. Tagore to follow.

In the large chamber beyond were three cylindrical assemblies of metal and crystal, more than a meter across and several meters long, glowing from within: at the core of each cylinder was an assembly of octahedral crystals, of a deep red-gold color.

"Carter Winston's ring," Dr. Tagore said. *"Dilithium."*

"What you asked to see." Krenn laughed again. *"Mirror* is an intermediate design . . . we're only using our existing equipment at higher power levels. The ship is always on the brink of overload. But there is a new generation coming, the D-6, which will make full use of the dilithium focus. And then, everything Admiral Shepherd said, will happen."

"But . . . you had it all along."

"There was a race, who called themselves Willall, who had it. But they were *kuve,* and did not know what they had. So the Empire took it, as was only fitting."

Dr. Tagore said, his voice rather small, "And now you have the report, and know how little we have. I am terribly stupid, Krenn. I still am not able to think as a Klingon."

"No, you do not," Krenn said. "Do you think the Council will believe that Starfleet freely gave them a complete report? They will read the report, and assume the truth is greater by a certain factor, and finally see themselves reflected. And the Federation, for its part, will assume we have stolen its knowledge, and we are equal on its level. And there will not be a war. This is what you wanted: I do not think its achievement makes you stupid."

"Oh, my," the Human said, "oh, my." He seemed quite shocked.

"Are you . . . all right?" Krenn said, in Federation. "I should not like . . . for you to die now." He had heard that old Humans sometimes died of shock.

"This one is very well," Dr. Tagore said. "This one is farther from death than in fifty years. I feel like . . . Lancelot, when his miracle came."

They rode forward again. The corridor from the lift door to the Transporter room was lined with ship's officers, all saluting, but with their weapons out of sight; Mak's doing, Krenn knew. Dr. Tagore nodded to them, as he passed; Krenn saluted. Maktai passed the two of them through the door.

Kelly was waiting at the transporter console. Dr. Tagore's bags were stacked neatly on the passenger discs.

"I think it has been an honorable mission," Dr. Tagore said, "even if not a glorious one. You realize, Krenn . . . there won't be any place in history to be written . . . for either of us."

"There are kinds and kinds of glory," Krenn said. "And that which is done before the naked stars—"

"Is remembered," the Human said. "Yes. I think that's history enough to make."

There was a tightness in Dr. Tagore's face: Krenn felt an overpowering ache in his own jaw. "Emanuel—"

The Human stopped just short of the transport stage, turned.

"I would tell you . . . on whatever ship I have, in the White Fleet or the Black . . . there will be a place for you, epetai-Tagore. Even if you do not take it."

Dr. Tagore's voice was very strong, in no way old. "And if I should hear that you have passed from this life, Krenn, I will mourn you . . . even if you do not want it."

Dr. Tagore stepped onto the disc. He held up his hand, palm forward. Krenn saluted, and Kelly. They held the gestures for a moment; then Krenn said "Energize," and there was the click of controls, and the silent, golden light, and then nothing.

Kelly reached to null the controls. Krenn said, "Wait."

"Captain?"

"If I ordered you to gather your gear, including your medical data, and beam down here, for . . . treatment, would you obey?"

"*Mirror* would then depart?"

"You would not be abandoned. You would wait for . . . a ship to return."

Kelly said, "Only the Ship's Surgeon may order medical leave. And the Surgeon may not be ordered in matters of medicine."

Krenn said, "The Security Commander's message from *Fury*—"

"You explained that all of the line were dead, Captain. That the name was free for any founder to take. This was in no way contradicted." She touched the transporter controls. "If I am ordered to beam down, I will obey. But if *Mirror* is to return here . . . I should like to return with it."

"Very well, Commander," Krenn said. He touched the communicator. "Crew to cruise stations. Prepare to get under way."

The atmosphere on the Bridge was foggy and thick, the temperature luxuriously higher than normal. Krenn breathed deeply, smiled, nodded to the Engineer: they had earned it. And there was power to spare.

He sat down in the Command Chair, noticing that the broken display had already been replaced. The main display showed the wreckage of Kian's squadron, some of it still glowing. A bit of the bombardment ordnance exploded, far away.

But it was not just Kian's squadron, of course. It was Kodon's. And Margon's. And others' as well. It was all in Section Two of the Red File. And when it was known that the war faction had almost gotten its wish—against a Federation that had dilithium, while almost destroying the Contacts Branch ship carrying that crucial information back to the Empire—

The Intelligence Master said he valued the Empire above all things, certainly above any faction of councillors. And Krenn believed that—though he had also arranged other outlets for Section Two.

And the faction that had brought about the death of Thought Admiral Kethas would themselves die of an Imperial displeasure, killed by their own squadron of ships.

The last move of the Reflective Game.

Krenn wondered if Meth would reward him with the truth about his birth. Certainly they had spent high energies, at an event horizon. Or would Meth keep the information, as he had kept Kelly's pattern, always just out of the reach of those he used as weapons?

Krenn smiled. Three years ago he had begun searching for Kelly's past, and Zharn's; and, almost by accident, he had found his own. Meth was correct: information was power, secrets weapons. Krenn thought how strange it was that this secret, that he was not the son of Rustazh, had made him even more the son of Khemara; given him exactly the weapon with which Kethas had tried to arm him. The weapon of patience, against which Klingons had no defense.

"Ready for orders, Captain," the Helmsman said.

"Course for Klinzai, direct, *zan* Kepool," Krenn told the Navigator. "*Zan* Klimor, Warp 4 until we're across the Zone . . . then Warp 6."

Krenn looked at the stars on the main display. Federation space, he thought, but the same stars. There was the answer to Dr. Tagore's question: Where could the one go? Anywhere: the naked stars were the same.

Too late now. If they ever met again, in this life or the next, he would have something to tell Emanuel.

The Human had been wrong about one thing, though. Dr. Tagore believed that Klingons kept their pain, their grief, to themselves, never shared it. And of course that was wrong.

Was not revenge, Krenn thought peacefully, the final reflection of sharing?

The stars streaked past, and the ship was gone.

Epilogue

Captain's Personal Log, Stardate 8405.15

I am . . . fascinated, as Spock would say.

I am reminded of something Abraham Lincoln is supposed to have said, when he met the author of *Uncle Tom's Cabin:* "So you are the little lady who started this big war." And I keep thinking of all those log entries I have made, indelible now, that refer to the Klingons as "vicious, heartless murderers," or the like. I did that very casually. Certainly the Klingon record has been far from gentle. But I think I shall be more careful now, in what I say for the record.

I know that most of the crew have read the book, either during leave or since; ship's library has printed nearly two hundred copies. (Spock provided the information . . . one of the few times I can recall having to ask him twice for something.) The response has been very quiet— the non-regulation hairstyles have all gone—but still it is there, and I'd be a poor captain if I didn't see.

Especially notable has been the lull in the war of words between Spock and Dr. McCoy. I suspect there has been a temporary truce, of sorts: Bones will not bring up Spock's episode in the Embassy game room if Spock will not mention McCoy in diapers.

And though I do not have words to tell them, I think all the more of both my friends for what I have read: and for those small glimpses I am grateful.

And for the reminder that the Federation has never been perfect, and never will be, I am grateful as well.

The book may, as Starfleet officially insists, be almost completely fictional. I should be sorry if that is so: truth is always more interesting. And I speak as a man who once . . . once long ago, in the city of New York . . . was tempted almost beyond reason to change history.

I feel a sort of bitterness now, one I am not sure if the author intended. Perhaps it is because I *have* seen how things could be made different, given only small changes: I think of the Klingons I have just read about, all of them now surely dead . . . and I think of how much we have lost, by not knowing them sooner.

End entry.

KAHLESS

Historian's Note

This story takes place in 2371, the eighth year of Jean-Luc Picard's command of the *Enterprise*-D—after the events chronicled in "All Good Things" . . . and prior to those described in *Star Trek Generations*.

Prologue

In ancient times, there was a road here.

But that was more than a thousand years ago, long after the end of the so-called heroic age. The rolling terrain had long since been claimed by flowering brush and snaking vines and a dense forest of gray-and-yellow-streaked *micayah* trees.

Which made it all the more difficult to excavate, thought Olahg, as he watched a half-dozen workmen finish clearing a stand of *micayah* with their hand tools. They could have used disruptors, but this forest was prized by those Klingons who lived in the vicinity, and it wouldn't be a good idea to cut down any more of it than they absolutely had to.

The clerics of Boreth, of whom Olahg counted himself a member, had plied the High Council for years to obtain permission to dig here. If they hoped to excavate other sacred sites, other locations where Emperor Kahless had walked, it was critical that they treat *this* place with respect.

By the time the work crew was done with Olahg's appointed, twelve-meter-square plot, the *micayah* were gone. So were the mosses and shrubs and flowering plants that had grown in the spaces between them. All that was left was the pungent smell of *micayah* sap, unraveling in the wakening breeze to the shrill protest of distant treehens.

The foreman of the crew stood up straight. Turning to Olahg, he grinned through his sweat and his long black beard. A Klingon's Klingon, he had a brow heavy with thick hornlike ridges.

"How's that, Brother? Clean enough for you? Or shall I cut the rest away with a dagger?"

The initiate swallowed, dismayed by the foreman's gravelly voice and broad shoulders. "It is clean enough," he confirmed, and watched the crew move to the next designated section, where another cleric awaited them.

Olahg sighed. He had never been one for confrontation. Nor was he built for it, with his skinny limbs and his slight, fragile frame.

Certainly, that quality had not made his life easy. It had caused him to fall from favor with his father rather early in his youth, and all but ensured him a desk job in some deadly-dull Klingon bureaucracy.

Then, several months ago, Olahg had heard the Call. He had hear-

kened to the small, insistent voice within, which had urged him toward
the teachings of the legendary emperor Kahless.

It was the Call that had brought him to the planet Boreth and its
shadowy mountain monastery, and placed him in the company of the
other clerics. And it was the Call that had convinced him to spurn
worldly things, embracing a life of pious contemplation instead.

Olahg had fully expected to spend the remainder of his worldly
existence that way—sitting around a smoking firepit with his brethren,
seeking visions in the scented fumes. He had grown comfortable with
the prospect. He had even convinced himself that he was happy.

However, only a few weeks after his arrival on Boreth, the wisdom
of Kahless began to lose its appeal. Or perhaps not the wisdom itself,
but the rather austere way in which it was handed down to Kahless's
disciples.

He came to long for a more personal relationship with the object of
his admiration. He yearned for an audience with the great, glorious
Kahless himself—or, failing that, the being made from Kahless's
genetic material who had been named the Empire's ceremonial
emperor a few years earlier.

But petition as he might, Olahg could not seem to win such an audience. He was told time and again that Emperor Kahless was too busy,
that his duties kept him away from Boreth—though when that changed,
he would surely visit the monastery.

When he could find the time.

Even though it was in that monastery that the clone had been created. Even though it was the community of clerics on Boreth to whom
the emperor owed his very existence.

The idea was a festering wound in Olahg's soul. He couldn't sleep
for the ingratitude of it, the injustice—the need he couldn't seem to fill.

And the spiritual Kahless was no more accessible. Though Olahg
sat before the prayer pit until his face grew raw with its heat, no visions
came to him. It was as if he had been abandoned, spurned by the icon
of his faith as surely as he had been spurned by everyone else in his
life.

Koroth, chief guardian of the monastery, had told him that Kahless
was testing him, that the emperor had something special in mind for
him. But as much as Olahg honored and respected Koroth for his
insight, that was difficult for him to believe.

More and more, he felt alone, apart. And he came to resent the very
personage he was supposed to worship.

Shaking his head, the initiate surveyed the patch of earth that had
been cleared for him. The severed ends of stray *micayah* roots still
stung his nostrils with their pungency. Later, the excavation teams

would move in—not only here, but in all those other places the ground had been cleared.

Then the digging would begin in earnest. For, according to the clerics' best guess, this was the area where the historical Kahless made camp on the long trek from his fortress to *Sto-Vo-Kor*.

Sto-Vo-Kor, of course, was the Klingon afterlife, to which Kahless disappeared after his death. It was a leap of faith to believe in such a place, but Olahg had done so wholeheartedly. At least, in the beginning.

The initiate knelt and picked up a handful of earth. It was rife with tiny bits of rock.

Was it possible that Kahless had really stopped at this spot and laid down his burden? That he had stretched out beneath the heavens here? Perhaps even spent his last night on Qo'noS in this place, breathing the fragrant air and taking in the sight of all the stars?

Allowing the loose earth to sift through his fingers, Olahg stood and brushed off his palms. It would be difficult to find conclusive proof that Kahless had been in this spot. After all, nearly seventy-five generations had come and gone since. Even if such evidence had existed once, he doubted that it would have survived intact.

That was not the way a cleric was supposed to think. It was not the way of faith. But it was the way he felt right now.

The initiate was about to look for his colleague Divok, to see if it was time for the midday meal yet, when he saw something glint in the rising sunlight. He smiled at the irony. Here he had just been thinking about what they might unearth, and an artifact had already presented itself.

No doubt, it would turn out to be a sign from Kahless that Olahg's faith had been well-placed, and that the universe's cosmic plan would now be revealed to him. He grunted derisively. Yes—and after that, spotted *targs* would sing Klingon opera from the rooftops.

More likely, it was some piece of junk cast aside as someone strolled through these woods. Or maybe it was the tip of some bigger piece of garbage, discarded some years ago, when this forest wasn't quite so large.

At any rate, Olahg wasn't going to get his hopes up. Not by a long shot. He had done too much of that already.

Crossing the small, squared-off clearing, he saw that it was indeed a piece of metal that had caught the light. As he had suspected, it seemed to be the corner of something larger.

Olahg kicked at it, expecting the thing to dislodge itself from the ground. It didn't. It was too firmly anchored.

His curiosity aroused, he knelt again and dug around it with his fingers. It was hard work and it made his fingers hurt, but in time he exposed a bit more of the object. It looked like part of an oblong metal box.

Getting a grip on the box with both hands, he tried a second time to move it, but it still wouldn't budge. So he dug some more. And some more again, as the morning light grew hotter and more intense.

Little by little, making his hands raw and worn in the process, he came that much closer to unearthing it. Bit by bit, it revealed itself to him.

He could see there were symbols carved into it. Ancient symbols, he thought, though he didn't have the knowledge to confirm that. But they certainly *looked* ancient.

Or was it just that he *wanted* them to look that way? That he wanted this box to be of some significance?

As his fingers were cramping, he collected sticks and rocks from outside the clearing to use as tools. Then he set to work again. It took a while, but he finally scooped out a big enough hole to wrest the thing from the ground.

With an effort that made his back ache and strained the muscles in his neck, he heaved and heaved and eventually pulled it free. More curious than ever, he laid the thing on its side and inspected it.

It was about a half-meter long, made of an alloy he had never seen before, and covered with the markings he had noticed earlier. The metal was discolored in some spots and badly rusted in others, but all in all it was remarkably well preserved.

That is, if it was anywhere near as old as it looked. And, the initiate reminded himself, there was no guarantee of that.

He picked it up and shook it. It sounded hollow. Yet there was something inside, something that thumped about.

Turning it over, Olahg saw what might once have been a latch. Unfortunately, over time it had rusted into an amorphous glob. He tried to pry it open with his fingers, but without success. Finally, he picked up one of the rocks he had gathered—the biggest and heaviest of them—and brought it down sharply on the latch.

It crumpled. The box opened a crack.

Only then did it occur to the initiate that he might be overstepping his bounds. After all, this excavation was to have been an organized effort.

But he had come too far to stop now. With tired, trembling fingers, he opened the box the rest of the way.

There was a scroll inside. Like the box, it was not in the best condition. It was brown and brittle at the edges, fading to a dark yellow near the middle. And the thong that had held it together was broken, little more than a few wisps of dried black leather now.

Olahg licked his lips, which had suddenly become dry. A scroll was mentioned in the myth cycle, was it not? It was said that Kahless had left his fortress with such a thing in his possession.

But for it to have survived the long, invasive ages since? The seeping rainwater, the corrosive acids in the soil? Was such a thing possible?

Then he remembered—the work crew had torn apart the surface of the forest floor, along with the *micayah*. There might have been something—some rock, perhaps—protecting the box and its contents from the elements. Still, he didn't know if that could be an explanation or not. He was not a scientist. He was a cleric.

Carefully, ever so carefully, Olahg picked up the scroll and unrolled it. Fortunately, it didn't go to pieces in his hands. It was still supple enough to reveal its secrets to him.

The thing was written in a bold, flowing hand. However, it was upside down. Turning it around, he held it close and read the words inscribed in it.

The first few words gave him an indication of what the rest would be like—but he couldn't stop there. He felt compelled to read more of it, and even more than that, stuck like a fish on a particularly cruel and vicious spear.

For what words they were! What terrible words indeed!

The initiate's heart began to pound as he realized what he had stumbled on. His eyes began to hurt, as if pierced by what they had seen.

For if it was true—if the scroll was indeed what it purported to be—this was the work of Kahless the Unforgettable. Yet at the same time, it was the greatest blasphemy Olahg could imagine. He looked around, to make sure no one had seen him reading it.

No one had. The other clerics were all tending to their own sections. He could barely see them in their robes through the intervening forest.

He had to put the scroll back in the box. He had to make sure it was never seen. Not by anyone, ever.

Or . . . did he? The initiate swallowed, allowing his eyes to feast again on the scroll and its contents.

Certainly, one could call it blasphemy to let this get out. But it might be a greater blasphemy *not* to.

If this was the authentic word of Kahless, should it not be given a voice? Should it not be heeded, as the emperor no doubt intended—for why else would he have written it?

Olahg hesitated for a moment, his head feeling as if it would burst like a *caw'va* melon left in the sun. He had never in his life had to make this kind of decision. Nor was he likely to again.

Peace? Or truth? His hands clenched into fists. He pounded the ground on either side of the open scroll, hoping for an answer, wishing one would be handed down to him.

And then he realized . . . it already had been. He had been allowed to find the thing. He had been given a gift. And a gift, he had been taught, should never be wasted.

Rolling up the scroll, he secreted it in the folds of his robes. Then he walked away from the cleared patch of earth, through the still-dense forest of *micayah* trees.

None of the other clerics noticed. No one stopped him.

A sign that he was doing the right thing, Olahg inferred. If he traveled quickly, without rest, he could make it to the city by morning.

One: The Modern Age

The volcano shot glorious red streamers of molten rock high into the ponderous gray heavens. But that was just the first sign of its intentions, the first indication of its fury.

A moment later, in an angry spasm of disdain for the yellow and green plant life that grew along its black, fissured flanks, a tide of hissing, red lava came bubbling over the rim of the volcano's crater. The tide separated into rivers, the rivers into a webwork of narrow streams—each one radiating a horrible heat, each one intensely eager to consume all in its path.

In the distance, thunder rumbled. At least, it appeared to be thunder. In fact, it was the volcano itself, preparing to heave another load of lava out of the scorched and tormented earth.

The name of this severe and lonely place was Kri'stak. It was the first time the volcano had erupted in nearly a hundred years.

A Klingon warrior was making his way up the volcano's northern slope, down where the rivers of spitting, bubbling lava were still few and far between.

The warrior wore a dark leather tunic, belted at the waist and embossed with sigils of Klingon virtues. The shoulders of the garment were decorated with bright silver circlets. On his feet, he wore heavy leather boots that reached to midthigh; on his hands, leather gloves reinforced with an iron alloy.

The warrior's enterprise seemed insane, suicidal. This was a volcano in full eruption, with death streaming from its every fissure. But that didn't seem to dissuade him in the least.

Picking his way carefully over the pitted slope, remaining faithful to the higher ridges the lava couldn't reach, he continued his progress. When he reached a dead end, he simply leaped over the molten rock to find a more promising route elsewhere.

At times, the figure vanished behind a curtain of smoke and cinders, or lost his footing and slipped behind some outcropping. Yet, over and over, he emerged from the setback unscathed, a look of renewed determination on his face. Sweat pouring from his bright red brow, he pushed himself from path to treacherous path, undaunted.

Unfortunately, his choices were narrowing radically as he

approached the lip of the crater. There was only one ridge that looked to give him a chance of making it to the top—and that was guarded by a hellishly wide channel.

It wasn't impossible for him to make the leap across. However, as drained as he must have been by this point, and as burdened by his heavy leather tunic, it was highly unlikely he'd survive the attempt.

Spreading his feet apart to steady himself, the warrior raised his arms above his head and unfastened the straps that held his tunic in place. Then he tore it from him and flung it into the river of lava below, as if tendering a sacrifice to some dark and ravenous demon.

In moments, the tunic was consumed, leaving little more than a thin, greasy trail of smoke. Nor would the Klingon leave the world much more than that, if he failed.

But he hadn't come this far to be turned away now. Taking a few steps back until his back was to yet another brink, the warrior put his head down and got his legs churning beneath him: It was difficult for his boots to find purchase on the slick, steamy rock, but the Klingon worked up more speed than appeared possible.

At the last possible moment, he planted his right foot and launched himself out over the channel. There was a point in time, the size and span of a long, deep, breath, when the warrior seemed to hover over the crackling lava flow, his legs bicycling beneath him.

Until he completed his flight by smashing into the sharp, craggy surface of the opposite ridge. For a moment, it looked as if he had safely avoided the lava, as if he had come away with the victory.

Then he began sliding backward into the river of fire. Desperately, frantically, the warrior dug for purchase with fingers and knees and whatever else he could bring to bear—even his cheek. Yet still he slid.

The rocky surface tore at the warrior's chest and his face, but he wouldn't give into it. Slowly, inexorably, by dint of blood and bone, he stopped himself. Then he began to pull himself up from the edge of death's domain.

Finally, when he felt he was past the danger, he lay on the ground—gulping down breath after breath, until he found the strength to go on. Dragging himself to his feet, too drained even to sweat, he stumbled the rest of the way up the ridge like a man drunk with too much blood-wine.

At the brink of the crater, the Klingon fell to his knees, paused, and pulled a knife from the inside of his boot. It was a *d'k tahg,* a ceremonial dagger. Lifting a thick lock of hair from his head, he held it out taut and brought the edge of his blade across it. Strand by severed strand, it came free in his hand.

For a long moment, he stared at the lock of hair. Then he dropped it into the molten chaos inside the volcano, where it vanished instantly.

But only for a moment or two. Then it shot up again on a geyser of hot, sulfurous air. Except now it was coated with molten, flaming rock, an object of unearthly beauty, no longer recognizable as a part of him.

Mesmerized, the warrior extended his hand, as if to grasp the thing. Incredibly, it tumbled toward him, end over end. And as if by magic, it fell right into the palm of his gauntleted hand.

Bringing it closer to him, the Klingon gazed at it with narrowed eyes, as if unable to believe what had happened. Then, his glove smoking as it cradled the lava-dipped lock, he smiled a hollow-cheeked smile—and started his journey down the mountain.

Worf, son of Mogh, hung in the sky high above it all, a spectator swathed in moist, dark cloud-vapors, his eyes and nose stinging from the hot flakes of ash that swirled like tiny twisters through the air.

He hovered like some ancient god, defying gravity, hair streaming in the wind like a banner. But no god ever felt so troubled, so unsettled—so pierced to the heart.

For a moment, all too brief, he had been drawn to the spectacle, to its mysticism and its majesty. Then the moment passed, and he was left as troubled as before.

"Mister Worf?"

The Klingon turned—and found himself facing Captain Picard, who was walking toward him through the clouds as if there were an invisible floor beneath him.

The captain had come from the corridor outside the holodeck, which was still partially visible as the oddly shaped doors of the facility slid shut behind him. It wasn't until they were completely closed that Picard became subject to the same winds that buffeted Worf.

The captain smiled politely and tilted his head toward the volcano. "I hope I'm not interrupting anything important," he said.

Inwardly, the Klingon winced at the suggestion. Certainly, it had *seemed* important when he entered the holodeck half an hour ago. There had been the possibility of solace, of affirmation. But the experience had fallen far short of his expectations.

"No," he lied. "Nothing important. I am merely reenacting the myth of Kahless's labors at the Kri'stak Volcano."

Picard nodded. "Yes, of course . . . the one in which he dips a strand of his hair into the lava." His brow wrinkled as he tried to remember. "After that, he plunged the flaming lock into Lake Lusor—and twisted it into a revolutionary new form of blade, which no Klingon had ever seen before."

Worf had to return the human's smile. Without a doubt, Picard knew his Klingon lore—perhaps as well as the average Klingon. And in this case even better, because this particular legend had been nurtured by a select few until just a few years ago.

"That is correct," he confirmed.

Pointing to the northern slope of the volcano, he showed the captain Kahless's position. The emperor-to-be had hurled himself across the deep channel again—this time with a bit less effort, perhaps, thanks to the improvement in the terrain he was leaping from—and was descending the mountainside, his trophy still in hand.

It was only after much hardship that he would come to the lake called Lusor. There, he would fashion from his trophy the efficient and graceful weapon known as the *bat'leth.*

Picard made an appreciative sound. "Hard to believe he could ever have made such a climb in fact."

Worf felt a pang at the captain's remark. He must not have concealed it very well this time, because Picard's brow furrowed.

"I didn't mean to question your beliefs," the human told him. "Only to make an observation. If I've offended you—"

The Klingon waved away the suggestion. "No, sir. I am not offended." He paused. "It was only that I was thinking the same thing."

Picard regarded him more closely. Obviously, he was concerned. "Are you . . . having a crisis of faith, Lieutenant? Along the lines of what you experienced before Kahless's return?"

Worf sighed. "A crisis of faith?" He shook his head. "No, it is more than that. Considerably more." He watched the distant figure of Kahless descend from the mountain, making improbable choices to defy impossible odds. "A few years ago," he explained, "it was a personal problem. Now . . ."

He allowed his voice to trail off, reluctant to give the matter substance by acknowledging it. However, he couldn't avoid it forever. As captain of the *Enterprise,* Picard would find out about it sooner or later.

"You see," he told the human, "these myths—" He gestured to the terrain below them, which included not only the volcano but the lake as well. "—they are sacred to us. They are the essence of our faith. When we speak of Kahless's creation of the *bat'leth* from a lock of his hair, we are not speaking figuratively. We truly believe he did such a thing."

Worf turned his gaze westward, toward the plains that formed the bulk of this continent. He couldn't see them for the smoke and fumes emerging from the volcano, but he knew they were there nonetheless.

"It was out there," he continued, "that Kahless is said to have wrestled with his brother Morath for twelve days and twelve nights, after his brother lied and shamed their clan. It was out there that Kahless used the *bat'leth* he created to slay the tyrant Molor—and it was out there that the emperor united all Klingons under a banner of duty and honor."

"Not just stories," Picard replied, demonstrating his understanding. "Each one a truth, no matter how impossible it might seem in the cold light of logic."

"Yes," said Worf. "Each one a truth." He turned back to his captain. "Or at least, they *were*." He frowned, despite himself.

"Were?" Picard prodded. He hung there in the shifting winds, clouds writhing behind him like a monstrous serpent in terrible torment. "What's happened to change things?"

The Klingon took his time gathering his thoughts. Still, it was not an easy matter to talk about.

"I have heard from the emperor," he began.

The captain looked at him with unconcealed interest. "Kahless, you mean? I trust he's in good health."

Worf nodded. "You need not worry on that count. Physically, he is in fine health."

In other words, no one had tried to assassinate him. In the corridors of Klingon government, that was a very real concern—though to Worf's knowledge, Kahless hadn't prompted anyone to want to kill him. Quite the contrary. He was as widely loved as any Klingon could be.

"The problem," the lieutenant went on, "is of a different nature. You see, a scroll was unearthed alongside the road to *Sto-Vo-Kor.*"

Picard's eyes narrowed. "The road the historical Kahless followed when he took his leave of the Klingon people. That was . . . what? Fifteen hundred years ago?"

"Even more," Worf told him. "In any case, this scroll—supposedly written by Kahless himself—appears to discredit all the stories that concern him. It is as if Kahless himself has given the lie to his own history."

The captain mulled the statement over. When he responded, his tone was sober and sympathetic.

"I see," he said. "So, in effect, this scroll reduces Klingon faith to a series of tall tales. And the emperor—"

"To a charlatan," the lieutenant remarked. "It was one thing for the modern Kahless to be revealed as a clone of the original. My people were so eager for a light to guide them, they were happy to embrace him despite all that."

"However," Picard went on, picking up the thread, "it is quite another thing for the historical Kahless to be nothing *like* the legend."

"And if the scroll is authentic," Worf added, "that is exactly the message it will convey."

Below them, the volcano rumbled. The wind howled and moaned.

"Not a pretty picture," the captain conceded. "Neither for Kahless himself nor for his people."

"That is an understatement," the Klingon replied. "A scandal like this one could shake the empire to its foundations. Klingons everywhere would be forced to reconsider the meaning of what it is to be Klingon."

Picard's brow furrowed. "We're speaking of social upheavals?"

"Without a doubt," Worf answered. "Kahless revived my people's dedication to the ancient virtues. If he were to fall from grace . . ."

"I understand," said the captain. His nostrils flared as he considered the implications. "For a while there, Kahless seemed to be all that kept Gowron in his council seat. If that were to change, the entire diplomatic landscape might change with it. It could spell the end of the Federation-Klingon alliance."

"It could indeed," the lieutenant admitted.

He saw Picard gaze at the volcano again. Down below, Kahless had reached its lowermost slopes, though it looked to have cost him the last of his strength. Still, according to the legends, he would make it to the lake somehow.

"So that is why you constructed this program," the captain remarked out loud. "To play out the myths before your eyes. To test your faith in the face of this scroll's revelations."

Worf confirmed it. "Yes. Unfortunately, it has only served to deepen my doubts—to make me wonder if I have been fooling myself all along."

Still gazing at Kahless, Picard took a breath and expelled it. "I suppose that brings me to the reason I barged in on you like this." He turned to the Klingon again. "A subspace packet has arrived from the Klingon homeworld. It seems to be a transcript of some sort. I would have notified you via ship's intercom. . . ."

"But you were concerned," the Klingon acknowledged, "about the possible political implications."

"Yes," the captain confirmed. "Anything from Qo'noS makes me wary—perhaps unnecessarily so." He paused. "Any idea what it might be?"

Worf nodded. "I believe it contains the contents of the scroll," he rumbled. "As I requested."

"I see," said Picard.

At that point, he didn't ask anything of his officer. Nonetheless, the Klingon sensed what the captain wanted.

"After I have read it," he said, "I will make it available to you."

Picard inclined his head. "Thank you," he replied. "And please, continue what you were doing. I won't disturb you any further."

Worf grunted by way of acknowledgment and turned to watch Kahless begin his trek toward the lake. Out of the corner of his eye, he saw the captain make his way through the clouds and exit from the holodeck.

The Klingon sighed. He would read what was written in the cursed scroll soon enough. For now, he would track the emperor's progress from his place in the sky, and try again to stir in himself some feeling of piety.

Two: The Heroic Age

The chase was over, Kahless thought, bringing his lean, powerful *s'tarahk* to a halt. And a long, arduous chase it had been. But in the end, they had cornered their quarry.

The outlaws milled about in the foothills of the towering Uhq'ra Mountains, wary as a cornered *targ* and twice as restless. Sitting at the head of the emperor's forces, Kahless listened to his mount gnashing its short yellow tusks while he considered the enemy. As they were upwind, he sampled their scent. His nostrils flared with surprise.

There was not the least sign of fear in the brigands. In fact, when Kahless tried to make out their faces, he thought he could see their teeth glinting in the sun.

They were not to be taken lightly, he told himself. But then, cornered beasts were always the most dangerous kind.

"Kahless!"

Turning, he saw Molor riding toward him on his proud, black *s'tarahk*. Out of heartfelt deference to his master, Kahless pulled hard on the reins of his own beast. It barked loudly as it reared and clawed at the air, red eyes blazing, muscles rippling beneath its thick, hairless hide.

After all, Molor was no petty land baron. He was a monarch among monarchs, who in the course of his lifetime had seized half the world's greatest continent. And before long, if all went well, he would no doubt lay claim to the rest of it.

"My liege lord," said Kahless.

He had served Molor for seven years, almost to the day. And in that time, he had gradually won himself a post as one of the ruler's most trusted warchiefs. So when Molor rode up to him, his pale green eyes slitted beneath his long, gray brows, it was with a measure of respect.

"What are they doing?" asked Molor, lifting his chin-beard in the direction of the outlaws.

"Waiting," Kahless grunted.

"For us to make the first move," his lord suggested.

The warchief nodded his shaggy head. "It looks that way, yes."

Molor's *s'tarahk* pawed the ground and rumbled deep in its throat. "Because our numbers are about even," the ruler observed. "And because, with their backs guarded by the hills, they have the strategic advantage. Or to be more accurate, they *think* they do."

Kahless eyed him. "You believe otherwise?"

As Molor's steed rose up on its hind legs, the monarch's lip curled back. "What I believe," he said, "is that strategies only go so far. More important is what is in *here*." He pounded his black leather breastplate, for emphasis. "Our hearts. And their hearts. That is what a battle is about."

The warchief couldn't help but acknowledge the truth of that. He said as much.

Gazing at the outlaws, Molor laughed. "I will confide something to you, Kahless, son of Kanjis—for you have earned it."

The warchief made a sound of gratitude. "And what is that, my lord?"

"Battles are won and lost," said Molor, "before they ever begin. It is not the strength of one's sword arm that carries the day, but the manner and the timing of one's attack. And the look in one's eyes that says he will suffer nothing less than victory."

Kahless had never looked at it that way. But if it came from his lord, could it be anything but wisdom?

"The enemy may seem fearless now," Molor observed. "Eager, even. But then, they expect us to spend the afternoon talking, planning what we will do next. If we were to strike swiftly and unexpectedly, like a bird of prey, and show not an ounce of mercy . . ."

Molor grunted. "It would be a different story entirely, I assure you of that. Before they recovered from our first charge, you would see it in their faces—the knowledge that they will not live to see another dawn." He chuckled in his beard. "Fear. There is no more powerful emotion," he grated. "And to us, no more powerful friend."

As if they had heard and understood, the first line of *s'tarahkmey* rumbled and poked at the ground with their forelegs. A smile on his face, Molor nodded approvingly.

"Prepare yourself," he told Kahless, "and see if I am not right."

Suddenly, he raised his right hand. All eyes were drawn to it, instantly, as lightning is drawn to an iron rod in the midst of a thunderstorm. Then, with an ululating cry to spur them on, Molor dropped his hand.

Like bristling, black death itself, the emperor's first rank sprang forward as one. Molor himself served as its spearhead, with Kahless right beside him, their war-axes held high.

His heart beating like a drum, even harder and louder than the thunder of his s'tarahk's charge, the warchief tightened his grasp on the haft of his weapon. Up ahead, the outlaws loomed in the lap of the hills, scrambling about to brace themselves for the unexpected onslaught.

Then, almost before he knew it, Kahless was among them, slashing and cursing, whirling and rending. He could hear the bellows of warriors seeking their courage and the clangor of clashing weapons. He could smell the sweat of their beasts and the metallic scent of blood, feel the numbing impact of the enemy's weapons on his own.

This was battle. This was what it felt like to be a warrior, to pit strength against strength and fury against fury.

And as Molor advised, the warchief s actions were swift and ruthless. The blade of his axe grew slick with the outlaws' gore—and still he smashed and cut and clawed, meeting savagery with even greater savagery. He refused to let up, refused to stop until the last of the brigands cried for mercy.

Nor was the enemy the only one who bled and fell, to be crushed under the hooves of the snarling s'tarahkmey. Many of Molor's men perished that day as well. Kahless bore witness to it.

Then again, it was a good day to die. It was *always* a good day to die.

Only Molor had to live. It would be the greatest shame to Kahless and the rest of their army if their monarch fell in battle. It would be a failure that would haunt them the rest of their days.

So, even while he was trying to preserve his own life, the warchief was keeping an eye out for Molor. It was a good thing, too, or Kahless wouldn't have seen the outlaw giant cutting and slicing his way in the master's direction.

Of course, Kahless had noticed the giant before, catching sight of him as they pursued the brigands across the plains of Molor's kingdom. It would have been difficult *not* to notice; the man stood a full head taller than most of the other outlaws and had shoulders like crags.

Warriors that tall were often clumsy and plodding, but this one was an exception. As immense as he was, as difficult to knock down, he was also as quick with a blade as anyone Kahless had ever seen.

No one could seem to slow the giant down, much less stop him. And before long, he had hacked away the last of Molor's defenders, leaving the emperor alone to face his fury.

No—not quite alone. For as the giant's sword whistled for Molor's head, Kahless leaped from his *s'tarahk* and dragged his lord to earth, saving his life in the process.

When they hit the ground, Molor was stunned. But Kahless was not. Rising in his emperor's stead, he challenged the outlaw.

"My name is Kahless," he roared, "son of Kanjis. If you wish to kill my lord, you must kill me first!"

The giant leered at him, revealing a mouthful of long, stakelike teeth. "It will be my pleasure!" he spat.

He had barely gotten the words out before he lifted his blade and brought it slicing down at Kahless. But the warchief was quick, too. Rolling to one side, he got to his feet again and launched an attack of his own.

The giant parried it in time, but had to take a step back. It was then, in a moment of strange clarity, that Kahless remembered Molor's words: *"Strike swiftly and unexpectedly, like a bird of prey, and show not an ounce of mercy."*

Surely, the giant wouldn't expect him to press his attack—not when they were so clearly mismatched. But, heeding his master's advice, that is exactly what the warchief did.

He rushed forward and swung his axe with all his might. To his surprise as well as the giant's, he buried it deep in the place where the outlaw's neck met his shoulder.

The giant screamed, dropped his own weapon, and tried to pull the axehead free. But with his life's blood soaking his leather armor, he no longer had the strength. He sank to his knees, still striving with the axe.

Kahless didn't have the luxury of watching his enemy's blood pool about him on the ground. There was still work to do. Plucking up the giant's sword, which was not that much bigger or heavier than those he was used to, he whirled it once around his head.

Then, in a spray of blood, he used it to decapitate the mighty outlaw. As the giant's head rolled off his shoulders, it was trampled under the hooves of a riderless *s'tarahk*.

After that, the outlaws seemed to lose their lust for battle. And before the sun met the horizon, Molor's men had carried the day.

In the aftermath of the fighting, the monarch embraced Kahless and awarded him first choice of the spoils for his work that day. Molor slapped the warchief on the shoulder and said out loud that Kahless, son of Kanjis, was his fiercest and most loyal warrior.

In Kahless's ears, there could have been no more pleasing sound than the praise of his master, or the resultant cheers of his men. He had wrapped himself in glory. What else was there?

Three: The Modern Age

When the Muar'tek Festival comes to Tolar'tu, even the heavens lift their voices in celebration.

Kahless reflected on the uncanny accuracy of the saying as he made his way through the milling crowd toward the town square. The afternoon sky, packed tightly with low, brooding clouds, rumbled softly, as if in willing accompaniment to the brave sounds sent up by the festival musicians.

The Klingon felt himself drawn to the tumult—to the hoarse whistling of the long, tapering *abin'do* pipes, to the insistent strumming of the harps, and to the metallic booming of the *krad'dak* drums that echoed from wall to age-stained wall.

If all went well, the coming performance in the square and the mounting storm would pace one another like a matched pair of hunting animals, reveling in their power and their beauty as they ran down their quarry—only to reach it at the same time.

As Kahless edged closer to the ancient plaza and the space that had been cleared out in the center of it, he caught the briny scent of the fresh serpent worms offered by the street vendors. And as if that were not enough to set one's belly grumbling, one-eyed Kerpach—whose shop was set into the western wall of the square—was bringing out a particularly pungent batch of *rokeg* blood pie.

Glancing around, he saw that few of those who'd come here for the festival wore their everyday dark clothes without embellishment. That was a change. Just a few years ago, one might see only a few of the elderly sporting a blood-red glove or band in keeping with the festival's traditions. These days, even the smallest children wore red headbands as a matter of course.

But then, to this square which had seen so much, these were *all* children—young and old, traditionalist or otherwise. And it welcomed them with open arms, as long as there was joy and honor in their hearts.

After all, this was the oldest part of Tolar'tu, the only part that escaped the ravages of Molor more than fifteen hundred years ago. The town's ancient center, where—it might be said—Klingon civilization first took hold. *And had it not been for Kahless,* he mused, *even this place would have been consumed by the tyrant's greed.*

He took considerable pride in that accomplishment. Perhaps he was not the historical Kahless, as he'd once believed. Perhaps he was only a clone of that warrior-prince, created by the clerics of Boreth from the blood on an ancient dagger to restore a sense of honor to the Empire.

Still, he felt responsible for everything the first Kahless had accomplished. And why not? Could he not remember the salvation of Tolar'tu as if he had *been* there? Could he not recall in detail his every stroke against Molor's armies?

Thanks to the clerics, he had all his predecessor's memories—all his wisdom and ethical fiber. And, of course, all his good looks.

That was why he had to conceal his face under a hood sometimes—today being a case in point. Most days, he was glad to be the Empire's icon, a symbol held high for all to emulate. But even an icon had to be by himself once in a while, and now was such a time.

No sooner had Kahless edged up near the front rank of onlookers than the musicians changed their tune. The music became louder—more strident, more urgent. It sounded more and more as if the instruments were *yearning* for something.

And then that very *something* had the grace to appear. With a great, shrill burst of delight from the *abin'do* pipes, the afternoon's performers darted out into the center of the square. One was dressed all in red, the other all in blue. They glared at each other, feigning hatred, as if already in the midst of a savage combat.

To the audience's delight, the performer in red bellowed his purpose in a deep baritone: to teach his opponent a lesson about honor. A moment later, his opponent answered in just as deep a voice, echoing the words that had been handed down through the centuries. . . .

"I need none of your wisdom, brother."

The crowd cheered with mock intensity—and awaited the gyrations sure to follow the brothers' challenges. For this was no choreographed ritual, predictable in its every gesture. Though no injury was intended, there was no telling who would do what to whom.

And yet, when the performance was over, the actor in red would somehow emerge victorious. That was the only certainty in all of this, the only predictability—that in the end, Kahless would exact from his brother Morath the price of telling a lie.

Needless to say, this was only symbolic of the combat in which the *real* Kahless had engaged—a combat that lasted twelve days and twelve nights. Kahless recalled it as if it were yesterday—at least, the beginnings of it. The rest was all but lost in a stuporous haze, born of sleep deprivation and lack of nourishment.

But Morath had learned his lesson. And from that point on, he had never compromised the honor of his brother or his clan.

There in the square, the actors wove in and out of each other's grasp. They barely touched one another, but their grunting and their flexing gave the impression of unbridled exertion. Sweat poured from their temples and ran down their necks, turning their tunics dark with perspiration.

Up above, the stormclouds shouldered one another, as if to get a better view of the performance. Lightning flashed and thunder cracked unmercifully. And the musicians answered, not to be outdone, as the first fat drops of rain began to fall.

A second time, the actor in red called out to his adversary, demanding that he regret his act of betrayal. A second time, the actor in blue refused to comply, and the audience roared with disapproval.

As well they should, Kahless remarked inwardly. The only thing worse than incurring dishonor was refusing to recognize it as such.

He wished that puny excuse for a cleric—the one who claimed to have discovered that damned *scroll* on the road to *Sto-Vo-Kor*—could have been here to witness this. He wished the little *p'tahk* could see what *real* honor was.

Then, perhaps, he might understand the gravity of what he had done—the purity of the faith he had assailed, and the disgrace that attended such a bald-faced lie.

The scroll was a fake. No one knew that better than Kahless, who had lived the events it attempted to question.

For whatever reason, Olahg was lying through his teeth. But there were those who seemed to take stock in his blasphemy. After all, he was one of the clerics of Boreth, wasn't he? And as a result, beyond reproach?

In the end, of course, Olahg would be brought low for his deception. Kahless promised himself that. And like Morath, the damned initiate would pay the price for his crimes.

As Kahless emerged from his reverie, he realized the rain had begun to fall harder. Some of the onlookers, mostly old women and little children, went rushing for cover, of which there was blessed little in the square. But most stayed for the balance of the performance, which they sensed was not all that far off.

Sure enough, as the ground turned dark with heavy, pelting raindrops, the actor in red struck his adversary across the face—or so it seemed. Then again. And again. The actor in blue sank to his knees, defeated.

"I yield," he cried, again citing the ancient words.

Finally, the Klingon in red lifted the exhausted figure of Morath to the heavens and bellowed his triumph. It was echoed by the *abin'do* pipes and the *krad'dak* drums. And as the music rose to a harsh, discordant crescendo, lightning blanched the sky in a great, white burst of glory, blinding them all for a single, dizzying moment.

They were still blinking when the thunder descended on them like a horde of wild *s'tarahkmey,* crashing about their ears and drowning out all else. Only when it finally showed signs of relenting did the actor in red let his "brother" down, and both of them bowed deeply to the crowd.

The people thrust their fists into the air and beat on one another's shoulders, delirious with approval. Even Kahless found himself butting heads with a young warrior who'd been standing beside him, enjoying the performance.

The clone laughed. He was right to have come here, he told himself. This was what he had needed to lift his spirits. A reaffirmation of his legacy, an assurance that this was still Kahless's world and not that of some mewling degenerate seeking an undeserved place in the sun.

As the rain let up a bit, the actors gave way to a big, bald-headed Klingon in a large black robe. Kahless recognized him as Unarrh, son of Unagroth, a powerful member of the high council and one of Gowron's staunchest supporters.

Unarrh lived near Tolar'tu, in a place called Navrath. It must have been he who had sponsored the street drama. If so, it was only proper that he should address the crowd afterward.

"I trust you enjoyed the performance," said Unarrh, his teeth exposed in a broad, benevolent smile, his voice deep and inexorable as the tides of the Chu'paq Sea. "However, let us not forget the meaning of what we have seen—indeed, the meaning of the entire festival."

Good, thought Kahless. *That is what the people needed to hear, now more than ever. It was to Unarrh's credit that he should be the one to remind them of this.*

"Let us rejoice in the tradition handed down to us by our fathers," the council member intoned. "Let us place honor above all else, despite the temptations laid in our path by treacherous men—"

"How do you know?" called one of the warriors on the fringe of the crowd.

Heads turned with a rustling of cloaks and hoods. The rain beat a grim tattoo on the hard ground.

"How do you know," the man repeated, "that the cleric Olahg is treacherous? How do you know he's not speaking the truth?"

"That's right," called another warrior, from elsewhere in the assemblage. "He says he has proof."

"What if Kahless was a fraud?" asked a woman. "What if all the myths about him are lies—as dishonorable as those for which Morath was punished?"

"They are *not* lies," Unarrh maintained, anger flashing in his dark, expressive eyes. "The stories are as true now as they have ever been. In time, this upstart initiate will be exposed for the fraud he is. But until then, I will continue to believe in the virtues Kahless taught us— and more than that, in Kahless himself."

Well said, the clone cheered inwardly. *Surely, that would silence the doubters in the crowd.*

But it didn't. If anything, it made their voices stronger as they rose to meet Unarrh's challenge, their protests louder than the grumble of thunder from the persistent storm.

"What if Kahless did not invent those virtues?" asked the first man. "What if that was a lie too?"

"All our lives," shouted the woman, "we've believed in him, worshipped him . . . never suspecting our beliefs were based on falsehoods which bring dishonor to us all. What will we believe in now?"

"Rest assured," shouted Unarrh, "your beliefs were based on *truth.* Nothing can change that—certainly not a corrupt cleric, whose imagination exceeds his sense of propriety."

He darted a glance at a subordinate who was standing off to the side. Kahless knew the meaning of the gesture. Before long, the protesters would be picked out of the crowd and taken bodily from the gathering.

As they should be. Yet, the prospect was of no comfort to him. The spirit of the occasion had been ruined, at least from his point of view.

Kahless snarled. His joy turned to bile, he left the square and headed for his favorite dining hall.

Kahless grunted as he walked in, still hooded, and felt the warmth of the firepit on the exposed portion of his face. It was a good feeling.

Not that he was cold—at least, not on the outside. It wasn't even close to being winter yet. The fire felt good because it was a diversion—because it took his mind off what had happened in the main square.

Also, the clone was comfortable here. He had eaten his midday meal in this hall for the last week or so, having become a creature of habit since his "return" a few years ago.

There were three empty tables. One was near the firepit, used every day by an elderly man whose name he didn't know. The other two were located in the corners by the back wall.

One of them was *his.* Without removing his hood or his cloak, Kahless crossed the room and sat down.

In most places, a hooded man would have attracted attention. Stares of curiosity, perhaps a taunt or two. But not in this place.

It was run by an old woman whose husband had been killed long ago in the Romulans' attack on Khitomer. Widowed, left with little or no property, she had opened a dining hall in her native Tolar'tu, on one of the narrow, twisting streets leading to the main square.

Because of the location, the woman's first customers had been of the less-than-respectable variety—the kind with secrets to keep. She hadn't done anything to discourage them, so more showed up. And more.

It was the fastest way to build a business that she could think of. More importantly, it worked. Before long, the widow was dishing out more bloodwine and *gagh*—serpent worms—than anyone else in Tolar'tu.

And if the fare wasn't the best, and the walls were bare of decoration, so what? It was a refuge for those in need of one, and there was always someone with that kind of need.

Besides, Kahless had never felt comfortable lording it over others. Here, he didn't have to worry about that. And though the customers were rough-hewn, they weren't the kind to give up on tradition because of some worm-eaten, fungus-ridden scroll.

Before long, the serving maid approached him. She was a comely sort, though a bit too short and stocky for his taste. Then again, she *did* have a nice sharp mouthful of teeth. . . .

"What do you want?" asked the serving maid.

Kahless shrugged. "You?" he asked playfully. Even a man in a hood could enjoy flirting. Particularly now, when his spirits were low.

"Not if you were the emperor himself," she replied. "Now, if you're not hungry, I can—"

"No," he said, holding up a hand in surrender. "I know what it's like to incur your wrath. One can sit here until he dies of old age and never get a chance to order." He sat back in his chair. "How's the *targ?*"

"It was still alive a couple of hours ago." The serving maid looked around at the patrons. "Which is more than I can say for some of the clientele. But there's no heart left."

"Of course not." Kahless thought for a moment—but *just* a moment. "The liver, then. And bring it to me bloody."

She chuckled. "Is there another way?"

He watched the swing of her hips as she left him, then nodded appreciatively. He liked this place. He liked it a lot.

Out of the corner of his eye, he noticed two men walk in, their cloaks as dark with rainwater as his own. Like him, they left their hoods up to conceal their faces.

One of the men was tall, with an aristocratic bearing. The other was broad and powerful—almost as broad as Kahless himself. They looked around, then headed straight for the elderly man's table.

Apparently, the serving maid had noticed too. Halfway to the kitchen, she veered off and wound up at the table in question. The two men, who were about to sit down, turned to her.

"We're not ready to order yet," said the tall one.

The maid shook her head. "You misunderstand. I wasn't asking for your order." She pointed to the table. "This is taken."

The tall man glanced at the table, then at her, then laughed. "Taken, is it? You're joking, right?"

"Not at all," she replied. "There's a man named T'lanak who sits here every day. I don't know much else about him, but he's a steady customer, and we stand by our steady customers."

The broad man took a step toward the serving maid. He was smiling, but it was a forced smile, and Kahless had the impression it could easily become something else.

"This T'lanak isn't here now—and we are. Nor are we any less hungry than he's likely to be. Now go see to your other customers while we decide what we want to eat."

The clone frowned. He didn't like the way this Klingon was talking. As much as he would have liked to keep to himself a while longer, he wasn't going to stand here while two cowards bullied a serving wench.

He got up and approached the men. He wasn't more than halfway there before they noticed and turned to face him.

His voice was low and unmistakably threatening. "The serving maid gave you some advice. I suggest you take it."

The broad man tilted his head to get a better look at Kahless, though he couldn't see his face very well because of the cloak. Likewise, the clone couldn't see much of his adversary.

Then again, he didn't have to. Kahless didn't back off from anyone. In fact, he was actually hoping the situation would come to blows. As emperor, he seldom got the opportunity to engage another Klingon in combat. But as a hooded man in a place where everyone had a secret, it wouldn't be at all inappropriate for him to crack a few skulls.

"This is none of your business," the broad man told him.

Kahless grunted. "I've made it my business."

"Even if it involves the spilling of blood?"

The clone smiled. "*Especially* if it involves the spilling of blood."

The broad man's hand drifted toward his waist. Under his robes, no doubt, he had a weapon tucked into his belt.

Kahless prepared himself for his adversary's move. But before the broad man could start anything, his companion clamped a hand on his arm.

The clone looked at the tall man. For a moment, as their eyes met, he caught a glimpse of a long, lean face, with a clean-shaven chin and a wispy moustache that began at the corners of the man's mouth.

Then, perhaps realizing that he was exposed, the tall man lowered his face. Again, his cowl concealed him.

"This isn't worth killing over," the man said, his voice deep and throaty. "It's just a table, after all. And there's another for us."

The broad one hesitated, lingering over the prospect of battle. But in the end, he relented. Without another word, he followed his companion to the empty table and sat down.

Out of the corner of his eye, Kahless noticed that the serving maid was looking at him. Gratefully, he imagined. The clone turned and nodded, as if to say, *you're welcome*. With a chuckle, the wench stirred herself and went about her duties.

Kahless returned to his seat, quite pleased with himself. It was satisfying to engage an opponent eye to eye and stare him down. Not as satisfying as drawing his blood, perhaps, but pleasing nonetheless.

And yet, as he reflected on it, there was something about the encounter that didn't seem right. Something that didn't ring quite true. He glanced at the newcomers, who were conversing across their new table with their heads nearly touching. Only their mouths were visible.

They didn't look the least bit shaken by him. Nor should they have been, considering there were two of them, and neither looked feeble in any way. So why had they backed down so easily?

Unless, perhaps, they had even more reason to hide behind their cowls than he did? The clone nodded to himself. That must have been it.

In his mind's eye, he reconsidered his glimpse of the tall one's features. Long chin. Wispy moustache. The more he thought about it, the more it seemed to him there was something familiar about what he'd seen—something he couldn't put his finger on.

He scoured his memory. The man wasn't one of the clerics, was he? No, not that. A bureaucrat on one of the moons? He didn't think so. A retainer to some great House, then? Or a crewman on the vessel that had carried him to the homeworld from the *Enterprise?*

Then it came to him. The man was Lomakh, a high-ranking officer in the Klingon Defense Force. They'd met less than a year ago, at a ceremony honoring Gowron's suppression of the Gon'rai Rebellion.

At the time, Lomakh had been very much in favor— held in high esteem by both the Council and the Defense Force hierarchy. So why was he skulking about now? And who was he skulking *with?*

Pretending not to be interested in the pair any longer, the clone looked away from them. But every few seconds, he darted a glance in their direction, hoping to catch a smattering of their conversation.

After all, he had been created by the clerics with a talent for reading lips—one of the skills of the original Kahless. As long as he could see the men's mouths, he could make out some part of what they were saying.

Of course, in ancient times, a great many people could read lips, as it was essential to communication in battle and, thus, critical to their survival. It was only in modern times that the practice had fallen into disuse.

Fortunately, the two men were so intent on their own exchange, they didn't seem to notice the clone's scrutiny. With increasing interest, Kahless watched their lips move, shaping an intrigue that caught him altogether off-guard—an intrigue so huge and arrogant in its scope, he could scarcely believe it.

Yet there it was, no mistake. Sitting back in his chair, he took hold of his reeling senses. This was something he had to act to prevent— something he couldn't allow at any cost.

Abruptly, he saw a plate thrust before him. Looking up, he saw the serving maid. She was smiling at him with those remarkable teeth of hers.

"I hope you like it," she said, then turned and left.

Kahless glanced at the conspirators, whose heads were still inclined together. He shook his own from side to side. "No," he breathed. "I *don't* like it. I don't like it at *all*."

The question was . . . what would he do about it?

Four: The Heroic Age

As Kahless entered the village of M'riiah at the head of his men, he saw a flock of *kraw'zamey* scuttling like big black insects over a mound of something he couldn't identify. It was only when he came closer, and the *kraw'zamey* took wing to avoid him, that he realized the mound was a carcass.

The carcass of a *minn'hor*, to be exact. A burden beast, prized in good times for its strength and its ability to plow a field. By its sunken sides and the way its flesh stretched over its bones, Kahless could tell that the beast had died of hunger. Recently, too.

It was not a good sign, he thought. *Not a good sign at all.* And yet, he had found it to be pitifully common.

With a flick of his wrist, Kahless tugged at his *s'tarahk*'s head with his reins and urged it with his heels around the *minn'hor*. Otherwise, the *s'tarahk* might have been tempted to feed on the carcass, and there was still a possibility of contagion in these lands.

Riding between the huts that made up the village, he saw the central square up ahead. It was nothing more than an empty space with a ceremonial cooking pot set up in the center of it. At the moment, though it was nearing midday, there was nothing cooking. There wasn't even a fire under the pot.

Again, he had seen this before, in other villages. But that didn't make it any more pleasant.

Behind him, Kahless heard a ripple of haughty laughter. Turning, he saw that it had come from Starad. Truth to tell, he didn't like Starad. The man was arrogant, cruel and selfish, and he used his raw-boned strength to push others around. But he was also Molor's son, so Kahless put up with him.

Unfortunately, Starad wasn't his only problem. Far from it. There were others who grumbled at every turn, or whispered amongst themselves like conspirators, or stared hard at one another as if they'd break out into a duel at any moment.

That was what happened when one's warriors came from all parts of Molor's empire, when they had never fought side by side. There was a lack of familiarity, of trust, of camaraderie. And the wretched tedium of their mission only made matters worse.

As Kahless stopped in front of the pot, he saw that the villagers had finally noticed him. They were starting to emerge from their huts, some with children in their arms. A few looked almost as bony as the *minn'hor.*

An old man in a narrow, rusted honor band came out of the biggest hut. His cheekbones looked sharp enough to cut leather, and his ribs stuck out so far Kahless could have counted them at a hundred paces.

This, apparently, was the headman of the village. Its leader. It was to him Kahless would present his demands.

Nudging his *s'tarahk* in the man's direction, Kahless cast a shadow over him. "I've come on behalf of Molor," he spat. "Molor, who claims everything from the mountains to the sea as his domain and demands tribute from all who live here." He indicated the circle of huts with a tilt of his head. "You've neglected to pay Molor what's due him, either the grain or the livestock. Where is it?"

The headman swallowed, visibly shaken. Even before he opened his mouth to speak, Kahless had a fair idea of what the old one would tell him—and he wasn't looking forward to hearing it.

"We cannot give you the grain due our lord, the matchless Molor." The headman's voice quavered, despite his painfully obvious efforts to control it. "Nor," he went on, just as painfully, "can we submit to you the livestock required of us."

Kahless's stomach tightened. *Give me an enemy,* he thought. *No—give me ten enemies, all armed and lusting for my blood—and I will not complain. But this business of squeezing tribute from a scrawny scarecrow of a headman was not to his liking.*

Off in the distance, the *kraw'za* birds picked at the *minn'hor*'s corpse. Right now, Kahless felt he had a lot in common with those *kraw'zamey*.

He leaned forward in his saddle, glaring at the headman as if his eyes were sharpened bores. "And how is it that you cannot pay Molor his rightful tribute?" he asked, restraining his annoyance as best he could.

The man swallowed again, even harder than before. "Because we do not have it." He licked his dry, cracked lips. "You must know what it has been like here the past two years. First, the drought and the famine that followed it. Then the plague that ravaged our beasts." He sighed. "If there was nothing for us to eat, how could we put aside anything for tribute?"

Before Kahless knew it, Starad had urged his mount forward and turned its flank to the headman. Lashing out with his foot, Starad dealt the villager a solid blow to the head with the heel of his boot.

Unprepared for it, the headman fell like a sack of stones and slammed into the hard-packed ground of the square. A moan escaped him.

"You put aside your tribute *before* you eat," Starad snarled, "out of respect for your lord Molor."

Eyeing Starad carefully, a couple of the females moved to help the headman, who waved them back. Dusting himself off, he rose stiffly and faced Kahless once more.

"Starad," said Kahless, though he still stared at the villager.

He could see out of the corner of his eye that Molor's son was grinning at those he called his companions in the group. He had entertained them with his attack on the headman.

"Yes?" replied Starad, the grin still in place.

"Another stunt like that one," Kahless said evenly, but loud enough for all to hear, "and I'll put your damned head on a post—no matter *who* your father is."

The wind blew ominously through the village, raising spiraling dust demons as it went. For several long moments, Starad's eyes narrowed gradually to slits, and it looked as if he might carry the matter further. Then he whirled and maneuvered his *s'tarahk* back into the ranks.

A wise decision, thought Kahless. He'd had no choice but to reprimand the youth. Just as he'd have had no choice but to physically discipline Starad, even in front of these lowly tribute-dodgers, if Molor's son had piled a second affront on top of the first one.

A leader had to lead, after all. And like it or not, Kahless was the leader of this less-than-inspiring expedition.

Turning back to the headman, he saw that there was a dark bruise already evident on the side of the man's face. But it was not out of pity that Kahless pronounced his judgment—just a simple acceptance of the facts.

"There is no excuse for failing to pay your taxes," Kahless rumbled. He could see the headman wince. "But I will exact no punishment," he said, glancing sideways at Starad, "that has not been exacted already."

The villagers looked at one another, incredulous. Kahless grunted. "Do not rely on the *next* collector's being so lenient," he added and brought his mount about in a tight, prancing circle.

With a gesture for the other warriors to follow, he started to put some distance between himself and the village square—until he heard someone call out his name. A moment later, Starad rode past him and planted himself in Kahless's path, giving the older man no other option but to pull up short.

"What are you doing?" Kahless grated.

His tone of voice alone should have been enough to make Starad back down. It was a tone that promised bloodshed.

But Molor's son gave no ground. "There's no room for mercy here," he bellowed, making fast his challenge in the sight of the other warriors. "Molor's instructions were specific—collect the full amount of the village's taxes or burn it to the ground."

"There's no glory in such work," Kahless spat, sidling his steed closer to Starad. "I didn't come here to terrorize women and striplings, or to drive them from their hovels. If that's what Molor requires, let him find someone *else* to do it."

"What has glory got to do with it?" asked Starad. "When one pays homage to Molor, one demonstrates obedience to him."

Kahless leaned toward the younger man, until their faces were but inches apart, and he could smell Starad's breakfast on his breath. "You're a fool," he told Molor's son, "if you think I'll take obedience lessons from the likes of *you.* Now get out of my way."

Kahless's father was long dead, the victim of a cornered *targ.* But while he lived, Kanjis had imparted to his only child one significant bit of wisdom.

In every life, his father had said, there were moments like a sword's edge. All subsequent events balanced on that edge, eventually falling on one side or the other. And it was folly, the old man had learned, to believe one could determine on which side they fell.

Kahless had no doubt that this was such a moment. Molor's whelp might back down or he might not. And if he did *not,* Kahless knew with a certainty, his life would be changed forever.

As luck would have it, Starad's mouth twisted in an expression of defiance. "Very well," he rasped, his eyes as hard and cold as his father the tyrant's. "If you won't do your job, I'll see it done for you."

Spurring his mount, he headed back toward the center of the village. As he rode, he pulled a pitch-and-cloth-swaddled torch out of his saddlebag. And he wasn't the only one. Several others rode after him, with the same damned thing in mind.

Kahless felt his anger rise until it threatened to choke him. He watched as Starad rode by one of the cooking fires, dipped low in the saddle to thrust his torch into the flames, and came up with a fiery brand.

"Burn this place!" he thundered, as his *s'tarahk* rose up on its hind legs and pawed the air. "Burn it to the ground!"

Before Starad's mount came down on its front paws, Kahless had spurred his own beast into action. His fingers closed around the hilt of his sword and dragged it out of his belt.

Molor's son made for the nearest hut. Kahless measured the distance between himself and Starad's objective with his eye and feared that he wouldn't be in time. Digging his heels into his animal's flanks, he leaned forward as far as he could. . . .

And as Starad's torch reached for the hut, Kahless brought his blade down, cutting the torch's flaming head off. Wrenching his steed about sharply, Kahless fixed Starad on his gaze.

"Stop," he hissed, "and live. Or continue this mutiny and die."

With a slithering of his blade from its sheath, Molor's son chose the latter. "If I'm to die," he said slowly and dangerously, "someone will have to kill me. And I don't believe you have the heart to do it."

In truth, Starad was immensely strong, and skilled in swordplay beyond his years. After all, he'd had nothing but the best instructors since he was old enough to stand.

But Kahless had had a crafty old trainer of his own: the long, drawn-out border wars, which taught him more than if he'd had a courtyard full of instructors. He was willing to pit *that* experience against *any* man's.

"Have it your way," he told Starad and swung down from his beast, sword in hand. On the other side of the square, Molor's son did the same. In the next few seconds, their riding companions dismounted as well, forming a circle around them—a circle from which the villagers backed away, one of them having already grabbed the cooking pot.

It was understood by every warrior present that only one combatant—either Kahless or Starad—would leave that battleground on his feet. This would clearly be a fight to the death.

There was no need for formal challenges or ceremonies—not out here, in the hinterlands. Without preamble, Starad uttered a guttural cry and came at Kahless with a stroke meant to shatter his collarbone.

The older warrior saw it coming, of course—but it was so quickly and powerfully delivered that he still had trouble turning it away. As it was, it missed his shoulder by a mere couple of inches.

Starad's momentum carried him past his adversary. But before the echoes of their first clash had a chance to die down, Molor's son turned and launched a second attack.

This time, Kahless was better prepared for Starad's power. Bracing his feet wide apart, he flung his blade up as hard as he could. The younger man's blow struck sparks from the hard-cast metal, but could not pierce Kahless's defense. And before Starad could regain his balance, Kahless had sliced his tunic from his right shoulder to his hip.

No, thought Kahless, with a measure of satisfaction. *More than just the tunic, for there was a hint of lavender along the edge of the ruined leather.* He'd carved the upstart's flesh as well, though he didn't think the wound was very deep.

For his part, Starad didn't even seem to notice. He came at Kahless a third time, and a fourth, matching bone and muscle with his adversary, until the square rang with the meetings of their blades and dust rose around them like a dirty, brown cloud.

It was the fifth attack on which the battle turned. It started out like all the others, with Molor's son trying to turn his superior reach to his advantage. He began by aiming at his enemy's head—but when Kahless moved to block the stroke, Starad dropped his shoulder and tried instead to cut him at the ankles.

Kahless leaped to avoid the blow, which he hadn't expected in the least. Fortunately for him, it missed. But when he landed, he stumbled.

He was just starting to right himself when his heel caught on something and he sprawled backward. At the same time, Starad came forward like a charging beast, his sword lifted high for the killing downstroke.

Kahless knew that someone had taken advantage of his vulnerability to trip him. He even knew who it was, though the man might have concealed it from the others. But there was no time for accusations—not with Starad's blade whistling down at him.

He rolled to one side—but not quickly enough. Before he could escape, the finely honed edge bit deep into his shoulder, sending shoots of agony through his arm and leaving it senseless as a stone.

Striding forward, Starad brought his blade up again—apparently his favorite line of attack. Kahless could see the purplish tinge of gore on it—the younger man's reward for his last gambit.

The sight of his own blood was maddening to Kahless. It gave him the manic strength to get his legs underneath him, to try to lift his weapon against this new assault. But again, he saw, he wouldn't be fast enough. Starad would crush his other shoulder, leaving him completely and utterly defenseless.

He clenched his teeth against the expected impact, knowing it was treachery that had cost him this battle. But treachery, he knew, was part of life.

Then something flashed between him and Starad—something small and slender and bright. It caught the younger man in the side, forcing him to loosen his grip on his weapon and hit the ground instead of his target.

Out of the corner of his eye, Kahless saw a warrior step back into the crowd, lighter by the weight of a throwing dagger. He vowed to remember the man, just as he would remember who had caused him to lose his footing a moment earlier.

In the meantime, there was still a battle to be fought. Kahless scrambled to his feet and raised his blade before him, albeit with one hand. By then, Starad had pulled out the dagger in his side and balanced it in his left hand. It was clear what he intended to do with it.

Seeing that he had no time to lose, Kahless lunged as quickly and forcefully as he could—closing the distance between them so the dagger couldn't be thrown. With a scowl, Starad brought his blade across to intercept his enemy's.

But just this once, he was too slow. In one continuous motion, Kahless thrust his sword deep into the younger man's side and followed it with his shoulder, bringing Starad down like a tall tree at a land-clearing feast.

They landed together, Kahless on top of his enemy—and his first thought was of the dagger. Taking a chance, he let go of his hilt and used his right hand to snatch at Starad's wrist.

There was still a lot of strength left in Molor's son—so much, in fact, that Kahless nearly lost the struggle for the dagger. But in the end, he forced Starad to plunge the thing into the ground.

Weaponless, hampered by the sword in his side, Starad clawed at Kahless's face, scoring it with his nails. But the older man managed to squirm free, to lurch to his feet, and to grab hold of the sword that still protruded from between Starad's ribs.

He pulled on it, eliciting a groan from Molor's son. With a sucking sound, the blade came free.

Kahless felt the weight of the sun on his face. His wounded shoulder throbbed with pain that was only just awakening. Breathing hard, sweat running down the sides of his face into his beard, he bent to recover the dagger that had preserved his life and thrust it into his belt. Then he paused to survey his handiwork.

Starad was pushing himself backward, inch by painful inch—trying to regain his sword, which had fallen from his hands at some point and still lay a meter or so beyond his grasp. There was gore running from his mouth and his nose, and his tunic was dark and sticky where Kahless had plunged his sword in.

Molor's son was no longer a threat. Left to his own devices, he would perish from loss of blood in a matter of minutes. But despite everything, Kahless was inclined to give him one last chance—for by doing so, he'd be giving himself a chance as well.

A chance that Molor would forgive him. A chance that he might still have a place in the world.

Approaching Starad, so that his shadow fell across the man, Kahless looked down at him. Molor's son looked up, and all the hatred in him was evident in his bulging, bloodshot eyes.

"Yield," Kahless barked, "and I'll spare your life."

Starad kept on pushing himself along, though he never took his eyes off his enemy. Obviously, he had no intention of giving in.

Kahless tried again anyway. "Did you hear me, warrior? I'll let you live if you admit your mistake."

"I admit nothing," Starad croaked. "If I were you, Kahless, I would kill me—because otherwise, I *swear* I'll kill *you.*"

The older man scowled. There was no point in dragging this on. He was weak with blood loss himself and needed stitching. Raising his blade with his one good hand, he brought it down as hard as he could. Molor's son shuddered as the spirit passed out of him.

But Kahless wasn't through yet. Removing the dagger from his belt, he turned and threw it. Nor did the warrior who'd tripped him realize what was happening in time to avoid it.

There was a gurgling sound as the man tried to pull it from the base of his throat. He'd only half-succeeded when his legs buckled and he fell to his knees, then pitched forward face-first on the ground.

Kahless grunted. There was silence all around him, the kind of silence that one might fall into and never be heard from again. Withdrawing his blade from Starad's body, Kahless wiped it clean on the tattered sleeve of his wounded arm. He could feel the scrutiny of his warriors, but he took his time.

Finally, he looked up and commanded their attention. "Molor ordered me to burn this place if its taxes were not paid. I will not do that, nor will I allow anyone else to do it. If there is a man among you who would dispute that with me, as Starad has, let him step forward now. I do not, after all, have all day for this foolishness."

The bravado of his words far exceeded his ability to back them up. He was already beginning to feel light-headed, and he doubted he would survive another encounter. However, he knew better than to say so.

"Well?" he prodded. "Is there not one of you who thinks ill of me for breaking my promise to Molor?"

No one stepped forward. But one of them, the one who had thrown the dagger at Molor's son, drew his sword from his belt and held it high, so it caught the sun's fiery light.

A moment later, another of Kahless's charges did the same. Then another, and another, until every warrior in the circle was pledging his allegiance to the wounded man. Even those who'd ridden with Starad, and laughed at his jokes, and drawn their torches when he did. Their swords were raised as well.

Kahless nodded. It was good to know they were behind him.

But at the same time, he recognized their foolishness. He had made a pariah of himself. He had begun a blood feud with the tyrant Molor, the most powerful man in the world.

Kahless had nowhere to go, no place he could call home. And no idea what he would do—in the next few minutes, or hours, or days.

No—that wasn't quite true. There was one thing he knew he would do. Eyeing the warrior who had taken the dagger in his throat, he walked over to him, ignoring the mounting pain in his shoulder.

Bending, Kahless withdrew the blade from below the man's chin. Then he walked over to the warrior who had thrown it in the first place.

"Here," he told the man. "I believe this is yours."

"So it is," the warrior replied. He accepted the dagger and replaced it in its sheath, which was strapped to his thigh.

"What's your name?" asked Kahless.

The warrior looked at him unflinchingly, with dark, deep-set eyes. "Morath," he answered. "Son of Ondagh."

Kahless shook his head. "To follow me is to invite Molor's vengeance. You must be a cretin, Morath, son of Ondagh."

Morath's dark eyes narrowed, but there was no spite in them. "No more than you, Kahless, son of Kanjis."

The warchief couldn't help smiling at that. Then, out of the corner of his eye, he saw someone approaching. He turned.

It was the village headman. Behind him, a couple of women had come out with wood for the cooking pot. Another man was setting it up again in the center of the square.

"Your wound," said the old man. "It must be cauterized and bathed, or it will become infected and you will lose the arm."

Kahless couldn't help but see the wisdom in that. Bad enough to be hunted by Molor, but to do so with only one hand . . .

"All right," he said, loud enough for all his warriors to hear. "We'll wait long enough to lay hot metal against my wound. Then we will ride."

But he still had no idea where they would go or what they would do. Unfortunately, he had never been an outlaw before.

Five: The Modern Age

As Kahless marched the length of the long corridor that led to the Klingon High Council Chamber, he could hear the resounding clack of each footfall. He had grown to like that sound, to look forward to it—just as he had grown to appreciate the venerating looks he got from the warriors standing guard along the way.

It was right that his footsteps should resound. It was right that warriors should look at him with respect and admiration in their eyes. After all, he was *Kahless*.

But even here, the emperor saw, the scroll had taken its toll on him. The guards didn't look at him quite the same way as he passed. Instead, they peered at one another, as if asking: Is it true? Can he be the utter fraud they've made him out to be?

The muscles in Kahless's jaw tightened. He wished he had Olahg's scrawny neck in his hands, for just a minute. He would repay the initiate tenfold for the damage he had done.

Regaining control, he saw the doors to the central chamber were just ahead. Kahless resolved not to glance at anyone else along the way, but to keep his gazed fixed on the entrance. *Remember who you are,* he told himself. *Remember and be proud.*

He didn't pause at the doors, as other Klingons did. It was his right as emperor—even one who wielded no political power—to come and go as he pleased. Laying a hand on either door, he pushed them open.

Gowron was sitting in the leader's seat at the far end of the chamber, conferring with one of his councilors. When he saw Kahless make his entrance, he paused for a moment, then dismissed the councilor with a gesture.

Kahless stopped, allowing the echoes of the man's footfalls to become lost under the dark, vaulted roof. Gowron sat back in his seat and assessed his visitor, his eyes giving no clue to his emotional state.

The emperor grunted softly. Gowron was very good at that, wasn't he?

"What do you want?" asked the council leader, his voice—like his eyes—as neutral as possible.

Kahless straightened to his full height. "I would speak with you privately, son of M'rel."

Gowron considered the request for a moment. Then he looked to the guards who stood at the door and made a sweeping motion with his arm. Kahless didn't look back to see how it was done—but a moment later, he heard the heavy, clanging sound of the doors as they were shut.

It was quiet in the chamber now. The only sound was that of their breathing—until Kahless spoke up again.

"I believe there is a conspiracy," he said, seeing no reason to be circumspect. "A plot against you and your regime—and therefore, against me as well."

Gowron's brows met over the bridge of his nose. He started to smile as if it were a joke, then stopped himself. "And who do you believe is conspiring against us?"

Kahless told him about the incident in the dining hall. About Lomakh, and the things he had seen Lomakh say. And, finally, he told Gowron what he thought it all meant.

The council leader stared at him. "Why *them?*" He tilted his head. "They have always been among my greatest supporters. Why would they see fit to turn against me now?"

"One might look at a *thranx* bush for seven years," said Kahless, "and conclude it was incapable of flowering. But if one came back in the eighth year, one would see a vast profusion of flowers."

Gowron scowled. "In other words, they've been nurturing a plot against me for some time? And I was simply not aware of it?"

"It is certainly possible," Kahless agreed. "The question is—what are you going to do about it?"

Gowron's scowl deepened, his eyes like flat, black stones. "I will do nothing," he replied at last.

If this was humor, the emperor didn't appreciate it. "Nothing?" he barked, his words echoing around him. "Against a threat of this magnitude?"

The council leader leaned forward in his chair. "If there *is* a threat," he rejoined. "I have seen no evidence. All I have to go on is the account of a single individual—an individual with a great deal on his mind right now, who may have perceived a conspiracy where none existed."

Kahless could feel the old anger rising inside him. It was all he could do to keep from challenging Gowron to combat.

"You doubt my *word?*" he seethed. "You think I've made this up?"

"I think you believe what you believe," the other man responded, leaning back ever so slightly. "However, under the circumstances, your beliefs may not be grounded in reality. And I cannot accuse my right hand of clawing at my throat until I have seen its fingers reaching for it."

Kahless felt the anger bubble up inside him, refusing to be denied. "I saw what I saw!" he thundered, until the rafters shook with it. "And if you will not defend your Empire, I will!"

Gowron's eyes flashed with equal fire. But before he could answer, the emperor had turned on his heel and was headed for the exit.

Had it been anyone else, Kahless knew, the council leader would have rewarded his impertinence with a swift and violent death. But scroll or no scroll, he was still Kahless. Gowron didn't dare try to kill him, no matter how great the insult.

What was more, Kahless had suffered the greater affront. The accuracy of his observations had been questioned, as if he were some drooling half-wit, or a doddering old warrior who had outlived his usefulness. Gowron's words stung him like *pherza* wasps as he threw open the doors and stalked back down the long corridor beyond.

Seeing his anger, the guards on either side of him looked away. *A wise move on their part,* he thought. He was in no mood for further impudence on the part of his inferiors.

Until recently, Kahless told himself, Gowron's regime had benefited mightily from the emperor's popularity. Only now, as the controversy concerning the scroll reached new heights, did Gowron seem eager to disassociate himself from Kahless—to keep the clone at arm's length.

Kahless's mouth twisted into a silent snarl. Regardless of how Gowron had treated him, he could not let the Empire fall. And yet, he couldn't very well face the threat of Lomakh and his conspirators alone.

He needed help. But from whom? Who could he enlist in his cause?

Not the clerics who created him. They were thinkers and philosophers, useless in a situation like this one. And there was no one else he could trust implicitly, within the council chamber or without.

No . . . wait. There *was* someone he could place his faith in.

Someone *outside* the empire . . .

Six: The Heroic Age

There was a village in the distance, the largest one they'd seen since Kahless and his men had fallen afoul of Molor's power. The dark tower of its central keep danced in the heat waves that rose off the land, surrounded by equally dark walls.

A deep, slow-moving river irrigated the fields and the groves of fruit trees that radiated from the village like the spokes of a wheel. The wind brought the smell of the *minn'hor* droppings commonly used as fertilizer. Swarms of blue-gray treehens scuttled across the land, screeching as they hunted for parasites.

Kahless used the back of his hand to rid his brow of perspiration. Removing his water bladder from his saddle, he untied the thong that held its neck closed, lifted, and drank. At least they'd had no shortage of water as they traveled north, away from Molor's capital—and the river up ahead would provide them with even more.

He wished the same were true of their food supplies. Their military provisions had run out long ago, and thanks to the famine the year before, it was almost impossible to find fresh game for the fire. As a result, they'd had to subsist on a diet of groundnuts and stringy *yolok* worms.

"I wouldn't mind stopping here," said Porus, the eldest of them. He'd been in Molor's service longer than even Kahless himself, but he hadn't liked their orders back in M'Riiah any better than the warchief had. "I'm weary of slinking around like a *p'tahk,* and this place looks prosperous. I'll wager they have plenty to eat, and then some."

Morath, who sat on Kahless's right flank, nodded wistfully. "I'll wager you're right. Their location on this broad old river must have helped them during the drought." He bit his lip. "But we don't dare stop here."

"Why not?" asked a third warrior, a wiry, one-eyed man called Shurin. "What harm could it do to cajole some bread from the local baker? Or better yet, to swipe it while he's not looking?"

Kahless shook his head slowly from side to side. "No," he said, "Morath is right. Once the villagers get an idea we're outlaws, they'll report our whereabouts to the tyrant. And then a good meal will be the *least* of our problems."

With that, he pulled on the reins and pointed his beast's head toward a bend in the river. There were plenty of trees and bushes there to conceal them while they filled their waterskins. As his men fell into line behind him, he could hear them moaning about what they'd missed.

"I wonder how these people prepare *rokeg* blood pie," Porus sighed. "Baked in spices? Or in its own juices?"

"Spices," decided Shurin. "Definitely."

"How do you know?" asked Porus.

"Because that's the way I like it," returned Shurin. "If I can't have it in any case, why not imagine I'm missing the best?"

Kahless cursed the circumstances that had put him and Molor at odds. After all, he'd been as loyal a soldier as anyone could ever want. He'd been brave and effective. He deserved better.

Why couldn't he have been sent to collect taxes from a village like this one, where they had enough to pay and be done with it? Then he might have been gnawing on *bregit* lung and heart of *targ* instead of dreaming about them.

But fate had given him no choice in the matter. How could he have burned M'riiah, with all the misfortunes it already had to endure? Molor might as well have asked him to flay the flesh from his shoulders.

Given a second chance, he knew, he would do the same thing all over again. He would like it no better than the first time, he would drag his feet—but he most certainly would do it. And if *that* was not some particularly virulent form of insanity, he didn't know what *was*.

Kahless grunted pensively—then looked around at his companions. *And yet,* he thought, *if I am insane, I am not the only one. If I am diseased, my men are doubly so. And Morath most of all.*

The man had risked his life for a warchief he barely knew, just to ensure a fair fight. Given Starad's size and prowess, Morath had to have believed he was wagering on a losing cause. But, fool that he was, he had wagered nonetheless.

And when the fight was over, and Morath had had every chance to fade into obscurity, he had chosen to raise his sword and lead the cheer for Kahless instead. The warchief shook his head.

Unlike the others, Morath was closemouthed, his motivations difficult to plumb. He didn't speak much of where he came from or how he had been raised, or how he had come to join Molor's forces.

Nor would Kahless make an attempt to pry the story from him. If the younger man wished to keep his own counsel, he would have every opportunity to do so. The warchief owed him that, at least.

Up ahead, the gray and yellow *micayah* trees swayed in the wind, their slim, brittle leaves buzzing like strange insects. Kahless urged his mount toward an opening between two of the largest specimens, through which the glistening surface of the river was blindingly visible.

The animal trotted along cheerfully, for a change. *The prospect of a good watering would do that to anyone,* thought Kahless. Cool shadows caressed him as he ducked his head to avoid a low-slung branch.

He had almost reached the river bank when he heard a cry downstream, to his left. His first thought was that he'd led his men into an ambush. His second was that Molor would have fewer outlaws to worry about tonight when he took his evening bath.

However, as Kahless slipped his sword free, he saw it wasn't an ambush at all. Not unless Molor's warriors were all females these days, and naked ones at that.

What's more, they hadn't noticed his approach. They were too busy shrieking with glee, too busy pounding at the surface of the water in an effort to drench one another—though they were already as drenched as one could be. Clearly not the behavior of steely-eyed assassins.

Kahless couldn't help smiling. The females were so lovely, so tempting as they raised rainbow-colored sprays with their splashing, their dark hair making slapping sounds as it whipped about their heads. He'd had precious little time for lovemaking these past few years, in Molor's employ. Now he was forcibly reminded of what he'd missed.

"What have we here?" murmured Shurin, as he caught up with his chief.

Porus chuckled. "Something tastier than blood pie, my friend. Our reward, perhaps, for sparing M'riiah?"

"Not likely," grunted Kahless, putting his cohorts on notice. He wasn't about to let anyone take advantage of these females. They had enough enemies without making more.

On the other hand, there was no harm in watching, was there? Certainly, Morath didn't think so. He was so intent on the females as he nudged his beast up near the bank, Kahless thought the man's eyes would boil.

"Look at you," Porus jibed, elbowing Morath in the ribs. "One would think you'd never seen a wench before."

Morath shot him a look that was altogether too serious. "That would be none of one's business," he hissed.

But before he could say any more, his mount gave in to temptation—and surged forward over the riverbank, landing with a noisy *plash* in the shallow water beyond.

Suddenly, the females' heads turned. For a moment, no one moved and no one spoke, each group seemingly paralyzed as it took stock of its situation. Then the naked ones struck out for the nearest bank.

For no reason he could identify at the time, Kahless brought his animal about and guided it through the trees. Up ahead, he could see the females scrambling for their garments in a little clearing, where they had hung them on the lower branches.

Without even bothering to put their clothes on, they scampered away through the woods. Not that there was any reason to flee, thanks to Kahless's prohibition—but they had no way of knowing that. Amused, he watched them run, fleet as any animal and twice as graceful.

All except one of them. The tallest and most beautiful stood her ground all alone, having grabbed not her clothes but a long, deadly dagger. As Kahless spurred his *s'tarahk* to move closer to her, he saw her eyes flash with grim determination.

He knew that look. This female had the heart of a warrior. He liked that. He liked it a lot.

Kahless heard his men emerge from the woods to assemble behind him. The female's eyes darted from one to another of them, but she didn't run or drop her weapon or plead for mercy. Yes, a warrior's heart indeed.

"My father warned me that Molor's warriors might be about," she said, with just a hint of tremulousness in her voice. "Collecting Molor's stinking taxes," she went on. "But foolish me, I didn't listen—and this is the result." She raised her chin in a gesture of defiance. "Still, I'll make some of you sorry you thought to lay a hand on me."

Kahless heard his men laugh deep in their throats. With a gesture, he silenced them, though he himself was grinning like a *kraw'za*.

"We were once Molor's warriors," he told the woman. "But we're not that anymore. In fact, he would be happier if we were hanged with our own intestines. And rest assured, we have no intention of laying a hand on you."

The female's eyes narrowed. "Not Molor's men? Then you must be . . ."

"Outlaws," said Kahless, confirming her suspicions. "And since I have spared your life, I ask a favor in return."

"A favor?" the female echoed.

He nodded his head. "We could use some food and a comfortable place to sleep for the night—somewhere we'll be safe from the lord of this place. We don't want to find ourselves his prisoners in the morning." He paused. "That is, if it's not asking too much."

For the first time, a smile tugged at the corners of the female's mouth. "I think I can give you what you want," she said. "But I'll make no guarantees about keeping your presence here from Lord Vathraq. After all, it's his hall you'll be sleeping in."

"His hall . . . ?" Porus muttered.

The female nodded. "He is my father."

Seven: The Modern Age

As Worf entered the captain's ready room, he had expected only Picard to be waiting for him. He was surprised to see that there was another figure as well—a figure whose drab, loose-fitting garb marked him as one of the clerics of Boreth.

And not just *any* cleric. Closer scrutiny showed Worf that the shadowed face beneath the cowl was that of Koroth—chief among those who had dedicated their lives to the preservation of Kahless's traditions.

Koroth inclined his head out of respect for the lieutenant. After all, it was Worf who had forced a meeting of the minds between Gowron and the clone, affording the emperor an honorary place in the council hall.

The security chief returned the gesture of respect. Then he looked to his superior for an explanation.

"I am as much in the dark about this as you are," Picard informed him. Casting a glance in the cleric's direction, he added: "Our guest asked that you be present before he told us what his visit was about."

There was just the slightest hint of resentment in the captain's voice, but Worf noticed it. After one had served with a commanding officer for more than seven years, one came to know his reactions rather thoroughly. However, the Klingon doubted that their visitor had picked up on it.

Koroth fixed Worf with his gaze. "I've come on behalf of Kahless," he declared. "The *modern*-day Kahless."

"The clone," Picard confirmed.

The cleric nodded, though it was clearly not the description he would have preferred. "Yes. You see, he is in need of help—and he hopes you two will be the source of it."

The captain shifted in his seat. "Why *us?*" he asked.

"Because he knows he can trust you," Koroth told him. He was still looking at Worf. "After all, you were the ones who helped him come to an understanding with Gowron. If not for you, the Empire might have split into bloody factions over their conflict."

True, thought Worf. *Though it was Gowron, as leader of the High Council, who still wielded the real power.*

"What *exactly* does Kahless wish us to do?" Picard inquired.

The cleric shrugged. "Unfortunately, he did not provide me with this information. Nor did I press him for it, as he seemed reluctant to speak of the matter. My mission was simply to alert you to Kahless's need . . . and to give you the coordinates of a Klingon colony in the Nin'taga system, where Kahless wishes to meet you at a designated time."

The captain eyed his security chief. Worf knew that look as well. It meant Picard had come up with some answers of his own, which he would no doubt wish to test.

"I don't suppose this has anything to do with the *scroll?*" the captain ventured.

Koroth scowled. "I would be surprised if it did not. The scroll has been a source of great discomfort to him. In fact, to all of us. I wish Olahg had never found the cursed thing."

"Has it been authenticated?" Picard asked.

The cleric shook his head. "Nor do I believe it will be. I have publicly demanded that it be subjected to dating technologies, to prove its fraudulence. However, it may be too late to bury the controversy the scroll has created." Koroth sighed audibly. "One thing is certain—Kahless needs your assistance now, before things get any worse."

Worf didn't doubt it. Kahless would not have called on them for any small problem. Whatever trouble the scroll had birthed, it was something big. He hated to think *how* big.

But in the end, it didn't matter *why* Kahless had requested their help—only that he *had*. Surely, Picard would see that.

"Will you honor the emperor's request?" asked the cleric.

The captain drummed his fingers on the desk in front of him as he looked from Koroth to the lieutenant and back again, mulling the situation over. After a while, he stopped.

"All right," he told the cleric. "If there's a problem in the Empire, I suppose I must investigate it, at least. Give me the time and coordinates of the rendezvous and I'll be there."

Koroth turned to Worf. "And you, Lieutenant?"

Worf indulged himself in a typically Klingon remark: "Can I let my captain risk his life alone?"

The cleric smiled a thin-lipped smile. "No," he said softly. "Not if you are the sort of a warrior the emperor believes you to be."

The lieutenant grunted. As Picard's duty was clear, so was his—to respond to Kahless's summons as quickly as possible, and to gauge the danger to both the Empire and the Federation.

But despite his brave remark, he didn't feel inspired by the undertaking. Not when all he believed about Kahless seemed to have been built on a foundation of lies.

Commander William Riker was sitting in the center seat on the bridge, staring at the Byndarite merchant ship hanging off their port bow. He didn't like the idea that something was going on and he didn't know what or why.

First, the Byndarites had hailed the *Enterprise*—an unusual event in itself, given the aliens' customary lack of interest in dealing with the Federation. Then the commander of the Byndarite vessel had asked to speak with Captain Picard—and Picard alone, though it was Riker who had command of the bridge at the time.

Naturally, the first officer had alerted the captain as to the request. Understandably intrigued, Picard had asked Riker to put the communication through to his ready room.

But the captain wasn't the only one curious about the Byndarites'

intentions. And the first officer only became more curious when Picard
gave the order to lower shields.

To Riker, that meant only one thing. Someone was beaming aboard.

Someone who insisted on a certain amount of secrecy, the first officer discovered a moment later. Otherwise, the visitor would have
arrived in one of the ship's several transporter facilities, instead of
beaming directly into the captain's ready room.

Trying to contain himself, Riker had remained patient—even when
he saw the turbolift open and deposit Worf on the bridge. A little taken
aback, he had watched the Klingon join Picard.

What did Worf have to do with the Byndarites? he had wondered. He
was still wondering some ten minutes later when the aliens retrieved
their mysterious envoy—or so his monitor indicated.

A moment later, as the first officer watched, Worf had emerged from
the captain's ready room. But he hadn't provided an explanation. He
hadn't even glanced at anyone on the bridge. The lieutenant had simply reentered the turbolift and disappeared.

Which left Riker where he was now, staring at the Byndarite as it ran
through some engine checks. Apparently, it was about to depart, taking
its mystery along with it—and leaving the first officer in the dark.

Of course, the captain wouldn't let him languish there for long.
There were few matters he didn't share with his senior staff, no matter
how sensitive or restricted they were.

That was one of the advantages of serving under someone with as
much clout as Jean-Luc Picard. He could bend the rules a little, and no
one at Starfleet Command was likely to complain.

Not that he would let just anybody in on a high-priority matter. Only
those officers he trusted.

Abruptly, the captain's voice flooded the confines of the bridge.
"Number One?" he intoned.

Ah, thought Riker. *Right on time.* "Yes, sir?"

"I'd like to see you in my ready room as soon as possible."

"Right away, sir," said the first officer.

Relinquishing the bridge to Commander Data, he got up, circum-
navigated the curve of the tactical console and made his way to the
ready room door. A moment later, he heard the single word, "Come."
Right now, it was a welcome word indeed.

As the door slid open, it revealed Picard. He was sitting at his desk,
chair tilted back, looking contemplative. Lifting his eyes, he gestured
to the chair opposite him.

"Have a seat, Will."

Riker complied. "This is about our mysterious visitor?" he asked. It
wasn't really a question.

The captain nodded. "Koroth. One of the Klingon clerics we had aboard a year and a half ago."

"Ah," said the first officer. *So* that's *who it was.* "One of the people who created the Kahless clone."

"Precisely. And since the clerics have no ship of their own, and Koroth wished to remain anonymous, he took advantage of his familiarity with the Byndarites to secure passage."

Riker understood. Boreth was on the outskirts of the Empire—and therefore nearly in the path of one of the Byndarite trade routes.

"But that doesn't explain what Koroth was doing here," the first officer pointed out. "Or why he felt compelled to be so secretive."

"No," Picard conceded. "Apparently, he was acting as a go-between. It seems Emperor Kahless desires a meeting with myself and Mister Worf."

Riker looked at the captain. "Why couldn't Kahless tell you that himself?"

Picard frowned. "I don't know—though Koroth implied we would find that out in due time. We have only one clue. Not long ago, a scroll was discovered on the Klingon homeworld—a scroll that seems to debunk a great many Klingon legends. Particularly those dealing with the historical Kahless."

"I see," said the first officer.

"Mister Worf received the content of the scroll via subspace communiqué recently. He's agreed to make it available to you and the other senior officers, in case it becomes necessary to familiarize yourselves with it. I recommend you take a glance at it—just in case."

Riker smiled uncertainly. "In case *what?*"

The captain sighed. "I don't know that either, I'm afraid. If I were you, I would be ready for anything."

The first officer grunted thoughtfully. "If you say so, sir."

"I do. Dismissed, Number One."

But Riker didn't leave. He just sat there, trying to decide how best to phrase what he wanted to say.

Picard's brow wrinkled. "Was there something else, Will?"

"Yes, sir. I don't suppose you've forgotten why you chose me to be the first officer of the *Enterprise?*"

The captain considered the question for a moment. "Because of that incident on Altair Three, you mean. The one where you forbade your captain to go on an away mission on the grounds it was too dangerous. When I read about it in your file, it showed me what you were made of—that you had the guts to stand up for what you believed in."

"That's right," Riker confirmed. "You might say a bell went off in my brain back on Altair Three. A warning bell."

Picard smiled. "Any reason that incident should come to mind right now?"

The first officer nodded. "That bell is going off again. You're responding to the request of someone who tried to deceive you once before."

It was hard to argue with that. Koroth and his clerics had tried to convince not only the captain, but the entire quadrant, that Kahless the clone was in fact Kahless the Unforgettable. And they had nearly gotten away with it.

"Even if you think you can trust him," Riker went on, "you're headed for the Klingon Empire—hardly the safest venue in the quadrant. And on top of it, you don't know what you'll find when you get there."

Picard met his gaze. "All true, Number One. And if the situation were different, I would feel compelled to consider your argument. However, Kahless specifically asked for *me* to meet with him. Also, I have visited the homeworld before. I will hardly be a babe in the woods there."

"And if it turns out to be a trap?" Riker suggested.

The captain's mouth became a thin, hard line. "Then I shall no doubt wish I had listened to you. But my instincts tell me it's not a trap, Will. And there is a Klingon expression . . ."

The first officer saw where Picard was going with his remark. *"DujIIj yIvog,"* he declared.

"Trust your instincts," Picard translated. "Exactly."

Riker thought for a moment. "All right," he agreed at last. "We'll *both* trust your instincts, sir."

Alexander was doing his quantum mechanics homework—or trying to—when he heard the whisper of an opening door and saw his father walk in. Right away, the boy knew that something was up. After all, Lieutenant Worf didn't normally visit in the middle of his shift.

Then, just in case Alexander had any doubts, he saw the expression on his father's face. It was an expression he'd seen before, a funny mixture of reluctance and determination.

The reluctance part had to do with his having a son on board—someone he had to raise and protect—and that meant not exposing himself to danger any more than he had to. He hadn't shared any of that with the boy, but Alexander had figured it out all the same.

As for the determination . . . the boy wasn't quite sure about that. But he could guess.

Sighing, Alexander leaned back from his computer terminal. "You're going on a mission, aren't you?"

His father looked at him. "Yes," he admitted. "And there is a chance I will be gone for some time."

The boy nodded. "Can I ask where you're going? Or has the captain asked you not to say anything?"

Worf scowled. "In fact, he has. But I can tell you this much—it involves the Empire."

"You're going to the homeworld?"

His father shrugged. "Possibly."

"In secret?" Alexander pressed.

"In secret," his father confirmed.

"How will you get there?"

"More than likely, we will be transported by the Pescalians."

Now it was the boy's turn to frown. "The Pescalians? But I thought you said their ships were held together with spit."

Worf harrumphed. "Perhaps I was exaggerating. In any case, we will rendezvous with one of their vessels in an hour."

Alexander felt a lump in his throat—the one he got whenever his father left on some dangerous assignment. And by the sound of it, this one was pretty dangerous.

"Who's *we?*" he asked.

"The captain and I," Worf replied.

Well, that was a bright spot. Alexander trusted the captain. He was a smart man. And Starfleet wasn't eager to lose him if they could help it.

"Okay," the boy said, not wanting his father to see his fear. "Have a good trip."

Not that Worf would have scolded him for being afraid. They had come to an understanding about Alexander's human side, the quarter of his heritage he had received from his mother's mother. But it was considered bad luck for a Klingon to leave in the midst of sorrow.

"I will try," his father agreed. "In the meantime, keep up your schoolwork. And your *bat'leth* practice."

Alexander nodded. "I will."

"And if you need anything, you can turn to Counselor Troi. She will be glad to help in any way she can."

The boy knew that without Worf's having to say it. He liked Counselor Troi. And so did his father, though he sometimes didn't seem eager to admit it—even to himself.

"Don't worry," said Alexander. He smiled. "I'll be fine."

Worf looked at him. His eyes gleamed with a touch of pride. "Good. I'll see you when I get back."

"Sure," the boy told him, faking an assurance he didn't quite feel. "When you get back."

A moment later, his father was gone.

Eight: The Heroic Age

Hungry as he was, Kahless had a hard time keeping his mind on the food that writhed and steamed and bled on Lord Vathraq's table. Of course, his men had no such problem.

They heaped their plates high with heart of *targ* and serpent worms, with warm, soft *tor'rif* bread and dark, sweet *minn'hor* cheese. They slacked their thirst with fragrant bloodwine, poured by Vathraq's servants. And they gorged themselves as if they didn't know where their next meal was coming from, which was no more or less than the truth.

Kahless, on the other hand, was too busy watching Vathraq's daughter to pay much attention to food.

Her name was Kellein, and in all his years he had never seen anything like her. At first glimpse, back at the river, he had appreciated her courage above all—despite her nakedness. Now, as he watched her move from table to table, seeing to it that everyone was amply served, he took time to appreciate her more obvious attributes.

The way her hips swayed beneath her long, belted tunic, for instance. Or the sharpness of her teeth. Or the shape of her eyes, as brown and oval as *en'tach* leaves in the spring.

Kahless would have guessed that she was twenty years old, perhaps twenty-two. Yet she was wearing a *jinaq* amulet on a silver chain, signifying that her parents had only in the last year deemed her old enough to take a mate.

By that sign, the warrior knew her to be only eighteen. It made her defiance in the river seem even more impressive to him.

Instinctively, he tried to catch her eye. To communicate without words his body's yearning for her. But Kellein didn't look his way.

Cursing himself, Kahless drained a goblet full of bloodwine. *Why should she?* he asked himself bitterly. *All I am is a stinking outlaw, a man with no standing and no future. She'd be better off with a half-wit for a mate than a man marked for death by Molor.*

Abruptly, the warchief heard a clamor at the far end of his table. Turning, he saw Vathraq standing with a goblet in his hand, pounding on the wooden boards for silence.

It took a while, but he got it. Smiling like someone who'd had too much bloodwine—which was true, if the stains in his ample gray beard were any indication—Vathraq raised his goblet in Kahless's direction.

"For my guest," he bellowed. "Kahless the Unconquered, Bane of the Emperor Molor. May he feed the tyrant his own entrails!"

There was a roar from Vathraq's people, most of whom were as drunk as he was. As they echoed the toast, they drummed their fists against their tables, making the rafters ring with their noise.

But Kahless didn't like the sound of his host's words. Getting up, he felt himself sway a little—a sign that he'd had more wine than he thought. But he spoke nonetheless.

"I have no intention of going anywhere near Molor, much less feeding him his entrails. In fact, I want to stay as far away from him as I can."

Vathraq roared with laughter. "Whatever you say," he replied. "Don't worry about us, brave Kahless. We'll keep your secret." He turned to his some of his people. "Won't we?"

They howled their approval. Kahless shook his head, intent on dispelling any illusion they had created for themselves.

"No," he shouted. "I mean it. We're outlaws, not idiots. No one can get within a mile of Molor, anyway."

But Vathraq and his people only laughed even louder. Dismissing them with a wave of his hand, Kahless sat down again. Obviously, they would believe what they wanted to, no matter what he said.

But as he poured another goblet full of bloodwine, the warchief saw Morath looking at him from across the room. Of all his men, only Morath seemed clear of eye, free of the wine's influence. And he had a distinct look of disapproval on his face.

Kahless could guess why, too. If he had learned one thing about Morath, it was that the man had principles—the kind that didn't allow him to let a falsehood go uncorrected.

The warchief grunted. Some falsehoods weren't worth worrying about, he mused. Turning away from Morath, he drained his goblet, allowing his troubles to drown themselves one at a time.

Nine: The Modern Age

Picard materialized on a smooth, black plateau open to a glorious, red-orange sky. The air was cool, with a strange, spicy scent to it. Beyond the precipice before him, a good hundred and fifty meters below, a Klingon colony sprawled across a ruddy brown landscape.

Turning to his left, he saw that Worf had taken shape beside him. That was something of a relief. He hadn't particularly trusted the transporter unit in the Pescalian cargo ship that had brought them here.

Then again, they hadn't had much choice in the matter. The captain couldn't have taken the *Enterprise* into Klingon territory without notice—not unless he wished to start a war with Gowron.

"Worf!" boomed a deep voice from behind them. "Captain Picard!" The captain turned—and saw Kahless emerge from behind a rock formation. The clone grinned. As he closed with them, a curious-looking amulet swung from a thong around his neck.

"It is good to see you again," he said. "Both of you. In fact, you don't know *how* good."

"It is good to see you as well, Emperor," Worf responded.

Kahless clasped his fellow Klingon by the forearm, then repeated the gesture with Picard. The captain winced. The clone was as strong as ever.

"You look well, Emperor," Picard said.

Kahless shrugged. "I am well," he replied, "despite what you may have heard." He looked past the human at the installation below them. "Strange. I have never been to this world before, but it feels familiar here."

He paused to consider the place for a moment. Then, slowly, a smile broke out on his face.

"T'chariv," the clone whispered.

"In the north?" asked Worf.

Kahless nodded. "Of course, the sky was this color only at sunset. But the shape of the settlement, the way it nestles in the hills . . ." He grunted. "It's T'chariv, all right. The place where the original Kahless called the outlying provinces to his banner."

Picard didn't say anything. Neither did Worf.

The clone looked at them. "Yes," he added, responding to their unspoken question. "I am *sure* the original Kahless visited T'chariv. Any person or thing that says otherwise is a liar."

Again, the captain withheld comment. Until the scroll was determined to be authentic or otherwise, he couldn't offer any encouragement. What's more, the clone knew it.

"In any case," Kahless went on, "I didn't bring you here to reminisce with me. There is treachery afoot. Treachery which will tear apart the Klingon Empire if left to run its course."

Picard couldn't help but be interested. "Treachery from what quarter?" he inquired evenly.

The emperor grunted. "I take no pleasure in saying this—but it is my duty as emperor." He paused for effect. "Apparently, the Klingon Defense Force is undertaking a military coup designed to unseat Gowron and the rest of the council."

"How do you know this?" asked Worf.

"I know," said Kahless, "because I saw two of the conspirators whispering in a dining hall in Tolar'tu, during the Festival of Muar'tek—and nearly every day since. Fortunately, I can still read lips as well as ever."

Picard looked at him skeptically. "But the leaders of the Defense

Force were handpicked by Council leader Gowron. They have sworn to defend him with their very lives."

Kahless's eyes blazed. "That," he told the human, his voice thick with revulsion, "is why they call it *treachery*." He turned his head and spat. "Believe me when I say there's a scheme against Gowron. And certainly, that would be bad enough. But the conspirators also mentioned Olahg's scroll—said it had enabled them to get their rebellion under way."

"How so?" asked Worf.

The clone made a gesture of dismissal. "The rebels are embracing it as evidence that I am not worth their respect. That Kahless the Unforgettable is not what he seems—and never was."

Worf scowled. "And in many instances, you were all that kept the people from rising up against Gowron."

"Exactly," said the clone. "Without me to bolster him, Gowron is all too vulnerable. Mind you, he's not my idea of a great leader, but he's a damned sight better than the alternative."

Picard agreed. Gowron, at least, was still an ally of the Federation. The next council leader might not be so inclined.

His eyes losing their focus, Kahless pounded his fist into his other hand. "I wanted to confront the conspirators right then and there. I wanted to stand on their conniving necks and watch their blood run out on the floor." He sighed. "Then I realized I wouldn't be tearing down the rebellion—only lopping off one of its limbs."

"And that's when you came to us?" the captain asked.

The clone shook his head. "First I went to Gowron, for all the good it did. He didn't believe I'd uncovered a threat. He thought I was seeing these things because I wanted to—because I needed to feel important."

Picard didn't want to say so, but he had some doubts himself. *And so would Worf,* the captain thought, if he knew the Klingon's mind.

This business with the scroll was clearly making Kahless wary. More than likely, he was imagining things. Lots of people whisper in dining halls, but that doesn't mean they plan to overthrow the government.

"You don't believe me," the clone said suddenly, noticing some nuance in Picard's expression. He looked at Worf, then back to the captain again. "Neither of you. You're as incredulous as Gowron was."

"Forgive me," Picard replied, "but there's no proof—"

"I know what I'm talking about!" Kahless thundered. "You want proof? Come with me to the homeworld and I'll *give* you proof!"

The captain didn't think that would be a good idea. He said so. "It was a risk just coming to this colony world. Returning with you to

Qo'noS would place Federation-Klingon relations in considerable jeopardy."

The clone's nostrils flared. "They are in considerable jeopardy already, Picard, though you refuse to see it. Knowing me as you do, how can you place so little trust in me? How can you ignore the possibility that I'm right—and that the Empire stands on the brink of revolution?"

Picard had to admit the Klingon had a point. With little or nothing in the way of facts at this juncture, he would be taking a risk either way. And if there was a conspiracy after all—and he ignored it—he would have to live with that oversight the rest of his days.

He turned to Worf. "What do *you* think, Lieutenant?"

The security officer didn't like to be put on the spot like this. The captain knew that from experience. On the other hand, Worf had the firmest grasp of the situation. If anyone could divine the truth about this "conspiracy," it would be the son of Mogh.

For a long moment, Worf looked Kahless square in the eyes. Then he turned to Picard. "I think we ought to go to the homeworld," he said at last.

The captain was still leery of the prospect. However, he had placed his trust in his security officer.

"All right," he concluded. "We'll go."

Kahless smiled. "You won't regret it," he said.

Tapping his wristband, he activated his link to whatever vehicle awaited him. It was the same kind of wristband Picard himself had used to maintain control of *Enterprise* shuttles.

At the same time, the captain tapped his communicator and notified the Pescalians they wouldn't be going back with them. At least, not yet.

"Three to beam up," the clone bellowed.

A moment later, Picard and the others found themselves on the bridge of a modest cruiser. As with all Klingon vessels, the place was small, stark, and lacking in amenities. Quarters were cramped and lights were dim. The bridge had three seats; Kahless took the one in the rear, leaving his companions the forward positions if they wanted them.

"Break orbit," the clone commanded, speaking directly to the ship's computer. "Set course for Qo'noS, heading three four six point one. Ahead warp factor six. Engage."

The captain felt the drag of inertia as the ship banked and leaped forward into warp. Even for a small and relatively unsophisticated vessel, its damper system left something to be desired.

Then again, Kahless probably preferred it that way. The rougher, the better, Picard mused.

"The journey will take a couple of days," the clone informed them. "When you tire, you'll find bunks in the aft cabin." He jerked a thumb over his shoulder for emphasis. "Back there."

Picard nodded. "Thank you."

He recalled the last time he was on a Klingon vessel. He had been on a mission to investigate Ambassador Spock's activities on Romulus. From what he remembered, his cabin had been sparsely furnished and eminently uncomfortable. He resigned himself to the likelihood that on a cruiser this size, the accommodations would be even worse.

Worf looked around. "Nice ship," he observed.

Kahless grunted. "Gowron gave it to me, though I don't think he expected I'd use it much. And truthfully, I haven't."

Again, Picard found his eyes drawn to the amulet on the clone's chest. He was starting to think he'd seen such a thing before in his studies of Klingon culture, though he wasn't sure where.

"You like my amulet?" asked Kahless.

The captain was embarrassed. "I didn't mean to stare."

"You need not apologize," said the clone. "It is called a *jinaq*."

Picard nodded. He remembered now. Klingon men used to wear them when they were betrothed to someone. Did that mean Kahless intended to marry?

"I have no lover," the clone informed him, as if he'd read the captain's mind. "Not anymore, at least—not for fifteen hundred years or more. But I wear it still, out of respect for her."

"I see," said Picard.

He made a mental note to ask Worf about the applicable myth later on. It sounded interesting—and if it would shed more light on Kahless for him, it was well worth the time.

Ten: The Heroic Age

Kahless sat back heavily in his sturdy wooden chair, his head spinning like a child's top. The food and the bloodwine had been more than plentiful. And in all fairness, Vathraq wasn't the *worst* storyteller he'd ever heard, although he came close.

But the warchief was restless under his host's vaulted roof. So, as the revelers' eyes grew bloodshot on both sides of the overladen table, and their speech thickened, and the hall filled with smoky phantoms born of the cooking fires, the guest of honor left the feast.

No one seemed to notice as he made his way out of the great hall, or as he crossed the anteroom and exited the keep. And if anyone did notice, they didn't care enough to say anything.

The evening air was cold and bracing after the warmth of Vathraq's feast—like a splash of melt from a mountain spring, clearing his head and tightening the skin across his face. Breathing it in deeply, he felt as if he'd regained some semblance of his wine-dimmed senses.

A dirt track began at his feet and twisted tortuously between a couple of dark, blockish storage buildings, then reached through the stronghold's open gates to the river road beyond. Kahless caught a glimpse of the cultivated *tran'nuc* trees that grew between the road and the riverbank, and the sweet, purplish fruit that drooped heavily from their thorny black branches.

Vathraq hadn't served the *tran'nuc* fruit because it wasn't ripe yet, nor would it be for a couple of weeks. Kahless knew that because his family had had a tree of their own when he was growing up.

Still, he hadn't bitten into a *tran'nuc* fruit since he left the capital months earlier. And he might not have a chance to taste one again, the way Molor was hunting him.

He could feel the warm rush of his own saliva making his decision for him. Wiping his mouth with the back of his fat-smeared hand, he set out for the gate and the trees beyond. The sentries on the wall turned at his approach. He called up to them, so there would be no surprises.

They swiveled their crossbows in his direction, just in case he was one of the tyrant's tax collectors trying to deceive them. Then one of them recognized him, and they let their weapons fall to their sides. It was unlikely that they'd have shot at him anyway, considering he was *leaving* the compound, and doing it alone at that.

Once past the gates, he felt the wind pick up. It lifted his hair, which he'd left unbraided. The broad, dark sky was full of stars, points of light so bright they seemed to stab at him.

Kahless grunted. What *wasn't* stabbing at him these days?

Leaving Vathraq's walls well behind him, Kahless crossed the road and approached the nearest *tran'nuc* tree. As he moved, the river unfolded like a serpent beyond its overhanging banks, all silver and glistening in the starlight. It seemed to hiss at him, though without malice, as if it too had had its fill this night.

Arriving at the foot of the tree, he reached up and tore a fruit from the lowest branch. In the process, he scratched himself on one of the long, jagged thorns. A rivulet of blood formed on the back of his hand, then another.

Ignoring them, he bit into the fruit. It was riper than he'd imagined, sweet and sour at the same time. But as he'd already gorged himself on Vathraq's food, he had no room for the whole thing.

Tossing the sweet, dark remainder on the ground, he waited for the *yolok* worms to realize it was there. In a matter of seconds, they rose up beneath it, their slender, sinuous bodies white as moonlight. The fruit began to writhe under their ministrations, and then to disappear in chunks as they consumed it with their pincerlike jaws.

Before long, there was only a dark spot on the ground to show that the *tran'nuc* fruit had ever existed. Kahless snorted; it was good to know there were still *some* certainties in life.

He turned to the river again, observing the ripple of the winds on its back. He had forgotten how good it could feel to have a full belly and the prospect of a warm place to sleep. He had forced himself to forget.

Of course, he could have had this every night, if only he'd gone along with Molor's orders back at M'riiah. If he had returned from his mission, the blood on his sword testament to his hard work, and remained the tyrant's most loyal and steadfast servant.

Molor treated his servants well. He would have given Kahless all the females he wanted, and all the bloodwine he could drink. And in time, no doubt, a hall of his own, with a wall for his trophies and a view of his vassals working in the fields.

But if he had torched the village as he was supposed to, all the bloodwine in the world wouldn't have soothed him at night. And the stoutest walls couldn't have kept out the ghosts of M'riiah's innocents.

The outlaw snorted. Why had the tyrant set such a task before him anyway? Why couldn't he have sent one of his other warchiefs—one with a quicker torch and a less tender conscience?

Kahless shook his head angrily. *I've got to stop playing "what if" games,* he told himself, *or they'll drive me mad. What's done is done, for better or worse. And is that any different from what I—*

Before he could complete the thought, Kahless realized he was not alone. His eyes slid to one side, searching for shadows; there weren't anyway. Nor could he find a scent, given the direction of the wind. But he sensed someone behind him nonetheless, someone who had apparently made an effort to conceal his approach.

Kahless's thumbs were already tucked into his belt, and his back was to his enemy. As subtly as possible, he moved his right hand toward the knife that hung by his thigh and grasped it firmly. Then he lifted it partway from its leather sheath.

Listening intently, he could hear the shallow breathing of his assailant, even over the sigh of the wind. In a minute, maybe less, the *yolok* worms would have another meal—and a meatier one.

He waited for a few impossibly long seconds, the hunter's spirit rising in him, the blood pounding in his neck like a beast tearing loose of its chain. His lips curled back from his teeth, every fiber of his being caught in the fiery fever of anticipation.

Finally, the moment came. Clenching his jaw, Kahless whirled, blade singing as it cut the air, heading for the spot between his enemy's head and his shoulders. His eyes opened wide, drinking in the sight of surprise on the intruder's face, exulting in the prospect of the blood that would flow from his—

No!

Muscles cording painfully in his forearm, he stopped his blade less than an inch from its target. The oiled surface of the knife glinted, reflecting starlight on the smooth, gently curving jaw of Vathraq's daughter. Her neck artery pulsed visibly beneath the metal's finely honed edge.

And yet, she didn't flinch. Only her eyes moved, meeting Kahless's and locking onto them. They were pools of darkness, full of resentment and anger.

But nothing to match his own. Lightning-swift, Kahless flicked the blade back into its sheath and snarled like a wounded animal.

"Are you mad?" he rasped. "To sneak up on me like a—"

He never finished. Kellein's open hand smashed him in the face, stinging him as he wouldn't have imagined she could. He took a half-step back, stunned for the moment.

But she wasn't done with him. Slashing him with her nails, oblivious to the knife he still held in his hand, she sent him staggering back another step. With his left hand, he caught one of her wrists and squeezed it hard enough to crush the bones within.

His intention was to make her stop until he could put his knife away, then use both hands to subdue her. But before he could carry it out, his back foot slipped on the uncertain ground of the riverbank. He felt himself falling backward and braced himself for the chill of the current.

But instead, he felt something hard rush up to meet him, half-pounding the breath out of him. Then there was another impact—that of a weight on top of him. *Her* weight.

It was only then he realized that they had fallen onto a gentle slope just beneath the bank. In the season of Growing, this ground would be submerged by the flood; now, it was dry.

Kahless found that he was still grasping Kellein's wrist with his free hand. Tightening his grip on it, he glared at her, his face mere inches below hers. He could feel the warmth of her breath on his face, smell the wildflowers with which she'd adorned herself for the feast.

Pleasant sensations, under other circumstances. But here and now, they only made him angrier. Remembering his knife, he plunged it into the soft earth beside him.

Kellein planted the heel of her hand on his chest and tried to get up—but he wouldn't let her. Though Kahless's strength was greater than hers, she tried a second time. And a third.

His lip curled. "You followed me out here," he growled accusingly.

"And what if I did?" she returned, her teeth bared in an anger that seemed every bit as inflamed as his.

"What were you thinking?" he thundered. "Why did you come up behind me without warning?"

Kellein's eyes narrowed, making her seem even more incensed than before. "Why," she asked—her voice suddenly husky with something quite different from anger—"do you *think?*"

Suddenly, Kahless understood. All too aware of the hard-muscled angles of Kellein's body, he caught her hair in his fist and drew her face down until her mouth met his.

He tasted blood—though it took him a moment to realize it was his own, wrung from a lip Kellein had just punctured with her teeth. He didn't care, not in the least.

In fact, it made him want her that much more.

In the aftermath of passion, Kahless lay with his back against the ground and Kellein's head on his shoulder. Lightly, she ran her fingernails across his cheek, tracing what seemed to him to be arcane emblems.

Praxis had risen in the east. In its light, Kellein's skin took on a blue-white, almost ethereal cast. She was too beautiful to be of this world, yet too full of life to be of the next.

"What?" she asked suddenly.

He looked at her. "How did you know I was thinking of something?"

Kellein grunted. "You are always thinking of something. If you weren't, Molor would have caught you a long time ago."

Kahless smiled at that. "But how did you know *this* thought had to do with *you,* daughter of Vathraq?"

She shrugged and looked up at the stars. "I just knew," she told him.

"Did you also know *what* I was thinking?"

Kellein cast him a sideways glance. "Don't play games with me, Kahless. I don't like games."

"I don't either," he admitted. "It is only that . . ."

"Yes?" she prodded.

"Where I come from, this means we are betrothed."

Kellein laughed. It was the first time he'd heard her do that. Normally, he would have liked the sound of it—except in this case, he felt he was being mocked. He said so.

"I am not mocking you," she assured him.

"It does not *have* to mean we're betrothed," the warchief told her, snarling as he gave vent to his anger. "It does not have to mean *anything*. We are not in my village, after all."

"I am not mocking you," Kellein repeated, this time more softly. "I was laughing with delight." She propped herself up on one elbow and looked deeply into his eyes. "What we did just now . . . it means the same thing to *my* people that it does to *yours*."

His anger faded in the wake of another emotion—a much milder one. "You would betroth yourself to me? An outlaw with no future?"

"Not just any outlaw," Kellein said. "Only Kahless, son of Kanjis, scourge of hill and plain."

Kahless was filled with a warmth that had nothing to do with the bloodwine. Taking her head in his hands, he drew her to him again.

"You should do that more often," he told her.

She raised her head. "Do what?" she asked.

"Laugh," he answered.

"Oh," she said. *"That."* There was a note of disdain in her voice. "I have never been the laughing kind." And then, as if she had been carrying on a separate conversation in her own head, "I will make you a *jinaq* amulet just like mine. That way, everyone will know we belong to each other."

"Yes. Everyone will know. And all through the Cold, whenever I touch it, I will think of you."

For a moment, Kellein seemed surprised. "Through the Cold . . . ?"

Kahless nodded. "I mean for my men and I to lose ourselves in the mountains. To give Molor time to forget we exist. Then, when the hunt for me has abated somewhat, I will send them away to seek their separate fortunes, unburdened by their association with me. And you and I will go somewhere the tyrant can't follow."

"I could go with you *now*," she suggested. "To the mountains, I mean. I could remain at your side the long Cold through."

"No," he told her. "It wouldn't work for me to have a mate when none of the others do. It would cause jealousy, dissension. Besides, if Molor were to catch us, the worst he could do is kill us. A female, especially a strong one, would be handled much worse."

Kellein ran her long-nailed fingers through his hair. "But you'll come back in the Growing." It wasn't a question. "And then you'll ask the Lord Vathraq for his daughter's hand in marriage."

He grunted. "I will indeed. That is, if I'm still alive."

She eyed him with a forcefulness he had never seen in a woman before. It robbed him of his breath.

"You'll still be alive," Kellein told him, "if you know what's good for you."

Eleven: The Modern Age

Alexander couldn't sleep. He stared at the ceiling, imagining fleecy sheep leaping over fences in a land of rolling, green hills. They leaped one at a time, making long, lazy jumps.

It didn't work. It had *never* worked. And it didn't make it any easier that he had never seen an actual sheep in his whole, entire life.

The only reason Alexander even tried counting sheep was that his mother had suggested it to him. He clung to things he remembered about her a little more than was absolutely necessary.

Like the way she used to sneak up on him and hug him when he wasn't expecting it. Or the way she would recite nursery rhymes to him, which she claimed were from Earth but sounded more Klingon than human.

Little Red Riding Hood, for instance. Didn't that one end with a woodchopper slicing a wolf into bloody bits?

Then there was Snow White, where an evil stepmother poisoned the heroine of the tale with a piece of fruit. K'mpec, who led the High Council before Gowron, died after being poisoned.

And what about the Three Billygoats Gruff? Unless Alexander was mistaken, that was about an animal who butted his enemy off a bridge and saw him drown in the waters below. If that wasn't Klingon, what was?

The boy sighed. He missed his mother.

And now, at least for a while, he missed his father as well. He wished Worf had been able to tell him something more about his mission. It would've made the darkness a little less dark if he knew something. *Anything.*

Suddenly, he remembered. His father had received a subspace message recently. Alexander hadn't thought to ask about it at the time, assuming it was something official or Worf would have discussed it with him.

But now he wondered. Could it have had something to do with the mission his father was on now? If that was the case, there would be some evidence of it in the ship's computer system.

Swiveling in bed, Alexander lowered his feet to the floor, got up, and padded over to the computer terminal in the next room. At the same time, he called for some illumination.

As the lights went on, the boy deposited himself on the chair in front of the computer screen. Then he accessed the log for this particular terminal. It showed him a long list of communications, the vast majority of them from other sites on the *Enterprise*.

There was only one from off-ship. And its origin was the Klingon Empire!

Alexander's hands clenched into fists. His instincts had been right on target so far. Now it was a matter of bringing the message up on the screen.

If it was classified information, he would be out of luck. No one could get into those files without Starfleet priority clearance. And even if he could somehow hack his way around that fact, he wouldn't. He liked the officers on this ship too much to get in trouble with them.

With a few touches of his padd, the boy established that the message wasn't classified after all. But it *was* restricted to this terminal and one other—the captain's.

And Captain Picard had gone with Alexander's father on the mysterious mission. *The pieces are starting to fall into place,* thought Alexander. Whatever was in the message, it had something to do with Worf's being called away.

Of course, he could tear the cover off this mystery right now. Tapping again at his padd, he called up the file.

What he saw came as a surprise to him. There was no call for help. In fact, it wasn't really a message at all. It was a history of some kind.

Curious, he read a few lines. And then a few more. It talked about Kahless and the kinds of things he did when he was young, but it didn't seem to jibe too well with what Alexander knew of him. In fact, it seemed to be talking about someone else altogether.

Intrigued, the boy propped his elbows on his desk. Resting his face in his hands, he read on.

Picard couldn't help frowning a little as he followed Kahless and Worf into the dining hall in Tolar'tu. After all, his hood was hardly a foolproof disguise. Anyone who had an opportunity to peer closely inside it would realize in a moment he was no Klingon.

All the more reason not to attract undue attention. Keeping his eyes straight in front of him, the captain felt the warmth of the firepit as he crossed the room.

There was a table in the corner with room for three. Kahless gestured, and they all sat down. Taking a moment to survey the place, Picard decided it was just as the clone had described it.

Nearly everyone was wearing a hood. Most were sitting alone, minding their own business, but there were pairs and trios as well. And everyone spoke in such low voices it was difficult to hear what they were saying.

The captain turned to Kahless. "Are they here?" he whispered.

The clone shook his head. "Not yet. But soon." He eyed Worf. "And you will recognize Lomakh when you see him, I promise. That is, if you look closely enough."

Picard and his security officer exchanged glances. Worf sat back in his chair and frowned.

No doubt, the lieutenant was wondering if he'd done the right thing encouraging his captain to come here. The closer they'd gotten to the dining hall, the more skeptical Worf's expression had become.

Still, Picard mused, *they had ventured this far. As the expression went, in for a penny, in for a pound.*

He had barely finished the thought when the door opened and two men walked in. One was tall, the other shorter and broad. Like everyone else here, they wore cowls to conceal their features.

Kahless turned to his companions. Picard could tell from the gleam in the Klingon's eye that these two were the ones he'd warned them about. Nonetheless, Kahless felt compelled to underline the point.

"It's them," he breathed.

Worf looked past him at the newcomers. They sat down at a table on the other side of the room and bent their heads until they were almost touching.

"You see?" Kahless commented. "Do they not look like conspirators?"

The captain sighed. The newcomers looked no more conspiratorial than anyone else in the place. "You said Mister Worf would recognize one of them."

The clone nodded. "Yes. The tall one."

Worf's eyes narrowed in the shadow of his hood. "I cannot tell from here," he decided. "I will need a better look."

"Then by all means, take one," Kahless urged.

His frown deepening, the security officer got up and crossed the room to the firepit. Once there, he made a show of warming his hands by its flames. Then he returned to the table.

"Well?" Kahless prodded.

Worf paused for a moment, then nodded. "I believe the tall one is Lomakh. I do not recognize the other."

"Then you see what I am saying," the clone hissed, triumphant. "What would Lomakh be doing in a place like this, concealing his face with a hood . . . unless it was to plan Gowron's overthrow?"

"Unfortunately," said Picard, "he could be doing a great many things." He was still unconvinced.

"I told you," Kahless insisted. "I read their lips. I saw them speak of plucking Gowron from the council like a fattened *targ.*"

As on the colony world, the captain turned to Worf, relying on his judgment and his expertise. "What do you think?" he asked.

The lieutenant sighed. "As an officer in the Defense Force, Lomakh is taking a risk coming here. It does not make sense that he would do so—unless he deemed it a greater risk to conduct his conversation elsewhere."

"In other words," said Picard, "you agree with the emperor's assessment of the situation."

Again, Worf paused a moment, ever cautious. "Yes," he replied at last. "For now, at least, I agree."

The captain absorbed the response. As far as he was concerned, they had seen enough. They could go.

But if they left without eating, Lomakh might notice and wonder about it. And if he really was part of a conspiracy, it might then dig itself an even deeper hole, from which it would be impossible to extricate it. So they hunkered down within their cowls and stayed.

A couple of minutes later, a serving maid came over. The clone ordered for all three of them. Fortunately, Picard was a connoisseur of Klingon fare, so he would arouse no suspicion in that regard.

His only disappointment was the lack of fresh gagh. Apparently, he would have to settle for the cooked variety.

The food wasn't long in coming. But at Kahless's request, they lingered over it, giving him more time to read lips and gather information. In the end, he failed to discover anything useful.

After a rather extended stay, Lomakh and his crony paid for their meals and left the place. The captain felt a bit of tension go out of him. Lomakh hadn't seemed to pay any undue attention to them. Apparently, they had been careful enough to avoid suspicion.

Finishing their food, which was as tasty as the clone had predicted, they gave Lomakh enough time to make himself scarce. Then Kahless took care of their bill and they departed.

Outside, the air was chill and the sun was beginning to set, turning the sky a few shades darker in the west. Obviously, they had been in the dining hall longer than Picard had imagined.

As they retraced their steps toward the main square, which was a good half-kilometer distant, the captain asked "Now what?"

Kahless looked at him. "I was hoping you would have a suggestion, Picard. After all, the captain of the *Enterprise* must wield considerable power."

Picard understood the implication—or thought he did. "Not the kind you need, I'm afraid. We can't exactly assume orbit around Qo'noS, beam down a security team, and place Lomakh under arrest. That is, if we even believed that was a good idea."

"Which it is not," the clone agreed. "As I myself pointed out, Lomakh is only a part of this. If we were to arrest him, we would never expose the rest of the conspiracy." His eyes narrowed beneath his bony brow. "I was speaking more in terms of your influence,

Picard. Surely, the Federation maintains spies within the Empire, who would—"

The captain looked at him. "Spies?" he repeated. He laughed. "Whatever gave you that idea?"

Kahless returned the look. "It is only logical. With the surgical techniques available, I imagine—"

"The Empire and the Federation are *allies,*" Picard asserted. "We have no spies among the Klingons."

The clone smiled a thin smile. "Either you are naive or you seek to conceal the truth, human. I will give you the benefit of the doubt and embrace the first possibility."

The captain shook his head. "I am neither concealing anything nor am I naive. We conduct no espionage within the Empire, period."

Kahless harrumphed. "Then your Starfleet Headquarters informs you of every move it makes—without exception?"

Picard could see this was getting them nowhere. "Believe what you like," he said. "The bottom line is I have no influence here, no resources. If we are to expose Lomakh's conspiracy, we will have to resort to other means."

The clone frowned. "Very well. If you won't help, or can't, we can always call on our—"

Picard looked at him, wondering why he'd stopped in midsentence. Then he saw the masked figures emerging from the alleyway to Kahless's right, each of them clutching a three-bladed *d'k tahg* in either hand.

Even as the captain prepared himself for their onslaught, he spared a glance in the opposite direction—and saw more trouble coming from the alley opposite. Altogether, it looked to be six or seven against their three. Fortunately, Picard and his allies weren't entirely unprepared.

They hadn't been able to carry phasers off the *Enterprise,* for fear of being identified by them—and disruptors might also draw undue attention. But everyone carried a blade of some sort, and Kahless had seen to it they were no exception.

Slipping his *d'k tahg* free of the sheath on his thigh, the captain braced himself. Before he knew it, one of their assailants was on top of him. Twisting quickly to one side, Picard narrowly avoided disembowelment. And as the Klingon's momentum carried him past, the human slammed his hilt into the back of the warrior's head.

The masked one hit the ground and lay still. Picard barely had time to kneel and pick up a fallen *d'k tahg* before the next assault came. This time, perhaps seeing what the captain had done already, his adversary approached more slowly and deliberately.

Then, with a viciously quick and accurate lunge, he stabbed at

Picard's throat. The human fended off the attack with one of his own blades and countered with a backhand slash of his own. The Klingon leaped back, and the slash fell short.

Almost too late, Picard turned and realized what was really happening. The frontal assault was only a decoy, so a second Klingon could stab him from behind. Reacting instantly, he ducked—and the second assailant sailed over his head, confounding the first.

That gave the captain a chance to see how his companions were doing. He noted with relief that they were both still alive. There was blood running down the side of Worf's face and Kahless had a wet, dark rent in the shoulder of his tunic, but their wounds weren't slowing them down.

Picard watched as Worf lashed out with his foot, cracking an opponent's rib, then faced off with another. And Kahless wove a web of steel with his dagger, keeping two more at bay.

As the captain turned back to his own assailants, he found them separating in an attempt to flank him. A sound strategy, he thought. Cautiously, he backed off, hoping to buy some time.

It would have been the right move, if not for the recovery of the Klingon he thought he'd knocked unconscious. Hearing the scrape of the warrior's boots, Picard whirled in time to catch a downstroke with crossed blades—but the maneuver left him open to the other two.

The captain could almost feel the shock of cold steel sinking into his back. But it never came. Instead, he saw his adversary withdraw into the alley that had spawned him. Turning, Picard saw the other masked ones retreating as well.

Then he saw why. A group of warriors were approaching from the direction of the dining hall, eager to even the odds. Fortunately, there was nothing a Klingon disliked more than an unfair fight.

Kahless started after the masked ones, caught up in a bloodlust, but Worf planted himself in the clone's way and restrained him. Seeing that his officer would need some help, Picard added his own strength to the effort.

"Let me go!" bellowed Kahless, his eyes filled with a berserker rage.

"No!" cried Worf. "We have got to get out of here, before people start asking questions!" Then he caught sight of the captain and his lips pulled back from his teeth. "Sir!" he hissed. "Your hood!"

Picard groped for it—and realized it had fallen back, exposing his all-too-human face to those around him. He pulled it up again as quickly as he could and looked around.

As far as he could tell, no one had seen him. The newcomers were far too eager to plunge after the attackers to notice much else.

Worf turned back to the clone. "Now we have even more reason to leave," he rasped.

Kahless scowled and made a sound of disgust deep in his throat. Thrusting Worf away from him, he probed the wetness around his shoulder with his fingers. They came away bloody.

"The *p'tahkmey,*" he spat. "This was a perfectly good tunic. Mark my words, they'll pay for ruining it."

"You'll need medical attention," remarked Picard.

The Klingon looked at him and laughed. "For what?" he asked. "A flesh wound? I've done worse to myself at the dinner table."

Then he gestured for Picard and Worf to follow, and started for the square again. Behind them, their rescuers were still hooting and shouting, but there was no din of metal on metal. Apparently, the attackers had gotten away.

The captain saw Worf turn to him, his brow creased with concern. "Are you all right, sir?"

Picard nodded. "Better than I have a right to be. And you?"

The Klingon shrugged. "Well enough."

The captain cast a wary glance down an alley as they passed it. "It seems we were not as circumspect as we believed. Someone realized we were on Lomakh's trail and sent us a message."

Worf grunted in agreement. "Stay clear of the conspiracy or die."

Kahless looked back at them. "Is that what you'll do, Picard? Stay away, now that I've shown you the truth of what I said?" His eyes were like daggers.

The captain shook his head. "No. Staying away is no longer an option. Like it or not, we're in the thick of it."

The clone smiled, obviously delighted by the prospect. "You know," he told Picard, "we'll make a Klingon of you yet."

Then he turned his massive back on them and walked on with renewed purpose. After all, his point had been made, albeit at the risk of their lives.

Twelve: The Heroic Age

Kahless cursed deep in his throat. His breath froze on the air, misting his eyes, though it couldn't conceal the urgency of his plight.

Up ahead of him, there were nothing but mountains, their snow-streaked flanks soaring high into wreaths of monstrous, gray cloud. As his *s'tarahk* reared, flinging lather from its flanks, the outlaw chief turned and saw the army less than a mile behind them.

Molor's men. With Molor himself leading the hunt.

Again, Kahless cursed. The tyrant had come out of nowhere, surprising them, rousting them from their early Cold camp. He had forced them to fly before his vastly more numerous forces, and the only direction open to them had been this one.

So they'd run, and run, and run some more, until their mounts were slick with sweat and grunting with exhaustion. And all the while, Kahless had had the feeling they were being herded somewhere.

His feeling had been right. Now they were pinned against a barrier of steep, rocky slopes, which their *s'tarahkmey* had no hope of climbing. They had no choice but to turn and fight, and acquit themselves as well as possible before Molor's warriors overran them.

Nor would their deaths be quick—Kahless's, least of all. Molor had to be half-insane with his thirst for vengeance. Starad had been the most promising of his children, after all. The tyrant would make his son's killer pay with every exquisite torture known to him.

As Molor's forces grew larger on the horizon, the outlaw glanced at his men. They were watching their pursuers as well, wondering how they could possibly escape. Kahless wondered too.

No doubt, the tyrant had been tracking them for some time, feeding on rumors and *s'tarahk* prints, edging ever closer. That was the way he stalked those who defied him—with infinite patience, infinite care. And then he struck with the swiftness of heat lightning.

And this trap—this too was in keeping with Molor's method. Many was the time Kahless had engineered just such a snare, in his days as the tyrant's warchief. And to his knowledge, no one had ever escaped.

"Tell everyone to be ready," he barked, eyeing Morath and Porus and Shurin in one sweeping glance. "Molor won't hold any councils when he arrives. He'll pounce, without warning or hesitation."

For emphasis, Kahless drew his sword, which had become nicked from hewing tough, gnarled *m'ressa* branches. But he had had little choice. It was either that or go without cover from the snow and rain.

"Kahless!" called a voice.

He turned and saw Morath sidling toward him on his *s'tarahk*. His deepset eyes were darker than ever—but not with hopelessness, the outlaw thought. It seemed to him the younger man had an idea.

Kahless couldn't imagine what it might be, or how it could possibly help. But he wasn't about to reject it out of hand.

"What is it?" he snapped, never quite taking his eyes off the approaching line of Molor's men.

Morath came so close their mounts were nearly touching. "I've been in these hills before," he said. "At least, I think I have. It was a long time ago."

Kahless had no time for fond reminiscence. "And?"

"And I think there's a way out," Morath declared.

The outlaw looked at him. "What way?" he asked. "Are you going to sunder the mountains and let us through? Because there's no way I can see to get *over* them."

Morath ignored the derision in the older man's voice and pointed to the gray slopes towering behind them. "We don't have to make it *over* them," he insisted. "We only have to make it *into* them."

Kahless was sure Morath had gone insane, but there was no time to argue with him. Scowling, the outlaw signaled to the others to follow. Then Morath took off, with Kahless right behind him.

Despite his leader's skepticism, the younger man seemed to know exactly where he was going. Turning first this way and that, as if negotiating an invisible trail, he urged his *s'tarahk* ever upward. And if the slopes grew steeper as he went, that didn't seem to faze him in the least.

From behind, Kahless could hear the cries of Molor's men. They were gaining on them now, perhaps half a mile away at most. If Morath was going to work some magic, it would have to come soon.

Suddenly, though the outlaw chief had had his eye on Morath from the beginning of their ascent, the younger man seemed to drop out of sight. Thinking Morath might have fallen into an unseen crevice, Kahless dug his heels into his *s'tarahk*'s flanks and urged the beast forward.

But it wasn't a crevice that had devoured Morath. It was a narrow slot in the mountainside, just big enough for a warrior and his mount to fit through. Morath stopped long enough to beckon his comrades— to assure them with a gesture that he knew what he was doing.

Then he vanished into the slot.

Still wondering where Morath was leading them, Kahless guided his *s'tarahk* into darkness. The walls of the slot scraped his legs where they straddled his beast, but he got through.

Further in, there was a strange sound, almost like the sighing of the north-country wind. It took the outlaw a few seconds to realize it was the murmur of gently running water.

It was shattered by a splash. As Kahless's eyes adjusted to the scarcity of light, he saw Morath moving forward like a shadow, a web of perfect ripples spreading out around him. Gritting his teeth, Kahless followed him into the icy water. Behind him, others were doing the same.

It was some kind of underground stream, flowing from a high point in the mountains. A mysterious black river which had carved a path for itself over the centuries, known only to the tiny creatures who must have inhabited it. And, of course, to Morath.

After a while, there wasn't any light to see by, no matter how well

Kahless's eyes had adjusted. He was forced to travel blind, listening for the snuffling of Morath's mount up ahead and heeding the man's occasional word of guidance.

Fortunately, they didn't have to remain in the river for long. When several minutes had gone by, it seemed to Kahless that the level of the water was dropping. A couple of minutes more and they were on solid rock again.

"Morath," the outlaw rasped, careful to keep his voice low.

Molor couldn't have reached the opening in the mountainside yet, but even so, he didn't want to take a chance on making any noise. Why give the tyrant any help in discovering their exit?

"What is it?" asked the younger man.

"Where does this lead?"

"To another stream," Morath told him, "more treacherous than the first. And from there, to a beach by the sea."

Kahless could scarcely believe what he'd heard. "But the sea . . ."

"Is ten miles distant," the younger man finished. "I know."

The outlaw would normally have been annoyed by the prospect. However, the trek might well prove to be their salvation.

Molor would have a hard time finding the slot. And when he finally discovered it and realized what had happened to them, it was unlikely he'd follow them into what could easily turn out to be an ambush.

Despite himself, the outlaw laughed softly. "That's twice you've saved my hide now," he whispered to Morath.

There was silence for a while. Then Morath spoke again.

"I would have preferred to stay and fight," he said, "if our forces had been more equal."

The chief shook his head. Morath was still young. With him, it was easy to forget that.

"As far as I'm concerned," Kahless replied, "each morning I wake to is a victory. There's no shame in running if it allows you to survive."

Morath didn't speak again as he led them through the darkness. But Kahless could tell that his friend disagreed.

Thirteen: The Modern Age

Despite his acquisition of a seat on the High Council, which had brought with it the governorship of the colony world Ogat, Kurn didn't seem to have changed much since Picard saw him last. The Klingon was still lankier than his older brother, favoring what the captain understood to be their mother's side of the family.

As they entered the garden of standing rocks, Kurn was conversing in bright sunlight with a shorter, stockier Klingon, whose jutting brow was easily his most distinguishing characteristic. Both men wore stately robes, which gave them an air of haughty authority.

At least in Kurn's case, that illusion was quickly dispelled. When Worf and his companions caught his eye with their approach, Kurn grinned like a youth reveling over his first hunting trophy.

"Worf! Brother!" he bellowed, so that the greeting echoed throughout the garden. "Let me look at you!"

Picard's security chief was just as glad to see Kurn. However, as always, he was somewhat less demonstrative in his enthusiasm.

Growing up in an alien culture—that of Earth, for the most part— Worf had learned all too well to hide his innermost feelings. His stint on the *Enterprise* had encouraged him to open up somewhat, but old habits were hard to break.

Kurn pounded Worf on the back and laughed: "It is good to see you, Brother. I miss your companionship."

"And I, yours," the lieutenant responded. "Though I see you have managed to keep busy, with or without me."

Kurn grunted and made a gesture of dismissal. "Serving on the Council is more drudgery than I had expected. It leaves little time for my more pleasant duties—like the inspection I've agreed to carry out today."

Picard saw Kurn's companion approach them then, as if that had been his cue. He inclined his head respectfully—though his dark, deepset eyes were clearly drawn to Kahless more than to Worf or the captain.

"This," said Kurn, "is Rajuc, son of Inagh, esteemed headmaster of this academy. You will find him to be a gracious host."

Rajuc smiled, showing his short, sharp teeth. "My lord governor is too generous with his praise. Still, I will do what I can to make you comfortable here." He turned to Kahless. "I have long been an admirer of your exploits, Emperor. This institution is honored beyond measure by your presence."

Kahless shrugged. "Tell me that after I've bloodied your furnishings and ravaged your women," he instructed.

For a moment, the headmaster seemed to take him seriously. Then his smile returned. "You may do your worst, great one—and I will be honored to be the first to match blades with you."

Beaming, the clone slammed his fist into Rajuc's shoulder. "That's the spirit," he hissed. "Give ground to no one."

"I never have," the headmaster informed him, warming to the subject. "Especially not to the rumor-mongers who would have us believe

Kahless was a fraud. I assure you, Emperor, I place no credence at all in the scroll they claim to have found. As far as I am concerned, the stories we learned as children contain the truth of the matter."

Kahless looked as if someone had rammed him in the stomach with the business end of a painstik. "Indeed," he said tightly. "I am grateful for your loyalty, son of Inagh."

No doubt true, thought Picard. *However, the clone didn't seem to like being reminded of the scroll—not in any context. It was quite simply a sore subject with him.*

"You will be interested to know," Rajuc continued, "that our eldest students plan to reenact Kahless's departure for *Sto-Vo-Kor* in two days' time." For the sake of protocol, he included Worf and Picard in his glance. "Perhaps you can stay long enough to see it."

"I am afraid not," Kahless replied. "As much as I enjoy such dramas, we have business elsewhere which cannot wait." He turned his attention to Kurn. "Which is what we came to speak with you about, Lord Governor."

Worf's brother inclined his shaggy head. "Of course, Emperor." He gestured to a remote cul-de-sac in the garden, obscured by tall, oblong boulders on three sides. "I believe you will find that spot over there to your liking." Placing his hand on Rajuc's shoulder, he added: "I will see you shortly, Headmaster. There is still much we need to discuss."

Rajuc inclined his head again—first to Kurn, then to Kahless, and finally to Worf and Picard. Then he departed.

"He does good work here?" asked the clone.

Kurn nodded. "Fine work. He turns out warriors of the highest caliber."

"Good," Kahless remarked.

Then, taking Kurn's arm, he led him toward the cul-de-sac. Nor did he wait until they reached it and took their seats to tell the governor why they had come. He began as soon as they were out of the headmaster's earshot.

As Picard watched, Worf's brother listened to Kahless's suspicions. It took a while, but Kurn didn't comment until he was certain the emperor had told him all he wished to tell.

"These are grave accusations," he said at last. "Had they come from someone else, I would have dismissed them out of hand. But from Emperor Kahless, the Arbiter of Succession, and my own brother . . ." Kurn scowled. "I will conduct an investigation through my contacts in the Defense Force. Then we will speak of a next step, if one is required of us."

Kahless nodded. "Thank you, son of Mogh. Worf told me you would not fail us."

Kurn flashed a smile at his brother. "Yes, he *would* say that." With that, he rose. "Unfortunately, I must complete my review of the Academy. But if you can linger a while, we'll eat together. I know of a feasting hall in town where the heart of *targ* is worth dying for."

"Done," replied Kahless, obviously cheered by the prospect. "We'll meet back here just before dusk."

"Before dusk," Kurn agreed. He acknowledged Picard, then Worf. "I will see you later, Brother."

"Yes, later," the lieutenant repeated.

He watched his brother leave them with a vaguely uncomfortable expression on his face—one which didn't escape the captain's notice. What's more, Picard thought he knew the reason for it.

"He was holding something back," he said to Worf. "Wasn't he?"

The lieutenant was still watching his brother withdraw. "Or covering something up," he confirmed, with obvious reluctance. "But what?"

Kahless looked at them. "What are you saying?" he asked.

Worf drew a deep breath, then let it out. "I am saying," he explained, "that my brother lied to us when he said he would help. There is something preventing him from doing so—though I cannot imagine what it would be."

The clone eyed him. "You're sure of this?"

The lieutenant nodded. "Regretfully, I am sure of it. And I intend to confront him with it when the opportunity presents itself."

"Dinner would be such an opportunity," the captain suggested.

Kahless made a sound of disgust. "Why wait for dinner? Let us pin him down now, while his lie is still fresh on his lips. Who knows? Maybe he's part of the damned conspiracy."

Worf grabbed him by his arm. Instinctively, Kahless spun around, ready for anything.

"My brother is not a traitor," the lieutenant snarled.

The emperor's eyes narrowed. "Then let him prove it."

And without waiting to see if his companions would follow, the clone took off after Kurn with that swaggering, ground-eating pace by which he'd become known.

Worf made a noise deep in his throat and followed. Picard did his best to keep up, though it wasn't easy. Klingons were damned quick when they wanted to be.

But just as Kahless caught up with his prey, Kurn was swarmed by a group of young admirers—warriors-in-training, wearing the black-and-crimson colors of their academy. The governor had barely expressed his surprise before he was assailed with questions—mostly about his encounters with the Romulans following Gowron's succession.

Kurn would likely have answered them, too, had Kahless not

shooed the youngsters away like a gaggle of young geese. When the emperor wanted something, he tolerated no delays.

Worf's brother looked at Kahless, no doubt trying to conceal his displeasure at the students' dismissal—but falling short. "Is something wrong?" he asked.

Worf answered for the emperor. "You *know* there is, Brother. You lied to us when you said you would investigate Kahless's concerns. And I want to know why."

"Yes," the clone added. "Unless you're a conspirator yourself. Then you may want to go on lying."

Kurn bared his teeth. For a moment, he glared at Kahless and then Worf, apparently liking his brother's challenge even less than the emperor's audacity. Then his temper seemed to cool.

"All right," he said. "I *was* deceiving you. But I had the best of intentions. And I am *not* a conspirator."

"There is a Terran expression," Picard remarked, "about the road to Hell being paved with good intentions. I'd like to hear more before I decide to exonerate you."

Kurn's nostrils flared. Obviously, this was information he wasn't eager to part with. He looked around and made certain they were alone before continuing.

"Very well," the governor growled. "But this must not become common knowledge, or I'll *truly* have become a traitor."

Worf thrust his chin out. "You *know* none of us will repeat anything you tell us."

Kurn thought for a moment, then nodded. "I believe you're right." He heaved a sigh before he began. "The reason I wished to dissuade you from investigating the Defense Force is simple. Close scrutiny of its activities would have revealed a significant number of concurrent absences on the parts of two particular officers—a male and a female, each one with a mate outside the Defense Force."

Picard grunted. The Klingon family was held together by almost feudal bonds. Such philandering was a violation of those bonds—at least, on the part of the male Klingon involved.

The female's situation was different. She could have initiated a divorce anytime she wanted—though she apparently had her reasons for not doing so.

Kurn turned to Picard. "This is not a thing to be taken lightly," he explained, just in case the captain didn't understand. "The response of the cuckolded husband, in this case, must be to seek revenge—as if a challenge had been made. Worse, the cuckolded wife in this situation may have her husband slowly drawn and quartered by four powerful burden beasts—while his lover is forced to watch."

"And yet," said Picard, "they risked this. And despite the fact that your society frowns on it, you yourself condone it."

Kurn scowled at the remark. "You must understand, Captain. These philanderers are members of prominent Houses, which have long been allies of Gowron. If their affair became public, it would drive a wedge between their families and severely erode Gowron's power base."

Kahless snorted. "So these liaisons must be kept secret?"

"Exactly," said Kurn. He turned to his brother. "Of course, if you and your companions had proof of your claims, that would be a different story. But until you do, I cannot help you."

Picard looked to his lieutenant, but Worf said nothing. Apparently, he accepted Kurn's answer as sufficient. Morality aside, the captain wasn't sure he disagreed, given the importance of Gowron's survival as Council Leader.

This time, Kurn didn't bother with niceties. He merely turned his back on them and resumed his progress toward the academy's main hall.

In other words, Picard thought, *they had gained nothing at all.* Frowning, he watched Worf's brother disappear into the building—and with him, their best hope.

Kahless looked to Worf, then Picard. "What now?" he asked. "Who else can we turn to, if not Kurn?"

The words were barely out of his mouth when an explosion ripped through the academy building like a fiery predator, shattering the peacefulness of the grounds and sending debris flying in every direction.

Worf's eyes flashed with anger and fear. "Kurn!" he wailed—and went running toward the site of the explosion, where flames were already starting to lick at the ruined masonry.

A moment later, the captain and Kahless took off after him. Picard could hear shouts of fury arising from the building. Also, cries of agony. Unfortunately, all of them were the voices of children.

Before they could reach the building, a door burst open and a gang of students came rushing out, carrying an adult—Rajuc. The captain winced at the sight of the headmaster. The man was half-covered with blood and his arm hung limply at his side, but at least he was still alive.

Brushing past the students and their burden, Picard followed Worf into the edifice itself—or what was left of it. A ruined corridor stretched out in either direction, choked with rubble.

At one end of it, the captain could see a gaping hole in the ceiling, where daylight tried to lance its way through a curtain of rising smoke and flames. As he approached it, following Worf's lead, he caught a glimpse of the carnage behind the curtain.

A lanky figure was hauling smaller ones away from the blaze. He raised his head at their approach, his face smeared with soot and taut with urgency.

It was *Kurn*.

"There are more of them back there!" he bellowed over the roar of the fire and the screams of the injured. "Some may still be alive!"

But it was clear that some were not. The bodies of dead students littered the hallway, having come to rest wherever the explosion cast them. Their postures were painfully grotesque.

Picard wanted to rearrange them, to give them some measure of dignity in death. But there was no time. His priority had to be the survivors.

For what seemed like an eternity, the captain pulled out child after child from the burning building. Some were conscious, some were not. Some were badly wounded, others only dazed.

There were still others to be saved—no one knew how many. But just as Picard was running back inside for another survivor, an even bigger explosion wracked the building.

He was deafened by it, thrown off his feet as the floor beneath him shivered with the impact. He found himself pressed against a slab of stone, the skin of his cheek scraped and bloody.

As the captain rose and regained his bearings, he saw a huge ball of fire blossom into the sky. In its wake, all was silent. There were no screams from within, no sound of life at all. And by that, he knew there was nothing more they could do in this place.

But if he stayed, the fire would consume him. So Picard dragged himself outside, where the surviving students had been arrayed on the short, red *en'chula* grass.

That's when he saw Worf heading toward him, the Klingon's countenance full of horror and rage. The captain waved his officer back.

"There's no one left in there," he shouted, striving to be heard over the groans of the wounded. "If they weren't dead before, they're dead now."

But Worf didn't stop. Wild-eyed, he kept on going, aiming for the burning pile of rubble that was all that remained of the academy.

"Lieutenant!" Picard cried. "Worf!"

His officer didn't heed him. Instead, as if bent on suicide, he plunged into the maze of flames.

The captain started after him, but he felt himself grabbed from behind. Whirling, he saw it was Kahless who had grabbed him, and Kurn wasn't far behind.

"Let me go!" Picard shouted. "It's Worf! He's gone back into that inferno!"

"Then he's dead!" the clone roared back at him. "You cannot throw your life after his!"

Kurn didn't say a thing. He just stared at the blazing ruin. But by the look in his eyes, the captain could see Worf's brother had given up hope as well.

Cursing beneath his breath, Picard tried to pull away from Kahless. But the clone was too strong, and the human was too drained from his rescue efforts. In time, the captain ceased his struggles and gazed narrow-eyed at the academy building.

He could feel the heat of the conflagration on his face. Even here, it made the skin tighten across his face.

By then, Picard told himself, Worf had to have perished. No one could have survived. He didn't want to believe it, but he couldn't see any way around it.

Suddenly, against all common sense, the captain caught sight of something moving in the debris. Something that made a path for itself between the flames. Something that staggered out through a gap in what had once been a wall.

It was Worf.

His face was blackened with soot, his clothing full of smoke and red-hot embers. And somehow, against all odds, he had not one but *two* young Klingons slung over his shoulders.

Rushing to him, the captain helped relieve Worf of his burden. With Kurn's help, he lowered one of the students to the ground. Though badly burned and bleeding from half a dozen places, the child was still breathing. He had a chance to live.

Not so with the other one, the youth Kahless had wrested from Worf's shoulders. He was blackened beyond recognition, a lifeless husk. But in the chaos within the building, there couldn't have been any way to tell that. Worf had just grabbed him and run.

As for the lieutenant himself, he was on all fours, helplessly coughing out the acrid fumes that had invaded his lungs. As someone came and took the living child away, Picard went to Worf and laid a hand on his powerful shoulder.

The Klingon's head came about sharply, his eyes smoldering no less than the inferno from which he'd escaped. Shrugging the captain off with a growl, he got to his knee and turned away.

Picard wasn't offended. He understood. His security officer had been reduced to instincts in his attempt to save those children. And his instincts were not pretty by human standards.

No, he realized suddenly—there was more to it than that. A great deal more. Standing, he recalled the story he had read several years earlier in Worf's personnel file.

As a child of six, Worf had accompanied his parents to the Khitomer outpost, on the rim of the Klingon Empire. It was an installation devoted to research, to scientific pursuits. Nonetheless, the Romulans attacked the place without warning, brutally destroying the four thousand Klingons who lived there—Worf's parents included.

Buried in the rubble, in danger of suffocation, Mogh's son would have died too—except for the Starfleet vessel *Intrepid,* which arrived in time to search for survivors. A team located a faint set of life signs in the ruins and began digging. It was Sergey Rozhenko, a human, who saved the Klingon's life and later adopted him.

The captain could only imagine what it had been like to be trapped in all that debris, small and alone, despairing of assistance yet hanging on anyway. Or how Worf had felt when he'd seen the stones above him coming away, to reveal the bearded face of his savior.

That's why he had refused to leave those two children behind. That was the force that had impelled Worf from the conflagration against all odds. The Klingon remembered the horrors of Khitomer. He could not do less for those students than Sergey Rozhenko had done for him.

Even as Picard thought this, he heard a call go up, a wail of pure and unadulterated pain. A moment later, a second call answered it, and then a third. Before he knew it, every survivor, child and adult, was crying out to the smoke-stained sky above them. Worf too.

This wasn't the death song the captain had heard before—the ritual howl of joy and approval meant to speed a warrior's soul to the afterlife. This was an admixture of fury and anguish, of ineffable sadness, that came from the darkest depths of the Klingon heart.

Those who died this day had been denied the chance to become warriors. They had been slaughtered like animals on the altar of greed and power. And no one here, Picard included, would ever forget that.

The murderers of these children had to be brought to justice. There was no other way the captain would be able to sleep at night.

"Whoever did this," said a hollow voice, "was without honor."

Picard turned and saw it was Kahless who had uttered the remark, his throat raw from crying out. And he was standing beside Kurn— hardly an accident.

Worf's brother didn't turn to look at the clone. But in his eyes, the captain could see the reflection of the burning academy. Kurn's jaw clenched, an indication of the emotions roiling within him.

"Obviously," said the governor, in a soft but dangerous voice, "the conspiracy is real. And this attack was directed at *me,* on the assumption I would move to help you uncover it." He grunted. "Me, a member of the High Council—as if that meant anything."

"The question," Kahless responded pointedly, "is what you are going to do about it."

This time, Kurn looked at him. "What I will do," he said, "is put my loyalty to the lovers aside—and help in whatever way I can."

The clone nodded, satisfied. Then, despite the weariness they all felt, he went back to see to the survivors, who were being tended to by those adults who had survived unscathed.

Suspecting that Worf and his brother might have several things to say to each other, the captain fell in behind Kahless. After all, Picard had a brother too. He knew how exasperating they could be.

Fourteen: The Heroic Age

Snow was falling in great, hissing dollops, making it difficult to see the trees even thirty meters in front of them. But it wasn't falling so heavily Kahless couldn't see the hoofprints between the drifts, or catch the scent of the wild *minn'hor* herd that had made them.

"We're gaining on them," Porus observed with some enthusiasm, his ample beard rimed with frost.

"Slowly," Shurin added. He snorted. "Too slowly."

Kahless turned to the one-eyed man. Like the rest of them, his cheeks were sunken from not having eaten in a while.

"We're in no hurry, Shurin. It's only the middle of the day. Why push the *s'tarahkmey* if we don't have to?"

Morath said nothing. That wasn't unusual. He only spoke if he really had something to say.

As the outlaw chief negotiated a path through the forest, he became aware of the *jinaq* amulet pressed against his chest by the weight of his tunic. And that made him think about Kellein.

Around her father's village, it would be Growing season in another month or so—time to pursue the promise he had made to her by the riverbank. And pursue it he would.

It was madness, of course. Though he wanted Kellein as he'd never wanted anything or anyone in his life, all he could give her was the life of an outlaw. And he had learned how hard that life could be.

All Cold long, he and his band had been on the move, always looking back over their shoulders, always wondering when Molor would swoop down on them like a hunting bird. Hell, Kahless hadn't gotten a good night's sleep since he killed the tyrant's son—except for the night he'd spent by Vathraq's keep.

If he stayed in this realm, Molor would track him down. If not in

Cold, then in Growing; if not during the day, then at night. Kahless had
no illusions about that.

That was why he had to reach the southern continent. True, it was a
harsh and backward place, largely untouched by civilization. Life there
would be punishing, and rewards few.

But at least he and Kellein would be safe from the tyrant's hatred.
With luck, they might find some measure of happiness together. And if
they were truly lucky, if the ancient gods smiled on them, their children
would never have to know the name Molor.

All Kahless had to do was make his way into one of the tyrant's port
towns. And hire a vessel with a greedy captain, who knew his way
across the sea. And when he had done that, he would—

Suddenly, the outlaw realized how absurd it all sounded. How
impossible. Chuckling to himself, he shook his snow-covered head.

How would he pay for their passage? And what seafarer would defy
the all-powerful Molor to help a scraggly renegade?

It was an illusion, a pipedream. And yet, it was one he would wrestle into truth. Somehow. For Kellein's sake.

"Kahless!" a voice hissed at him.

It was Shurin. The one-eyed man pointed through the sheeting
snowfall at a wide brown smudge in the distance. Kahless sniffed the
air.

It was the herd, all right. Perhaps a dozen of the beasts, enough to
keep them fed for a week or more. Nodding at Shurin to acknowledge
the sighting, Kahless reached for the bow he'd made, which was
secured to the back of his saddle.

He could hear the flapping of leather as the others did the same. Of
course, they didn't have to worry about the *minn'hormey* hearing them.
They were still a good distance from the herd and the thick, falling
snow dampened all sounds.

As long as Kahless and his men remained downwind of the beasts,
they wouldn't have any trouble picking them off. An easy kill, he
thought—though small compensation for the scarcity of such herds, or
the painstaking time it took to find them.

Raising his hand, the outlaw gave the signal for his men to urge their
mounts forward. Then he himself dug his heels into the flanks of his
s'tarahk. The animal picked up its pace, gradually narrowing the gap
between hunter and prey.

The *minn'hormey* didn't seem to suspect a thing. They maintained
their slow progress through the wood, their shaggy hindquarters sway-
ing from side to side, their horned heads trained squarely on what was
ahead of them.

Kahless sighted a particularly slow *minn'hor* and was about to take it down when he felt a hand on his arm. Turning, he saw Morath's ruddy, snow-covered face. In the swirling gray of the storm, the younger man's eyes looked like dark caverns.

"What?" asked Kahless.

Morath pointed—not at the herd, but at something off to the left of it. Something that moved with a purpose similar to their own.

There were four-legged predators in this place, but they didn't hunt in packs. And besides, these shapes were too tall to be animals. Klingons, then. Mounted, like Kahless's men. And after the same *minn'hormey.*

The other band must have spotted them at about the same time, because the riders hung back from the herd. With another hand signal, Kahless gestured for his own men to slow down.

The *minn'hormey* kept going, still unaware of their danger. The wind howled and writhed, sending spindrifts whirling through the forest. And all the while, the two hunting parties sat their mounts, eyeing one another.

Sizing one another up. After all, they were Klingons.

Finally, Kahless spoke, shouting to make himself heard over the storm. "This herd is ours. If need be, we'll fight for it."

On the other side, one figure separated itself from the others. His hair was the color of copper, gathered in ice-encrusted braids. "So will we," came the answer.

Kahless licked his lips. The last thing he wanted was to lose men over a meal. But he didn't know when the next one would come along, and he had no stomach for *s'tarahk* meat.

Morath and Porus had positioned themselves on either side of him. He glanced at them, making sure of their alertness. They held their bows at the ready, waiting for him to give the word.

But the leader of the other band acted first. With a bloodchilling cry, he raised his arrow to eye level and let it fly.

It sliced through the snow, missing Kahless by no more than an inch, and buried itself in a tree behind him. The outlaw chief's teeth clenched. Roaring a challenge of his own, he shot back.

A moment later, the forest was alive with swarms of wooden shafts. There were grunts of pain and angry curses, all muffled by the storm. The *s'tarahk* under Porus shrieked, spilling him in its agony.

Kahless didn't like this. They could fire back and forth for hours, with no clearcut victor—except the damned *minn'hormey,* who would go free in the meantime. It was time to remember Molor's advice and take the bloody battle to the enemy.

Replacing his bow on the back of his saddle, Kahless took out his blade and spurred his mount forward. The animal responded with a gratifying surge of speed, putting him face to face with the enemy leader before anyone could stop him.

Another of Molor's lessons sprang to mind—cut the serpent's head off and the rest of it will die. With this in mind, Kahless took a swipe at the enemy leader's chest.

But the man was quicker than he looked. Ducking low, he let the blade pass over him. Then he reached out and grabbed Kahless's wrist.

At the same time, he drew a weapon of his own—a sword which had clearly seen better days. But it was still sharp enough to sweep a warrior's head off his shoulders.

Kahless had no intention of being the head in question. Lunging forward, he grabbed his enemy by the forearm.

The two of them struggled for a moment, whirling about on their s'tarahkmey, neither daring to let go of the other. Then, as one or both of them lost his balance, they toppled into the snow.

By then, Morath and Porus and the others had come crashing after their chief, breaking branches and trampling saplings in their way. But the other band leaped forward to meet them.

Kahless and his adversary were like a rock in the middle of a strong current. The battle raged around them as they rolled on the ground, each struggling for leverage with savage intensity.

Suddenly, Kahless's foot slipped out from under him, and the other man gained the upper hand. Twisting his wrist free, he smashed Kahless across the face with the hilt of his sword. A second time. And again.

For Kahless, the world swam in a red haze. And when it cleared, his enemy was sitting astride him, sword raised high, ready to plunge it deep into his naked throat.

Kahless groped for the handle of his weapon, but it wasn't there, and he was too dazed to search for it. He tried to push his enemy off, but it was no use. His strength had left him along with his senses.

"Tell me your name," said the man, "so I may honor it when I speak of our battle around the campfire."

The outlaw chief laughed at his own helplessness, spitting out the blood that was filling his mouth. "You'd honor me?" he grated, his voice sounding a hundred miles distant. "Make it Kahless, son of Kanjis, then. Or Molor himself. Or whoever you want."

What did he care? He'd be dead by then.

But as Kahless's words sank in, a change came over his enemy's face. A look of uncertainty, the outlaw thought. At any rate, the sword remained high.

"You are . . . Kahless?" the man demanded sharply. "In truth?"

The outlaw nodded. "I am." He squinted through the prismatic snow that had gathered on his eyelashes. "Do I know you?"

His enemy shook his head from side to side, his copper-colored braids slapping at his cheeks. "No," he said. "But I know *you.*"

Suddenly, the man was on his feet, waving with his sword at the other combatants. "Stop," he cried. "All those who follow Edronh, put down your weapons. These warriors are our friends!"

Kahless thought he was dreaming, or addled by all the punishment he'd taken. Klingons didn't stop in the middle of a life-or-death struggle to declare their enemies their allies.

Or did they?

All around him, the enemy stopped fighting. Kahless's men looked at one another, unsure what to make of this. And as the outlaw chief himself got to his feet, he didn't know what to tell them.

Then the leader of the other band knelt before Kahless and laid his sword at Kahless's feet. When he spoke again, it was in a voice filled with deep shame and embarrassment.

"We yield to bold Kahless, who leads the fight against the tyrant. Had we known from the beginning whom we faced, we would never have raised our bows against him."

The son of Kanjis began to understand. Edronh and his men were outlaws too—the kind Kahless had hunted when he was still in the tyrant's employ. And like Vathraq to the south, they believed Kahless was leading a revolt against Molor's rule.

He was about to correct the notion when he realized how foolish it would be. The truth would only start their bloody battle all over again. And by keeping his mouth shut, by going along with the lie, he would get them the *cob'lat*'s share of the hunt.

Grabbing a tree for support, because his head still swam with the other man's blows, Kahless dismissed the conflict with a sweep of his arm. "It was an honest mistake. I will not hold it against you, nor will my men."

To cement his promise, he eyed as many familiar faces as he could find with a single glance. They seemed to understand, because to a man they nodded back. All except one, that is.

Only Morath looked away from him, reluctant to be part of the falsehood. The younger man was scowling as he stuck his sword in his belt. *It was all right,* Kahless thought. *Some day, Morath would learn.*

A young warrior, even younger than Morath, approached Kahless. Like his chief, he laid his sword in the snow.

"It is an honor to meet you," he said.

The enemy leader—no longer an enemy at all now, it seemed—grinned at the young one. Then he turned to Kahless.

"My youngest son," he explained. "His name is Rannuf."

Kahless nodded. "In that case, I'm glad we didn't kill him. Now, my friend, about the herd . . ."

"We'll take it down together," suggested Edronh. "But you may take the bulk of the provisions. We know these hills as we know our own swords. We can always find another herd."

Kahless smiled. This was better than leaving corpses in the snow. Much better. And all it had cost them was a single lie.

Fifteen: The Modern Age

Deanna Troi spotted the boy in the corridor outside the ship's classrooms, on his way to the turbolift. She hurried after him, calling his name.

"Alexander?"

The boy turned and stopped to wait for her. The Betazoid smiled.

"I almost missed you," she told him. "I meant to be here ten minutes ago, but my work ran a little long today."

Alexander looked at her, his dark brows coming together at the bridge of his nose. "Is everything all right?"

She knew exactly what he was asking. *Damn,* she thought. *Here I am, trying to ease Worf's absence, and I find a way to alarm the poor kid. Some counselor you are, Deanna.*

"Everything's fine," she assured him, "as far as we know."

Troi had to add the caveat, just in case. After all, away missions included their share of tragedies, and the Klingon Empire was more perilous than most other destinations.

Alexander seemed to relax a little, but not completely. "So why were you in such a hurry to see me?"

The counselor shrugged. "No reason in particular. It's just that I haven't had a chance to spend any time with you since your father took off, and I thought you might like to keep me company while I have a sundae in Ten-Forward. Of course, you *could* have one yourself, so I don't look like too much of a glutton."

The boy normally smiled at her silliness, but not this time. "Okay," he said without enthusiasm. "I guess."

"That's the spirit," she told him, wishing she meant it.

Worf looked around the bridge of Kurn's ship. It wasn't much bigger or more comfortable than the one in which Kahless had brought them to Ogat. But it had four seats, one in the center and three on the periphery, and that made it possible for them all to be on the bridge at once.

At the moment, Kurn was in the center seat, checking to make certain they were still on course. After all, Klingon vessels of this size had a tendency to veer slightly at high speeds.

Kahless was pacing the corridor that led to the vessel's sleeping quarters, occasionally striking a bulkhead with a mere fraction of his strength. It was as if the ship were a *s'tarahk* and he was urging it into a gallop, eager to get on with his self-appointed mission.

Captain Picard was sitting at the station closest to the main viewscreen, his blunt, human features illuminated by the lurid light of his control panel. He seemed absorbed in the readings of the alien monitors.

Sitting next to the captain, one panel over, Worf watched him. There was something he needed to say, but he was having difficulty finding the words to say it.

After a moment or two, he gave up. He would just have to say what he felt, and hope that would be enough.

"Sir?"

The captain turned to him, so that the control lights lit up only half of his face. "Yes, Lieutenant?"

Worf frowned. "Sir, I must apologize for the way I acted on Ogat. At the academy, I mean."

Picard nodded. "After you emerged from the burning building, and I attempted to console you."

"Yes," said the Klingon. "I pulled away from you in a most unseemly manner. But I assure you, it was not my intention to offend you. Or to seem ungrateful for your—"

The captain winced and held up his hand. "Please, Mister Worf. There is no need for you to go on. First off, it's much too painful for me to watch. And second, I was not offended."

The lieutenant looked at him. "But the way I acted was hardly in keeping with Starfleet protocol."

Picard leaned closer. "That is true. However, you were under a great deal of strain at the time. We all were. And as you have no doubt noticed, we are not now wearing Starfleet uniforms. It occurs to me we can make some allowances if we wish."

The Klingon breathed a little easier. "Thank you, sir."

For a second or two, the captain smiled. Then he said, "You are quite welcome, Lieutenant," and went back to scrutinizing his control panel.

His duty discharged, Worf sat back in his chair. He was fortunate to have a commanding officer who understood—at least in some small measure—what the Klingon was going through.

Normally, he would have been able to control his more feral instincts, no matter the provocation. Serving on the *Enterprise* had made him skilled at that. But this was different.

The killing of children was a provocation that went to the heart of his being—and not just because it was dishonorable, or because it stirred the memories of his experiences on Khitomer.

Worf was a father. And not so long ago, he had considered sending his son to the academy on Ogat, to make him more of a Klingon.

That was why the faces of those children had cut him so deeply, with their bloodless lips and their staring eyes. That was why he had lost control of himself and reverted to savagery.

Because to him, every one of those faces had been Alexander's.

Troi found Will Riker in the captain's ready room, taking care of ship's business at the captain's computer terminal. As she entered, he leaned back in his chair, his expression speaking volumes.

"And people ask me why I turned down my own command," he sighed.

"Red tape?" she asked.

"By the cargo hold full," he said. "What can I do for you, Deanna?"

"It's about Alexander," she told him. "He's not himself lately. And I think I know why."

Riker guessed at the answer. "The boy's having a hard time coping with his father's absence?"

"Certainly," said Troi, "he's worried about his father coming back in one piece—but not as much as you might think. He has a lot of confidence in Worf, after all."

"Then what's on his mind?" the first officer asked.

The counselor frowned. "Alexander wouldn't tell me, of course. It's as if he's trying to be like his father—strong and silent. So on a hunch I checked the computer log, to see if he'd been exposed to anything disturbing."

"And?" said Riker.

Her frown deepened. "I found out he had read those scrolls the captain told us about. The ones concerning Kahless."

The first officer regarded her, then leaned forward and tapped out a few commands on his padd. A moment later, he read the information contained on the screen.

"I see what you mean. Alexander accessed the contents of the scrolls night before last. And it seems he spent quite a bit of time with them." He shrugged. "Now what? Are you going to confront him with this?"

Troi shook her head. "No. As much as he likes me, as much as he trusts me, I don't think I'm the one he wants to talk to."

It took the first officer a moment or two to figure out what she meant. "You mean you want *me* to talk to him?"

"It would be a big help," the Betazoid noted. "Besides, it'll give you a chance to see how much fun my job is."

Riker eyed her. "If I'd wanted to be a counselor, Counselor, I would've applied to the University of Betazed." His features softened. "On the other hand, I can't let poor Alexander swing in the wind. Just what is it you'd like me to do?"

Troi told him.

Sixteen: The Heroic Age

It was the season of Growing.

The river that led to Kellein's village was swollen with flood, rushing between its banks as if it had somewhere important to go. The overhanging *micayah* trees were sleek and heavy with dark green nuts, which somehow managed to hover just above the glistening water.

As Kahless led his men along the same path he'd traveled the year before, Vathraq's village loomed ever closer. He recognized the dark walls, the dark keep, the dark tower. The rows of fruit trees that extended in every direction. And of course, the smell of manure.

It was just as he remembered it. More than ever, he was aware of the *jinaq* amulet his betrothed had given him. It lay against his chest, a promise yet to be fulfilled.

Kahless smiled at the thought of his betrothed. He imagined the look on her face when she spotted the outlaw band making its way down from the hills. The joy in her sharp-toothed grin, the quickening of her pulse.

He almost wished he could catch her bathing again and surprise her as he had before. But that would be too much to ask, he knew. It was ample cause for thanks that he had made it through the Cold.

As he led his men closer, the track dipped and then rose again, lined now on the river side with *tran'nuc* trees. Their purplish fruit were still puny things, waiting for late in the season to grow fat and flavorful.

He remembered how he had staggered out of Vathraq's house and tasted one—just before he'd tasted Kellein, and she him. Perhaps, he thought, I should bring one with me as a luck charm. Then he again felt the amulet under his tunic and knew that was all the luck he needed.

"Kahless," said Morath, who had come up beside him.

The outlaw was smiling as he turned to his friend. "Yes? What is it?"

Morath seemed intent on something in the distance. He squinted in the sunlight. "Something is wrong."

"Wrong?" Kahless echoed. He could feel his heart start to beat faster. "In what way?"

Following Morath's gaze, he saw what the man was talking about. One of the gates in the wall ringing the keep had been left ajar.

"It's only a gate," said the outlaw.

But he knew better. And so did Morath, by his expression.

"Where are the sentries?" asked the younger man.

Kahless repeated the question to himself. Granted, it was the middle of the day, but danger could appear at any time. Vathraq wouldn't tolerate such an oversight . . . if that was all it was.

Placing his hand on the hilt of his sword, he eyed the place in a new light. The quiet, which had seemed so natural only a few moments ago, seemed ominous now. And Vathraq's house, which had been so inviting, began smelling a lot like a trap.

If Molor discovered Kahless was taken in by these people, he might have left some men there to watch for the outlaw's return. Certainly, stranger things had been known to happen.

"A wise man would withdraw," Morath remarked.

Kahless looked at him. "Turn from a fight? That's not like you, my friend."

The younger man grunted. "I said a *wise* man would withdraw—not that we would. And if I know you, we will not."

True, thought the outlaw. *After all, this wasn't simply a matter of their own preservation. If the keep had been taken by Molor's men, Kellein was a captive—perhaps worse.* Kahless couldn't tolerate the thought of that.

"Follow me," he advised Morath. "But be wary."

"I am always wary," his friend replied.

Little by little, Kahless urged his *s'tarahk* up the river road, toward the open gate. His senses prickled with awareness, ready for the least sign of an ambush. But he couldn't find any.

At least, not at first. However, as they came closer to the gate, he distinctly heard something rustling within the walls. The swords of Molor's men, perhaps, as they drew them from their belts? Their arrows, as they fit them to their bowstrings?

The outlaw had to make a decision, and quickly. Should I charge the gate, he asked himself, in an effort to surprise the *p'tahkmey?* Or continue this slow progress, waiting to see how far I can get before they stop me?

Before Kahless could come to a conclusion, the whisper of movement within the walls became a storm of activity, punctuated by high-pitched cries of annoyance. Before his eyes, a huge, black cloud erupted around the keep.

A flock of *kraw'zamey,* protesting loudly as they headed for the slopes beyond the river. The outlaw swallowed, his mouth as dry as dust.

This was no trap. Carrion birds didn't abide the presence of Klingons. Nor did they gather except where there was sustenance for them.

If Molor's men had been here, they were gone now. But that was no comfort to Kahless. Clenching his jaw so hard it hurt, he dismounted and walked the rest of the way to the gate. Then he went inside.

What greeted his eyes was a slaughterhouse. Vathraq's warriors choked the space between the walls and the keep with their gutted, lifeless bodies. Fleshless skulls grinned up at him with bared teeth and hollowed-out eyes, picked to the bone by the beaks of the *kraw'zamey.*

Molor's men could still have been inside the keep, awaiting them, but Kahless no longer cared. He was too overcome with fear for his beloved, too caught up in a current of dread and fascination to worry about himself.

Crossing the courtyard, he tore open the doors to the keep. Inside, it was silent as a tomb. Putting one leaden foot in front of the other, he made his way past the antechamber into the great hall.

Vathraq was sitting on his high wooden throne, just as Kahless remembered him. Except now he was slumped to one side, a blackened hole in his chest where an arrow had pinned him to the chair, and his eyes were sunken and staring.

His people lay scattered about, draped over serving tables or crumpled on the stone floor, cut down at the brink of the firepit or tossed inside to char and burn. No one had escaped, young or old, male or female.

No one except Kellein. Try as he might, Kahless couldn't find her body. It gave rise to a single, reckless hope.

Perhaps she had eluded Molor's hand. Perhaps she had been away at the time. Or she had seen the tyrant's forces in time to hide herself.

Perhaps, against all odds, she still lived.

Kahless felt a hand on his shoulder. Whirling, he saw that it was only Morath. But his friend had a grim expression on his face, even grimmer than was called for.

Suddenly, the outlaw knew why, and his heart plummeted. "Kellein . . . ?" he rasped, his throat dry with grief.

Morath nodded. "Upstairs," he said.

Rushing past him, staggering under his load of anguish, Kahless left the feast hall and found the steps that led to the higher floors. His men, who had been searching the place while he lingered downstairs, stood aside for him as he barreled his way up.

At the head of the stair, he found her. She was sprawled in a pool of dried blood, a sword still clasped tight in her hand.

Kellein's eyes were closed, as if she were only sleeping. But her skin was pale and translucent as *pherza* wax, and there was a track of blackened gore from the corner of her mouth to the line of her jaw.

The outlaw didn't have the heart to inspect her wounds. Slowly, carefully, he touched his fingertips to her lips. They were cold and stiff as stone. Sorrow rose up in him like a flood.

Only then did he notice the thong around her neck and reach inside her tunic to take out her *jinaq* amulet. Cradled in his hand, it sparkled gaily in the light from a nearby window, affirming her vow.

Clumsily, with fingers that barely seemed alive, Kahless took out his own amulet and held it beside hers. As intended, they were identical. He and Kellein had planned to wear them at their mating ceremony.

Without meaning to, he began whispering the words he would have spoken. "I pledge my heart and my hand to you, Kellein, daughter of Vathraq, and no other. I am your mate for the rest of my days."

They were more than words to him, though his beloved had passed through the gates of Death. Kahless knew then and there he would never take another mate as long as he lived.

Indeed, why live at all? Why bother? With Kellein gone, what was there to live for?

Nothing, the outlaw screamed in the darkness of his despair. "Nothing!" he bellowed, making the hallway ring with his anger and his pain.

Blind with bitterness, Kahless drew his sword from his belt and raised it high above his head. Then, with all his strength, he hacked at the floor beside Kellein. One, twice, and again, raising white-hot sparks, until the gray metal of the blade finally relented and shattered on the stones.

The pieces skipped this way and that, then were still. As still as Kellein, Kahless raged. As still as the heart inside him.

Delirious, writhing inside with agony, he fled. Down the stairs, out of the antechamber and across the blindingly bright courtyard. He staggered past the corpses of Vathraq's defenders, through the gates to the walled town, and out to the river road.

His *s'tarahk* stood there with all the others, taut and nervous though it didn't know why. It raised its head when it saw him coming.

With a growl, he threw himself into the saddle and dug his heels into the animal's sides. Startled, it bolted forward, taking him down the road as fast as it could carry him.

He didn't know where he was going or why. He just knew he wanted to die before he got there.

Seventeen: The Modern Age

Kurn's estate on Ogat wasn't far from the academy. As dusk fell, Picard stood in its rambling main hall, a mug of tea warming his hands. He stared out a window at the darkening sky.

Several silvery shapes, each too big and irregularly shaped to be a star, reflected the light of the homeworld's sun. Testimonies, the captain mused, to the Klingon tendency to fragment themselves at every opportunity.

Once, more than seventy-five years ago, there had been a moon in these heavens. Called Praxis, it supplied the Klingons with more than three-fourths of their energy resources. Then, due to years of overmining and insufficient safety precautions, a reactor exploded—contaminating the homeworld's atmosphere, poking great holes in its delicate ozone layer, and creating a quirk in its orbit.

Klingon scientists had turned pale as they anticipated the result. In half a century, Qo'noS would have become a lifeless husk, abandoned by its people. Of course, there were ways to save it, to preserve Klingon culture and tradition. But they were expensive ways—made implausible by the size of the Klingons' military budget.

There was but one option. The High Council opened a dialogue with the Federation, aiming for peace between the two spacefaring entities. Once that was accomplished, funds could be diverted from military uses to the rescue of the homeworld.

As it turned out, peace was not an easy row to hoe. Factions in both the Klingon hierarchy and the Federation tried to halt the process at every turn. There was considerable hardship, considerable violence. Nonetheless, by dint of courage and tolerance and hard work, a treaty was signed.

There would be peace between the Federation and the Klingon Empire. But that didn't mean the Klingons would stop warring with each *other.* Not by a long shot.

Over the next seventy-five years, the complexion of the High Council changed again and again. The story was always the same—some rising power challenging an established one at the point of a sharpened *bat'leth.* And no sooner was the upstart ensconced on the council than some newcomer appeared to challenge *him.*

As a young man, Picard had heard about the Klingons' overwhelming thirst for power, which made them tear at each other like ravening beasts. He had accepted it, but he had never truly understood it.

Now, he understood it all too well. It wasn't power that motivated the Klingons so much as instinct. It was in their nature to fight. If they couldn't battle an outside foe, they would battle each other.

Hence, this conspiracy to overthrow Gowron, which had begun to carve its bloody path to the council chamber. Perhaps the captain would not have been so angered by it, perhaps he could have accepted it better, if its victims had not been innocent children.

Turning, he saw Worf and Kahless standing by the hearth, staring into its flames. Picard could only imagine what they saw there.

Chaos? Destruction? The deaths of multitudes? Or the irresistible glory of battle? Even in his officer's case, he wasn't entirely sure.

Abruptly, the doors to the chamber opened and Kurn returned to them. Closing the doors behind him, he glanced at the captain.

"As you suggested," he said, "I've arranged with Rajuc to report my death in the explosion. Also, the deaths of several other adults. With luck, our enemies will believe you three perished as well."

Kahless nodded. "Well done, Kurn. If they think we're dead, they will lower their guards. And it will give us the opportunity to strike."

"Yes," the master of the house agreed. "But strike *how*, my friend? Where do we begin?"

The clone made a sound of disgust. "I had entertained the hope you could speak to Gowron for us. I thought you would have his ear."

Kurn shook his head. "Gowron has changed. He has forgotten who supported him when the House of Duras went for his head. I no longer understand what he is thinking half the time."

"Surely," said Picard, "the firebombing of the academy should be enough to arouse his suspicions."

"He will say it could have been an accident," Kurn argued. "Or the work of someone other than a conspirator."

"Still," Worf maintained, "if we had proof, he would have to act on it. He would have no choice."

"Yes," Kahless agreed. "Something he can hold in his hands. Something tangible. But then, obtaining such proof has been our problem all along."

"Something tangible," the governor echoed.

There was silence for a moment. Picard was at a loss as to how to proceed. So were the others, apparently.

Finally, it was Worf who spoke. "If there was a bomb," he said slowly, still honing the idea in his own mind, "there will be fragments of it in the academy's wreckage. And while they are not the sort of proof we are looking for, they may provide us with a way to obtain that proof."

Kahless's eyes burned. He nodded. So did Kurn.

Unfortunately, the captain didn't quite know what Worf was talking about. But he imagined he was about to learn.

The broad, powerful leader of the conspiracy made his way through the hot, swirling mists of the cavern, his only garb a linen loincloth. The mists stank of sulfur and iron and the pungent lichen that grew here, and they were like fire on his skin.

But those who frequented the steambaths of Ona'ja'bur lived years longer than their peers. Or so it was said—mostly, the conspirator suspected, by the crafty merchants in the town down the hill, which profited greatly from the armies of visitors.

Of course, the conspirator had never put much credence in the tales about the baths. He would never have come here strictly out of concern for his health. Rather, it was the need for a meeting place far from the scrutiny of others that had drawn him here.

Not too long ago, he would have considered conferring with his comrades at the dining hall in Tolar'tu. But clearly, that was no longer an option. When his comrades were discovered there, it had rendered that venue useless to all of them.

Nor would this one be any more useful, were it not for the lack of visitors to the baths at this time of year. After all, they needed their privacy as well as their anonymity.

The conspirator sat and waited, as far from the battery-powered safety globes as possible. They were only vague, blue-white balls of incandescence in the distance. Fortunately, he didn't have to wait long before he saw a figure emerge from the mists.

It was Lomakh, looking thinner and considerably less distinguished in his loincloth than in his body armor. But then, the conspirator thought, that was probably true of everyone—himself included.

Lomakh inclined his head. "I am glad you could come," he said, his voice as harsh as ever, even subdued in a whisper.

"Likewise," said the conspirator. And then, because he was not by nature a very patient individual: "What news do you have?"

His companion sat down beside him. "Good news, most likely."

"Most likely?" the conspirator echoed.

Lomakh shook his head. "The groundskeeper at the academy, the one we hired to plant the bombs?"

"Yes? What about him?"

"He was killed in the explosion, the idiot. Therefore, we have not been able to corroborate the deaths of our enemies."

The conspirator cursed. Some little thing was always going wrong. "What of our sources elsewhere on Ogat?"

"Those, at least, seem to confirm that our action was successful. So far as they can tell, Kahless and his friends are no more."

The conspirator relaxed somewhat—but not completely. "Continue your investigation," he said, "but keep it discreet. We don't want to give ourselves away as we did before."

Lomakh scowled at that. "It was the sheerest coincidence that Kahless spotted us in that dining hall."

"Of course it was," he replied, allowing a note of irony to creep into his voice. "I just want to make sure there are no *further* coincidences."

As it happened, Fate had been their friend as well as their enemy. After a couple of days of their dining-hall meetings, Lomakh had realized that he and Kardem were being watched, and had arranged for the watcher to be killed by street mercenaries.

But that was the day the watcher's allies had chosen to show up. In the melee that followed, one of them was revealed as a human—a human called "Captain" by a comrade.

Few humans had ever set foot on Qo'noS. One of them, the famous Arbiter of Succession, fit the description provided by the street mercenaries. And of course, he was the *Captain* of the *Enterprise.*

What's more, if Jean-Luc Picard was on the homeworld, could his Lieutenant Worf have been far behind? And would they not have enlisted the aid of Worf's brother Kurn in short order?

Still, it was not clear who had summoned them—who the mysterious, cowled watcher was in the dining hall—until they had gotten word from one of their sources at Gowron's court.

Apparently, the Kahless clone had come to the council leader with some interesting suspicions. But from what their spy could gather, Gowron had declined to help, asking for some proof of the so-called conspiracy.

Would Kahless have given up, then? Allowed a plot of some consequence to hatch without his doing something about it? Certainly not. But where else could he have gone for help?

To the captain of the *Enterprise,* perhaps? It made some sense. And it went a long way toward explaining Picard's presence in Tolar'tu.

Just in case, the conspirators had determined Kurn's schedule and planted their firebombs wherever they could—knowing the governor's estate was too well-guarded for them to reach him there. As a result, the academy hadn't been the only place targeted for destruction—just the place where Kurn had received his visitors.

With luck, their other bombs would go unused. But the leader of the conspiracy wasn't quite ready to concede that.

He sighed. "Even if we were successful on Ogat, Kahless may have managed to spread word of his suspicions. There may be others working against us even as we speak."

"Then we will find them," said Lomakh. He closed his fingers into a fist and squeezed. "And we will crush them."

"No," the conspirator declared. "That is not enough. We must speed things up, if we are to accomplish our objective."

The other Klingon looked at him. "How much faster can we go, my lord? It is a tricky thing, this reshaping of public opinion—especially when it involves as beloved a figure as Kahless."

The conspirator had to acknowledge the wisdom of that. When the clone's death became common knowledge, he would become an even tougher adversary. Nothing was harder to fight than a memory.

He peered into the mists, as if seeking an answer there. "Nonetheless, there must be a way to accelerate our plan."

Lomakh grunted. "We cannot tamper with the testing of the scroll, if that is what you mean. If it proves authentic, as we believe it will, the finding must be beyond reproach."

The conspirator bit his lip. His companion had a point. Yet there had to be something they could do besides bide their time. Perhaps it would take some time to think of it.

As he thought this, he saw two vague figures striding through the sulfurous mists. Not toward them exactly, but close enough to overhear their conversation. The conspirator felt his jaw clench.

He did not wish to invite any more exposure. They had had more than their share already and been fortunate to get away with it. With a glance, he informed Lomakh that their meeting was over. Nor was Lomakh inclined to protest, silently or otherwise.

Instead, he got up and walked away, pretending they didn't know each other at all. A moment or two later, he vanished like a wraith into the roiling clouds of steam.

The leader of the conspiracy frowned. He would not have to sneak around like a Ferengi much longer, he promised himself. Soon he would be sitting in the high seat in the central hall, where Gowron sat presently.

Then, he mused, things would be different. The Empire would shrug off its ties to the cursed Federation and find other allies. Not the Romulans—someone else. Allies of the Klingons' choosing, willing to observe Klingon rules and serve Klingon purposes.

That was the trouble with the rebellion the House of Duras had launched a couple of years ago. The Romulans had been pulling the strings, rendering Duras's sisters and his heir mere pawns in their scheme. And if Gowron had been toppled, the Romulans would have ruled the Empire.

Not so with *this* rebellion. The conspirator would be beholden to no one for his ascent to power. Not even Lomakh and Kardem and Olmai, and the others who did his bidding.

His ties with them were already growing strained. And the last thing he wanted was to surround himself with proven traitors. Better to find supporters among the well-fed and the content, and not have to look for the glint of a knife's edge in every mirror.

The conspirator smiled. Soon, he thought. Soon it would all be in his capable hands. And what did it matter if some blood was shed along the way, even the blood of innocent children?

What was a council leader, anyway, if he did not spill *someone's* blood from time to time? What was the use of being in the high seat if one did not hold the power of life . . . and death?

Eighteen: The Heroic Age

As his *s'tarahk* left Vathraq's village behind, Kahless heard someone call out to him. Looking back over his shoulder, he saw that Morath was following on his own beast.

The younger man was only fifty meters behind and gaining. With a burst of speed, Morath closed the distance even more. But by then, Kahless had turned away again.

He wanted no part of what Morath wished to tell him. He wanted no part of anything except oblivion.

"Kahless!" the younger man cried out again.

Ignoring him, the outlaw kept on going. But soon, Morath pulled even with him. And though he didn't say anything, he stared at his friend with those dark, piercing eyes of his, until Kahless could take no more of it.

The outlaw glanced at Morath. "Leave me alone."

Morath shook his head. "I will not."

"And why not?" growled Kahless. "Why can't you let me suffocate in my misery, damn you?"

"Because it is your fault the villagers are dead," Morath replied. "Because it is you who murdered them. And you cannot leave until you have made retribution for your crime."

Kahless rounded on him, his anger rising high enough to choke him. "Me, you say? Did I take a blade to Kellein? Did I pin her father to his throne with my arrow?" His teeth ground together. "I had nothing but respect for those people. Respect and gratitude!"

Morath kept pace with him, relentless. "Then why did you allow them to become close to you, when all you could expect was the tyrant's hatred? Why did you let them believe in your rebellion, when none of it was true?"

Kahless didn't have an answer for that. He found that his hands had turned into tight white fists around his reins.

"I'll tell you why," said Morath. "To suit your purposes. To fill your belly. Or sate your lust."

The reference to Kellein filled Kahless with a blind, consuming fury. With a sound like a wounded animal, he threw himself at Morath and dragged the man off his mount.

Before Morath knew what was happening, Kahless struck him with all his strength. Again. And again, staggering him. The hills echoed with each resounding impact.

For the first time, Kahless saw anger in the younger man's eyes—a cold, deadly anger. The next thing he knew, Morath had taken his sword in his hand. Kahless stared at him, wondering if this was the way he was going to perish—and not much caring.

But a moment later, Morath's rage cooled. He tossed the sword away. And, with blinding speed, dealt Kahless a savage blow to the jaw.

The outlaw spun around and nearly fell, but he put out a hand to right himself. Then, like a charging *targ,* he went after his friend. Nor could Morath move in time to avoid him.

They hit the ground together, clawing and pounding at one another. Kahless grabbed his adversary by the hair and tried to dash his brains out on a piece of exposed rock. But Morath used both hands to push Kahless's chin back and finally broke the older man's hold.

They wrestled like that for what seemed a long time, neither of them gaining the advantage, neither coming close to victory over the other. Kahless felt as if he had fallen into a trance, as if his arms and legs were striving on their own without his mind to guide them.

But there was a struggle in his mind as well—not with Morath himself, but with Morath's accusations. He was grappling with shame and guilt, trying to free himself though he knew he would never be free again.

At last, exhausted in body and spirit, he and Morath fell apart from one another. As Kahless rolled on the ground, his muscles aching as if he'd wrestled a mountain instead of a man, he nonetheless found the strength to glare at Morath.

"Leave me," he demanded. "Go back to the others and let me drown in the depths of my pain."

His face scored and smeared with dust, Morath shook his head. "No," he rasped. "You've lied. You've shamed yourself and all your ancestors. The blood of an entire village is on your hands, as surely as if you had put them to death yourself."

Kahless closed his eyes against the accusation. "No," he insisted. "Molor killed them. *Molor!*"

"Not Molor," said Morath. *"You!"*

The outlaw couldn't listen to any more of the man's libels. Raising himself to his knees, he gathered one leg underneath him, then the other. Staggering over to his *s'tarahk,* who had been gnawing on groundnuts by the side of the trail, he pulled himself onto the animal's back.

Somehow, he sat up and took the reins in his hands. "Go," he told the *s'tarahk.* "Take me away from this place."

The beast began to move, its clawed feet padding softly on the ground. But after a while, Kahless heard a second set of clawed feet behind him.

With an effort, he turned and saw a haggard-looking figure in pursuit. It was Morath, sitting astride his own *s'tarahk,* only his eyes showing any life. But they accused Kahless as vigorously as ever.

The outlaw turned his back on his pursuer. *Let Morath dog my steps all he likes,* he thought. *Let him follow me day and night. If he keeps at it long enough, he can follow me to* Gre'thor.

Nineteen: The Modern Age

Alexander eyed the lanky Klingon standing not two paces away from him, armed with a wicked-looking *bat'leth.* A bar of light from a hole in the cavern roof fell across the Klingon's face, throwing his knife-sharp features into stark relief.

The boy moved sideways, placing a milk-white, tapering stalagmite between them. The scrape of his feet on the stone floor echoed throughout the dark, musty space. Chuckling to himself, the Klingon followed, shifting his weapon in his hands to allow him more reach.

"You shouldn't have come here," the Klingon rasped.

"I go where I please," the boy piped up, though his heart wasn't really in it.

Without warning, his adversary struck in a big, sweeping arc—one meant to separate Alexander's head from his shoulders. Somehow, the boy got his *bat'leth* up in time to block the blow.

The cavern walls rang with the clash of their blades, just as if this had been a real place and not a holodeck recreation. Alexander's opponent made a sound of disgust in his throat, just as if he were a real being and not an amalgam of electromagnetic fields and light projections.

Quickly, the boy moved to the other side, taking advantage of another stalagmite to buy himself some time. But, enraged by his failure to deal a mortal wound, the Klingon moved with him.

"You were lucky that time," he growled.

"We'll see about that," Alexander countered.

But he knew the Klingon had a point. The boy wasn't concentrating as hard as he should have been. He was too distracted, too concerned with events outside the program.

Even his retorts to the warrior's taunts seemed hollow. And usually, that was his favorite part of the exercise.

Alexander had received the program as a gift from his father on his last birthday. Of course, birthday gifts were a peculiarly human tradition, but Worf had grown up on Earth and was familiar with the practice.

"Tell me," his father had asked, "is there anything in particular you would like? Something from Earth, perhaps?"

The boy had shaken his head. "What I want," he'd said, "is another *bat'leth* program. I'm kind of getting tired of the one in the town square. I mean, it's so easy once you get the hang of it."

That seemed to have surprised his father. But it also seemed to have pleased him.

"I have just the thing," he told Alexander. "And you'll find it a lot more difficult than the one you have now, I assure you."

He was right. This one *was* a lot more difficult.

Actually, it was an adaptation of a program Worf himself had used when he first arrived on the *Enterprise.* Of course, a Klingon had been inserted in place of a Pandrilite and it was restricted to Level One, whereas Worf had bumped it up to Level Three at times. But otherwise, it was pretty much the same.

For instance, if his adversary's *bat'leth* connected, it would hurt like crazy. All the more reason, thought Alexander, not to let it do that.

The Klingon struck again, this time coming from above. Anticipating the move, the boy stepped to the side and launched an attack of his own—a swipe halfway between the vertical and the horizontal.

It wasn't the best countermove Alexander had ever made. Far from it, in fact. But fortunately for the boy, his opponent had overextended himself.

Before the Klingon could withdraw again, Alexander dealt him a nasty blow to the left shoulder. If an adult's strength had been behind the blow, it might have made a bloody ruin of the joint.

As it was, it didn't even pierce the Klingon's body armor. But it did make his arm twitch—an indication that the boy had done some damage after all. Gritting his teeth, the warrior switched his *bat'leth* to his other hand.

Alexander was about to try to capitalize on his enemy's weakness when he saw an irregular pattern open in the stone wall. Of course, that wasn't going to stop the Klingon.

He launched another assault, this time one-handed. Still, it was every bit as vicious as the first. The boy stepped back and nearly tripped on a stalagmite, but managed to keep his feet. And somehow, he deflected the attack.

Then, before he could be pressed any further, a voice said: "Freeze program."

The Klingon stopped moving. Alexander noted how much less threatening his adversary looked frozen in midmaneuver.

"Sorry to interrupt," said Riker, stepping through the opening. Behind him, one of the ship's corridors was visible. Bright, austere, and streamlined, it provided a jarring contrast to the subterranean depths of the cavern. "I just thought I'd look in on you. See how you were doing, you know?"

The boy looked at him. "I guess."

The first officer indicated Alexander's *bat'leth* with a tilt of his chin. "You've gotten pretty good with that thing."

Alexander knew it was less than the truth. His friend was just being kind. "Not as good as I'd like," he said.

Riker regarded him. "In that case, maybe I can help." He looked up at the ceilingful of stalactites. "Computer. I'd like a *bat'leth,* appropriate size and weight."

A moment later, a blade materialized in his hands. He hefted it, then nodded his satisfaction and eyed Alexander.

"Ever heard of anbo-jytsu?" he asked.

The boy shook his head. In fact, he hadn't heard of it. And more to the point, he had no idea what it had to do with his combat program.

The Klingon named Majjas sat in his heavy, carved chair against the far wall of his central hall, his white hair glistening in the light from several tall windows. He smiled beneficently.

"This is quite a day," said Majjas. "Not only do I have the pleasure of meeting the Emperor Kahless and renewing my acquaintance with the sons of Mogh, though that would be honor enough. I am fortunate to have beneath my roof the esteemed Arbiter of Succession."

Picard smiled back. It wasn't just the slightly ironic twist the Klingon put on the word "esteemed" that elicited the human's admiration.

It was the fact that Majjas had not waited for his wife to make introductions, but had glanced at each of his visitors in turn and identified them all without the slightest hesitation.

Not bad for a blind man, the captain thought. *Especially one without a VISOR to rely on.*

Apparently, Majjas had lost his sight several years ago in a weapons-room accident on a Klingon bird-of-prey. The scars that wove their way through the flesh around both his eyes bore mute testimony to that—though it was difficult to see the man's eyes themselves, slitted as they were and hidden beneath large, bushy white brows.

Kahless must have been surprised by Majjas's feat as well, because he grunted approvingly. "I see the stories about you are true," he remarked. "Majjas, son of Eragh, is as canny a warrior as ever served on a Klingon ship—and your blindness has not changed that."

Of course, Picard mused, *the old man would have had warning of their visit. Kurn would have seen to that before he took them off Ogat in his private vessel. But still, to know each of them by their footsteps— or perhaps their scent—was certainly an accomplishment.*

Majjas chuckled. "The Mogh family is coming up in the world," he jibed, "to be traveling in such distinguished company." Leaning closer to Kahless, he added: "For the record, I do not care in the least whether the scroll is authentic. I, for one, will always believe in the Kahless of legend. Now," he continued, leaning back in his chair, "what sort of impulse has brought you to my humble abode?"

No sooner had Majjas completed his question than a quintet of females emerged from a back room, carrying trays full of decantered drink and brazen goblets, and writhing gagh in bowls of supple, red *m'ressa* twigs.

The captain couldn't help noticing how beautiful they were. In a savage way, of course.

"My daughters," said the old man, his smile broadening—though from his tone of voice, it was clear even to Picard that Majjas would have liked a strong son to go with them.

As one of the trays was placed in front of him, the captain poured himself a goblet full of black Klingon wine—but declined when offered the gagh. He had eaten on the way here, after all.

Worf was the one who finally answered Majjas's question. "You have been a friend of my family for years," he told his host. "Since before Kuru and I were born."

"Since before your father was born," the old man interjected. "And a difficult birth it was."

Worf grinned. "I stand corrected, honored host. Since before our *father* was born." He paused. "I remember my father saying no one knows armaments like Majjas—regardless of whether they are daggers or disruptor cannons, phasers or photon torpedoes."

"Your father did not lie," the old man agreed. "That's what comes of serving on a Bird-of-Prey all one's life."

As Picard looked on, Worf's smile disappeared. "I am glad to hear that," the lieutenant said. "We need such expertise on our side."

"Your *side?*" Majjas echoed. "Then am I to understand you're at odds with some other House?"

"With *someone,*" Kahless interjected. "Though it may be a great deal more than a simple conflict between Houses." He glanced meaningfully at the old man's wife, a slight woman with sharp features. "Perhaps this is something you alone may wish to hear, Majjas."

Their host shook his white-maned head. "My wife and my daughters—young as they are—are more than ornaments in this hall. You will not have occasion to regret your trust in them."

Kahless inclined his head, to show his compliance with Majjas's terms. If the old man couldn't see him, at least his wife could. Then the clone went on to describe all they'd learned—starting with his observations at Tolar'tu and ending with the bloodshed at the academy on Ogat.

By the time he was done, Majjas was scowling in his wispy, white beard. "You are dealing with cowards," he concluded, "and worse. But I see what you mean—this is more than a feud between Houses." The muscles in his temples worked, evidence of his determination to help. "What service may I perform for you, my friends?"

The captain watched as Worf opened the pouch on his belt and removed its contents, then placed them in their host's hands. Examining the metal fragments with his fingertips, Majjas harrumphed.

"Pieces of a bomb casing," he announced. "No doubt, from one of the firebombs your enemies set off at the academy. And what is it you wish to know about these pieces?"

"We were hoping," said Picard, "that you could provide us with some clue as to their manufacture. Preferably, something that might lead us to our enemies."

Our enemies, thought the captain. It was a phrase any ambassador in the Federation would have frowned on. However, it seemed eminently appropriate at the moment.

Majjas turned the shards over and over in his hands. "A clue, eh? I can tell you this—they're made of *mich'ara,* an alloy most often used in heating elements, since it conducts thermal energy so well. But for a time, it was *also* used in the making of explosive devices."

Picard nodded. Now they were getting somewhere. "For a time?" he prodded. "But no longer?"

"That is correct," said the old man. "The practice stopped when cheaper alloys were introduced, which could be applied to the same purpose."

Worf s eyes narrowed. "Then not *every* armory would provide our enemies with access to such a device."

"True," Majjas confirmed. "In fact, to my knowledge, there is only *one*. It is on Ter'jas Mor, not far from the city of Donar'ruq."

Worf smiled as warmly as the captain had ever seen him smile. "The House of Mogh is once more in your debt, my friend. If there were some way to repay you for your assistance . . ."

Their host shrugged. "You could take me with you," he suggested.

A silence fell . . . until Majjas began to laugh out loud in his beard. His daughters looked at one another with relief—the same sort of relief Picard himself was feeling.

"You may relax," the old Klingon assured them. "I don't expect you to drag a blind man along. But if circumstances were different, it would be good to strike a blow again for the Empire." He sighed. "I tell you, I would have enjoyed that to the bottom of my heart."

"How long will you be staying here on B'aaj?" asked Majjas's wife, the epitome of Klingon gentility—though she must have already known the answer.

"I regret," Worf told her, "that we cannot remain here as your guests. Our mission is too urgent for us to delay."

"Except to finish your wine," the old man stipulated.

"Of course," Kahless replied. "It would be dishonorable to do otherwise." And with that, he drained his goblet.

Worf cleared his throat, causing Majjas to turn in his direction. "There is one other thing."

"And that is?" the old man inquired.

"I ask that you—and your family—refrain from mentioning you even glimpsed us. After all," said Mogh's elder son, "one never knows whom one can trust at times like these. And as far as our enemies are concerned, we are dead."

"Dead?" repeated Majjas. He laughed some more. "Some would say that is even *worse* than being blind."

Kahless stood and put his goblet down on a table made for such a purpose. "I am afraid," he said, "it is time to take our leave of you now. And if my companions are too polite to hurry out of your hall, I will bear the blame on my own shoulders."

But he hadn't offended their host, Picard observed. Far from it. Majjas's grin was so wide, it looked painful.

"Don't worry," the old man told them. "I am not offended, Emperor. Rather, I am honored. Have a safe trip, my friends. It is a dark and dangerous road you have chosen."

"That it is," Kahless agreed. And without further conversation, he led the way out of Majjas's house—leaving Picard and the others no choice but to follow.

Twenty: The Heroic Age

For two days, Kahless drove his *s'tarahk* mercilessly, pausing only for the animal to munch on grass and groundnuts, and to water itself. Its rider, on the other hand, neither ate nor slept.

His mind had long ago settled into the rhythm of the beast's progress, avoiding anything so painful as a thought. Day turned into night, night became day, and he barely noticed.

But all the while, Morath was right behind him. He stopped when Kahless stopped and went on when Kahless went on. He didn't attempt to overtake him, or to speak with him again, only to haunt him from a distance.

At one point, just as twilight was throwing its cloak over the world, Kahless came to a fast-rushing stream. Seeing no way to go around it, he urged his *s'tarahk* to enter the water. But the beast wouldn't move.

It dropped to its haunches, then fell over on its side, exhausted. And in the process, Kahless fell to the ground as well.

He looked back. Morath was sitting on his mount, saying nothing, making no move to come any closer. Only staring, with those dark, baleful eyes of his. But his stare was an accusation in itself.

Kahless grunted derisively. "Are you still here?" he asked.

Morath didn't answer. He simply got down off his *s'tarahk* and let the animal approach the stream. As it drank, Kahless grunted again.

"Have it your way," he said.

Kahless considered his mount again. The *s'tarahk* wasn't going anywhere in its depleted condition—not for a while. The outlaw was tired too. Taking his sleeping mat off the beast's back, he rolled into it and closed his eyes against the starlight.

It was possible that Morath would kill him while he was asleep. But Kahless didn't care. It would be as good a death as any other, and he wanted more desperately than ever to end his suffering.

Kahless woke with first light. The sun's rays were hot on his face and blinding to his eyes.

For a moment, staring at the *s'tarahk* grazing placidly beside him and the blanched hills all around, he didn't know where he was or how he had gotten there. For that moment, he knew peace. Then he remembered, and his load of misery crushed him all over again.

A shadow fell over him. Turning, he saw Morath standing there. As before, the younger man accused his comrade with his eyes.

"What is it you want from me?" asked Kahless.

Morath grunted. "I want you to pay for what you've done."

"Pay how?" asked the outlaw.

The other man was silent. It was as if he expected Kahless to know the answer. But Kahless knew nothing of the kind.

With an effort, he got up, his muscles sore from striving against Morath the day before, and limped over to his *s'tarahk*. The beast looked rested. That was good, because he didn't intend to pamper it.

There was a pit in his stomach, crying out to be filled. Kahless ignored it. Dead men didn't eat.

Getting back on his mount, the outlaw turned it north again. It wasn't as if he had a destination—just a direction. He would follow it until he could do so no longer.

But Morath wasn't done with him. Kahless could tell by the shadow the man cast as he mounted his *s'tarahk,* and by the scraping of the animal's claws on the hard, dry ground behind him. Morath followed him like a specter of death, unflinching in his purpose—whatever it was.

Not that it made any difference to Kahless. He was too scoured out inside to play his friend's games, too empty of what made a Klingon a Klingon. Nothing mattered, Morath least of all.

For a total of six days and six nights, Kahless led Morath high into the hills. Twice, they were drenched to the bone by spring sleet storms, which came without warning and disappeared just as suddenly. Neither of them cared much about the discomfort.

On some days, they wrestled as they had that first time, consumed with hatred and resentment for one another; on others, they simply followed the track on their poor, tired beasts. With time, however, their wrestling matches became shorter and farther between.

After all, their only sustenance was the water they came across in streams running down from the highlands. Neither of them ate a thing. They left to their mounts the few edible plants that grew along the path.

There was no conversation either, not even as prelude to their strivings with one another. Neither of them seemed to find a value anymore in speech. On occasion, Kahless saw Morath speaking to himself. But the outlaw wasn't much of a lip-reader, never having seen the need for it, so he couldn't discern the sense of the other warrior's mutterings.

Finally, on the morning of the twelfth day, in the shadow of a great rock alongside a windy mountain trail, Kahless woke with the knowledge that he could tolerate Morath's presence no longer. One way or the other, he had to be rid of the man.

Turning, Kahless eyed his comrade, who had more than once saved his life. When he spoke it was with a voice that sounded strange and foreign to him, a voice like the sighing of the wind in a stand of river reeds.

"I will go no further, Morath. I cannot stand the thought of looking back and seeing you following me. We'll wrestle again, eh? But this time, only one of us will walk away."

Morath shook his head. "No, Kahless." His voice was thin and harsh as well. "If you want to grapple, fine. But I have no more intention of killing you than I do of being killed myself."

Days ago, Kahless would have been moved to anger. Now, the remark only annoyed him, the way a mud gnat might annoy a *minn'hor* calf.

"Then I'll take my own life," he told Morath. "That will do just as well." He looked around. "All I need is a sharp rock . . . or a heavy one. . . ."

"No," said the younger man. "I won't allow it." As obstinate as ever, he placed himself in his companion's way.

Kahless eyed him. As far as he could tell, Morath meant it. Besides, there weren't any rocks around that filled his need.

The outlaw sighed. "What do you want of me?" he asked, not for the first time. He was surprised to hear a pleading quality in his voice, a weariness that went down to his very soul. "You mentioned a price, Morath. I'll pay it—I'll pay anything, if you'll only tell me what it is."

Morath's lips pulled back over his teeth, making him look more like a predator than ever. "Pay with your life then."

Kahless tilted his head to look at the man. "Are you insane? I offered to end my life with my own hands. Or if it's vengeance you want—"

The younger man shook his head. "No, not vengeance," he insisted. "There's been altogether too much slaughter already. What I ask for is not a death, Kahless—but a *life*."

Only then did the outlaw begin to understand. To pay for what he'd done, he would have to dedicate his life to those who had perished. He would have to become what Vathraq and the others thought he was.

A rebel. A man devoted to overthrowing the tyrant Molor.

At first, he balked at the idea. The tyrant was too powerful. No one could tear him down, least of all a pack of untrained outlaws, led by a man who had lost his stomach for fighting.

On the other hand, what was the worst that could happen? He would die. And right now, he welcomed death like a brother.

"A life," Morath repeated. It was more of a question than anything else.

The wind blew. The sun beat down. One of the *s'tarahkmey* grumbled and scraped the ground with its claws, looking for food.

At last, Kahless nodded. "Fine. Whatever you say."

"Then get on your *s'tarahk*," said the younger man, his voice flat and without emotion, "and be the renegade you let others believe you to be."

Kahless straightened at the harshness of the retort. "Not yet," he said.

Morath looked at him. No doubt, he expected to have to argue some more. But it wouldn't be necessary.

"First," said Kahless, "I need something to eat."

Approaching a patch of groundnuts on shaky legs, he knelt and began to wolf them down. After he had taken a couple of mouthfuls, Morath joined him. They ate more like *targs* than men.

Then, their bellies full for the first time in many days, they mounted their beasts and turned back toward Vathraq's village.

At night, when Kahless was unrolling his sleeping mat, Morath began to speak. He was not a man given to long utterances, but this time he eyed the stars and spoke at length.

"My father," he told Kahless, "was a strange man. He was raised as a devotee of the old gods. It was to them he cried out for help when my mother was giving birth to me.

"The gods, he said, promised him their assistance. Nonetheless, my mother died. My father lashed out at his deities, calling them deceivers—and smashed all the little statues of them that stood around the house. Thereafter, he hated deceit above all else.

"Somehow, I thrived. But my father neither took another mate, nor did he conceive another child. There were only the two of us, and he raised me with an iron hand.

"When I was five years old, he almost killed me for telling a small, inconsequential lie. Shortly thereafter, while I still bore the bruises of his beating, our house was set upon by reavers—cruel Klingons who obeyed no laws, self-imposed or otherwise.

"My father fought bravely—so bravely a chill still climbs my spine when I think about it. I remember being surprised that this was the same man who had beaten me so, protecting his son and his hearth with such feverish intensity.

"And I?" Morath grunted bitterly. "I ran away and hid in the woods, afraid to fight at my father's side—caught in the grip of wild, unreasoning terror. In the end, the reavers proved too much for Ondagh, son of Bogra. They killed him and took everything we had of value.

"Only when they were gone did I come out of hiding and see what they had done to my father. I knew that I should have fallen at his side, but I had not—and nothing could ever change that. Unable to bear my burden, I tried to run away again—this time, from my father's ghost.

"For a long time, I wandered the wide world, looking for a way to rid myself of my guilt. One day, after many years had passed, I came upon a still, serene lake and bent to drink from it.

"Then I recoiled—for it was my father's reflection I saw in the tranquil waters. And I realized I had been given a second chance. I would be Ondagh—not as he was, but as he could have been. I would brook no deceit, neither from man nor god. And I would never run away from anything again."

Having said his piece, Morath unrolled his own mat and lay down on it. In a moment or two he was asleep.

Kahless looked at his friend for a long time, beginning to understand why Morath did the things he did. Then, at last, he too fell asleep.

Kahless and Morath came in sight of Vathraq's keep twelve days after their departure. To the outlaw's surprise, his men were still waiting for him, still eyeing the horizon.

By then, of course, they had burned all the corpses, as much to deny the *kraw'zamey* a meal as to discourage the spread of disease. Unfortunately, that made it worse for Kahless. The mangled shapes of death held less terror for him than their empty aftermath.

The outlaw himself said nothing about the time he was gone. Morath didn't say much either. But he did mention how sore he was from wrestling with Kahless, and pretty soon the others picked up on it.

Before long, the story became amplified. The outlaw and his friend had wrestled in the hills for twelve days and twelve nights, it was said, through heat and storm and all manner of hardship. Of course, no one could figure out why they would want to do that.

Nor did Morath disabuse them of the notion. Even for him, apparently, it was close enough to the truth.

Twenty-one: The Modern Age

Picard breathed in the cold air and observed the contingent of Klingons on the next plateau, perhaps a hundred meters below him and his companions.

Their dark hair was drawn back and tied into ponytails, in the manner of Worf's. In the flat, gray light of predawn, their white *mok'bara* garb looked strangely serene against the coarse, black rock and the omnipresent tufts of hardy, red *en'chula* grass.

Of course, the Klingons themselves were anything but serene. Focused, yes. Entranced, perhaps. But serene? Even in the practice of so demanding a discipline, Klingon serenity was a contradiction in terms.

Anyone who doubted that had only to witness what the captain was witnessing—the ferocity with which these practitioners assailed one another, launching kick after deadly kick and blow after crushing blow, and following each with a guttural shout of exultation. Fortunately for them, none of these assaults found their targets—for as skilled as they were at attacks, they were just as skilled at avoiding them.

It was a mesmerizing spectacle, the captain mused. Like a spider of many parts weaving a continuous, flashing web. Or a particularly vicious species of bird writhing in a torturous form of flight, the reasons for which were lost in its genetic past.

Picard had seen Worf teach the *mok'bara* exercises to a dedicated few on the *Enterprise,* Beverly and Deanna among them. However, those maneuvers were to these as a jog in the woods was to the Academy marathon. Neither Beverly nor Deanna would have lasted more than a few brief seconds in so violent and rigorous a ritual.

"I am amused," Kahless hissed.

He was careful not to speak so loudly that he'd draw the attention of the martial artists below—though with all the bellowing going on down there, such care seemed rather unnecessary.

"In my day, there was no such thing as this. . . ." He turned to Worf. "What did you call it?"

The lieutenant scowled. *"Mok'bara,"* he replied.

"This *Mok'baaara,"* Kahless finished, butchering the word as if on purpose. He shook his head. "In my era, life itself contained all the exercise one would ever need. And if one still craved action at the end of the day, there was always the requisite afterdinner brawl."

Worf harrumphed. Clearly, thought Picard, his officer didn't appreciate the clone's disparagements.

"The ritual provides more than exercise," the lieutenant explained. "It helps one to set aside distractions—to concentrate on the advancement of one's spirit."

Kahless clapped him affectionately on the back. "I don't mean to offend anyone, Worf—and certainly not my closest companions. If you want to perform pantomimes in your night clothes, I have no objections."

Kurn looked at the clone. "With all due respect, Kahless, I can see why you were never revered as a diplomat."

"To *Gre'thor* with diplomats," Kahless spat—*Gre'thor* being the Klingon equivalent of Hell.

After some of his experiences with diplomatic envoys, the captain was inclined to agree. But, not for the first time since he'd embarked on this mission, he held his tongue.

Abruptly, he noticed the first brazen rays of the sun sneaking over the cliffs to his right. He turned to Worf, who'd mentioned earlier that the ritual would end when dawn touched the plateau.

"Lieutenant?" said Picard, by way of a reminder.

Worf glanced at the cliffs and nodded. "We should start down now."

Without further ceremony, he retreated from the edge of their rocky plateau and made his way across it toward a steep, winding path. By following this path, the captain knew, they would end up exactly where they wanted to be—and with any luck, see just whom they wished to see.

Their descent took them around a natural column of crags and boulders, one of many that seemed to punctuate the landscape. Though Picard's interests leaned more toward archaeology than geology, he resolved to learn someday what sort of forces created these structures.

As the sky continued to lighten above them, they came to the end of the path and gathered in a hollow. By peering through a cleft in the rocks, they could see the slope just below the *mok'bara* practitioners' plateau. To be sure, it was a gentler way down than the one they'd just taken—but more importantly, it narrowed to a point right near the cleft.

They'd barely arrived when the martial artists began to descend. It was remarkable how calm they seemed, after the effort they'd put into their ritual just a few moments earlier.

The Klingons were conversing quietly, nodding, even smiling at one another. It seemed to the captain they'd come from a sewing bee instead of a potentially lethal combat.

"Which one is Godar?" Kahless asked softly.

"He is the last of them," Kurn replied. "As always. You see him? The tall, wizened-looking one with the simple chin-beard?"

"Ah, that one," said Kahless, craning his head to get a better angle. "And you believe he can be trusted?"

Worf's brother grunted. "I believe so, yes."

"You seem to trust a great many people," the clone commented.

"Like you," Kurn told him, "I have no choice."

In moments, most of the *mok'bara* practitioners had passed the cleft on their way down from the plateau. None of them seemed to notice Picard and his companions. But after what had happened in Tolar'tu, that was little assurance in the captain's eyes.

As Kurn had indicated, Godar was the last of them. He too appeared unaware of the quartet that had traveled so far to speak with him. That is, until Kurn croaked his name.

At first, the man seemed confused as to who might have called him. Then he happened to glance in the direction of their hiding place.

Under similar circumstances, Picard thought, *he himself might have cried out in surprise—or bolted, fearing an ambush.* But Godar did neither of these things. Still invigorated by his exercises, he simply altered his stance a bit, ready to take on whatever awaited him.

"Who is it?" he rasped, darting a sideways look at his fellow practitioners, who seemed not to have missed him—at least not yet. "Speak quickly—and give me a reason not to warn the others."

"It's me," Worf's brother whispered. "It's Kurn, son of Mogh."

Immediately, Godar's expression changed. He became more curious than wary. "Come forward, so I can see it is really you," he demanded.

Worf's brother complied with Godar's wishes. As the hollow filled with sunlight, the man saw the truth of the matter—and grinned.

"Kurn," he said. "You Miravian slime devil!"

Reaching in, he grasped Kurn's arm in a handclasp reserved for brothers and close allies. "What in the name of *Fek'lhr* are you doing on Ter'jas Mor?" He squinted. "And who the blazes is in there with you?"

Kurn moved aside, so the older man could get a better look into the hollow. "You will find," he explained, "that I travel in unusual company."

As Godar spotted Worf and then Picard, his elderly brow creased with curiosity. And when he realized that Kahless was with them, the crease became a deep, dark furrow in the center of his forehead.

"Unusual company indeed," the man murmured. He turned back to Kurn. "And how does this involve *me,* son of Mogh?"

As he did at Majjas's house, Worf's brother explained what was going on. However, he left out Majjas's name, referring to the blind man simply as "an expert in armaments."

The *mok'bara* practitioner nodded. "And since I was once the master of the defense armory on this world, you believe I can tell you who might have stolen the bomb."

Worf shrugged. "If anyone knows the people who worked there, it would be you. If you were pressed to come up with a name . . ."

Godar didn't respond right away. Finally, after what seemed like a long time, he came up with not one name but two—and a bit of information to back up his suspicions.

"Mind you," he told them, "I don't know for a fact that they're guilty. I'm only guessing."

Kurn snorted. "A guess from Godar, son of Gudag, is better than a certainty from anyone else. I thank you, my friend—and I trust you will keep the matter of our survival a secret."

The *mok'bara* practitioner laughed softly. "I haven't lived *this* long by betraying my friends, Kurn. Your secret is safe with me." He gazed downslope again. "But if I don't hurry, my companions will wonder what kept me so long. Follow the path of honor, Son of Mogh."

And with that, he was gone. Picard looked at Kurn. "I assume we'll be paying our bombing suspects a visit."

Kurn nodded. "You assume correctly."

"Then what are we waiting for?" asked Kahless.

"We're not," Worf's brother replied.

Pulling up his sleeve to expose the remote control band on his forearm, he tapped in the necessary information. Then he activated the link to his vessel's transporter system.

The captain felt a brief thrill, something like a low-voltage electrical current, running through him—the earmark of Klingon transporter technology. A moment later, he was back on Kurn's ship—though with what they knew now, he was certain he wouldn't stay there very long.

Twenty-two: The Heroic Age

Kahless looked at all those who had assembled in the village of T'chariv, along the edge of the northern forests. His own men were only a small part of the crowd that huddled under a gray sky, surrounded by low wooden houses and a flimsy-looking barricade.

Last of all, the outlaw glanced at Edronh, the man he had fought over the *minn'hor* herd nearly a year ago. Edronh nodded, and Kahless looked back at the funeral pyre that stood behind him.

Torch in hand, he approached the pyre, with its burden of half a dozen corpses. The wind whistled in his ears, whispering things he didn't want to hear or know about.

Touching his torch to the kindling beneath the wooden platform, he waited until the fire caught. Then he watched as logs were placed on the burning branches, feeding the flames until they enveloped the bodies above. Finally, assured that all was as it should be, he withdrew to stand by Edronh.

As the fire danced around the pyre, Kahless looked deep into the outlaw's eyes. He saw the sort of agony there that he himself had known. The kind of torment only the loss of a loved one may bring.

He wanted desperately to look away. But he couldn't, not ever again. He could ignore the wind, but not what he saw in a man like Edronh.

If he was to lead a rebellion as so many wished him to, he would have to understand their pain. He would have to distill it, like blood-wine. And he would have to give all of Molor's people a taste, so they would know what they were fighting for.

Out of the corner of his eye, he could see Morath staring at him, silently keeping him to his promise. But Kahless no longer fomented rebellion for Morath's sake alone.

Now he did it for himself as well—and for Kellein. He had discovered it was the only thing that made his heart stop hurting for her, the only balm that worked for him.

Had he been the one to die instead of Kellein, she would have made the rest of her life a tribute to him. She would have turned her sorrow and her anger into something useful—and deadly.

Could he do any less?

"Rannuf," Edronh whispered, the flames reflected in his eyes as they picked at his child's bones. His wife moved closer to him, to give comfort and to take some. "My son," he said, "my strong, brave son."

Kahless nodded as a bone popped and sparks flew, rising like a swarm of fiery insects among the twists of smoke. "Rannuf," he echoed.

Edronh turned to him. "You knew him, my friend. He laid his sword before you, that day in the woods. You saw his courage, his manliness."

I saw how young he was, Kahless thought. *How excessive in his eagerness.* But he didn't mention that.

"Rannuf was a warrior," he said. "He died defending his people against the depravities of Molor."

That much was true. The tyrant must have gotten wind of the things Edronh was saying about him. And though Edronh and his men were outlaws, every outlaw had kin somewhere. Once Molor had determined where that somewhere was, the rest was simple.

He had sent his soldiers to T'chariv with fire and sword, just as he had once sent Kahless himself. Unfortunately for Rannuf, he had been home at the time, visiting his mother and his younger brother. Seeing what the tyrant's men intended, he had met them blow for blow.

But the soldiers were more numerous than the village's defenders and had killed them to a man—then lopped off their heads for good measure. The only good fortune was that the soldiers had spared the village itself, their point having been made.

Do not think to defy your lord Molor, they had said—if not with their tongues, then with their sharp-edged swords. After all, no one can hope to stand against him.

In the last half-year, that message had been carved like a bloodeagle from one end of the tyrant's domain to the other. Vathraq's village had only been the beginning. Nor would T'chariv be the end.

Kahless looked at Edronh. "It would be a shame," he said, "if Rannuf were to go unavenged."

The other man bit his lip. Clearly, he wasn't as enthusiastic about revolution as he had been.

Until now, Edronh had thought himself too far north to feel Molor's sting. To his everlasting regret, he had learned that was not so. Having seen Rannuf's mangled body, having lifted it in pieces onto the pyre, he had become wary.

But if he was to have a hope of toppling the tyrant, Kahless needed men like Edronh. Men who could not only fight, but spread word of their struggle to others.

"I had a lover," he told Edronh, plumbing the depths of his own sorrow. "We were betrothed before you and I met. But before I could return to her, Molor crushed her village and everyone in it."

The other man looked at him. "The tyrant is everywhere."

Kahless grunted. "Because we allow him to be everywhere. Because we sit in our own separate hideaways and wait for him to bring us misery."

Edronh's eyes narrowed. "What are you saying?"

"Only this," said Kahless. "That it is not enough to speak of rebellion, as we have done in the past. It is time we let our swords do our speaking for us. Together, as one army, we can show Molor what misery truly is. And in time, we can destroy him as surely as he destroyed Rannuf."

Edronh seemed to be mulling it over. After a while, he spoke in a voice thick with emotion.

"I have only one other son, my friend. I could not bear to lose him as I lost Rannuf."

Kahless eyed him sternly. Perhaps it was not enough to distill the pain of Molor's victims. Perhaps he needed something more.

And instinctively, he seemed to know what that something would be.

"Then you will lose more than your sons," he told Edronh. "You will lose everything."

Edronh shook his head. "Everything?" he echoed.

"Everything that matters," the outlaw explained. "The day we met, Edronh—you remember it?"

The other man said he did. "As if it were yesterday."

"You spoke to me of honor that day—the honor a warrior may accord another warrior, whom he has come to respect. But there is another kind of honor, my friend. It is the kind a man must seek in himself—a love of virtue he must not abandon, no matter the consequences—or else admit to the world he is less than a man."

Edronh's features hardened, as if he had been challenged. "I am a man, Kahless. I have never been anything less."

"Then fight," the outlaw spat. "Fight for your honor, your dignity. Fight to make this land free of Molor's tyranny."

Edronh grunted. "Brave words, Kahless. But I fear to take part in a halfhearted venture—one which would spur Molor to even greater atrocities."

The outlaw nodded. "I understand. And I swear to you, we will finish what we start, or I am not the son of Kanjis. I will not lay down my sword until the tyrant is dead—or *I* am."

Edronh measured the size of Kahless's conviction—and found it sufficient. He clapped his friend on the shoulder.

"I will not lay down my sword either, then," he promised. "From this day on, I fight at your side. And so do all those who ride with me."

Kahless smiled. "I want more than that, Edronh. I want you and your men to go out as messengers—to speak with everyone you know, every hearth you can find. Tell them I am gathering an army to march against Molor in the tyrant's own stronghold. Tell them I am doing this for the sake of their honor." His smile widened. "And tell them they will never have a chance like this again."

Edronh smiled too, though the flames of the funeral pyre turned his eyes to molten gold. "I will do it. You have my word."

Kahless could almost hear the pounding of the blacksmith's hammer as he forged the first link in his chain of rebellion. But it was only one link, he had to remind himself. He would need an entire chain before he could challenge the likes of Molor.

Feeling someone's stare on the back of his neck, he turned. Morath was looking at him. The younger man seemed pleased.

Kahless nodded at him. It had begun.

Twenty-three: The Modern Age

Unlike his captain, Riker had never been to the Klingon Homeworld. But he was familiar enough with Worf's holodeck programs to know which cavern he was standing in.

It was called DIS jajlo', literally "dawn cave." He didn't know how it had gotten that name, since the shaft of light that came from above was only visible in midday.

At least, that was true of the real DIS jajlo', back on Q'onoS. In this program, for all he knew, the shaft of light never moved.

Right now, nothing else was moving either. With a single command, he had frozen Alexander's Klingon adversary in place. And the boy himself was so focused on the first officer, he might as well have been frozen too.

Well, thought Riker, I *seemed to have piqued his interest. Now it's time to follow through.*

"Anbo-jytsu," he said, "is a martial art form back on Earth—a one-on-one confrontation, much like the one you're involved in now." He raised his chin to indicate the Klingon warrior. "Of course, there are some differences. In anbo-jytsu, you wear a padded suit and your weapon is a stick three meters long. On one end of the stick, there's a proximity detector. You need that because you're wearing a blindfold the whole time you're at it."

Alexander looked at him. "A blindfold?" he echoed.

"Right—you can't see. That makes it pretty important to have a good sense of balance. And to be able to anticipate your enemy's moves. Here, let me show you what I mean."

Again, the first officer looked to the stalactite-riddled ceiling of the cavern. "Computer, I need a blindfold."

A band of white cloth materialized in Riker's hand. Grasping it, he approached the Klingon warrior. Then the first officer tied the blindfold around his head, covering his eyes, and raised his *bat'leth* in front of him.

"Computer," he called, "resume program."

Riker heard the rustling that meant the warrior had come back to life. Taking a step back, he felt for a stalagmite with his heel—and found one. That told him how far backward he could go.

A moment later, he heard the derisive grunt that signified the Klingon's recognition of what he was facing. Clearly, he didn't expect a man who couldn't see to put up much of a fight. Under normal circumstances, he'd probably have been right.

But the first officer had been honing his skills at anbo-jytsu since he was eight years old. He no longer needed a proximity detector to sense an attack coming, or to know what to do about it. And even though he had a *bat'leth* instead of a three-meter-long staff in his hand, a two-handed weapon was pretty much a two-handed weapon.

Listening carefully, Riker heard a sharp intake of breath. Bracing himself, he allowed his instincts to take over. Without actually thinking about it, the first officer found himself moving to block a blow from the warrior's right hand.

Careful to remain balanced, attentive not only to what he heard but also to what he smelled and felt in the movements of the air, Riker parried a second attack from the same quarter. And a third.

Apparently, the Klingon was going to keep trying the same thing, over and over again. Either he had some idea that the human was more vulnerable there or the warrior was himself limited. Say, by a wound he'd sustained before Riker arrived.

There was only one way to find out. Before his opponent could strike again, the first officer shifted the *bat'leth* in his hands and swung hard at the Klingon's left side. He heard a cry of apprehension, then felt his blade connect with something solid. It made a *chukt* as it sliced through leather body armor and maybe flesh as well.

The warrior cried out, then made a shuffling sound. A moment later, Riker heard him grunt as he hit the ground. Then there was a clatter, as of something metal.

"Freeze program," he said.

Removing his blindfold, the human surveyed his handiwork. The Klingon was on his back, clutching his left arm. His face was a mask of pain, his *bat'leth* lying at the base of a stalagmite.

Riker turned to Alexander, who was looking at him with a new respect. The first officer smiled. "I guess you get the picture."

The boy nodded. "But how did you—?"

"Practice," Riker told him. "Want to give it a shot? I'll be your sparring partner."

"Okay," said Alexander.

Coming around behind him, the first officer placed the blindfold across the boy's eyes and tied it. Then he stepped in front of him with his *bat'leth*.

"Here we go. Keep your feet wide apart for balance. With all these stalagmites around, it's easy to trip. Now, listen as hard as you can, and tell me what I'm doing."

Taking care not to make too much noise, Riker moved to his right. At first, the boy seemed confused. Then he turned in the right direction.

"That's good," said the first officer. "You've got sharp ears."

This time, he moved to the left. Again, Alexander hesitated for a second. Then he seemed to find Riker's position.

The first officer didn't say anything right away. He wanted to see if the boy wavered in his conviction. But Alexander continued to stare in the same direction.

"Excellent," the first officer noted. "Keep trusting your senses and you'll be fine. Now, the toughest test of all."

Moving to his right again, he shifted his *bat'leth* from one hand to the other, making enough noise to give the boy a fighting chance. Then he raised the weapon high and brought it down slowly toward Alexander's shoulder.

The boy reacted in plenty of time, but held his *bat'leth* in position to stop a thrust, not a downward stroke. Only at the last second did he realize his mistake and bring his blade up over his head—just in time to ward off the attack.

Riker was impressed. Alexander was doing things it took him years to learn. But then, the boy was part Klingon. He had a warrior's instincts imprinted in his genes.

Alexander grinned. "I did it!" he cried.

"You sure did," said the first officer. "You can take off your blindfold now."

Still grinning, the boy did as he was told. He got a kick out of seeing Riker just where he expected to see him.

But a moment later, his joy faded. Apparently, he had remembered whatever it was he had on his mind.

"Something wrong?" asked the first officer.

Alexander sighed. "You know there is. Otherwise, Counselor Troi wouldn't have sent you to talk to me."

Riker had to smile. "It was that obvious, was it?"

The boy nodded. Placing his back against a stalagmite, he slid down the side of it and came to a stop when he reached the ground.

The first officer sat, too. "So? Do you want to get it out in the open, or do I just mind my own business?"

Alexander pretended to inspect his *bat'leth*. "We can talk," he said.

"Is it about the scrolls?" Riker asked. "The ones that suggest Kahless isn't all he's cracked up to be?"

The boy looked up at him. "You know I was reading them?" Then he must have realized how easy it would have been for the first officer to determine that. "Of course you do. You're in charge of the ship. You've got access to everything."

"Well?" the first officer prodded. "Is that it? You're disillusioned by what you read?"

He fully expected Alexander to nod his head. Instead, the boy shook it slowly from side to side.

"Don't tell my father, but I don't care how many days Kahless wrestled his brother, or how hard it must have been to plow his father's fields with his *bat'leth,* or how terrible a tyrant Molor was." He shrugged. "They're terrific stories, sure, and I love to listen to them—but they're just stories."

Alexander went back to inspecting his weapon. There was a discomfort in his features that Riker hated to see there.

"To me," the boy went on, "being a Klingon isn't about being like Kahless. I hardly know Kahless. It's about being like my father."

The first officer smiled. *Funny thing about sons,* he thought. *No matter how different they may be from their fathers, they always want to idolize them.*

But he still didn't understand why Alexander was upset. "I don't get it," he said. "If what you read in the scrolls didn't bother you—"

"It *did.*" Alexander's brow creased. "But not because *I* was disappointed. It bothered me because I know how my father feels about those stories. I don't want *him* to be disappointed."

Riker grunted. Obviously, the boy had zeroed in on the truth.

First, he had seen Worf receive a subspace packet. Then his father had taken off on a secret mission in the Empire. Coincidence, maybe. But coincidences were seldom what they seemed.

Alexander couldn't have discovered any of the details of the venture, of course—couldn't have guessed that the captain and Worf were investigating a conspiracy to overthrow Gowron and throw the quadrant into disarray.

But he seemed to understand the significance of the scroll. He had sensed that what was at stake was nothing less than the Klingon faith. And he knew how very much that faith meant to his father.

"You're a very clever young man," the first officer told his young companion.

The boy looked at him, his brow still heavy with concern. "Thanks." He got up. "I think I've had enough training for today."

Riker got up too. "Same here." He looked at the ceiling of the cavern. "Computer, end program."

A moment later, the cavern and everything in it—the wounded warrior, the blindfolds and the *bat'lethmey*—gave way to the stark reality of the black-and-yellow hologrid. As they headed for the door, it opened for them.

The first officer wanted to tell Alexander that everything would be all right. He wanted to assure him that Worf would come back with his faith intact. But he couldn't.

This wasn't a folktale. This was the real world. Here, nothing was certain. One had to take one's chances and hope for the best.

As they exited from the holodeck into the corridor outside, Riker put his hand on the boy's shoulder. Alexander looked up and managed a smile, as if he shared the first officer's thoughts.

"It's all right," he said. "I'll be okay. Really."

Riker stopped. As he watched, wishing he could have done more, the boy headed for his quarters.

Twenty-four: The Heroic Age

Kahless whirled on his *s'tarahk* and cut at his adversary with his sword. With a speed born of self-preservation, the soldier parried the blow with a resounding clang, then launched an attack of his own.

But Kahless's first cut had only laid the groundwork for his second. Ducking to avoid his enemy's response, he struck hard at the man's flank.

The soldier couldn't react in time. Kahless's sword bit deep between two ribs, eliciting a scream. Then, while the man was at a disadvantage, the rebel sat up again and delivered the deathstroke.

As the soldier fell from his mount, his throat laid open, Kahless turned and surveyed the barren hillside he had chosen. No one else was coming for him. Satisfied that he was safe for the moment, he surveyed the changing terrain of the battle.

It was his first full-scale clash with Molor's forces—a clash designed to test the mettle and dedication of his ragtag army. So far, it seemed to him, the battle was more or less even. To their credit, the rebels were holding their own.

Still, they could be overrun if some pivotal event went against them. The same with the tyrant's army. That was the way of such conflicts—Kahless knew that from his service to Molor during the border wars.

He was determined that if the battle turned, it would do so in the rebels' favor. That meant he could not simply wait and hope—he had to make something happen on his own. And he knew just what that something might be.

Cut off a serpent's head. Had that not been the tyrant's own advice to him in the border wars?

Seeking out the warlord in charge of Molor's forces, he found the man directing a charge against the rebels' flank. Kahless smiled to himself. He couldn't see who the warlord was for the hair that obscured his face, but it didn't matter. He would bring the man down or die in the attempt.

Spurring his *s'tarahk* with his heels, he sliced his way through the ranks of the enemy. When he was close enough, he bellowed a challenge—one that could be heard even over the din of battle. As he'd hoped, the warlord turned to him.

And Kahless realized then whom he'd challenged. The man's name was Yatron. And like Starad, he was Molor's son.

The rebel clenched his teeth. He had already earned the tyrant's hatred many times over, hadn't he? What difference did it make if he gave Molor one more reason to despise him?

"Kahless!" bellowed Yatron, consumed with rage.

He seemed to recognize his brother's killer. And judging by the expression on his face, Yatron had no intention of adding to his father's miseries. Digging his heels into the flanks of his *s'tarahk,* he charged at Kahless, his sword whirling dangerously above his head.

Raising his own blade, Kahless charged too. They met in an empty space, each trying to skewer the other with the force of his attack. But somehow both of them escaped untouched, their only injuries the numbness in their sword arms.

Yatron whirled and hacked at the rebel's head, but Kahless was ready for him. Turning the weapon away, he stabbed at the warlord's chest. Fortunately for Yatron, he was quick enough to catch the stroke and deflect it.

For a long time, they exchanged brutal blows, neither of them giving an inch. Kahless was gouged and cut and battered, but none of his wounds were enough to slow him down.

It was the same for Molor's son. As many times as the rebel tried to slice him or run him through, Yatron always eluded the worst of it—and came back for more.

Kahless's sword became too heavy to swing. His throat grew raw with the dust he raised. And still he fought on.

Finally, he saw an opening—a hole in the web of steel Yatron wove about himself—and took advantage of it. Reaching back for whatever strength he had left, the rebel brought his blade around in a great and terrible arc.

When he was done, Yatron lay in the dirt, clutching at his entrails. Exhausted as he was, Kahless didn't let him lie there that way for long. As he'd shown mercy to one of Molor's sons, he now showed mercy to the other.

Done, he thought. *The serpent's head is off.*

The rebel paused for a moment, chest pounding, sweat streaming down both sides of his neck. It was a moment too long.

Out of the corner of his eye, he saw something bearing down on him. Too late, he turned and brought his sword up. He had time to glimpse a flash of teeth and a pair of murderous eyes before he felt a sword bury itself in his side.

With a sucking sound, it came out again. Kahless bit back a cry of agony and clutched at the neck of his *s'tarahk,* trying desperately to steady himself. He could feel his strength ebbing, feel his side growing cold and wet with blood.

His attacker spun about and came back at him to finish the job. Somehow, despite his agony, Kahless found the strength to lash out backhanded.

He was lucky. The edge of his blade caught his enemy in the forehead, sending him twisting down to the ground.

The outlaw had no time to congratulate himself. He was losing his grip—not only on the reins, but on his senses. The battle churned and tossed about him like an angry sea, disorienting him until he didn't know up from down.

Kahless was weak from loss of blood, and it was getting worse. If he was to achieve victory today, he would have to hurry. Hanging on as best he could, he raised his sword with a trembling arm.

"Their warlord is dead!" he thundered, though the ground seemed to reach up at him. "Without him, they are no better than we are!"

His words seemed to have the desired effect. With cry upon cry, his warriors surged against Molor's forces like a ponderous surf, a force that would not be denied.

The outlaws shoved the tyrant's men back. And again, and further still. And moments later, Molor's army broke like a dam trying to hold back a flood.

Kahless yelled at his men, urging them on. But he himself didn't have the strength to dig his heels in and follow. His hands and feet had become cold as ice, his vision had grown black around the edges.

Finally, mercifully, the ground rushed up at him. He had no choice but to give in to the darkness.

Twenty-five: The Modern Age

The installation that included Ter'jas Mor's defense armory was so big and stark and gray, Picard had trouble believing even a Klingon would have found it esthetically pleasing. But then, it was built more for security than esthetics.

And certainly, under normal circumstances, the place's state-of-the-art security systems would have kept intruders from getting in. But these were not normal circumstances—and Kurn, with his thorough knowledge of Defense Force design methods and codes, was hardly the average intruder.

Kahless grunted. "I never thought the day would come when Kahless the Unforgettable wore a mask like a lowly sneak thief." Reaching underneath his hood, he scratched some part of his face to relieve an itch.

"I sympathize," said the captain.

He, too, felt funny wearing a mask—and he doubted that Worf and Kurn liked it any better. Among Klingons, as in many other cultures, masks were badges of dishonorable intent.

However, it was important that they not reveal themselves here in the heart of a Defense Force installation. Hence the additional precautions, which included concealing themselves in the shadows until their prey entered their trap.

Picard had barely completed his thought when he heard footfalls approaching from the far end of the alley. Exchanging looks with Worf, he pressed his back that much harder against the wall that concealed them.

As their objective came closer, the captain all but stopped breathing. It was important that this be as quick and silent as they could make it. If anyone else heard what was going on, all their hard work might go for nothing.

Luck was with them. The Klingon armory worker didn't have the slightest inkling they were about. Without a care in the world, he approached his door and tapped in the security code on the well-worn padd beside it.

It wasn't until the door began to slide aside that he heard even the slightest sound. And turned. And opened his mouth to cry out.

But by then, it was too late. Grasping the man by the back of his neck, Kahless pushed hard—sending him hurtling into his abode, where he sprawled on the hard, smooth floor.

Twisting about to see who had attacked him, the Klingon might have had ideas about getting up or sounding an alarm—but it was too late for that as well. Worf was already standing over him, the disruptor in his hand pointed directly at the center of the Klingon's forehead. And at this range, it was highly unlikely he would miss.

Of course, as far as Picard could tell, Worf had no intention of using the weapon, except as a bluff. But the object of their attentions didn't know that.

Picard touched a wall padd beside the door and the metal panel slid closed. That left the four of them alone with their newfound friend.

"What . . . what is it you want from me?" the Klingon grated.

He was a lean man with a head that somehow seemed too large for his body. Though his skin was dark, his eyes were large and blue, and his only real facial hair was a tuft of beard in the center of his chin.

Kahless knelt beside the armory worker and grabbed a fistful of his tunic. When he spoke, his voice dripped with deadly intent. *What's more,* the captain thought, *the clone wasn't just pretending— he meant it.*

"What do we want?" Kahless echoed. "We want to know what possessed you to steal a bomb from the place where you're employed."

The man shook his head vigorously. "Whoever you are, you're mistaken. I stole no bomb."

Kahless leaned closer, his eyes smoldering through the slits in his mask. "Do not lie to me, *p'tahk.* I hate liars more than anything. Now tell me—why did you take the bomb? Do you get some sort of perverse satisfaction from destroying innocent children?"

"I know nothing of this," their host complained. "You must be thinking of someone else."

Kahless tilted his head as he studied the worker. "Perhaps you are right. Perhaps we have the wrong man."

Abruptly, he struck the Klingon across the face with his free hand. The captain winced beneath his mask and the worker flung his hands up to protect himself from a second blow.

But it was unnecessary. Kahless had made his point.

"Perhaps that is so, Adjur, son of Restagh. Perhaps we have made a mistake. But," the clone growled, "I do not think so. I think we have *precisely* the man we are looking for."

"We know you stole the bomb," said Worf, a voice of reason in comparison to Kahless. "Tell us who else was involved. Your accomplices, your contacts in the Defense Force, everything. Or you will not live long enough to regret the blood you've shed."

The Klingon looked from one masked and hooded face to the next, his blue eyes full of fear. By now, he must have known how slim his chances of survival were—unless he cooperated.

There was still the chance that he was telling the truth, of course, and was completely innocent of the charges against him—but Picard doubted it. He'd been a captain long enough to know when someone had the stench of treachery about him—and this one stunk to high Heaven.

"All right," Adjur relented. "I'll talk." His eyes narrowed. "But first, you must tell me what you meant about the children."

Was it possible he didn't know? Certainly, his question seemed sincere enough. Or was he simply building a case for his ignorance?

Kurn spat. "The bomb was used to destroy an academy. Some of the victims weren't tall enough to cut your throat."

That got a reaction from the Klingon—an expression of shame and disgust. "I did not know," he swore heatedly. "If I had, I would never have gotten involved with them."

"With who?" asked Kahless.

Adjur scowled. "The one who came to me was a Klingon named Muuda. He's a merchant of some sort."

"Tell me more," the clone advised him.

Adjur's scowl deepened. "Muuda said he represented a conspiracy to overthrow Gowron, and to replace him with someone else. But he never said who the other conspirators were or who they proposed as council leader."

"And you didn't care enough to ask?" Worf prodded.

The armory worker shrugged. "What difference would it have made to me? Besides, Muuda was willing to offer me latinum in exchange for my cooperation. One in my position does not often get such an offer."

"Who else accepted this offer?" asked Kahless.

Adjur went silent. "No one," he said.

Based on Godar's comments, they suspected otherwise. This was their chance to have the suspicion corroborated.

"A lie," snarled the clone, tightening his grasp on the Klingon's tunic. "Tell me the truth, son of Restagh, or I'll see to it you never walk the same way again."

Adjur swallowed. "His name is Najuk, son of Noj. We made the deal with Muuda together. Najuk got one bomb and I got another."

Picard nodded. Godar had been correct. Besides, he recalled seeing two separate explosions at the academy.

Kahless pulled the armory worker's face closer to his own. "Listen carefully," he rasped. "I should turn you in for what you've done—but I won't, if you continue to help me. I want to know how to find this Muuda."

Adjur saw he had little choice in the matter. "That goes for all of you?" he asked. "You won't turn me in?"

"All of us," Worf confirmed.

That was good enough for Adjur. "He lives on Kerret'raa, just north of the city of Ra'jahn. He once described the place to me."

"Anything else we should know?" asked Kurn.

The armory worker thought for a moment. "Yes. You'll know Muuda at a glance because he has only one arm. He lost the other in a battle with the Romulans twenty years ago."

Kahless made a sound of disgust as he thrust Adjur away from him.

"A real patriot, this Muuda. Good. Then we won't have to twist off his other arm to get some information out of him."

The armory worker must have thought his ordeal was over. But as the clone turned away from him, Kurn pinned Adjur hard against the wall. Behind his mask, the governor seemed to be smiling.

"If I were you," he said, "I would pack up and run. *Tonight.* Otherwise, you will be *kraw'za* food before you know it."

The Klingon looked confused. "But I told you what you wanted to know. You said you wouldn't turn me in."

"And we won't," Kurn assured him. "But that doesn't mean we won't tell the families of those who were killed."

Adjur paled. His eyes grew larger than ever. "You wouldn't," he moaned.

Worf's brother didn't answer. He just released the armory worker as if he were some diseased animal. Then he tapped the appropriate keys on his wrist controller.

The next thing the captain knew, they were back on Kurn's ship, and its master was setting the controls for Kerret'raa.

Twenty-six: The Heroic Age

Like a man who had discovered how to see for the first time, Kahless opened his eyes. He was standing in a courtyard.

The stones beneath his booted feet were small and gray, deftly cut and fitted together. The walls around him were gray as well, and taller than he had ever imagined walls could be. Even the barriers around Molor's fortress at Qa'yarin seemed small and frail-looking by comparison.

The doors to the keep here were made of heavy wood, and bound between sheets of tough, black iron. As Kahless watched, they opened for him. A din of music and laughter poured out, making the courtyard ring. Curious, he ventured inside.

There was no one in the anteroom to ask him his name or his business there, no one to stop him. Glad of it, he hurried on into the feast hall.

It was huge and imposing, with beams and poles and rafters made of rich, red *teqal'ya* wood and a flock of exotic birds roosting in the recesses of its high vaulted ceiling. The place was ringed with benches, on which sat a veritable host of armed men. And in the center of the hall, two warriors in leather armor clashed and clattered and raised a terrible commotion with their swords, though neither seemed to sustain any wounds.

Kahless shook his head in wonder. *Whose hall was this? How had he gotten here? And who were these warriors?*

Suddenly, he noticed that someone was standing next to him. Expecting a threat, he whirled.

But it wasn't a threat. A cry stifled in Kahless's throat. Reaching out, he touched the side of Kellein's face with infinite gentleness.

"How . . . ?" he stumbled, drinking in the sight of her.

Kellein grasped his hand and placed it against her breast. He could feel her *jinaq* amulet.

"Do not ask how," she told him. "Nor when, nor where, nor why. Only trust that I am who I seem I am, and that we have a pitifully short time to be together."

He drew her closer. "Kellein . . . I wish I . . . if only . . ."

She shook her head. "You did not fail me, Kahless, son of Kanjis. I was meant to perish along with the rest of Vathraq's people. There is nothing you could have done about it."

He couldn't accept that. "But if I had turned down your father's invitation, if I had kept riding—"

"The same thing would have happened," Kellein insisted, "albeit it in a different way. We were meant to find this place."

Kahless looked around and realized where he was. He swallowed hard. Until now, it had only been a legend to him, a tale told to children around the fire. Now it was wonderfully, painfully real.

"Enough of me," his betrothed said. "I need to speak of you, Kahless. Soon, you will leave this place, because you do not belong here. And when you return to the world, there is something you must do."

He looked around at the warriors seated on the benches, and he began to see among them faces that he recognized—faces of men who fought beside him on the frontier. And also, the faces of those who had fought against him.

Finally, he turned to Kellein again. Her hair was black as a *kraw'za's* wing and her eyes were green as the sea. She looked every bit as strong and defiant as the day he saw her in the river.

"I don't want to go anywhere," he told her. "I want to stay."

Her eyes flashed. "No, Kahless. You *must* go back. You have come a long way toward tearing down the tyrant Molor, but there is yet much to do."

"Molor means nothing to me," he declared. "The rebellion means nothing, except for my promise to Morath. I would give it all up in a moment to have you with me again."

Even before Kellein spoke, he knew the truth of the matter. "It is not possible," she said. "At least, not now. You have a destiny to take hold of—and in their hearts, all who follow you know that. But to succeed in your quest, you will need a sword."

Kahless shrugged. "There are plenty of swords in the world."

She grasped his arm. "No. This one is different. It will be a friend to you in battle. It will make you unbeatable."

Kahless wanted to laugh, to tell her that a sword was no better than the warrior who wielded it. But he could see his Kellein was not in a joking mood.

"Listen carefully," she told him.

Kellein gave him directions on how to make the sword. First, he had to take a lock of his hair and dip it in the hot blood of the Kri'stak Volcano. Then he had to cool the thing in the waters of Lake Lusor. Finally, he had to twist it just so.

"Only then," she said, "will you have the kind of weapon you need to overthrow the tyrant." She squeezed his hand harder than ever. "Only then will you achieve a victory unequaled in the history of the world."

Kahless moved his fingers into the softness of her hair. He didn't want to be talking with her about swords and tyrants. He wanted to tell her how much he ached for her still, how he would never forget what she meant to him.

But before he could utter a word, Kellein faded like smoke on the wind. And before he knew it, he held nothing in his hands but empty air.

He would have bellowed then like a wounded *minn'hor*, making the rafters ring with his agony, except someone had leaped off one of the benches and was approaching him. Someone he knew all too well.

It was Starad, Molor's son. And he was whole again, unscathed.

The warrior had a sword in his hand, and it seemed he was looking for trouble. But something told Kahless that he could not be harmed here. After all, Kellein had said he had a destiny to seize elsewhere.

"Kahless?" Starad laughed, brash as ever. "Is it really you?"

The rebel held his ground. "You can see it is."

Molor's son stopped in front of him and sneered. "I know what you're up to, Kahless. But you're just a *yolok* worm beneath Molor's boot. Oh, maybe you'll win a battle or two, but in the long run you can't hope to accomplish anything." He leaned closer to the rebel, grinning with his long, sharp teeth. "Why not give yourself up and save everyone some trouble?"

Kahless could feel his own lips pulling back. "You were a fool when you were alive, Starad. I never thought to seek your counsel then, so why would I heed it now?"

Molor's son raised his sword before his face. Catching the light, the blade glinted murderously.

"Ignore me if you want," he rasped, "but you will not be able to ignore my father's power. When the deathblow falls and your wretched rebellion falls along with it, you will remember me." His eyes slitted with barely contained fury. "You will remember Starad."

Kahless cursed him. "You think I wanted this?" he hissed. "You think I wanted to be hunted like an animal? To see my mate lying dead on her father's ground? To be deprived of comfort everywhere I turn?"

Starad opened his mouth to reply—but nothing came out. And a moment later, he had faded to smoke, just like Kellein before him.

Kahless felt a hand on his arm. He turned and found himself face to face with Rannuf, Edronh's son. The boy was just as he had been in the forest that snowy day, ruddy-cheeked and full of life.

"Rannuf," he said, his anger abating. In its place, he felt only heavy-hearted remorse. "I am sorry you had to die. Believe me, I wish it were otherwise."

Rannuf shook his head. "You misunderstand, Lord Kahless. I have not come to exact an apology from you, or to blame you for my death. I have come to warn you about impending treachery."

"What treachery?" the rebel asked.

"It is my father," Rannuf explained. "Edronh plans to sell you out to Molor's forces. He grows weary of losing his family and his possessions—weary of the bloodshed. The only way it will end, he believes, is when the tyrant has your head."

"No," said Kahless. He shook his head. "That is not possible. Edronh has never shown me anything but loyalty."

The youth smiled grimly. "Molor might have said that about *you* once, my lord. Men change."

Kahless frowned. He couldn't ignore Rannuf's advice—not under the circumstances. It was said the dead had knowledge that was denied the living.

"All right," he replied. "What does your father intend to—?"

He never finished his question. Like the others, Rannuf wavered and blew away on a puff of air.

Kahless turned to the center of the hall, where the two warriors were still raising a terrible noise. The multitude of spectators egged them on from their seats. Up above, strange birds flew from one rafter to the next.

Kellein had said he didn't belong here. It seemed to him that she was right—that he wasn't meant to leave the world of the living quite yet. But how was he supposed to get back?

What offering did he have to make, and to whom? There was no sign

*of the serpent said to guard this place and keep it inviolate, or of the
ancient ones who had challenged it. . . .*

Just as he thought that, the hall itself began to quake and come
apart, as if under the influence of a powerful wind. Oblivious to it, the
warriors on the benches continued to cheer for one fighter or the other,
and the birds continued to fly. But Kahless could see the hall shiver and
dissipate, and its occupants along with it.

Finally, he himself began to lose his shape, to twist in the wind and
drift away. He cried out . . .

. . . and found himself sitting upright in a tent, the air cold on his skin.
His heart was pumping like a bellows and his eyes stung with sweat
that had pooled in the hollows of their sockets.

Kahless wasn't alone, either. Morath was sitting in a corner, alongside Porus and Shurin, and a heavyset man he didn't recognize at first.
Then he remembered. The man's name was Badich. He had professed
to be a healer when he joined them.

"Kahless is awake!" snapped Shurin.

Morath got to his feet and came closer. "He looks better, too. I think
the fever has broken."

"What did I tell you?" asked Badich, getting to his feet as well,
albeit with a good deal more difficulty. "It was the poultice I made him.
There's nothing it can't cure."

"How long have I been here?" asked Kahless.

"Two days," said Porus. "Your wounds became infected. You were
so feverish, we thought we had lost you. How do you feel?"

Kahless didn't answer him. He just grabbed his tunic and slipped it
on. It wasn't easy, considering he hurt in a dozen places, all of which
were dressed and bandaged.

"What are you doing?" asked Morath.

Kahless found his belt and cinched it around his waist. Then, with
an effort, he pulled his boots on.

"Where's Edronh?" he wanted to know.

The others looked at one another. Judging by their expressions, his
question was a surprise to them.

"Edronh?" echoed Shurin. "What difference does it make?"

"It makes a difference," Kahless insisted. "Where is he?"

Porus shrugged. "With his men, I suppose."

Kahless grunted. "Let us see if that is so."

Doing his best to forget how much he still ached, he emerged from
the tent. It was dusk. The fires of his followers stretched for a distance
all around him.

"Edronh and his men are *that* way," said Morath. He pointed in the direction where the sky was lightest and the stars already dwindling. "They're guarding our front against the enemy."

"Show me," Kahless ordered.

Morath led him and the others to the place where Edronh was supposed to be encamped. Neither the northlander nor his warriors were anywhere to be seen, nor had their fires been tended lately.

"Maybe we were wrong," said Porus. "Maybe they bedded down somewhere else."

Kahless sniffed the wind. Nothing yet. But soon, there would be plenty.

"You were not wrong," he told Porus. "They were supposed to be here and they are not. They are off betraying us instead."

Morath looked at him, his brow wrinkled with concern. "How do you know that?" he demanded.

"I heard it in a dream," Kahless replied. "Now listen closely. We have to move before Molor takes Edronh's treachery and skewers us on it." He turned to Porus. "Stay here with a hundred warriors. Pretend to sleep, but keep your blades at hand."

"And what of the rest of us?" asked Shurin.

Kahless clapped him on the shoulder. "The rest of us will slip away quietly and take up positions along the enemy's flank."

"But the enemy is not in the field," Badich protested. "He *has* no flank."

"Not yet," Kahless agreed. "But he will soon enough."

Twenty-seven: The Modern Age

As Picard and his comrades materialized on the perimeter of Muuda's estate, the first thing that struck the captain was the heavy-handed showiness of the place. It was not a tribute to elegance by any standard, Klingon or otherwise.

All around the low-lying *m'ressa*-wood structure, there were ornate fountains of polished marble and overgrown *tran'nuc* trees and elaborate stone paths leading through seas of ruby-red fireblossoms.

And statues. Lots of statues.

Ironically, the largest of them depicted Kahless's epic struggle with the tyrant Molor. In this particular piece, they were locked in hand-to-hand combat, their *bat'leths* broken and lying in pieces at their feet. Both were bleeding from a dozen wounds, eyes locked, muscles straining in a life-or-death battle that would decide the fate of a civilization.

The clone had apparently noticed the statue as well. "Nice likeness," he grunted matter-of-factly from beneath his cowl. But he said nothing more on the subject.

Of course, if the scroll were to be believed, Kahless's encounter with Molor had been of a different nature. But if the clone wasn't inclined to comment, Picard wouldn't either.

There was no evidence of a security system on the grounds or around the house. Apparently, Muuda had spent all his *darsekmey* on his esthetic, unable to imagine that his deeds would come back to haunt him.

But haunt him they would, and with a vengeance. Picard and his allies would see to that.

Proceeding along one of the wildly meandering stone paths, the four of them made their way to a window in the back. Worf peered inside, then turned to face the others.

"There are warriors inside. Females as well," he said, his mask muffling his voice. "But they all appear to be asleep, some with bottles of *warnog* in their hands."

Kurn grunted. "Drunk. Muuda must have thrown a party with his latest infusion of blood money."

Kahless nodded. "The same sort of blood money he used to buy this estate and furnish it with heroic images. I say we burn it down and him with it—give him a taste of what he did to those children."

"*After* we've dragged some information out of him," Kurn noted.

"Yes," said the clone. "Afterward, of course."

The captain looked at them with some alarm. But Worf made a gesture of dismissal, indicating it was only talk. The Klingons wouldn't incinerate these people any sooner than Picard would.

It wouldn't be honorable. And to some Klingons, honor was still an issue.

"Come on," said the lieutenant.

He moved to the next window and looked through it. This time, the captain saw Worf's lip curl in disgust. When he turned to them again, he didn't report out loud as before. He just tilted his head to indicate Muuda was inside.

Kahless didn't hesitate. Taking out his *d'k tahg,* he turned it pommel-first and smashed the window glass. Then he vaulted through the aperture, oblivious to the shards that still stuck to the frame.

In rapid-fire succession, the others followed. As Picard leaped through the ruined window, he saw a one-armed Klingon lying in a bath of faceted obsidian, surrounded by three levels of steps. Despite the noisiness of their entrance, Muuda was still unconscious.

But then, *warnog* had that effect. Warriors had been known to sleep for days after a particularly generous dose of the beverage.

Not so the two females who had shared Muuda's bath. Eyes wide, they slithered out of the water and ran for the door, naked as the day they were born. But Kurn blocked their way, his drawn dagger enough of a threat to stop them in their tracks.

They hissed at him. "Let us go," one of them insisted, showing her teeth. "We have done nothing wrong."

"Get back," the governor instructed, obviously not in a mood to argue the point.

Worf grabbed a couple of robes hanging on a wall rack and threw them at the females. "Clothe yourselves," he told them. "Then find a corner and be still. Cooperate and we'll leave you unharmed."

Ultimately, the females had little choice. Catching the robes in midair, they put them on and relegated themselves to a corner of the room. But even then, they were far from docile-looking.

Having dealt with Lursa and B'Etor of the House of Duras, the captain knew how big a mistake it would be to underestimate the "gentler" Klingon sex. He resolved to keep an eye on the females until they were done with their business here.

Advancing to the bath, Kahless walked up the steps and reached for Muuda's hair, which lay spread about his shoulders. Grabbing a lock in his fist, the clone tugged without mercy.

Crying out, Muuda brought a bottle out of the water with his good hand. Out of instinct, he tried to strike Kahless with it. But the clone batted it away. A moment later, it shattered on the floor, leaving an amber-colored pool on the stone.

"Muuudaa," growled Kahless, drawing the name out, making it plain it left a bad taste in his mouth.

The Klingon in the bath looked up at him through bloodshot eyes, still half in an alcoholic stupor. But he wasn't so drunk he didn't know what kind of danger he was in.

"Who . . . who are you?" he stammered.

The clone took out his dagger and laid its point against Muuda's cheek. "I will ask the questions here," he said.

Realizing this was no dream, the Klingon swallowed. "Yes," he agreed. "You will ask the questions."

"You bought two bombs from a pair of armory workers on Ter'jas Mor," Kahless told him. "Bombs intended for use in an academy on Ogat. But you didn't see them planted yourself. You were merely a go-between—a middleman. Who was it you bought the bombs for?"

Muuda swallowed again, even harder than before. Obviously, he was thinking of what would happen to him if his employers discovered he had identified them. But he also had to be thinking about the more immediate danger—the masked intruders in his bath chamber.

Noting Muuda's indecision, the clone flicked the point of his dagger, breaking the skin of the Klingon's cheek. He winced as a droplet of lavender blood emerged.

"I asked you a question," Kahless hissed. "I expect an answer."

Muuda glared at him. "All right," he said, slurring his words. "I'll tell you. Just let me up. It is cold in here."

The clone shook his head. "Not a chance, *p'tahk*. You will have plenty of time to warm yourself when we are done here. Now who was it?"

Seeing his ploy wouldn't work, the Klingon acquiesced. He told them not only who was involved in the plot, but the role each of the conspirators had assumed in it.

It was just as Kahless had been telling them all along. These people were some of the most highly placed officers in the Klingon Defense Force. And there was one name that was not associated with the Defense Force, but was nonetheless more important than all the others.

"All well and good," said Worf. "But what proof do we have that this *ko'tal* is telling the truth?"

The merchant licked his lips. "There is a way to prove it," he replied. And he informed them of it.

When Muuda was done, the clone took his knife back and sheathed it. "That is more like it," he said. "Now we leave you to your newfound wealth and your companions. But trust me, coward, when I say you will not have long to enjoy them. The innocents you killed will not soon be forgotten."

Picard saw the look in Muuda's eyes. The Klingon believed it. No doubt, it would take the pleasure out of his revels, knowing how short-lived they would be. At least, the captain wanted to think so.

With a jerk of his shaggy head, the clone advised them it was time to withdraw. The warriors in the house might come out of their drunken sleep at any moment, and it would be tempting fate to stay and lock horns with them.

Instead, Kahless slipped out of the window, and the others followed. Before Muuda and his females could sound the alarm, Picard saw the glimmer in the air that signified their transport.

Twenty-eight: The Heroic Age

Kahless and his men had barely settled in when Molor's army.began to move, charging headlong without the least bit of caution. After all, the enemy's warchiefs expected the rebels to be helpless and exposed. Thanks to the warning Kahless had received, they were neither.

He waited only until Molor's soldiers had moved past them and were on the verge of the rebel camp. Then, with guile and fury and righteous indignation, he attacked. The tyrant's men never knew what hit them.

The outlaws cut through them like a scythe, harvesting death, irrigating the ground with the blood of their adversaries. Kahless searched for Edronh across the battlefield, but never found him. It wasn't until later that he realized why. Apparently, Morath had found him first and showed him the error of his ways.

In the end, Kahless routed Molor's men, sending away half the number that had come after him. It was his second great victory in three days. More importantly, it showed his followers they could go nose-to-nose with the best-trained army in the world.

When the combat was over, and Kahless was surveying the field with Morath at his side, he remembered another bit of advice he had gotten in his dream. Unfortunately, he could not take it literally.

A lock of hair was not a good thing to make a weapon of, no matter how cleverly it was twisted. Nor was the crater of an active volcano any place for a man who still clung to sanity.

Still, Kellein's directions made a kind of sense if one looked at them the right way. A sword like that would be more than a means of killing one's adversaries. It could become a symbol.

Of self-reliance. Of freedom. And ultimately, of victory.

"I need a metalsmith," Kahless said out loud.

Morath looked at him. "Right now?" he said.

"Right now," the rebel confirmed. "And so he will have something to work with, I will need twenty swords plucked from the hands of the enemy's corpses. And of course, whatever he needs to make a smithy."

His friend grunted. "Did you hear about this in your dream as well?"

Kahless nodded. "As a matter of fact, I did."

As it happened, there were several metalsmiths among the rebel forces. The best one was Toragh, a man with short, gnarly legs, a torso like a tree trunk, and biceps each the size of a grown man's head.

"You want what?" asked Toragh, after Morath and Porus had brought him to Kahless's tent.

A second time, the rebel chieftain showed the metalsmith what he wanted, carving the same shape into the soft dirt. "Like so," he said. "With a grip here in the center, and an arc here, and cutting edges all around."

The metalsmith looked at him as if he were crazy. "I have been at this for twenty years, and I have never heard of anything like this. How did you come up with it?"

"Do not ask," Morath advised him.

"Where I got the idea is not important," Kahless added. "What is important, metalsmith, is whether or not you can make it for me."

Toragh stroked his chin as he considered the design in the dirt. Finally, he nodded. "I can make it, all right. But it will not be easy. A weapon like this one will require a steady hand at the bellows, or the balance will be off—and balance is everything."

"I will work the bellows myself if I have to," Kahless replied. "Rest assured, you will have everything you need."

Toragh eyed him. "And you're certain this will help us to tear down the tyrant?" He seemed skeptical.

Kahless laughed. "As certain as the bile in Molor's belly."

Twenty-nine: The Modern Age

Propelled by only a fraction of its impulse power, Kurn's craft drifted ever closer to the subspace relay station that hung in space dead ahead. Picard had seen plenty of such stations before, but never one operated by the Klingon Defense Force.

The difference was pronounced, to say the least. Though the station's sole function was to transmit data from one place to another, its architecture was so severe as to look almost ominous. The captain wouldn't have been surprised if it turned out to be better armed than some starships.

It wasn't long before they got a response from the station. A lean, long-faced Klingon with a thin mustache appeared on the monitor screen set into Kurn's console. His garb suggested that he was in command of the facility.

"Who are you and what do you want?" the Klingon grated. His eyes, one dark brown and the other a sea green, demanded an answer.

In any other culture, Picard knew, this would have been a sign of disrespect, perhaps even a challenge. However, Klingons did not waste time with amenities. They simply said what was on their minds.

Still, Kurn put on a show of anger. As he had explained minutes earlier, the best way to deal with a bureaucrat was to seem even more annoyed than he was.

"I am Kurn, son of Mogh," he grated. "Governor of Ogat and member of the High Council."

The station commander's eyes narrowed. "I have heard of Kurn. But for all I know, you could be a slug on the bottom of Kurn's boot."

Worf's brother made a sound deep in his throat. "Then look for yourself. Bring up my file image and compare it to what you see."

The station commander wasn't about to take anyone at his word. Barking an order to an offscreen lackey, he glared at Kurn—as if trying to decide what to do with him if he *wasn't* the council member.

A few moments later, the same lackey whispered in the station commander's ear. A look of confusion passed over the Klingon's face, like the shadow of a cloud on a sunny day.

"You do indeed appear to be Kurn," he said finally. "But according to our information, Kurn is supposed to be dead."

Fortunately, Worf's brother was prepared for this. Tossing his shaggy head back, he laughed out loud. "Dead?" he roared. Abruptly, he leaned forward, so that his face was only a couple of inches from the monitor. "Tell me, son of a *targ*—do I *look* dead to *you?*"

The station commander swallowed. "No," he conceded, "you do not."

"Then lower your shields," said Kurn, pressing his advantage, "and prepare for our arrival."

The Klingon on the relay station hesitated—but only for a moment. Then, looking as if he'd just eaten something distasteful, he turned and barked an order over his shoulder.

"Our shields have been lowered," he reported. "You may beam aboard the station whenever you please."

That was Picard's cue. Still wearing the cloak he had used on Ter'jas Mor, he picked up the hood and brought it down over his face. After all, it would arouse instant suspicion if a human were to beam aboard alongside Kurn.

Since Kahless and Worf might also have been recognized, they donned their hoods as well. Only Kurn went bareheaded.

Picard and his lieutenant set their disruptors on stun. However, their companions, Klingons through and through, did nothing of the sort.

Worf's brother then reached for the remote transporter controls set into his armband. He tapped out the proper sequence and glanced at the captain—as if to make certain he was ready for what would follow.

Picard was ready, all right. The next thing he knew, he was standing on what appeared to be the relay station's main deck, almost face-to-face with the Klingon he'd seen on the monitor.

Kurn interposed himself between them, so the station commander wouldn't be tempted to try to peer inside the hood. Of course, that didn't stop the other Klingons present.

Each of them looked up from his duties and wondered at the newcomers. The captain noted that the Klingons were all armed—not that that was a surprise. And he was certain *their* disruptors weren't set on stun.

"I want to download secured transmission records," Worf's brother announced. "My ship's computer is ready and waiting. All I need is your help to get past the security codes."

The station commander glanced at Picard, Worf, and finally Kahless. Then he turned back to Kurn.

"You travel in mysterious company," the Klingon observed.

"My choice of companions is not your concern," Kurn snapped. And then, to throw out a bone: "A man in my position finds the best bodyguards he can, Klingon or otherwise. Now, the help I asked for?"

The station commander frowned. Obviously, this wasn't going to be as easy as they had hoped.

"You have not yet stated your reasons for coming here," he maintained. "It's one thing to allow you entry, considering your position with the Defense Force. But to circumvent the security codes, I would require clearance from the homeworld. I have not received any such clearance."

Kurn grunted. "And if I told you I was here on Council business? And that the Council does not wish its dealings to be known beyond these bulkheads?"

The station commander thrust out his beardless chin. "In that case, I would *still* require some form of—"

Kurn didn't allow him to finish his statement. Instead, he backhanded the Klingon across the mouth with a closed fist, sending him staggering into a bulkhead. When the station commander looked at him again, there was hate in his eyes and lavender blood running down his chin.

But by then, Worf's brother was aiming his disruptor pistol at the Klingon's forehead—just as his companions were pointing theirs at the various other personnel on the station.

Kurn took a step closer to the station commander, keeping his weapon level. The look in his eyes said he wouldn't think twice about using it. In fact, he might relish the experience.

"Thank your ancestors I am a merciful man," Kurn bellowed. "But I will not ask you again." He tilted his head to indicate the communications console at one end of the room. "Do it—or you will wish you had."

Suddenly, Picard heard a shout from somewhere behind him. He whirled just in time to see yet another Klingon emerge from behind a sliding door—a Klingon with a weapon in his hand. He must have been working in a storage area when Kurn's group arrived.

And now, he had returned to the main deck—only to see his comrades held at disruptor-point. Under the circumstances, the man's reaction was understandable. The captain sympathized.

But that didn't mean he was going to stand there and present an easy target for the Klingon's disruptor fire. Ducking to his right, he watched the disruption beam pass him and strike a bulkhead, where it disintegrated a good part of the thing before its destructive energies wore themselves out.

That could have been me, Picard told himself. At the same time, he returned his adversary's blast—crumpling the Klingon where he stood.

It might have ended then and there. However, their comrade's entrance gave the stationkeepers the chance they'd been looking for. Or so it seemed to the captain, as the place turned into a chaotic mess of hurtling bodies and flailing limbs, not to mention the occasional errant disruptor beam.

"Watch out!" cried a familiar deep voice.

Before Picard could determine what he had to watch for, he saw Worf rush past him—in order to meet another Klingon head on. The human winced at the bone-jarring sound of their clash, and was only slightly relieved when he saw his officer had come out on top.

A disruptor beam sizzled by his ear. Turning, Picard aimed at the source of it and let fly with a beam of his own.

It hit a stationkeeper's hand and knocked the pistol out of it. And before he could recover, Kahless slammed his fist into the Klingon's jaw, sending him sprawling.

But before the captain could seek out another target, he felt something strike him in the back of the head. There was a moment or two that seemed very long, much too long, and then the floor rose up to meet him with a sickening impact.

Tasting blood, Picard turned his head to see what was going on. Something descended on him—something big and dark and powerful-looking. He was about to lash out at it with the heel of his foot when he realized it was Worf.

"Captain," said his tactical officer, evincing obvious relief. "When I saw you go down, I was afraid they had—"

Picard waved away the suggestion. "The point is, they didn't," he said. With Worf's help, he got to his feet and surveyed the place.

About half the stationkeepers were unconscious. The rest of them were gone without a trace. Fortunately, the station commander was among those who still remained.

With Kahless's help, Kurn dragged the Klingon over to the main console and placed the commander's hand on the appropriate padd—the customary Defense Force security bypass. Abruptly, the console lit up with a pattern of green and orange lights.

"Qapla'," said Kahless, smiling.

"Qapla' indeed," agreed Kurn, as he set out to download the transmission records. It only took a minute or so, once they had access to

the system. Had it been a Federation system, it wouldn't even have taken that long.

"Your computer has the information?" the clone asked.

Worf's brother nodded. "The transmission is complete."

"Good," said Kahless.

Lifting his disruptor pistol, he trained it on the console and fired. The thing was consumed in a matter of seconds.

"Now," he declared, "these burden beasts will be unable to call for help when they come to."

In fact, the "burden beasts" in question were already stirring. Picard looked at Kurn, who nodded once and worked the controls on his armband.

The captain drew his next breath on Kurn's ship. Kahless snorted, a sound of triumph. Worf eased himself into the pilot's seat and brought the ship about as his brother went to the sensor panel.

Picard joined Kurn. "No sign of any transmission, I trust?"

Without looking up, Kurn shook his head. "None. And to my knowledge, there are no backup systems. Klingons are not enamored of redundancies."

Except when it comes to parts of your anatomy, the captain thought, remembering how Worf's biological redundancies had enabled him to walk again after his back had been broken. But as with so much else, he didn't say it out loud.

"Wait," said Kurn. "There *is* a transmission."

Kahless came over to see it with his own eyes. "I do not understand," he said. "I destroyed the communications panel. You all saw it."

"It is not coming *from* the station," Worf's brother explained. "It is being sent there from somewhere *else.*"

The emperor snorted. "That's more like it. What does it say?"

Kurn brought it up on his monitor. Of course, Picard couldn't read Klingon very well. He had to wait for the others to provide a translation.

But after only a few moments, he could tell that the news was not good. Suddenly, Kahless blurted a curse and turned from the console.

The captain looked to Kurn. "What is it?" he asked.

"It is about the scroll," Worf's brother told him. He glanced at the emperor. "It was tested for authenticity—and it passed. Apparently, even the clerics of Boreth are now satisfied the thing is authentic."

Thirty: The Heroic Age

In the center of Tolar'tu, Kahless held Shurin's battered body in his arms and roared at the gathering storm. Rain fell in heavy, warm drops, mixing with Shurin's blood and marking the dirt at the rebel's feet.

"This was my friend," Kahless cried. "Shurin, who never knew his father or mother, who lost an eye fighting Molor's wars. Yet he saw more clearly than most men, for he was among the first to turn against the tyrant."

With a sudden heave of his powerful arms, the outlaw raised Shurin's loose-limbed corpse to the heavens. More importantly, he made it visible to the vast mob gathered before him—an assemblage of rebels that packed the square from wall to wall and squeezed into the narrow streets all around.

Nor was he the only one with a dead man in his hands. There were hundreds of others clasped by friends and kin, grim evidence of the efficiency of Molor's soldiers and the sharpness of their swords.

But for every rebel that fell, two of the tyrant's men had gone down as well. For every one of Kahless's outlaws, two of Molor's soldiers. And in the end, that had been enough to save Tolar'tu from destruction.

Not all of it, unfortunately. Not the outer precincts, where the enemy had smashed and burned and gutted at their warlord's command. But thanks to the courage of these rabble and riffraff, this square and the buildings around it had gone unscathed.

"What will I tell this man of courage," Kahless raged, "when I see him on the far side of Death? What will I say took place after he left us? What tale will I bear him?"

There were responses from the crowd, guttural demands of vengeance and promises of devotion. He couldn't make out the exact words for the echoes. But he could see the expressions on the rebels' faces, and by those alone he knew he was reaching them.

Strange, the outlaw thought. *He had always been able to reach them this way, hadn't he?* He had just never paused to reflect on it. Kahless raised Shurin's body a little higher.

"Will I tell him his comrades came as far as Tolar'tu, then faltered? That at the last, they spit the bit and allowed his death to come to nothing? Or will I tell him we persevered, and went on to Qa'yarin, and trampled the serpent there under our heel?"

This time the answer was so deafening, so powerful, Kahless thought the buildings around him might crumble after all. It was like being in the center of a storm, the likes of which the world had not known since its beginnings—a tempest made of men's voices and clashing swords and a yearning so fierce no enemy could stand against it.

Truth to tell, Shurin had broken his neck falling off his *s'tarahk* in the midst of the battle. Kahless himself had seen the beast stumble and throw the man to the ground, and he had seen Shurin lie still as other beasts came and trampled him.

It might not have been that way if the man hadn't had too much bloodwine the night before. Or if he had slept more instead of rolling gaming bones halfway to morning.

But that was not the picture the outlaw wished to paint—and since he had been the only witness to Shurin's death, he could paint it as he liked. The one-eyed man would be an asset in death as he was in life. A hero if necessary, a martyr if possible. Shurin himself would have laughed at the notion, but he was no longer alive to have a say in the matter.

Lowering Shurin's corpse, he laid it on the ground. Then he stood again and waited for just the right moment.

"Wait!" Kahless shouted suddenly, as the cheers began to die down. "Stop! What in the name of our ancestors are we doing?"

The throng grew quiet, peering at him through faces caked with dirt and blood. *What sort of question is that?* they must have wondered.

"Are we insane?" the outlaw asked. "Just because we have triumphed in a few small skirmishes, does that make us think we can win a war? Molor is no petty despot, cowering in his keep. He is the master of all he sees, power incarnate, the hand that clutches the throat of the world entire!"

There were protests, some of them heartwarmingly savage. But Kahless had more to say. As it happened, a lot more.

"And who are we to dare this?" he bellowed. "Not soldiers, not warriors, only old men and children who have become skilled at pretending. We have learned to fool ourselves. We have learned to believe we can tear down the mightiest tree in the forest, when all we have in our hands are our fathers' rusted *d'k tahgmey!*"

"No!" cried a thousand voices.

"Lies!" thundered a thousand more.

"We are warriors!" they rumbled. "Warriors!"

"For that matter," Kahless roared, "why should we fight at all? For honor? For dignity? We have none of these things—and we deserve none! We are outlaws and worse, less than the dirt beneath the tyrant's feet!"

"More lies!" came the thunderous reply.

"We are Klingons!" they stormed.

"Molor will fall!"

"For honor!"

"For freedom!"

And on and on, one shout building on another, until they were all one cry of rage and purpose, one savage chorus with but a single idea burning in their minds—to tear down the one who had brought them so much misery. To pry Molor loose from his empire and grind his bones to dust.

And as if in support, the skies answered them, crashing and lightning and pelting them with rain. But the rebels didn't budge. They stood there, their hearts raised as high as their voices, and let the water from the heavens run over them and cleanse them.

Kahless smiled, but only to himself. They had needed their spirits bolstered after such a hard fought and bloody battle. And with the power he had discovered in himself, he had done what was necessary.

Molor might beat them yet. He might show them the depth of their foolishness at Qa'yarin. But it would not happen because the rebels' courage had not been fanned to a fever pitch. If they failed, it would not be because Kahless had not done his part.

And who knew? Perhaps in ages to come, warriors would sing of the battle at Tolar'tu, and the speech a rebel had made there. Not that it mattered to Kahless if he was remembered or not.

He glanced at Morath, who was in the first rank of onlookers. The younger man remained calm and inscrutable as ever, as the rain matted his hair and streamed down his face.

Morath was truly the backbone of this rebellion. Kahless might have been its voice, its heart, but it was his friend who made it stand straight and tall and proud.

Well done, Morath told him, if only with his eyes. *You have put the fire in them. You have spurred them as no one else could.*

Had he been aware of the way Kahless had ennobled Shurin's clumsiness, he would no doubt have disapproved. But he did not know, and the outlaw had no intention of telling him.

In his own way, he had kept his vow, made in the depths of weariness and madness in the hills north of Vathraq's village. And he would continue to abide by it a little longer, until either he died or Molor did.

Then, either way, his work would be done. If the outlaw succeeded, Morath could have Molor's empire, to do with as he wished. And if Kahless fell short, Morath could make of that what he wanted as well.

Feeling a hand on his shoulder, he turned. It was Porus, who had suffered a cut to his brow during the battle. Rain was already dripping from his chin and the end of his nose.

"Enough," he said. "The troops are gnashing their teeth in anticipation of Qa'yarin. Right now, we have to dispose of poor Shurin."

Kahless nodded. "You're right. I will see to it."

Porus waved away the suggestion. "I can do it. You have done the work of a thousand men this evening."

The outlaw shrugged. "If you say so."

Still standing there in the center of the square, he watched as Porus began organizing the construction of a funeral pyre. Of course, they would need a great many of them. Tolar'tu had never seen so much blood.

Nor had An'quat before it. Or Serra'nob. Or any of the other places where they had clashed with Molor's forces.

As Morath joined him, Kahless grunted. "Once the rain stops, there will be a fire that will be seen for a hundred miles around."

"And bodies enough to keep it going for a day and a night," Morath added. "But that is the price of victory. Of freedom. Of honor. Nor will it compare to the flames that will rage outside the tyrant's citadel."

The outlaw nodded. "One way or the other."

Thirty-one: The Modern Age

On the bridge of Kurn's vessel, Kahless found a seat and lowered himself into it. He looked drained. Lifeless. Crushed by the reality he had hoped so fervently to deny.

Picard sighed and went to the emperor's side. What could he say? "Are you all right?" he asked at last.

Kahless was on his feet suddenly, his anger twisting his features as he thrust them like a weapon into the captain's face. "What do *you* think?" he roared.

Picard said nothing, but stood his ground. After a moment, the clone lumbered past him and stared out an observation port.

"Am I all right?" Kahless repeated, every word as sharp as a dagger. He shook his head. "I am far from all right. The conspirators were correct all along, Captain. Kahless was a fraud—and therefore, so am I."

His fists clenched at his sides and trembled in white-knuckled rage. Then the emperor's right hand reached up, tore at something near his neck and cast it on the deck beside him.

It was the *jinaq* amulet—the one the historical Kahless had received from his lover as a sign of their betrothal. Picard looked at Worf's brother and saw the expression of worry on his face.

If the clone was modeled after someone who never existed, Kurn seemed to say, what chance did they have? Was Gowron's reign not doomed, no matter what they did to preserve it?

And if all they had believed in until now was a fraud, a mockery, should they even try?

It was Worf who finally provided the answer. Getting up from his pilot's seat, he approached Kahless. For a moment, he simply regarded the emperor, as if weighing what to do next. Then he knelt, retrieved the amulet, and stood up again.

"I believe this is yours," he said, holding the thing out in the palm of his hand.

Kahless turned to him and growled: "Leave me be, Worf."

"I will not leave you be," the lieutenant told him, "until you return this to the place of honor where it belongs."

Apparently, that was not what the emperor wished to hear. With a bellow of rage and pain, Kahless lashed out and struck Worf across the face with the back of his hand. As the cabin echoed with the sharp, explosive sound of the blow, Worf took a couple of steps back.

But he didn't fall, as the clone might have expected. Instead, he came forward like a wild *targ*, grabbed Kahless by the front of his robe, and pinned him against the nearest bulkhead.

"Are you out of your mind?" the emperor bellowed, his eyes bulging with outrage. "I have *killed* men for far less!"

"Then kill *me*," Worf advised him, showing no fear. "But not before I have had my say."

Opening his hand, he showed Kahless the amulet. The emperor bared his teeth at the sight of it, then turned his face away.

"Get it away from me!" he cried.

He tried to wriggle free from Worf's grasp. But the lieutenant, quite a powerful individual in his own right, would not let him go.

"Not so long ago," Worf snarled, "you told me the *original* Kahless left us a powerful legacy. A way of thinking and acting that makes us all Klingon. If his words hold wisdom—if the philosophy they put forth is an honorable one—does it really matter what Kahless himself was like?"

The lieutenant thrust the amulet at the clone, who snatched it away from him. Then Worf released him and took a step back. But Kahless didn't strike the lieutenant again, nor did he turn his back. He went on listening to what Worf had to say.

"What is important," the lieutenant went on, in an even yet forceful tone, "is that we follow his teachings. For, at least in this case, the words are more important than the man."

The clone stood there for a moment, the *jinaq* amulet in his hand, the muscles in his jaws working furiously. It looked to Picard as if he were chewing something tough, something difficult to swallow—and perhaps he was.

Worf had thrown his own words back in his face—the same words Kahless had uttered on the *Enterprise*. Like it or not, the clone couldn't dismiss them out of hand. He had to consider them.

"What about the people?" Kahless asked at last. "They will shun me. They will call me a fraud—and a liar."

"Perhaps a few of them," said Worf. "But not all. Not the head-master of the academy we visited, or blind Majjas. They and all the other Klingons who want a Kahless—who *need* a Kahless—will make the leap of faith, just as they did when they found out you were a clone."

"I wish I could believe you," Kahless told him.

"You must," Worf replied. "Our people care less about the scroll's authenticity than they do about what Kahless taught them. Only give them time and you will see I am right."

For what seemed like a long while, the clone was silent, the *jinaq* amulet resting in his large, open hand. Picard wondered if Worf's little pep talk had worked . . . or if Kahless was as resigned to failure as before. A moment later, he received his answer.

Closing his fingers around the amulet, the emperor held it against his chest. The glint of purpose returned to his eyes. Raising his chin, he looked at his companions.

"Very well," he agreed. "We started this together. We will see it through together. And in the end," he went on, a smile playing at the corners of his mouth, "let our enemies beware."

Thirty-two: The Heroic Age

Molor's citadel bulked up huge, dark, and foreboding against the gray, brooding sky. Its battlements bristled with a thousand archers, and there were a thousand more within its gates.

Still, the road that led to this pass had been no less formidable and Kahless had traveled it without faltering. With luck, he and his men would not falter now either.

"The tyrant is within our grasp," said Morath. His *s'tarahk* pawed and snuffled the ground.

The outlaw turned to him and snorted. "Or we are within his. It all depends on your perspective."

Kahless was whole again, recovered from the wounds he had suf-fered at Tolar'tu. In fact, he had never felt stronger in his life. Constant strife had a way of hardening a man.

Looking back over his shoulder, the outlaw surveyed the ranks of his followers, who were nearly as numerous as Molor's soldiers and twice as eager. A mighty siege engine constructed of sturdy black *skannu* trees rose up in the midst of them—a fifty-foot tall monster with a battering ram slung from its crossbar and a platform big enough for a hundred archers.

Such devices had been used in the past, when a great many lords vied for supremacy on the continent. But never had one so large and sturdy been built. Then again, no one had ever tried to take a fortress like this one.

It had been difficult to haul the towering *skannu* trees out of the steep valleys south of here, but they had had no other option. If they were to break the tyrant's power, they would need the proper tools.

At least, that had been Morath's contention. And Kahless had come to see the wisdom in it—just as he now saw the wisdom in most everything his friend said or did.

The outlaw had accomplished everything Morath had required of him. He had forged a rebellion out of countless tiny uprisings and dissatisfactions, and with it had shaken the foundations of Molor's supremacy. But without the younger man's part in it, the rebellion would never have lasted this long or come this far.

Kahless was just the point of a dagger, the razor edge. Morath was the one who cut and thrust with it.

Porus rode up to them, his face dirty with the dust of the road. Squinting, he scanned Molor's defenses.

"Too bad we all could not have lived to see this," he rumbled. Then he turned to his leader. "When do we attack?"

Kahless frowned. If it were the tyrant sitting outside these gates and someone else were within, the assault would already have begun.

"Now," he replied.

Gesturing, he ordered his men to bring up the siege engine. With a collective grunt, they put their backs into it.

As the engine rumbled forward on massive wooden wheels, the outlaw glanced at the faces of the tyrant's archers. Even from this distance, he could see the apprehension there, the realization that they were not as safe within their walls as they had imagined.

He laughed a hollow laugh. Vathraq's walls hadn't kept Molor from murdering Kellein. Why shouldn't he return the favor?

But the engine alone would not carry them to victory. At another signal, his most agile warriors climbed the monstrous timbers of the thing, their bows slung over their backs.

When they reached the platform, they took up their positions and knelt. Of course, Molor's archers would have an advantage over them, firing down from a greater height. But Kahless's archers were not

charged with tearing down the gates. They were only there to provide
cover fire, so those below could do their job.

Faster and faster the engine rolled, heading for the great, iron-bound
doors to the tyrant's citadel. Kahless himself rode beside it, raising his
bat'leth to the heavens and bellowing a challenge to the enemy.

The sense of it did not matter, only the sound itself. Hearing it, each
of his warriors took up the cry, until it drowned out the rumble of the
engine's wheels with its thunder and echoed back at them from Molor's
walls.

The outlaw ignored the arrows that rained down on them, taking the
mounted and those on foot alike. His place was in the lead, no matter
the danger. Anything less would have been a breach of his promise to
Morath.

He would sooner have died than breach that promise. And just in
case he came to feel differently at some point, Morath was right beside
him to remind him of it.

As they approached the gates, Kahless clenched his teeth with
determination. Rocks, not just arrows, were pelting the ground all
around him. Warriors died in agony and were flung from their screaming *s'tarahkmey*.

But this was just a taste of the carnage to come. Just the merest hint
of the blood that would be spilled this day.

As if to underscore the thought, the outlaw wheeled on his *s'tarahk*
and uttered a new command. Heeding it, the archers on the siege
engine braced themselves—and those on the ground gave it one last
push. Despite its terrible weight, the thing surged forward.

It couldn't go far on its own, Kahless knew. But it didn't have to.
Molor's iron-bound gates were only a couple of yards away.

With an earsplitting groan, the engine's front wheels slammed into
the gates. A second later, the immense battering ram swung forward.
Unlike the engine itself, nothing had stopped its progress yet.

Then that changed. The ram struck the gates, sending up a
whipcrack of thunder. The outlaw's bones shuddered with the impact.

"Again!" he cried.

As his archers provided cover, his ground forces drew the ram back
and then drove it forward again. The gates creaked miserably, like a
mighty animal in awful pain. But they didn't yield. At least, not yet.

A second time, the ram was drawn back and thrust forward. And a
third. But it was only with the fourth blow that the mighty gates began
to cave inward. The rebels bellowed, drawing courage from it.

The fifth stroke sounded like rocks breaking; it caved the gates in
even more. And the sixth burst them open at last, giving the invaders
access to what was inside.

Like *yolok* worms reaching for an especially luscious piece of fruit, Kahless and his warriors swarmed around and through the siege engine. After all, the thing had done its job. The rest was up to the strength of their arms and the hatred in their Klingon hearts.

The courtyard was packed tight with defenders. But they wielded long, heavy swords and axes, the kind warriors had used for hundreds of years. They were not made for infighting.

The rebels' *bat'lethmey* were a different story entirely. Lighter, more versatile, they represented a huge advantage in close quarters. And Kahless had equipped fifty of his best fighters with them.

Cutting and slashing, the outlaw led the way into the citadel, with Morath barely a step behind. Nor did Kahless's warriors disappoint him. Battering and thrusting, they followed him inch by bloody inch.

The fighting was intense, unlike anything the outlaw had seen before. But his *bat'leth* served him well. Like a hunting bird, it swooped and swooped again, each time plucking a life from the enemy's midst.

Blood spilled until it was everywhere, making the ground slick beneath their feet. Warriors fell on both sides, slumped on top of one another, glutting the confines of the courtyard with their empty shells.

And still the two sides battled, matching blow with clanging blow, war cry with earsplitting war cry, neither side willing to yield. Kahless's men fought for freedom from the tyrant, Molor's men because they feared his wrath. But in the end, both sides suffered their share of casualties.

Nor did the outlaw wade through the struggle unscathed. By the time he came within reach of the tyrant's keep, he was bleeding from a dozen wounds. But he was only vaguely aware of them, his heart pounding too hard for his head to keep up with it.

A year earlier, he would never have imagined this—would never have believed it possible. Yet here he was, a mighty force behind him, knocking on the tyrant's door. With a vicious uppercut, he dispatched one defender, then skewered another one on his point. A backhanded blow sent a third warrior to the afterlife.

Suddenly, the inner gate was naked before him. Lowering his shoulder, he slammed into it with all his strength. It didn't budge. And the siege engine wasn't narrow enough to make it into the courtyard.

But there was more than one way to skin a serpent. Raising his *bat'leth* as high as he could, he sent up a cry for help. And before he knew it, a dozen rebels had appeared to add their strength to his.

Morath, of course, was the first to lean into the gate with his friend. Digging in with their heels, the others did the same. Then they pushed as hard as they could, grunting with the effort.

At first, there was no more progress than when Kahless had tried it himself. But a few seconds later, the outlaw heard the shriek of bending iron.

"Harder!" he roared. "We are almost in!"

They drew deeper, finding strength they did not know they had, and used all of it against the gate. There was another shriek of twisting metal, and all of a sudden the thing surrendered to them.

Flinging the gate wide, Kahless took in the sight of Molor's torch-lit anteroom. It was full of tall, powerful warriors, who grinned at him with eyes full of venom and mouths full of sharpened teeth.

The tyrant's personal guard, two dozen strong. The most devastating fighters the world had ever known. Or so it was said.

Kahless tightened his grip on his *bat'leth*. One way or the other, he repeated to himself, remembering the words he had spoken at Tolar'tu. One way or the other.

Then, as a handful of his men clustered about him, he raised his weapon high and charged into the midst of the enemy.

Thirty-three: The Modern Age

The house was an impressive one, broad and angular as it bulked up against the faintly pink underbelly of the sky. It dwarfed the other buildings in this wealthy and less-traveled part of Navrath.

Still, Lomakh was no longer quite so awed by it as he had once been. After all, he had visited the place several times in the last year, on the occasion of one splendid feast or another. Its owner—a wealthy and prominent member of the high council—was quite fond of extravagant celebrations.

And not just feasts. He liked to sponsor local festivals and opera performances as well. But he most enjoyed inviting people to his home.

During one such revelry, the council member had shown Lomakh his family armory—and invited the Defense Force officer to join a young but burgeoning conspiracy. Of course, the wealthy one had done his research. He knew Lomakh was disaffected with Gowron's reign and bold enough to do something about it.

Lomakh had hesitated—but only for a second or two. Then he had pledged himself to their common cause.

He was still pledged to it now, heart and hand. And though some small matters had not gone as smoothly as he would have liked, larger matters had more than made up for them.

In the end, the conspirators' victory seemed assured. The Empire was still reeling over the confirmation of the scroll's authenticity, the clone and his comrades had been destroyed in the explosions on Ogat, and Gowron was too stupid to believe in the threat right before his eyes.

By the time he gave the rumors of conspiracy any credence, it would be too late for the council leader and all his supporters. Gowron would be gone, and another raised in his place. And the alliance with the Federation would be a grim and distasteful memory.

Most important of all, Lomakh would be a man held in the highest esteem by Gowron's successor. Such a man could have most anything his heart desired—power, latinum, vengeance against old enemies.

Yes, the officer mused. *Things were going very well indeed.*

Such were Lomakh's thoughts as he approached the house's sturdy, *qava*-wood gates and the sensor rods on either side of them. Pulling the cowl of his cloak aside for a moment, he glanced over his shoulder to make sure no one had followed him through the streets. Apparently, no one had.

Satisfied, he moved forward to stand between the sensor rods and waited. He didn't have to wait long. In a matter of moments, the house guards had emerged from between the gates—a quartet of them, each one bigger and more hostile-looking than the one before him.

Familiar with their routine, Lomakh opened his cloak to show them the extent of his armaments. Removing his disruptor from his belt, he turned it over to the biggest of them. He kept his *d'k tahg,* however. It would have been a breach of propriety to strip a Klingon of *all* his weapons.

Satisfied, the guards escorted him through the gates and into the courtyard. On the far side of it, there was another set of gates, a bit smaller but otherwise identical to the first. There were sensor rods there too, in case the first set malfunctioned.

Lomakh passed between them without incident. As two of the guards opened the gates, he entered a pentagon-shaped anteroom. Just past it was the stronghold's central hall.

It wasn't quite as big as the High Council chamber and its ceiling certainly wasn't as high, but it was just as majestic and well appointed. And the high seat at its far end was, if anything, even larger and more formidable than Gowron's.

The one who occupied that seat was formidable too, the hairlessness of his large head accentuating the darkness of his brows. Right now, his face illuminated by the flames from freestanding braziers placed at intervals, the council member looked as hard and unyielding as stone.

At first, Lomakh believed his host was the only one who awaited him. Then, as he came closer, he realized there were other figures there.

Four of them, to be exact, all but obscured by the shadows outside the circle of torchlight. What's more, Lomakh recognized them.

Tichar. Goradh. Olmai. Kardem.

All high-ranking officers in the Klingon Defense Force. All, like Lomakh himself, key participants in the conspiracy. They turned at his approach, their eyes narrowing beneath the ridges of their foreheads.

What is going on? they seemed to ask. Lomakh wanted to know himself. He looked to their host for an answer.

Unarrh, son of Unagroth, looked back at him from his high seat. He leaned forward, so that the lines in his squarish face were accentuated and his eye sockets were swallowed in shadow. Only his irises were visible as pinpricks of reflected firelight.

"Lomakh," Unarrh rumbled. "Finally. Now tell me quickly, before my patience runs out—why did you call us here?"

"Yes," added Olmai, "tell us. I thought we had agreed not to meet in large numbers until the rebellion was well under way."

"I thought the same," spat Goradh.

"And I as well," added Tichar.

Lomakh shook his head. Clearly, he had missed something. Or *someone* had.

"I did not call anyone," he protested.

"What?" The council member's brows converged over the bridge of his nose. "Then why are you here?" he asked.

Lomakh indicated one of the other conspirators with a tilt of his head. "I received a message from Kardem, summoning me. Though I must admit, it seemed strange to me at the time."

Unarrh's eyes narrowed. He looked from one of his fellow conspirators to another. "Someone is lying," he said.

The Defense Force officers glanced at one another, hoping someone would step forward and tender an explanation. No one did.

The council member's eyes opened wide. He cursed lavishly beneath his breath. "This must be some kind of trap," Unarrh decided. "The best thing for us to do is—"

He was interrupted by a commotion in the corridor outside. A moment later, one of Unarrh's house guards came hurtling into the hall. Then another. Both sprawled on the floor, unconscious, bleeding from the head and face.

The other guards, Lomakh observed, were nowhere to be seen. He could only conclude they had been neutralized as well.

Immediately, his hand went to his belt, where it expected to find his

disruptor pistol. But of course, it was no longer there, so he had to settle for the ceremonial knife concealed in the back of his tunic.

Unarrh shot to his feet like a rearing *s'tarahk.* "What is the meaning of this?" he roared.

An instant later, the intruders entered the hall. First, a group of
three, one of whom seemed vaguely familiar even in darkness. Then
another group, cloaked and cowled like the conspirators themselves.

"Who are you?" Unarrh demanded. "By what right do you impose
yourselves on my house?"

By way of an answer, a member of the first group stepped forward
into the light from the braziers. Instantly, his features became recognizable. They were, after all, those of the honorable Gowron—son of
M'rel and leader of the Klingon High Council.

Unarrh's eyes took on an even harder cast. His voice was taut, commanding, as he addressed the council leader.

"I trust there is some meaning in this *somewhere,* Gowron. Because
if there is not, you will regret barging in on me like this."

The council leader scowled. "I assure you, Unarrh, I did not come
here simply to annoy you." He jerked his chin at the four who still
stood in the darkness, their faces concealed by their hoods. "It was they
who persuaded me. They claimed they had something to tell me—but
would not reveal it except in your presence."

Unarrh turned his gaze on the quartet. "And who are *they?*" he
rasped.

All four of them pulled back their cowls. Then they joined Gowron
in the circle of illumination.

Lomakh's mouth went dry as he saw who had come calling on him.
"Kahless . . ." he gasped.

The clone grinned fiercely. "Yes, Kahless, back from the dead. I
seem to specialize in that, don't I?"

Lomakh looked at the others, their faces revealed now as well. His
mouth twisted with hatred and frustration.

The sons of Mogh, Worf and Kurn. And the human, the damned
Arbiter of Succession—Picard of the Federation.

All alive. And from the look of things, undeterred in their pursuit of
the conspirators. Lomakh grunted softly, wondering what would come
next and how to play it.

"What interesting companions you have," Unarrh commented, glaring at Gowron and choosing to ignore the others.

Kahless chuckled, indicating the Defense Force officers with a
sweep of his arm. "I might say the same of you," he countered.

Unarrh's lips curled back, exposing his teeth. With obvious reluctance, he turned his gaze on the clone.

"I will not tolerate your presence here much longer," he snarled. "If you have something to say, say it."

Lomakh grunted. Unarrh must have known their conspiracy had been discovered. He was simply playing for time, trying to find out how much Kahless knew before making his move.

Or did the council member truly believe he could talk his way out of this? Lomakh tightened his grip on the dagger in his tunic—aware of the possibility that Unarrh's plans for saving himself might not include the preservation of his allies.

In the meantime, the clone had been digging in his belt pouch for something. He extracted it now and held it up to the light.

It was a computer chip—the kind used here on the homeworld, and therefore compatible with systems of Klingon manufacture. Lomakh tried to anticipate how it might incriminate them—and couldn't.

But he didn't have to wait long to find out.

"This chip," Kahless hissed, "contains information downloaded from a Klingon subspace relay station—one my comrades and I had occasion to visit recently." He smiled at Worf, who stood beside him.

"On the main communications band," the clone continued, "there is nothing more than the usual subspace chatter. But on a frequency normally left unused by the Defense Force, there is something more. . . ."

Lomakh knew what that something was, even before Kahless finished his thought. After all, he had taken part in it—in the early stages of the conspiracy, before Unarrh decided to clamp down on security.

". . . a record of several conversations," Kahless went on, "in which certain Defense Force officers repeatedly conspire to tear down the honorable Gowron. And the name Unarrh always seems to figure prominently in these discussions." The clone scanned the officers assembled, clearly enjoying himself. "It occurs to me all of those who took part in this conspiracy are now present in this hall." His smile broadened as he turned to Gowron. "A great convenience, if you ask me."

The council leader didn't say anything. But Lomakh wasn't blind. He could see Gowron's interest in the chip.

Worf took another step toward Unarrh and lifted his arm to point at the council member. "All along, you have claimed to be a supporter of Kahless and his orthodoxy. Yet you were nothing of the kind."

The hall rang and echoed with his accusation. Unarrh's eyes grew wide, but he said nothing in his defense.

"In truth," Kurn added, "you were the guiding force behind the rebellion all along—even before the scroll was made public."

Kahless handed the computer chip to Gowron. The council leader hefted the thing in his hand, then turned again to Unarrh.

"Bring me a playback device," he told his host.

"Unless you fear what is on it," Worf suggested, relentless in his pursuit of the truth.

Unarrh laughed an ugly laugh. "I fear nothing and no one." As he glowered at Worf, his eyes seem to burn in the firelight. "Especially a *p'tahk* who was discommendated for his family's treachery."

Worf was incensed. "Duras was the *p'tahk*, not I. And who are you to speak of treachery?" he thundered. "You, who would have torn the council apart without a second thought—though it was Gowron who raised you to your office in the first place?"

Unarrh turned a dark and dangerous shade of red. Reaching behind him, he produced a disruptor pistol—one even Lomakh hadn't known about. Apparently, the council member had anticipated some sort of trouble.

Before anyone could move, Unarrh took aim at one of Gowron's guards and pressed the trigger. A blue beam shot out and consumed the warrior in a swirl of rampant energies. Then the council member aimed and fired again, and Gowron's other retainer died in agony.

Lomakh had seen enough. Unarrh seemed to have decided he had run out of options—and was taking his best shot at survival.

Unfortunately, even if he destroyed all his enemies, he would have to explain his actions to the council. And they would not look kindly on his killing Gowron and Kurn—apparently without provocation.

More than likely, Unarrh would have to throw them a bone—a Defense Force officer or two, to punish as they saw fit. And Lomakh had no desire to be sacrificed in such a manner.

Let Unarrh fend for himself, he thought. *I will be elsewhere, making new allies, before he can point a finger at me.*

With a hiss of metal on molded leather, he drew his dagger and made a break for it. Nor were his fellow officers far behind.

Thirty-four: The Heroic Age

In Molor's anteroom, Kahless swung his *bat'leth* and struck down one of Molor's guards. Beside him, Morath disemboweled another.

For a time, the tyrant's retainers had held their own, even against greater odds. Perhaps twenty of the rebels lay stacked about them, blood running from twice as many wounds.

But now there were only a dozen defenders left, and none of them were grinning as eagerly as before. A couple barely had the strength to stay on their feet. Slowly but surely, the tide was turning against them.

"They're faltering!" Kahless cried. "It won't be much longer now!"

Still, every second they delayed him was like the sting of a *pherza* wasp. He wanted desperately to reach their master and see an end to this.

Blinking sweat from his eyes, Kahless hacked at another of Molor's warriors. The man stumbled backward, barely managing to deflect the blow in time. In another moment, he would come back with one of his own.

But in the meantime, the outlaw had a clear path to his goal—a long, straight hallway that led deeper into the bowels of the citadel. With a burst of speed, he seized the opportunity.

And Morath was right behind him. As always.

"Kahless!" he cried.

The outlaw turned, barely breaking stride. "What is it?"

"We should go back and finish them," Morath protested.

"No," said Kahless, firm in his resolve. "If you want to end this, I'll show you a quicker way."

Morath hesitated. But in the end, he came running after his friend. "All right," he said for emphasis. "Show me."

The outlaw pledged inwardly to do his best. Pelting down the long, echoing hallway, he tried to remember the layout of the place. After all, he had only been here a couple of times, and both seemed impossibly long ago.

At the end of the hallway, there was a choice of turnings. The corridor to Kahless's left was decorated with heroic tapestries and ancient weapons. The one to his right held a series of black-iron pedestals, each one host to something dark and hairy.

A head, the outlaw recalled. A *stuffed* head.

Turning to the right, he broke into a run again. As before, Morath followed on his heels.

"What are these?" his friend asked, referring to the heads.

"The tyrant's enemies," Kahless told him. "Though from what I've heard, they plague him no longer."

Unexpectedly, he drew courage from the sight. It was as if every shriveled, staring face was shouting encouragement to him, every hollow mouth crying out silently for vengeance.

These were his brothers, the outlaw told himself, his kinsmen in spirit. He would do what he could to see all their demands fulfilled— for if he did not, he would almost certainly join them.

The corridor ended in the beginnings of a circular stairwell, one narrow and smoothed by age. Hunching over, Kahless took the steep, uneven steps as quickly as he could.

"Where are you going?" asked Morath.

The outlaw stopped long enough to look at him. "You want Molor, don't you?"

The warrior's brow knotted. "How do you know he's up there?"

Kahless grunted. "I was one of his warchiefs, remember?"

"But you've never seen him defend against a siege," Morath protested. "He could be anywhere."

Kahless didn't answer. He just started up the stairs again. After all, he knew the tyrant as well as any man.

Besides, he had been gambling and winning battle after battle for months now. Why stop?

Halfway up the steps, he heard something. Barely a sound—more like the absence of one. Slowing down ever so slightly, he braced himself.

Suddenly, a spear came thrusting down at him. Though he was prepared, it was no easy task to batter it aside with his *bat'leth*—or to keep from staggering under the weight of the warrior who came after it.

Still, the outlaw managed to keep his footing, and to grab his adversary's wrist before the man's hand could find Kahless's throat. Then, off-balance as he was, he smashed his *bat'leth* into the guard's face.

There was no cry, no bellow of pain. Just a gurgle, and the man collapsed on him. Pressing his back against the wall, the outlaw allowed the corpse to fall past him, end over end. Farther below, Morath did the same.

It was not the last obstacle Kahless would face on his way up the steps. He had to dispatch two more warriors, each more fierce than the one before, in order to reach his destination. But reach it he did.

And all the while, Morath pursued him, ready to take his place if he was cut down. Fortunately for both of them, it was not necessary.

Reaching the top of the stair, Kahless emerged onto a dark, windowless landing. At the opposite end, he saw a door.

If he was right, Molor would be behind it. *And some guards as well?* he wondered. *Or had he dispatched them all already?*

Morath came up beside him. For a moment, both of them listened—and heard nothing. Shrugging, the younger man pointed to the door. Kahless nodded and took its handle in his hand. And pushed.

It wouldn't move. It had been bolted from the inside.

Clenching his teeth, the outlaw slashed the door with his *bat'leth*—once, twice, three times, until it was a splintered ruin. Then, with a single kick, he caved in the remains.

As Kahless had suspected, Molor was inside.

The tyrant was plotting his next move at his *m'ressa*-wood table. His large and imposing frame was hunkered over a map of his citadel, casting a monstrous shadow in the light of a single brazier.

The outlaw had looked forward to the expression on the tyrant's face when he saw his warchief coming back to haunt him—to exact revenge for Kellein, and for Rannuf, and for all the other innocents Molor had trampled in his hunger for power.

But what Kahless saw was not what he had expected. Halfway into the room, the outlaw stopped dead in his tracks, stunned as badly as if someone had bludgeoned him in the head.

"Blood of my ancestors," he breathed.

Molor looked up at him, his eyes sunken into his round, bony head like tiny, black dung beetles. The tyrant's skin was intricately webbed as if with extreme old age and riddled with an army of open purple sores. His once-powerful body was hollowed out and emaciated, his limbs little more than long, brittle twigs.

"Greetings," he rattled, his voice like a serpent slithering through coarse sand. "I see you've found me, Kahless."

Molor said the outlaw's name as if it fascinated him, as if it were the very first time he'd had occasion to say it out loud. His mouth quirked in a grotesque grandfatherly smile, revealing a mottled tongue and rounded, worm-eaten teeth.

A moment later, Morath came into the room behind his friend. Glancing at him, Kahless saw the horror on the younger man's face—the loathing that mirrored Kahless's own.

"As I expected," the tyrant hissed gleefully, "your shadow is right behind you."

Molor wheezed as he spoke, the tendons in his neck standing out with the effort it cost him. Spittle collected in the corners of his mouth.

"What happened to him?" asked Morath, seemingly unable to take his eyes off the tyrant.

"What happened?" echoed Molor, his voice cracking. "I'll tell you. I fell victim to the plague that's been killing all the *minn'hormey.*"

He tossed his head back and made a shrill, harsh sound that Kahless barely recognized as laughter. Threads of saliva stretched across the tyrant's maw. Then, with a palsied, carbuncle-infested hand, he closed his mouth and wiped the drool from his shriveled chin.

"Funny," he said, "isn't it? My physicians tell me the disease afflicts one Klingon in a thousand. And of all the wretched specimens on this wretched continent, whom should it bring down but the most powerful man on Qo'noS?"

Molor started to laugh again, but went into a coughing fit instead. He had to prop himself up on the table for support. When he was done, he looked up at his enemy again.

"I hope you are not disappointed," he rasped. "I would give you a fight even now, Kahless, but it would not be much of a match. You are such a strong and sturdy man still, and I . . ." The tyrant's face twisted with revulsion, with hatred for the reedy thing he had become. "I do not believe I would stand up to a stiff wind."

The outlaw shook his head. He had come here thirsting for vengeance with all his heart. But he knew now he couldn't slake that thirst. As long as he lived, he could *never* slake it.

He would get no satisfaction from killing a plague victim, no matter what Molor had done. But he couldn't let the *p'tahk* live, either. The tyrant had to pay for his crimes somehow.

With that in mind, Kahless used his left hand to remove his dagger from the sheath on his leg. With a toss, he placed it on the table in front of his enemy. It clattered for a moment, then lay still.

"What are you doing?" asked Morath.

"I am giving him a chance to take his own life," the outlaw answered, "before my warriors tear him limb from limb. It was more than he did for Kellein and her people. And it is certainly more than he deserves. But nonetheless, there it is."

Molor picked up the *d'k tagh* with a trembling hand. And with difficulty, he opened it, so that all three blades clicked into place.

"You're right," he told Kahless, as he inspected the weapon. "This is considerably more than I deserve. However—"

Suddenly, the tyrant's eyes came alive. He drew back the dagger with an ease that belied his appearance and balanced it gracefully in his hand.

"—it is precisely what *you* deserve, son of Kanjis!"

In that moment, the outlaw realized how badly he'd been duped. He saw all he had worked for—all his friends had given their lives for—about to vanish in a blaze of stupidity.

Before he could move, Molor brought the knife forward and released it. But something flashed in front of Kahless—and with a dull thud, took the blade meant for him.

Openmouthed, the outlaw stared at his friend Morath. The *d'k tahg* was protruding from the center of the warrior's chest. Clutching at it, Morath tried to pull it out, to no avail. Then, blood spilling from the corner of his mouth, he sank to his knees.

Kahless was swept up in a maelstrom of blind, choking fury. He turned to Molor, the object of his hatred now more than ever.

The tyrant was drawing a sword from a scabbard hidden underneath his *m'ressa*-wood table. With spindly wrists and skeletal fingers, Molor raised the weapon. And brought it back. And with a cry like an angry bird, braced himself for his enemy's attack.

But it did the tyrant no good. For the outlaw was already moving forward. Tossing the heavy table aside with his left hand, he brought his *bat'leth* into play with his right.

First, Kahless smashed the sword out of Molor's hand. Then, putting all his strength behind the blow, he swung his blade at the other man's neck. With a bellow—not of triumph, but of pain and rage—he watched the tyrant's head topple from his shoulders.

As Molor's skull clattered to the floor, followed by a splash of blood, the outlaw turned to Morath. His friend was sitting on his haunches, still trying to draw the *d'k tahg* from his chest. With Kahless watching, Morath toppled to one side and lay gasping on the floor.

Tossing his *bat'leth* aside, the outlaw fell to his knees and lifted his friend up in his arms. Kahless wanted to tell him there was hope he might outlive his wound, but he knew better. And so did Morath.

"This is wrong," the outlaw railed. "You cannot die now, damn you. Not when we have *won*."

"Your promise to me," Morath began, his voice already fading. "It is not yet . . . not yet done. . . ."

Kahless shook his head, his sweat-soaked hair whipping at his face. "No," he snarled, like a *s'tarahk* struggling against its reins. "I told you I would tear the tyrant down. And I have done that."

"A life," Morath reminded him, his mouth bubbling with blood. "You said you would pay with your *life*. The people . . . they still need you. . . ."

The outlaw's teeth ground in anger. But his friend was dying, having taken the dagger meant for Kahless.

How could he deny Morath this last request? How could he think of himself after all the man had done for him?

"A life," he echoed, hating even the sound of the word. His lip curling, he swallowed back the bile that rose in his throat. "As I promised you in the wilderness, a *life*."

Morath managed a thin, pale smile. "I will speak well of you to your ancestors . . . Kahless, son of Kanjis. . . ."

Then, with a shudder, his body became an empty husk.

The outlaw stared at the flesh that had once been Morath. He couldn't believe his friend was dead—and he, Kahless, was still alive. If anything, he had expected it to be the other way around.

Abruptly, all his exertions and his wounds tried to drag him down at once. He bowed his head under the terrible weight of them.

How could it have happened this way? he asked. *How?*

He was supposed to have gotten rid of all his burdens. Now he had undertaken more of them than ever. No longer merely a rebel hungry for vengeance, he would become a thrice-cursed king.

With a grimace of disgust, Kahless found the strength to get to his feet. Picking up Morath's body, he slung it over his shoulder. Then he righted Molor's *m'ressa* table and lowered the body onto it.

Grasping his *d'k tahg* by its handle, he tugged it free of his friend's chest. Then he tucked it into his belt, still slick with Morath's blood.

Finally, he turned back to Morath's body—to the eyes that still stared at him, refusing to release him from his vow. Kahless scowled. *Even in death,* he thought. *Even in death.*

He took a deep, shuddering breath. When warriors sang of this day, they would not forget the son of Ondagh. This, he swore with all his being.

And Kahless would remember too. Morath the warrior and the liberator, who was a better man than Kahless by far. Morath his pursuer and his tormentor, who was more a brother to him than a friend.

Unexpectedly, a wellspring of grief rose up in him, and he raised his voice in a harsh yell—just as he had raised it over the body of Kellein those long months ago. He yelled until he was hoarse with yelling, imagining that his noise was speeding Morath's soul to the afterlife.

Not that Kahless believed in such things. But Morath did. For his friend's sake, the outlaw would give in just this once.

There was just one more thing to do while he was up here. *Better to do it quickly,* Kahless thought, *before any more blood is shed.*

Molor's head was lying in a corner of the room, soiled with a mixture of gore and dust. Picking it up by the strands of hair still left on the tyrant's chin, he pulled aside a curtain to reveal another winding stair—a much shorter one, which led up to a high balcony.

One by one, he ascended the stone steps. The last time the outlaw had negotiated them, he hadn't been an outlaw at all, but chief among Molor's warlords. The tyrant had wished to show him what it was like to hold the world in the palm of one's hand.

Those days were long gone. Now it was *Molor* he held in his hand, and the world would have to find somewhere else to reside.

As Kahless emerged into the wind and sky, he saw the battle still raging below him on the battlements and in the courtyard. He could hear the strident clamor of sword on sword, the bitter cries of the dying, the urgent shouts of the living.

"Hear me!" he bellowed at the top of his lungs.

Not everyone turned to him at once. But some did. And as they pointed at him, amazed by the sight, so did others. In place after place, adversaries stepped back from one another, curious as to how the outlaw had reached Molor's balcony—and what that might mean to them.

Kahless filled his lungs. The wind whipping savagely at his hair, he cried out again.

"The tyrant Molor is dead! There is nothing left to fight for, you hear me? Nothing!"

And then, to substantiate his claim, he lifted Molor's head so all could see. For a second or two, he let it hang there, a portent of change.

Then, drawing his arm back, he hurled it out over the heart of the battle like a strange and terrible missile. It turned end over end, rolling high and far across the sky, until gravity made its claim at last and the thing plummeted to earth.

"There," the outlaw said, in a voice only he could hear. "That should put an end to it."

On shaky and uncertain legs, he came down from the balcony. Out of the wind, into the quiet and the shadows.

Now, he thought, *comes the hard part.*

Thirty-five: The Modern Age

Worf was closer than anyone else to Unarrh's high seat. When the council member started firing his disruptor at Gowron's men, the lieutenant knew he had only two choices.

He could retreat and flee Unarrh's hall—perhaps the safer route. Or he could go forward and try to wrest the disruptor from Unarrh's grasp.

In his years with Starfleet, the Klingon had learned there was no shame in retreating. Often, it was the wiser course. But in his heart, he was a warrior, and a warrior always preferred to attack.

Besides, it was a good day to die. And the rightness of his cause made it an even better day.

Lowering his head, he put aside any thought of danger to himself and charged the high seat. Just before he reached Unarrh, he caught a glimpse of his enemy's weapon, its barrel swinging in his direction.

Even as Worf hurled himself at the council member, he was blinded by the blue flash of disruptor fire. But a moment later, he felt the reassuring impact of bone and muscle as he collided with Unarrh.

Apparently, he thought, the blast had missed him. He was not dead—at least, not yet.

Then his momentum carried both him and Unarrh backward, toppling the man's chair in the process. They landed heavily on the stone floor, Worf's left hand gripping the council member's powerful wrist.

Unarrh tried to roll on top of him, to pin the lieutenant with his considerably greater weight—but Worf was too quick for him. Using a *mok'bara* technique he had demonstrated on the *Enterprise* only a week ago, he brought his right hand around his adversary's head and grabbed Unarrh by his left ear. Then he pulled as hard as he could.

Screaming for mercy, Unarrh rolled onto his back to lessen the pain. Taking advantage of the council member's discomfort, Worf smashed Unarrh's weapon hand against the floor. The impact was enough to dislodge the disruptor and send it skittering over the stones.

But Unarrh wasn't done yet. Far from it. Continuing to roll, he drove his elbow into Worf's ribs, knocking the wind out of the security officer—and forcing him to release Unarrh's ear. And once free, the council member lunged for his weapon again.

Still on his back, Worf grabbed Unarrh by his calf and kept him from reaching his goal. Then, flipping onto his stomach, he got to his knees to improve his leverage.

But Unarrh lashed out with his heel, hitting the Starfleet officer in the shoulder. The shock forced Worf to release him again—but the lieutenant wouldn't be denied. Leaping on Unarrh's back, he grabbed the back of the council member's hairless head as best he could.

With all his might, he drove Unarrh's chin into the stone floor. Not once, but three times. Finally, after the third blow, Unarrh went limp.

Just in case it was some kind of trick, Worf launched himself over his adversary and grabbed the disruptor. But it wasn't a trick after all. Unarrh remained right where he was, clearly unconscious.

The lieutenant snarled—all the victory celebration he would allow himself. Then he looked to his comrades.

Picard saw Worf topple Unarrh as Lomakh and his friends drew their daggers. Trusting to his lieutenant's fighting skills, he drew his own *d'k tahg* and blocked the entrance to the hall.

Unfortunately, there were other ways out—and the conspirators took one of them when they bolted. Seeing the way to the front door guarded, they fled the other way, deeper into Unarrh's mansion.

Even then, as it turned out, their path wasn't exactly clear. Kurn and Kahless managed to tackle two of the conspirators from behind. And a moment later, Gowron flung his knife into a third.

Two were still on their feet, however. As they disappeared, the captain raced after them. Crossing the hall, he saw Kurn tumble end-over-end with his adversary. But the clone was more expedient, slamming his opponent headfirst into a wall.

When the conspirator slumped to the floor unconscious, Kahless looked up and saw Picard. There were no words exchanged between them, but the clone seemed to understand two of the traitors were unaccounted for. Without hesitation, he joined the captain in his pursuit.

As they darted out of the hall into a curving corridor, Picard caught sight of their objectives. One was Lomakh, the conspirator they had spied on in Tolar'tu. The other was an even taller and stronger-looking Klingon named Tichar.

No doubt, Kahless would have been perfectly willing to take on both of the plotters by himself. Fortunately, that wouldn't be necessary. The clone may have begun this fight all on his own, but it wouldn't end that way. He had help now.

Meanwhile, Lomakh and Tichar led them through one winding passageway after the other, their heels clattering on the stone floors. But they couldn't shake their pursuers. Kahless was like a bulldog, refusing to let go. And though the captain was no longer the youth who had won the Academy marathon, he was hardly a laggard either.

Of course, their chase couldn't go on forever, Picard told himself. Sooner or later, Lomakh and his comrade had to hit a dead end of some sort. Then they would have no choice but to turn and fight.

Events quickly proved him right. Racing down a short, straight hallway, the captain got the impression of a large, dim room beyond. As he and the clone entered it, they saw it had no other exit.

Lomakh and Tichar were trapped inside. But that didn't mean they intended to go down without a struggle.

As luck would have it, they had stumbled onto an armory of sorts. There were bladed weapons of all shapes and sizes adorning the far wall, along with a variety of other, more arcane devices. Unarrh, it seemed, was a collector of such things.

First Lomakh reached for a *bat'leth,* then Tichar did the same. Grinning, they advanced on Picard and his companion, shifting their weapons in their hands as if looking forward to what would come next.

"Bad luck," Kahless muttered.

"It seems that way," the captain agreed.

He gauged his chances of getting past the conspirators to obtain a *bat'leth* of his own. The odds weren't very good at the moment. Gritting his teeth, he weighed his other options.

He and Kahless could give ground, perhaps go back the way they came. But if they went back far enough, Lomakh and Tichar might find a way out of Unarrh's complex. And once they did that, they would have a chance to escape.

Picard knew he couldn't live with himself if these two got away. He recalled the faces he saw in the ruins of the academy on Ogat—the faces of the innocent children who died at the hands of the conspirators.

No one should be able to do that with impunity, he thought. Lomakh and Tichar would have to pay for their crimes. And if they had some other outcome in mind, they would have to go through the captain in order to obtain it.

"Out of our way!" growled Lomakh.

"Not a chance in Hell," Kahless shot back.

"You'd rather die?" asked Tichar.

The clone's eyes narrowed. "There are worse things, *p'tahk!*"

Kahless's lips pulled back past his teeth in a feral grin. He rolled his *d'k tahg* in his hand. Clearly, he had come too far and fought too hard not to see this through to its conclusion.

Picard had to admire his courage and his persistence. Perhaps this was not the Kahless of legend, but the clone had the heart of a hero.

The conspirators seemed to think so, too. The captain could see it in their eyes, in the way they hunkered down for battle. Despite their advantage in the way they were armed, they knew this would not be easy for them.

For a moment, there was only the echo of advancing footfalls on the floor, and the glint of firelight on their blades, and the pounding of Picard's heart in his chest. Then Kahless sprang forward like a maddened bull and the combat was joined.

The armory clattered with the clash of metal on metal as the powerful Tichar met the clone's attack with his *bat'leth*. At the same time, the captain saw Lomakh come shuffling toward him sideways, bringing his weapon up and back for a killing blow.

Picard didn't waste any time. Darting in close, he ducked and heard the whistle of the blade as it passed harmlessly over his head. Then he stabbed at the conspirator with his *d'k tahg,* hoping to find a space between the Klingon's ribs.

It didn't work out as he'd hoped. Not only did Lomakh ward off his blow, he struck the captain in the mouth with the heel of his hand. Staggering backward with the force of the blow, Picard tasted blood. As he tried desperately to steady himself, he felt something hard smack him in the back—and realized it was the wall.

The conspirator's eyes gleamed as he saw his chance. With a flip of his wrists, he swung his *bat'leth* a second time. But Picard regained control in time to roll to one side, removing himself from harm's way.

The *bat'leth* struck the wall where he had been, giving rise to a spray of hot sparks. Enraged, Lomakh turned to his adversary and went for him again, thrusting with the point of his blade.

But this time, the captain had a better plan. After all, he had studied fencing as a youth, and his instructor had emphasized the importance of distance. Peddling backward suddenly, his dagger held low, he managed to keep his chin just beyond the leading edge of Lomakh's *bat'leth.*

As the conspirator came on, trying to extend his reach, Picard maintained his margin of safety. Then, without warning, he drove Lomakh's blade aside with a vicious backhand slash. His adversary lurched forward, unable to regain his balance, much less protect himself.

Taking advantage of the opening, the captain grabbed the front of Lomakh's tunic with his free hand and dropped into a backward roll. Halfway through the maneuver, he planted his heel in the Klingon's chest and allowed Lomakh's momentum to do the rest.

As Picard completed his roll, he saw the Klingon sprawl, a tangle of body and limbs and razor-sharp *bat'leth*. Lomakh bellowed with pain before he came to a stop. A moment later, the captain saw what had caused the warrior so much discomfort.

The *bat'leth* had imbedded itself in Lomakh's tunic, cutting through flesh as well as leather. With a guttural curse, the Klingon tore the blade free and staggered to his feet.

"For that," he spat, "your death will be slow and painful!"

Picard smiled grimly, caught up in the interplay of bravado. "This may surprise you," he said, "but I have heard that before."

Again, Lomakh charged him. And again, the captain let him think he was on the verge of achieving his goal. Then, at the last possible moment, Picard turned sideways, flung up his arms, and let the conspirator's *bat'leth* shoot past him.

As Lomakh followed through, the human brought the hilt of his dagger down on the base of the Klingon's skull. With a grunt of pain, his adversary fell to his knees. His weapon slipped from insensible hands. And before he could recover, Picard's knee was in the small of the Klingon's back.

Driving Lomakh down with all his weight, the captain gripped the conspirator's hair with his left hand and pulled. Then, with his right hand, he placed the edge of his blade against Lomakh's eminently exposed throat.

"*Bljeghbe'chugh vaj blHegh!*" Picard growled. "Surrender or die!"

The conspirator tried to twist his head free, but the captain only increased the pressure of dagger against flesh. He repeated the order, this time in the short form.

"*Jegh!*"

Lomakh groaned, awash with shame—but not so much he would die to rid himself of it. "*Yap,*" he rasped. "Enough."

Careful not to let his guard drop, Picard looked up—in time to see Kahless dodge a sweeping attack from Tichar. As the human watched, the clone struck back—once, twice, and again, battering down the conspirator's defenses. Tichar looked a little clumsier and a little more fatigued with each blow leveled against him.

But then, Kahless was wearing down too. Sweat streamed down either side of his face and his barrel chest was heaving for air. Besides that, there was a nasty cut on his forehead just below his hairline, and the blood from it was seeping into his eyes.

Finally, the clone seemed to find an opening, a gap in his opponent's defenses. Taking advantage of it, he darted in for the kill—and Tichar was too weary to stop him in time. With a savage *thukt,* Kahless's *bat'leth* buried itself deep in the conspirator's belly, just below the sternum.

The clone snarled as he drove his point upward, lifting his enemy off the ground despite his bulk. Picard winced as he watched Tichar scream in agony. Finally, Kahless let the conspirator down.

Tichar sank to his knees, mortally wounded. Applying his boot to the conspirator's chest, the clone pulled his blade free and let Tichar sprawl backward. Then Kahless turned to the captain and grinned through his own gore, more like an animal than a sentient being.

But then, thought Picard, *that is and always has been the nature of the Klingon dichotomy. Canny intelligence mingled with the most relentlessly violent impulses. A dream of greatness floundering in a sea of blood.*

Unable to contain his exuberance, the clone bellowed in triumph. He sounded like a storm, like a force of nature. The walls echoed with it and the rafters seemed to quiver.

This was joy pure and unbridled, an emotion as honest as it was repugnant to the human sensibility. It was Kahless's answer to those who questioned his authenticity, his challenge to those who would stand against him.

Here I am, he seemed to say. *Neither legend nor fraud, but a Klingon in all my earthly glory. Strive to be like me if you dare.*

Ultimately, that was his appeal—and his greatness. Kahless was the Klingon Everyman, a mirror in which every last son of Qo'noS might find the noblest parts of himself.

The captain was so taken with the passion of the clone's display, he almost didn't see Tichar sit up, mortal wound and all. And even when he saw it, all he could do was cry out.

"Kahless!" he roared.

But it was too late. With his last reserve of strength, the conspirator hurled his *bat'leth* at the clone. As it whirled end over end, Kahless saw the look in the human's eyes and turned.

He had no time to ward the *bat'leth* off—not completely. All he could do was bring his own weapon up and hope for the best.

Unfortunately, the clone's action didn't slow the blade down one iota. The *bat'leth* punctured his tunic in the center of his chest. Staggered, he sank to one knee.

His face a mask of pain, Kahless gripped the *bat'leth* with both hands and tugged it free. Then, with a curse, he flung it from him. The blade scraped along the floor.

"My God," whispered Picard.

Was it possible the Klingon had come all this way just to perish in the end? Could Fate be so cruel?

He saw Kahless find him with his eyes. For a moment, they stared at one another, neither one knowing what to expect. Then the clone's teeth pulled back in a grin again, and he howled louder than ever.

The captain stared openmouthed. He didn't understand. He had seen the point of the *bat'leth* bury itself in Kahless's chest.

But as the Klingon approached him, caught up suddenly in the throes of laughter, he made the answer clear. Reaching into his leather tunic, he pulled out the betrothal amulet he wore—the one modeled after that of the original Kahless.

It was badly dented. In fact, the closer Picard looked, the more it seemed to him the thing had taken the brunt of a *bat'leth* thrust.

"Apparently," the clone boomed, "there is something to be said for tradition after all!"

Before the armory stopped ringing with his words, reinforcements arrived in the form of Worf, Kurn, and Gowron. And several of Gowron's guards, whom he had left outside at first, were there to back them up.

Relieved, the captain released Lomakh and got to his feet. At last, he told himself, it was *over*.

Thirty-six: The Heroic Age

Emperor Kahless looked out the window. There were endless crowds gathered on either side of the road that led from his citadel—once Molor's citadel—to the eastern provinces. Though he hadn't shown himself yet, they were cheering and pumping their swords in the air.

The old warchief sighed. He had intended for only his closest friends and servants to know that he was leaving. Somehow, the word had leaked out.

"It wasn't me," said Anag.

Kahless turned to look at his chief councilor. Anag was a lean, dark-skinned man with a big, full beard. He was also Kahless's handpicked choice of successor.

"*What* wasn't you?" Kahless asked, confused by the declaration.

"It wasn't me who told the people of your departure," the younger man explained.

The emperor grunted. "Oh. That." He shrugged. "And if it *were* you, Anag? Would I have boiled you in *en'tach* oil for your transgression?" He laughed. "There hasn't been a secret kept in these halls since I took the tyrant's life. Why should my leaving be any exception?"

Anag frowned. "You are . . . certain about this?"

Kahless nodded. "I am certain. Let us not have this conversation again, all right? I am an old man. I need to leave under my own power, and I will not have the chance to do that much longer."

He went over to his bed, where he had left his traveler's pack—a cracked leather relic of his days as an outlaw. There were still a few things he wanted to add to it.

Anag shook his head. "I still don't see the need for it. If you died in your bed, what difference would it make?"

The emperor looked at him. "You are right."

His councilor seemed surprised. "About your staying, you mean?"

"No," said Kahless. "About your not understanding."

Morath would have understood. Hell, he would have come up with the idea in the first place.

After all, it had only been a few decades since Kahless overthrew Molor and united the Klingon people. But in that time, he had seen his deeds magnified into the stuff of legend. If he could make a myth of his passing as well, it would only strengthen his legacy.

And a true legacy it was. With the tyrant overthrown, he had given the Klingons a set of laws by which they could conduct themselves honorably. Naturally, the basis for those laws was the principles Morath had lived by.

Keep your promises to one another. Deal openly and fairly, even with your enemies. Fight a battle to its end, giving no quarter. And when it is necessary to die, die bravely.

His people had embraced these precepts as a man dying of thirst might embrace a skin full of water. What's more, they had been quick to give Kahless credit for them. But he had insisted that Morath be known as the source of their wisdom—thereby fulfilling the vow he had made to his friend more than thirty years earlier.

Kahless had also set free the provinces that used to pay Molor tribute, inviting them instead to join his confederacy of free states. As he could have predicted, the provinces swore allegiance to him—and instead of tribute, they now paid taxes.

The same situation, of course, but a different appearance. Over the years, Kahless had learned to play his role well.

Morath would no doubt have been proud of all his friend had

accomplished—if not of Kahless himself. After all, the emperor took no pride in what he had done for his people. His only motivation had been to please Morath's ghost—to keep his word to the man.

To remind himself of that promise, he had kept the dagger that killed Morath—still black with Morath's blood—in a glass case in his throne room. People had tried to confuse its significance, to say it was Kahless's blood on the thing—but again, he had insisted on the truth.

It was Morath's blood. *Morath's*. And it was important to him that they remembered that.

After all, Morath had been a man of honor. And Kahless himself was just a fraud in honor's clothing—a fake, playing the part of the beloved emperor—even if he was the only one who knew it. Fortunately, he would not have to maintain the pretense much longer.

"What is that?" asked Anag.

Kahless looked at the scroll in his hand—the last thing he meant to pack. He chuckled. "Nothing, really. Just a collection of maps to guide me in my travels."

It was a lot more than a collection of maps. It was an account of his life—not the one shrouded in legend, but a true story with all its blemishes. He believed it would be of value someday, when myths were no longer quite so necessary, and Klingons had learned to embrace truth.

His councilor sighed. "There's nothing I can say, then, to talk you out of this? Nothing I can do to make you stay?"

Kahless put his hand on Anag's shoulder. "You are a wise man," he said, "and an honorable one. But you talk entirely too much. Now come, son of Porus, walk me downstairs."

With that, he hefted his pack and made his way to the ground floor. Anag followed a step behind him, saying nothing, no doubt still puzzling over his emperor's motives.

Kahless wished he could have stayed and seen how Anag ruled. He wished he could have been assured of a smooth succession, and prosperity for his people, and the survival of Morath's laws.

But there were no assurances in life. He had learned that long ago. Men might keep promises, but Fate bound itself to no one.

The emperor reached the foot of the stairs, crossed the anteroom, and made his way out into the courtyard. The gates were open. Beyond them, he could see the multitude that had gathered on either side of the road.

Some of the faces closest to him were familiar ones. They were his retainers, those charged with seeing to his safety. No doubt, the news of his leaving had been more confusing to them than to anyone.

For a single, astonishing moment, he thought he caught a glimpse of Kellein in the crowd. She seemed to be waving to him, standing tall and beautiful in the fading light.

His heart leaped in his chest. How was it possible . . . ?

Then he realized his eyes were playing tricks on him, and his heart sank again. But then, that happened when one got old.

Putting one foot before the other, he walked out through the gates, leaving Anag behind. Nor did he look back.

On one side and then the other, people pushed out from the crowd to speak to him. To appeal to him with their eyes. To pose the same question in different forms, over and over again.

"Master, where are you going?" asked one of his retainers.

He smiled, exposing teeth that were still sharp and strong. "To a place called *Sto-Vo-Kor*," he answered. "Where no one lacks sustenance or bends his knee to anyone else. Where in every hall, the clash of swords rings from the rafters. And where men hold honor above all else."

In truth, he didn't know where he was going, or how long he would survive. But it didn't matter. Like an old *rach'tor* who couldn't hunt anymore, he knew it was simply his time to go.

"Where is this *Sto-Vo-Kor?*" asked a woman.

Kahless thought for a moment. Then he pointed to the evening sky, where the stars were just making their presence felt.

"There," he said.

Then he pounded the center of his chest with his fist. The impact made a satisfying sound.

"And here," he said.

Last of all, he pointed to his temple. He left his finger there for a moment.

"And here," he told his people. "That is where you will find *Sto-Vo-Kor.*"

Inwardly, he chuckled. Such a cryptic answer. If he was lucky, they would puzzle over it for a hundred years to come.

There were other questions, other pleas for him to stay, other blessings heaped on him. But he didn't stop to respond to them. He just walked east from the citadel, taking strength from their clamor.

Vorcha-doh-baghk! they cried. *Vorcha-doh-baghk Kahless!*

All hail! All hail Kahless!

It was easy for him to go. They *made* it easy. With their adulation to lighten the pack on his back, Kahless the Unforgettable carved his name into Klingon history.

At least for a while, he thought. No one knew better than Kahless that nothing lasts forever.

Thirty-seven: The Modern Age

Night had fallen in the city of Navrath, but the pinkish cast had remained in the sky. In the courtyard of what had been Unarrh's house until just a few moments ago, Picard and his three companions watched Gowron hold their computer chip up to the light of a coal-filled brazier.

It was strange to see a symbol of modern technology in such a stark and primitive-looking place, under such a primal, foreboding sky. But somehow, the smile that reshaped Gowron's face seemed even stranger.

The council leader did not often display a sanguine expression. It spoke volumes that he did so now.

"Empty?" Gowron echoed, eyeing Worf.

The lieutenant nodded. "Empty," he confirmed.

"Completely," Kurn added for emphasis.

"Though no emptier than Unarrh's head." Kahless laughed—wincing at the pain his quip brought on, but determined to ignore it.

Gowron's eyes narrowed as he tried to puzzle it out. "But you *did* visit the relay station, did you not?"

"That we did," the captain agreed. "And we downloaded the accumulated data, just as we described. However, the computer files were damaged in the melee. The parts we were interested in were wiped out, obliterated—though we didn't discover that until it was too late."

The council leader grunted—a sign of admiration, apparently. "Then it was all a deception. You had no incriminating evidence at all."

"However," Worf remarked, "Unarrh and the others didn't know that—so they provided the evidence themselves."

"Indeed," Gowron commented. He looked at the chip again. "And this is your only copy of what you downloaded?"

"It is," the lieutenant confirmed.

"Good," said the council leader. Dropping the chip in the dirt at his feet, he ground it beneath the heel of his boot. "Defense Force data is still Defense Force data. It is not," he remarked pointedly, "for public consumption."

Gowron might have dismissed them at that point. But he didn't. Apparently, he wasn't done with them yet.

"Needless to say," he remarked, "there is still a great deal of work to be done before we can identify the rest of the conspiracy—some of which may be closer to home than I would like."

"Needless to say," the clone echoed.

"However," said Gowron, "I want you to know you have my gratitude for what you have done. My gratitude and that of the Empire."

Picard grunted softly. Gratitude wasn't something one associated with the council leader either.

Kahless elbowed Worf in the ribs. "Tell our esteemed companion the Empire is quite welcome. However, its council leader could have ended this a long time ago, simply by heeding its emperor's concerns."

Gowron gazed at Kahless. But if he was angry, he didn't show it. In fact, the captain thought he saw a hint of admiration for Kahless there, no matter how well the council leader tried to conceal it.

"Perhaps," said Gowron. "Perhaps."

"Well," Picard interjected, "Lieutenant Worf and I would love to stay and chat. Unfortunately, we have other duties—that's the way of Starfleet. And Governor Kurn has been good enough to offer us a ride to the Neutral Zone." He eyed the most powerful Klingon in the Empire. "I'm glad everything worked out, Gowron."

The council leader inclined his head ever so slightly—a sign of respect. "No more glad than I am, Picard."

With that, Gowron crossed the courtyard and exited through the gate in the wall. The captain watched him go, knowing the man still had his share of battles to fight. One could not sit where he sat without looking over one's shoulder now and then.

Picard just hoped the pressures surrounding Gowron would never turn him against the Federation. The last thing he wanted was to cross blades with the son of M'rel.

For a moment, the courtyard was silent except for a rising wind. Then Kahless spat on the ground.

"He has the tongue of a serpent," said the clone. "If I were you in the Federation, I'd be wary of Gowron's gratitude—almost as wary as I would be of his enmity."

The captain silently noted the similarity between the Klingon's views and his own. "I will remember that," he promised.

"On the other hand," said Kahless, "you have nothing to fear from *my* gratitude. And I am grateful indeed." He turned to Worf, to Kurn, and back to Picard. "It was because of you three I was able to rescue the Empire—not to mention the ethos of honor that is its foundation. My namesake would have been proud of you."

"I think I speak for all of us," the captain replied, "when I say we were happy to be of service."

The clone eyed Worf. "I am indebted to you in particular, son of Mogh."

The lieutenant looked at him. "Me?" he echoed.

"Yes. It was you who made me see the truth—that it is not the myths that bolster belief in Kahless, but rather the idea of Kahless that bolsters belief in the myths."

Picard smiled. It was an interesting observation, all right. His security officer had developed a knack lately for coming up with the right insight at the right time.

Kahless clapped Worf on the shoulder. "I hope the majority of our people will end up hanging on to their beliefs, despite the scandals inscribed in that damned scroll."

"I believe they will," the lieutenant told him.

Now that he had time to think about it, the captain believed so, too. If he had learned one thing in all his years in the center seat, it was that a person's faith was often stronger than the most concrete scientific fact.

In time, he mused, this entire affair might become a historical footnote, nothing more. And while the name of Olahg would be forgotten, the name of Kahless would be revered for ages to come.

After all, he wasn't called Kahless the *Unforgettable* for nothing.

Epilogue

As Worf entered his quarters, he didn't ask for any illumination. It was the middle of the night, according to the ship's computer, and Alexander would be asleep in the next room.

The lieutenant smiled to himself. It was good to be back on the *Enterprise.* As much as he yearned sometimes to immerse himself in his Klingon heritage, it was here he felt most at home.

This was where his friends were. This was where his sense of duty called the loudest and was most resoundingly answered. Even Kahless had been able to appreciate that.

After all, a Klingon could be a Klingon anywhere—even all by himself, if necessary. Nor was it necessary to be raised as one to *be* one.

Being Klingon was a path one either chose or disdained, a way of looking at things with the heart as much as the mind. It was not always a clear path or an easy one, but it was always there if one looked hard enough for it.

Suddenly, he heard an intake of breath at the far end of the room. At the entrance to Alexander's quarters, a shadow moved.

"Lights!" said a voice, before Worf could make the same request.

A moment later, the lieutenant saw his son standing there in his bedclothes, squinty-eyed with sleep. But when the boy realized who had come in, a smile spread from one side of his face to the other.

"Father!" he cried.

Alexander crossed the room in a leap. Before Worf knew it he was holding the boy to his chest, slender but strong arms wrapped around his neck. The lieutenant grinned as if he were a child as well.

"Alexander," he replied.

Worf said nothing more than that, just the boy's name. But it carried all the depths and shades of emotion clamoring inside him.

"I was worried about you," Alexander confessed.

The lieutenant nodded. "I knew you would be."

Leaning away from him, the boy looked at him. "Did everything go all right? Is the homeworld okay now?"

"Yes," Worf assured him. "The homeworld is fine."

For now, he thought. *And for as long as Kahless and Kurn and others like them refuse to let their guards down.*

Alexander's eyes narrowed. "And what about you, Father? Are *you* okay?"

The Klingon was surprised by the question. "As you can see," he began, "I am in good health."

The boy shook his head. "No, I mean *inside*. Are you okay with what it said in the scrolls?"

Worf's first impulse was to scold his son for accessing what he had intended to be private property. Then he remembered that he hadn't left any instructions to that effect, or taken any precautions against Alexander's prying.

Based on such evidence, Deanna would have said he *wanted* the boy to see the scrolls. Subconsciously, at least. And he wasn't absolutely certain she wouldn't have been right.

"Yes," he answered, putting the lecture aside for another time. "I have accepted what it said in the scrolls. I am . . . okay."

Alexander smiled. "Good. I hate it when you're unhappy."

Worf eyed the boy. "Right now, it would make me happy to see you in bed. It is late and you have school tomorrow."

His son frowned. "Okay. But can you sit with me a while? Just a few minutes maybe, until I fall asleep?"

It was not the sort of request a Klingon child made to his parent. But then, the boy was only *three-quarters* Klingon.

"Actually," the lieutenant said, "I was about to suggest that myself."

As he returned Alexander to his room, Worf basked in the glow of his progeny. That was a part of being a Klingon too.

A very *important* part.